COMANCHE WOMAN

"A fast and furious read."
—*Belles and Beaux of Romance*

FRONTIER WOMAN

"A rousing, passion-filled story of a proud and
larger-than-life family."
—*Rendezvous*

"[Joan Johnston's] best story yet."
—*Old Book Barn Gazette*

THE LONER

"Fans of Ms. Johnston will recognize the family names of
the two Texas dynasties, Blackthorne and Creed. Rich
supporting characters generate a depth that shows
romance can be found at any age, in any walk of
life, and even with physical limitations."
—*Romantic Times*

JOAN JOHNSTON

SWEETWATER SEDUCTION

A DELL BOOK

SWEETWATER SEDUCTION
A Dell Book

PUBLISHING HISTORY
Dell mass market edition published January 1991
Dell mass market reissue / November 2004

Published by Bantam Dell
A Division of Random House, Inc.
New York, New York

ISBN 0-440-20561-1

Manufactured in the United States of America
Published simultaneously in Canada

OPM 20 19 18 17 16 15 14 13 12

*For my mother
Emogene Mertens,
a woman of indomitable spirit*

Acknowledgments

I am indebted to Ken Alstad's collection of *Savvy Sayin's* as a source for most of the cowboy wisdom found at the opening of each chapter.

I am also indebted to Edgar R. "Frosty" Potter, whose book *Cowboy Slang* provided inspiration and education on the succinct, pithy, cowboy way of saying things.

Finally, I want to thank my friend Mary Pershall, who, when I called her excited about an idea I had for a book, naturally assumed I would use a western setting to tell my story—which had never even occurred to me until she happened to mention it.

SWEETWATER
SEDUCTION

Chapter 1

The West is where water has the same value as blood.

☼ MISS EDEN DEVLIN, SPINSTER SCHOOLTEACHER, FELT a chill of foreboding as she watched Bliss Davis, a nester's fifteen-year-old daughter, and Hadley Westbrook, a rancher's sixteen-year-old son, making cow eyes at each other across the schoolroom. It wasn't that she disapproved of young love. In fact, at an on-the-shelf twenty-nine, she envied the blushing glow on Bliss's cheeks and the liquid warmth in her eyes that was sparked by Hadley's admiring gaze. What concerned Eden was the violent reaction their fathers would have if they discovered that their children didn't share their parents' enmity toward one another. Because, as sure as hell took sinners, Big Ben Davis hated Oakley Westbrook's guts.

To Miss Devlin's horror, it seemed the once peaceful community of Sweetwater was only one short step away from a full-fledged range war. Eden knew there were honest grievances between ranchers and nesters. The homesteading nesters had fenced water holes the ranchers needed for their cattle. The ranchers had retaliated by cutting fences and ruining crops. Cattle were being rustled in alarming numbers.

But Oak Westbrook had denied the ranchers were cutting fences. And Big Ben Davis had denied the nesters were rustling cattle. There seemed to be no hope of working out their differences peacefully.

With the exception of Bliss and Hadley, the animosity of the adult ranchers and nesters was being played out among their children at school, disrupting Miss Devlin's teaching efforts. It was a good thing she was a peace-loving woman, because Miss Devlin had a good mind to knock some heads together. She had about decided that if she wanted the sixteen young minds in her one-room schoolhouse to concentrate on geography and arithmetic and spelling again, she was going to have to do whatever was necessary herself to get the situation peaceably settled.

But first she was going to make sure that the love blossoming between Bliss Davis and Hadley Westbrook didn't provide the spark to ignite a blazing battle between ranchers and nesters.

"Children, you may pick up your lunch boxes now. Be sure to wear your coats if you decide to eat outside. I'm afraid we've seen the last of Indian summer."

Miss Devlin watched Keefe and Daniel Wyatt jostle Jett and Wade Ives as the four adolescent boys—once good friends—raced for the best seats at the picnic tables outside. The girls were no better. Sally Davis and Henrietta Westbrook, better known to her friends as Henry, fairly hissed at each other as they rushed for the sunshine. The Carson girls, Emmaline, Enid, Elaine, and Efrona, managed to stall long enough to irritate the twins, Glynne and Gerald Falkner. Even the youngest joined the shenanigans. Seven-year-old Elliott Wyatt yanked six-year-old Felicity Falkner's golden braid and then scooted for the door.

"Elliott!" Miss Devlin's voice held a ring of command that would have done a general proud. Elliott Wyatt skidded to a halt. Miss Devlin's voice was quiet but firm when she continued, "I believe you owe Felicity an apology."

"Aw shucks, Miss Devlin. Do I hafta?"

"Absolutely."

"Aw shucks. I'm sorry, Felicity," he said in a sullen voice.

"You stink like your cows and I hate you, Elliott Wyatt!" Felicity retorted.

"Felicity! That will be quite enough of that," Miss Devlin said, feeling the utter futility of her efforts even as she continued to make peace. "I want both of you to . . ."

What could she say? Make up and be friends? Hardly likely considering what they heard their parents saying at the supper table every night. No, the problem with the children wouldn't be resolved until the problem with the parents found a solution. Miss Devlin sighed.

". . . behave yourselves," she said at last. When Miss Devlin dismissed them, the two children bolted down the school steps like calves out of a loading chute.

Miss Devlin stepped in front of Bliss and Hadley as they reached the doorway. "I'd like to speak with both of you for a moment."

The nester's daughter and the rancher's son exchanged guilty glances that made Miss Devlin sigh again.

"Sit down, both of you." Miss Devlin watched as Hadley painstakingly pulled out a wooden bench and seated Bliss. It was true love, all right. "I want to speak frankly with both of you, because I think you're old enough to understand the importance of what I have to say."

Hadley and Bliss sat up straighter at this indication of their maturity.

"I've noticed lately that you both seem to have developed certain . . . feelings for one another."

Hadley reached out to grasp Bliss's hand, and their fingers automatically entwined. "I love Bliss, Miss Devlin,"

Hadley said in a solemn voice. "And I don't care who knows it," he added defiantly.

That was exactly what Miss Devlin had been afraid of. "You know the situation between ranchers and nesters is a powder keg just waiting for a spark to ignite it. What do you think your fathers would do if they knew about the two of you?"

Miss Devlin paused long enough for both young faces to flush before she continued. "I'm not going to say you shouldn't share these wonderful feelings you have for one another. But I'm going to ask you to be very careful about expressing your feelings where they can be observed."

"Why, Miss Devlin?" Bliss asked. "I love Hadley. We want to get married."

"Do you think Big Ben would approve of such a match?" she asked.

Tears appeared in Bliss's large blue eyes, and one spilled over. Hadley had to clear his throat before he could speak. "We plan to be married whether our parents approve or not."

"I can understand your feelings—"

"How can you possibly understand how we feel?" Hadley challenged.

Hadley said no more, just stared at her. Miss Devlin's lips took on a prunish look, and unflattering lines appeared around the edges of her mouth. Hadley was well aware that during the entire three years Miss Devlin had been teaching school in Sweetwater, she had never had a beau.

Miss Devlin had never had a beau in her entire life. Not that she had wanted one, of course. When she had left St. John's Academy for Orphans in Wichita at nineteen and headed north, the last thing on her mind had been finding a husband. She hadn't been sure exactly what she was looking for, she'd only known she had to go out into the world and seek it.

She would go somewhere and teach for a year, decide that the nebulous *something* she was looking for, but never able to define, was missing, and move on. It was a good thing teachers were so scarce, because after a while her reference letters always contained the acerbic warning, "While Miss Devlin is a superior teacher, she has not indicated a willingness to extend her stay beyond a single school term."

The day Eden arrived in Sweetwater, she had looked down into the lush green valley in which the small town was situated and felt her stomach tighten in recognition.

In the distance, beneath a towering cottonwood, a woman sat on a patchwork quilt holding a baby to her breast, while a man pushed a small boy on a wooden swing that hung from the same tree.

Several white frame houses boasted picket fences around the yards in front, and neat-rowed gardens out back. There were sod structures with dogs lolling in the dirt and long johns hanging on lines strung between oleander bushes. There was even a two-story stone mansion, with a manicured front lawn and a pale pink—yes, pink—gazebo out back.

Heart pounding with excitement, she had eyed the Powder River running like a blue crayon line down the center of the valley, surveyed the dark green pines overlooking the town from above, viewed the plowed fields that interrupted the miles and miles of grassy plains stretching as far as the eye could see, and thought: *This is it.* She couldn't explain her feelings, she only knew her heart had found a home.

Although Miss Devlin had stopped drifting once she reached Sweetwater, she had still avoided the usual courtship rituals. For her there had been no picnicking under the watchful eyes of the congregation at a church social. No stolen kisses on the porch swing. Not even a long, lazy stroll arm-in-arm along the river on a flower-scented summer evening. So Hadley had a good point. How could she possibly know how these two young lovers felt?

Miss Devlin swallowed over the unexpected lump in her throat. "Perhaps I should have said instead that I *sympathize* with your feelings, Hadley. It doesn't change my opinion about how you should act. I'm convinced your discretion is critical to keeping the peace," she finished with a hard-won smile.

Bliss looked up at Hadley with worried eyes. "Miss Devlin is right, Hadley. If Pa found out about us there's no telling what he'd do. I'd just die if the two of you got into a fight or . . . or worse. Maybe we should—"

"No! I won't stop seeing you, Bliss." Hadley clutched Bliss's hand and gazed down into her luminous eyes. "I need you. I love you. I can't give you up!"

"I love you, too, Hadley!" Bliss turned to Miss Devlin and pleaded, "What can we do?"

Faced with those impassioned speeches, Miss Devlin felt her heart go out to the young couple. She was more determined than ever to find a way to end this horrendous war, which was being waged without visible battle lines. "Try to be patient a little longer," Miss Devlin urged. "I'll be meeting with the Sweetwater Halloween Dance Committee this afternoon, which includes both your mothers. Maybe we can find a way to make things right again."

Hadley's voice was bitter when he said, "If the damned nesters hadn't fenced all the water holes none of this would have happened."

"It isn't all our fault," Bliss cried. "What about the ranchers cutting fences? My father lost nearly his entire wheat crop."

The young lovers looked at each other and acknowledged there was wrong on both sides. But what could they do? They were helpless pawns in an increasingly vicious game of wills.

"Right now, I think you should go eat your lunches," Miss Devlin said. "And remember what I said."

"We will, Miss Devlin," Bliss said.

"All right, Miss Devlin," Hadley muttered as he reluctantly separated his hand from Bliss's.

Miss Devlin spent the afternoon watching the hopeless look in Bliss's eyes, and the longing in Hadley's, with growing concern. Eden was intimately familiar with the classics, and she saw all the signs in their budding romance of a modern-day *Romeo and Juliet*. She was not about to stand around and watch a similar tragedy occur. When she got Regina Westbrook and Persia Davis in here this afternoon, she was going to give them both a good piece of her mind!

The children's departure from school that day was followed closely by the arrival of their mothers. Since she was still nursing, Amity Carson brought her six-month-old daughter, Edna, along. She made an insulting point of joining Persia Davis and Mabel Ives on the opposite side of the schoolroom from Regina Westbrook, Claire Falkner, and Lynette Wyatt. The barely veiled hostility between ranchers' wives and nesters' wives had Miss Devlin clenching her teeth in an attempt to keep her self-control.

"Welcome, ladies," she began. "I'm glad you could all be here this afternoon. We have a lot of planning to do to make the traditional Sweetwater Halloween Dance a success. First, there's something I think we need to discuss. Namely—"

At that point baby Edna burst into a long, loud wail.

"If you nesters insist on breeding children like rabbits," Regina muttered under her breath, "the least you can do is keep them equally quiet."

While Amity unbuttoned her dress to nurse the crying child, Persia jumped to her defense. "Better breeding like rabbits than looking like cows."

Regina rose to her feet, the fringe on her capelike black dolman quivering. She had always been sensitive about her large bosom, and Persia knew it. "How dare you!"

"The same way you do!"

Regina struck a militant pose as a torrent of voices joined Persia and Regina in reviling one another.

"Ladies! Ladies!" Miss Devlin's schoolteacher voice stood her in good stead, and the group fell silent. Eden took a deep breath, fighting for calm. "This isn't accomplishing anything."

"No, you're right," Regina agreed. "We're leaving." She turned like a queen surveying her court and bobbed her head farewell, nearly unseating the complicated black hat on her upswept snow-white hair. With dutiful obedience, Claire Falkner and Lynette Wyatt rose and followed her imperious exit out the door.

"Button yourself up!" Persia snapped at a startled Amity. "We're leaving too." Like an empress in her own right, despite her well-worn calico dress and scuffed black boots, Persia pulled her woolen shawl more tightly around her shoulders and led Amity Carson and Mabel Ives out of the schoolroom past the gape-mouthed teacher.

Miss Devlin stared in bemused wonder at the barren schoolroom. Not a woman given to swearing (it was beneath her intelligence), she resorted to a satisfyingly guttural "Oooooh!"

She sought calm by doing all the menial jobs that fell to her at the end of each school day. Once the blackboard was erased, she rearranged the benches behind the four rows of wooden desks, and checked to make sure the fire in the stove that heated the schoolroom was banked for the night. Finally, Miss Devlin took the broom from the corner and briskly swept the floor. She discovered a stray pencil and, pursing her lips at its well-chewed condition, set it back on Henry Westbrook's desk.

When Miss Devlin was done, she looked out over the pristine schoolroom and realized she hadn't found the calm she had sought. She gathered up the papers that needed grading and left, carefully closing the door behind her.

She headed off down the short, narrow dirt path that led to the home that had been built for the school's teacher. Eden loved the tiny white gingerbread-trimmed house, which was only a brisk ten-minute walk from the north end of town.

As she strolled homeward, a frown of concentration formed on her plain face. This wrangling had to be stopped. Nipped in the bud. Ended. But how? Lord have mercy. How?

Like all boys his age living in such an untamed country, Hadley Westbrook had responsibilities beyond his schooling that had to be tended to every day. But it was with growing reluctance that he forced himself to leave Bliss to take care of his chores. He stood with his arms around her, hidden by the copse of lodgepole pines that marked the divergent paths that led in one direction to the elegant two-story stone Westbrook mansion, and in the other to the dog-trot plank structure Big Ben Davis had built for his small family.

"I have to go, Bliss," Hadley said, leaning down to kiss her gently on the lips.

Bliss clung to him and when he tried to remove her arms from around his neck said, "I don't want you to leave, Hadley. Stay with me."

"You know if I don't pick up those supplies in town before dark, my father will have my head. I've got to go." He hugged her again and touched his lips to hers for what he told himself would be the last time before he got on with his chores. But young love being what it is, it was long moments later before he came to his senses. He was breathing hard, Bliss's dress was unbuttoned, and his sun-browned hands cupped her bare white breasts.

He jerked his hands away and stepped back. "Lord, Bliss! I don't know how I let myself get carried away like that. It's just that touching you is so sweet . . ."

He was afraid when she turned away that she might think he blamed her somehow for what had happened. But he was the one who couldn't seem to control himself. He was afraid to touch her even now, for fear he would get carried away again. The little whimpers he heard as she struggled to repair her clothing made his stomach clench.

"Bliss, I'm sorry. I'm sorry." His voice was ragged as he stepped up behind her and encircled her with his arms, grasping her hands to stop her frantic efforts to button her dress. "It's just that I love you so much. I . . . I don't want to lose control like I did before and . . ."

He hadn't meant for things to go so far that time. The tears streaking Bliss's pale face afterwards—even though she had said she wanted it as much as he did, and she didn't mind that they hadn't waited until they were married—well, he couldn't handle seeing her look like that again.

His fear that she was upset by his fervent lovemaking was soothed when she turned around and he saw the way she was looking at him, with her blue eyes soft and loving and dewy. He had to struggle not to drag her back into his arms.

"You're not the only one wanting," she admitted, her voice low and trembly. "I feel the same way. When you touch me I . . . I forget myself. I don't want you ever to stop!"

He pulled her into his arms after all and hugged her tight, his throat working as he tried to tell her how much it meant to hear what she was saying. But the words got stuck there, so he just felt them and hoped she would understand without his saying them back.

Bliss kept her head tucked into his shoulder so he couldn't see her face when she confessed, "I know it's supposed to be wrong to want you like this."

Hadley's arms tightened around her.

"But how can it be wrong when it feels so right?" she finished in an aching whisper.

Hadley didn't have an answer for her. He felt the same way. But he was stunned by what she said next.

"Let's run away, Hadley."

Hadley took Bliss by the shoulders and forced her to step back to face him. He looked deep into her blue eyes and said soberly, "I don't want to run away, Bliss. I want to stay here in Sweetwater and get married and raise our kids. My father's ranch will be mine someday. I already love the Solid Diamond like it was my own."

"Your father is never going to let us get married, Hadley. Neither is mine. You know it and I know it."

Hadley pulled Bliss back into his embrace, rocking her back and forth as he reassured her, "We'll be married, Bliss. When the time is right I'll talk to your father and mine and they'll see reason."

"When will that be?"

"Soon," Hadley promised. He pushed her away from him again and with a rueful smile finished buttoning up her dress. "It's time for you to get home and me to get on with my chores."

"Will you be coming to see me tonight, Hadley?" she asked, stepping toward him.

Hadley felt himself getting hard again just looking at her. He wasn't sure if it was the trusting look in her eyes or the soft brush of her belly against his that made up his mind for him, but there was no way he could deny her.

He made up his mind then and there that he wasn't going to let himself lose control again. She deserved better from him. He would share the touching caresses they both wanted, and kiss her silly in the bargain, but that was as far as it would go until they were married. If he was man enough to want her, he had to be man enough to do what was best for her without thinking about himself.

"All right, Bliss," he agreed. "I'll come an hour after dark. Meet me in the usual place?"

Bliss smiled and Hadley felt his heart begin to pound. "I'll be there, Hadley. I love you." With that, she turned and ran down the footpath leading to her home.

Hadley mounted his horse and raced toward the Solid Diamond to get the freight wagon he needed to pick up supplies in town. An hour later he was whistling as he pulled the team to a stop in front of the general store in Sweetwater. He saw Big Ben Davis the instant he entered the store. Bliss's father would have been hard to miss.

Hadley was easily as tall as Big Ben, but he was lean and lanky where Big Ben had a barrel chest and heavy thighs that were the result of years spent behind a plow. Hadley had often wondered how Bliss could be so beautiful when he compared her delicate oval face with its pert nose and bowed lips to her father's square jaw and blunt features. He supposed all those hours in the sun were the cause of Big Ben's craggy face. Bliss, he knew, was never without a bonnet to protect her complexion. Looking at Big Ben's gray-streaked brown hair, he marveled at Bliss's golden chestnut curls, which had been soft and silky in his hands the afternoon he made her his own.

Thinking of Bliss that way in her father's presence made Hadley uncomfortable, and he blurted a greeting to cover his distress. "Hello, Mr. Davis. How are you today?"

"What the hell does it matter to you how I am?" Big Ben replied.

Hadley forced himself to meet Big Ben's glare and cleared his throat to make sure he would have a voice to say, "Your daughter Bliss and I are good friends, Mr. Davis. I just wanted—"

"Nesters and ranchers can't be friends."

"But Bliss and I—"

Big Ben grabbed a fistful of Hadley's plaid wool shirt and pulled him close enough that Hadley could smell the licorice on the farmer's breath when he ranted, "You stay away from my daughter!"

When Big Ben let go, Hadley stumbled against a counter, and a wire potato masher, a fruit jar cover wrench, and a tinned kitchen skimmer all clattered to the wooden floor.

A nester standing near the register guffawed.

Hadley lost both his temper and his good sense. "I'll see Bliss whenever I please," he shouted. "And you can't stop me!"

"Oh, I'll stop you, boy. You set one foot on my place and I'll shoot you dead!"

In a small town like Sweetwater any kind of altercation could be expected to draw an audience. A gathering of both cowboys and nesters was on hand to hear the threats being aimed at Oak Westbrook's nearly grown boy by Big Ben Davis. It wasn't really clear whether it was a cowboy or a nester who threw the first punch. The only thing Hadley knew for sure was that it hadn't been either him or Big Ben.

By the time Sheriff Felton Reeves arrived on the scene, followed by Deputy Joe, who stayed carefully behind him, the rowdy free-for-all had spilled out of Tomlinson's General Store and into the street. Sheriff Reeves pulled out his Colt Peacemaker .45 and shot once into the air, freezing everyone in place. He took advantage of the moment of quiet to announce, "Anybody who ain't gone from here in one minute flat is going to spend the night in jail."

Sheriff Reeves was a big, blond-haired, blue-eyed man, with a friendly-looking face and a deadly aim. After two years with Reeves as the sheriff of Sweetwater, nester and cowboy alike had learned to respect his word. The crowd quickly began to disperse.

Big Ben Davis made a point of confronting Hadley one more time. The farmer wiped his bloody mouth with the back of his hand and said, "Just you remember what I said. You come near my girl and I'll kill you!"

It wasn't until he was halfway home that Hadley realized he hadn't picked up the supplies he had gone to town for. He started to turn around, but realized that his father's anger could hardly be worse than another scene with Ben Davis, so he kept on driving.

When he got home, he found horses tied up in front of the house that he knew from their brands belonged to Rusty Falkner, Cyrus Wyatt, and six other ranchers from surrounding spreads.

When Hadley walked in the front door, his mother took one look at his swollen face—he had a beauty of a black eye—and tried to haul him off to the kitchen in search of some steak to take down the swelling.

Hadley resisted her entreaties. "Where's Dad?" he demanded.

"He's in the middle of a meeting of the Sweetwater Stock Growers Association."

Hadley stared at the closed door of his father's study and frowned. "Have they heard what happened in town?"

"Your father got word of it a few minutes ago from one of the hands who was there and saw the fracas. A brawl, Hadley! In the middle of town. And over that Davis girl. How could you?"

"Her name is Bliss, Mother. And I didn't start it."

"That hardly matters under the circumstances. I'm sure your father is making arrangements right now to ensure the same thing won't be happening in the future."

"What do you mean? He's not going to do anything to Ben Davis is he?"

"Well . . . I . . . I'm sure I don't know about that."

Hadley feared the worst from what his mother hadn't said. He already had a hand on the door to his father's study before his mother realized what he intended to do. "You can't go in there, Hadley. Your father—"

Hadley stepped inside the room that served as a combination library, music room, and office for his father, shutting the door in his mother's face.

Oak looked up at his son from behind his rolltop desk, and after perusing the damage to Hadley's face said, "Sit down, Hadley. You've certainly earned the right to hear what we're planning."

Hadley edged over to the corner and sat down on the upright piano bench in time to hear Cyrus Wyatt say, "When does he arrive?"

"I don't know, exactly," Oak replied. "His telegram said he'd get here as quick as he could. I'd say by the end of this week, or the beginning of next, the troubleshooter we hired should be here."

"Troubleshooter? What's that?" Hadley's question was met by grim looks on the faces around the room.

Finally, Oak replied, "Just what you think it is, son."

"A hired gun?"

"One of the best," Oak said. "Maybe *the* best," he amended.

"Why do we need a gunfighter?" Hadley demanded.

"He's not just a hired gun," Oak explained. "He's a troubleshooter—someone who comes in to solve problems of any and every kind. We're hoping he can find out who's been rustling our cattle."

"And who's been cutting fences and laying the blame at our door," Cyrus Wyatt added.

"And if need be," Rusty Falkner said, "he can handle any other problems that crop up."

Hadley flushed as the men in the room stared at his battered face. "Ben Davis didn't start the fight."

"It doesn't matter who started it," Oak said, his teeth clamping on his cigar. "I heard about the threat Ben Davis made against you, and I heard why he made it. It's time Big Ben learned a few hard lessons."

Hadley rose abruptly from his seat. "I think you're making a mistake, Dad."

"Because you find a nester girl easy on the eyes, son, is no reason—"

"Don't talk about Bliss that way!"

"Look, son, maybe you'd better go let your mother take a look at those cuts on your face."

Hadley stood there, sickeningly aware of his inability to stop the events his father had set in motion. He had to see Bliss. He wasn't sure exactly what he would say to her, exactly what they could do. But he knew in that instant that he had to get to her and hold her in his arms.

He turned and bolted from the room. Hadley was running by the time he hit the front porch, not stopping to answer when his mother called out to him. By the time he found his horse in the barn and saddled him, it was dusk. All he could think about was what would happen if the troubleshooter his father had hired ended up killing Big Ben Davis. Would Bliss still love him then? Would she still marry him? He had to find out.

Hadley was so absorbed in his thoughts that he paid little attention to the night sounds around him as his horse made its way across the dusky landscape. It seemed forever before he arrived at the gate leading to Big Ben Davis's farm and reached out to free the latch. He glanced off toward the cottonwoods where Bliss usually had a warm blanket spread and waiting for him. They would wrap themselves up in it and hold each other close, shutting out the rest of the world.

Sometimes they talked about the uncertain future that lay before them. Sometimes they would stare at the sky and wonder if there were other beings out there somewhere among the stars. Eventually, they always turned to each other, and the passion that rose between them would leave them breathless and aching.

As he freed the gate, Hadley heard the distinct lever action of a Winchester rifle being cocked. He thought instantly of Big Ben's threat. He hadn't believed Bliss's father would really kill him, but apparently he had been wrong. Hadley knew he was an easy target outlined by the setting sun, but he tried to save himself anyway.

Luck wasn't with him.

Before he had even freed his boots from the stirrups, Hadley heard the sharp crack of the Winchester and felt a shocking jolt in his chest. In a reflex action his spurs dug into his horse's belly and the animal reared. Hadley lost his balance and, unable to hang on, tumbled to the ground in an undignified heap.

Hadley couldn't tell how bad he was hurt, but he was having trouble moving, and that scared him. He was bleeding pretty bad too. The whistling wind chilled him where blood quickly soaked his shirt. The sharp rock under his left buttock was killing him. He tried to get up, but his arms were as limp as a well-used rope.

That was when he realized that whoever had shot him—he refused to believe it was Bliss's father, although he could think of no other likely suspect—might come around to finish the job. And that really scared him.

But no one came.

That was when he figured the bushwhacker planned to let him bleed to death. It wouldn't take long if he kept on bleeding like a stuck hog.

He wondered what Bliss would think when he didn't show up. She would probably think he had decided not to tempt fate. He wondered, as he drifted into unconsciousness, who would console her at his funeral . . . if his father let her come . . . if her father let her go . . .

Chapter 2

Too little temptation can lead to virtue.

BLISS DAVIS HAD ONE DRIVING THOUGHT, AND THAT was to reach Miss Devlin. Everything had gone so wrong! Hadley had been shot practically on her doorstep last night, and she didn't know whether he would live or die. He had been taken home to the Solid Diamond, so she couldn't even be near him.

Sheriff Reeves had come to the farm today with Deputy Joe and arrested her father. Everyone had heard Big Ben's warning to Hadley in the general store yesterday and figured he had simply carried out his threat. Bliss didn't deny her father's temper, but she knew from experience he was more bark than bite. She simply couldn't imagine her father shooting anyone!

It was Saturday, and with all the chores she had to do with her mother, there hadn't been a chance for her to slip away. Once everyone had gone to bed, she had sneaked out of the house and started at a fast walk along the path toward school. She needed to talk to Miss Devlin. Miss Devlin would know what she should do.

Bliss was so absorbed by her woes, she didn't hear anyone approaching until she was practically surrounded by cowboys. She recognized the brands on their horses. They were from the Solid Diamond. Anxious for news of Hadley, she approached one of them. "I'm Bliss Davis. Please, have you heard anything about how Hadley is doing? Is he going to be all right?"

The Solid Diamond hands had been drinking in town at the Dog's Hind Leg Saloon. Ordinarily they would have shunned any cowpoke who even spoke a disrespectful word to a lady. But talk about the cold-blooded ambush of Oak Westbrook's son had inflamed already high tempers and put them in an ugly mood.

"That's her, fellas. The nester bitch whose father shot the boss's boy."

"My father didn't shoot anyone," Bliss retorted.

"Whatcha doing out here all alone, missy? Who you hopin' to meet?"

"No one," Bliss mumbled, startled by the malice in the cowboy's voice. Frightened, she started walking along the path again, but one cowboy spurred his horse to ride beside her. He leaned down and Bliss was assailed by the rank smell of cheap whiskey. "You're drunk!" she said in the most disdainful voice she could manage.

"Not hardly, little lady. Leastaways, not enough so's you'd notice the difference. Wanta come on up here and say howdy?"

"I most certainly do not!" Bliss was mortified by his words, horrified by his evident intention. Before she could take breath to scream, the cowboy had yanked her off her feet. He held her with one arm around her waist as he pressed his mouth against hers. His mouth was sloppy wet and his tongue nearly gagged her. Before he could do more, another cowboy had dismounted and dragged her down into his arms. He tripped on her trailing skirt and they both fell to the grassy ground.

"Please stop," Bliss cried. "Don't touch me. Let me go!"

The drunken cowboys encircled her, some reaching for her flailing arms while others tried to grab her kicking feet. The only sounds were the grunt of one of the men when she kicked him in the groin with her boot, and the foul oath of another as she bit into a hand that clasped hers.

"Let her go."

The three words hit the silence like bullets. The astonished cowboys stared in awe at the extraordinarily tall figure outlined by the scant moonlight. The man was dressed entirely in black from his hat right down to his boots. The wind lifted his black duster and spread it away from his body. It was too close to Halloween for the same thought not to have risen in every cowboy's mind: Was this apparition real? Or not?

Out of the corner of her eye Bliss saw the cowboy on the ground beside her reach for his gun and shouted, "Look out!"

The gun had barely cleared the cowboy's holster when a shot rang out. The cowboy slumped sideways with a loud groan, his bloody shoulder sliding across Bliss's skirt.

"Anybody else got any smart ideas?" the apparition demanded in a steely voice. When there was no answer the faceless voice ordered, "Get on your horses and get out of here."

The cowboys grabbed their wounded comrade and were on their horses and gone in a matter of moments. Bliss wasn't sure whether to be grateful or terrified. The cowboys' attack on her had left her quaking. As the apparition moved closer the trembling turned to terror.

"Please. Don't come any closer," she whispered.

"I don't mean you any harm."

His voice was reassuring, gentle almost. Bliss found that even more frightening. Perhaps he only meant to put her off her guard before he took her for himself.

"I only want to help you," the voice said.

Bliss was too petrified to move. Strong hands lifted her and she was cushioned against a broad chest. She squeezed her eyes shut, afraid of what she would see if she opened them.

"Are you all right?" he asked.

Bliss nodded her head vigorously, keeping her eyes closed. She thought she heard a chuckle.

"Can I take you somewhere?"

Bliss decided that no ghost she had ever heard of had a sense of humor. She opened her eyes and peered up into the moonlit face of the stranger who had rescued her.

"Why, you're handsome!" she said, her voice filled with indignation. Suddenly she realized what she had said and her hands rose to cover her face in embarrassment. "I don't believe I said that."

The man threw back his head and laughed. "Would you be happier if I looked fearsome?" he asked when he'd recovered his voice.

"Well, no. But you sure scared the liver out of me. I half expected you to be Lucifer himself," Bliss admitted.

The stranger's features hardened. "Some would say I am."

Bliss shivered.

"I'm scaring you again," he said, his lips pressed flat in disgust. "I'll take you home."

"Oh, no! I can't go home. I have to see Miss Devlin."

"Miss Devlin?"

"My teacher. Her house is down this path a little way. Please, I'll be all right. You can let me go now."

The stranger pursed his lips in thought, then marched off with her in his arms in the opposite direction from Miss Devlin's house.

"Really, I'll be fine," Bliss said. "I—"

"Be still."

Bliss shut her mouth and kept it shut while the cowboy set her down and mounted a black-and-white paint gelding she hadn't noticed before. He reached down and grabbed her under the arms and lifted her as easy as you please into his lap.

"I think I'll make sure for my own peace of mind that you reach this 'Miss Devlin' in one piece."

Miss Devlin sat bolt upright in bed when she heard someone pounding on her door. She didn't even stop to put on a robe or slippers, simply dropped the volume of Greek plays she was reading and ran to throw open the door. Bliss Davis stood on her threshold. The girl's torn blouse was grass-stained and fresh blood smeared her striped cambric skirt.

"My God, Bliss! What happened?"

The young woman threw herself into Miss Devlin's arms, babbling incoherently about Hadley and cowboys and some devil dressed all in black. "Oh, Miss Devlin, it was horrible. I was nearly . . . I was almost . . . Oh, Miss Devlin, you have to help me."

Miss Devlin felt Bliss trembling and her wrath grew for whoever had been so cruel as to molest the poor child. She settled Bliss on the brocade Victorian sofa in her parlor, unconsciously straightening the lace doily that protected the arm when Bliss knocked it askew. It was then she sensed the presence of someone else in the room.

Miss Devlin turned around and looked up—a surprise in itself since she was so tall—into the probing eyes of a man she had no doubt was Bliss's "devil dressed all in black."

His face was masked by shadows, yet she saw a jutting

chin (a sure sign of stubbornness), a blade of nose, sharp cheekbones, and dark, predatory eyes. It was the face of a hunter. Yet there was the look about him of the hunted—cautious, wary. From his challenging stance, however, she was certain he was the kind more inclined to fight than to flee.

Her heart was pounding, yet it wasn't fear she felt. He took another step inside the room, and the lamplight brought his face into definition. Upon a second, closer look she thought, *he likes to win, and probably does; he likes to be right and probably is;* and lastly, because she found his dark eyes and black, collar-length hair so compellingly attractive, she thought, *he's used to being fawned over by women, and they probably do.*

As a teacher, Miss Devlin knew there was always an exception to every rule. And in this man's case, she was it.

"Miss Devlin, I presume."

The sound of his voice, deep and melodious and touched with a hint of humor, made her shiver. She wasn't quite sure of the source of his levity, until she noticed his gaze lazily raking her from head to foot. It was only then she realized that her titian hair was haphazardly tucked up inside a quaint, lace-edged sleeping cap. She was also barefoot and dressed in no more than a plain cream-colored flannel nightshift which, mercifully, was roomy enough to completely disguise the feminine figure beneath it. To make her dishabille complete, she was still wearing her reading spectacles!

Despite her best efforts to prevent it, Miss Devlin felt a blush rising up her neck. By the time it had stained her cheekbones she possessed the appalling knowledge that if she didn't say something soon, the stranger would somehow divine her confused feelings.

"I'm Miss Devlin" was all she could manage. To her

dismay, the voice she heard was throaty, almost seductive. There was nothing the least bit schoolmarmish about it.

"Somehow you're not what I expected," he replied.

The grin that split his face gave Miss Devlin the goad she needed to get hold of herself. He certainly wasn't admiring her beauty; more likely he was ridiculing her appearance. Stunned at how totally she had succumbed to the mystery surrounding this dark stranger—who was openly laughing at her—Miss Devlin sought to gain control of the situation by taking the offensive.

"I don't allow guns in my house," she said in an icy voice.

The stranger looked down at the Colt .45 tied low on his right leg and then back up at Miss Devlin. "My gun goes where I go," he answered in equally daunting tones.

"Guns kill people," she said.

"Yes, they do," he agreed.

"I abhor violence."

"I'm a peaceful man."

Miss Devlin's mouth puckered. She arched her neck and looked down her nose at the gunman through her reading spectacles. It was a pose guaranteed to cow even the most argumentative man into submission. And to a point, it worked.

"I don't go looking for trouble," the stranger amended.

"But somehow trouble always finds you," Miss Devlin retorted, angry, but not sure why. "I've always suspected men like you wear guns in a futile effort to disguise your hebetudinous natures. And now I'm sure of it."

The word *hebetudinous* rolled off Miss Devlin's tongue with all the ostentation of the wise preaching to the foolish. It wouldn't be the first time she had called a man stupid to his face with a word he couldn't understand. She was certain *hebetudinous*, spoken with just the right note of condescension, was exactly what she needed to put this dark-eyed stranger in his place.

To her amazement the gunman retorted, "I've always suspected women like you use big words when they know they're in the wrong. And now I'm sure of it."

"Why you vainglorious, supercilious—"

"Use all the big words you want. Because I'm not the least bit *hebetudinous,* ma'am. Pardon me, that's *Miss* Devlin, isn't it?"

She retreated.

He advanced.

Miss Devlin stared in disbelief at the look on his face. She could have sworn he was actually *leering* at her.

Eden was shaken and hard-pressed not to show it. This stranger simply ignored the verbal no trespassing signs she had posted all around her. Under the circumstances she wasn't sure how to handle him—assuming he could be handled. Maybe conciliation was the better route. She decided to give it a try.

"Perhaps I was too hasty in my condemnation of you. I—"

"I wear a gun because I need it for my work," he continued inexorably. "And I use it only when I have no other choice."

Miss Devlin had been too concerned with the stranger's intimidating presence to concentrate on what he was saying. All at once it sank in. "My God! You're a hired gun?"

The stranger shrugged. "It's how I make my living."

"Surely no one asked you to come to Sweetwater."

The stranger remained silent, and Eden felt an awful sinking feeling in the pit of her stomach. She wasn't aware that her hand gripped her gown in front, bunching the soft material so her full breasts were outlined for the stranger's frankly interested gaze.

"Who hired you?" she demanded.

He raised a brow but didn't answer.

"We don't need anyone bringing trouble here," Miss Devlin said, unaware of the pleading tone in her voice or the two flags of color burning in her cheeks.

"Trouble is where you find it," he replied curtly. The stranger abruptly shifted his body away from Miss Devlin toward the bookcase along one wall.

Miss Devlin had no explanation for his sudden defection from the argument at hand, but she was grateful for the respite that allowed her to compose herself—which was when she realized that the way she was clutching her gown had outlined her breasts, right down to the nipples, for the gunman's perusal. She did her best to rearrange the nightshift into its former shapelessness, but nothing she did could conceal the fact she had a respectable bosom.

Feeling at a distinct disadvantage, she decided discretion was the better part of valor. She would save her arguments for another time and place. It was past time to get this stranger out of her house. When she cleared her throat, the gunman turned his dark eyes back on her.

"As I was saying," Miss Devlin began. "We don't want any trouble here in Sweetwater. So I think it's best—"

"After what happened to this girl tonight I'd judge there's already trouble in this valley. I'm here to take care of it."

"We don't need you here," Miss Devlin snapped, her gray eyes flashing. She stepped around behind the sofa— which seemed a safer distance from the stranger—and slipped a protective arm around Bliss's shoulder. "So you can turn right around tonight and go back where you came from before some other young woman is subjected to the same disgraceful treatment as this poor girl."

"I won't take blame for what happened to the girl."

"I'm sure you don't like taking blame for the kind of rowdy behavior cowboys like yourself impose on others, drinking—"

"Oh, no, Miss Devlin," Bliss interrupted. "This man *saved* me from the drunken cowboys. In fact, he shot one of them."

Miss Devlin mashed her lips together and glared at the stranger. There was an intense struggle going on between her good sense and her redheaded temper, and she thought it best to keep her mouth shut until she could say something nice, since she was in the presence of one of her pupils. The returning glint of humor in the gunslinger's eyes proved to be more than she could bear.

"Bliss, go in my bedroom and shut the door," she ordered.

"But Miss Devlin—"

"Go!"

The unaccustomed stridency in Miss Devlin's voice sent Bliss scampering to the bedroom. The instant the door shut behind her pupil, Miss Devlin confronted the gunslinger. "However nobly you may have acted tonight I know your kind too well to believe—"

Her eyes widened as he vaulted over the sofa as though it wasn't there. Suddenly they were face-to-face.

"And I know your kind, Miss Devlin," the gunslinger said in a silky voice.

He stepped forward.

She stepped back.

Miss Devlin opened her mouth to tell him to stay away from her, but nothing came out. She fought the urge to cross her arms over her bosom. He was standing so close now she could feel his breath on her face.

"Like I said, Miss Devlin. I know your kind."

His voice was low, and so seductive she was prepared for anything but what he said next.

"You're a straitlaced, stiff-necked, stuffy old spinster who lives her life through the experiences of others and—"

"How dare you!"

"Too close to the mark for comfort, *Miss* Devlin?" the gunslinger goaded.

Miss Devlin's open palm hit the gunslinger's face with a resounding *thwack*. Eden recoiled in surprise at what she'd done. She had never struck another human being in her life, and the fact she should resort to violence, when her supposed objection to the man was that he solved people's problems in a violent way, caused her face to whiten with mortification. And yet, to her utter horror, she found it impossible to utter the words of apology she knew were necessary.

"Get out of my house," she grated in a voice that was a mere whisper.

"I thought there might be more to you than met the eye," he said, rubbing his cheek. "You know, you should learn to control that educated tongue of yours. It's likely to get you into trouble someday." With a wink and a roguish grin he turned on his heel, spurs jangling, and strolled out the door.

"Oh, you—" Miss Devlin couldn't think of an epithet harsh enough for the scoundrel who had just sauntered away from her. She was used to having the last word, but since nothing (decent) came to mind, she settled for slamming the door hard enough after him to leave the windows rattling.

Miss Devlin looked down at her hands and realized they were trembling. What a horrible, despicable man! He was sure to cause trouble in Sweetwater. Why, that stranger—whoever he was—had already shot a man. Then he had sauntered in and out of her home, insulting her and threatening her, and—and never even told her his name!

She thought of the awful things he had said about her. Imagine calling her a *straitlaced, stiff-necked, stuffy old spinster.* She was no such thing! Well, perhaps at twenty-nine she must own up to the spinster part, but she was none of the others.

Besides, there were perfectly good reasons why she had never married. And no one could say she hadn't led a perfectly fulfilled life all these years without a man by her side. Why, she most certainly had!

Besides, if Miss Devlin hadn't rushed into marriage it was because she had learned from bitter experience that having a husband didn't necessarily ensure happiness. She had seen firsthand the pain and suffering that could result from loving the wrong man. Just such a tragedy had left Eden orphaned at eleven when she had buried her mother, a woman who had made the mistake of marrying in haste and for love. That was enough to give anyone pause for thought. Miss Devlin had simply taken twenty-nine years to think about it.

It wasn't that she hadn't dreamed about getting married *someday.* And lately, when she lay alone in her bed, she admitted she might have missed something by denying herself a husband and children all these years. With her thirtieth birthday looming on the horizon, she had begun actually making lists in her head, weighing all the advantages of marriage against the risks.

That was how Miss Devlin had come up with the notion that she might avoid her mother's mistake if she simply didn't fall in love with the man she planned to marry. Of course, Eden intended to like him a great deal. But that wasn't the same thing. As long as she didn't love him, she would never be vulnerable—he could never break her heart. All this assuming, of course, that she could find some man willing to marry her whom she also liked well enough to take for a husband. So maybe she had earned the unflattering title of spinster, but it was a title she was not averse to seeing changed.

"Miss Devlin?" Bliss's tentative inquiry from the bedroom door called Miss Devlin's attention back to the matters at hand. She squared her shoulders and turned to face Bliss.

"Why don't you come out here and sit down at the dining room table with me, Bliss. It's time we talked about what you're doing out of bed in the middle of the night."

There was enough scold in Miss Devlin's voice to make Bliss quail. Nonetheless, she lifted her chin and replied, "I had to come. There's something I have to tell you."

"What's so important it couldn't wait until Monday?"

Bliss paused dramatically and then blurted, "I'm going to have a baby!"

Burke Kerrigan spent the entire ride to Sweetwater mulling his reaction to the enigmatic Miss Devlin. There was a certain kind of woman he usually associated with, and it wasn't schoolmarms. Yet he had found himself baiting her and waiting to see if she would rise and take the lure. He had enjoyed sparring verbally with her. In fact, she was the first woman he'd known who'd given as good as she'd got.

He hadn't missed her physical reaction to him either, which had been totally female. He felt sure, however, seeing how flustered she had become, that she hadn't understood her feelings. It might be fun, he thought with a grin, to strip off all those straitlaced, stiff-necked, stuffy old layers to see what lay beneath her priggish spinster's facade. He suspected what he would find might be well worth the effort.

Kerrigan shook his head when he thought of the galling things he had said to the schoolmarm. Truth to tell, he had deserved her slap. He ran his tongue around the inside of his cheek. The lady sure packed a wallop. But she was a big woman. Not big, exactly, but tall. Not that he held that against her. In fact, he found something decidedly exciting about the thought of having that much woman in his arms.

He had been on the verge of thinking her plain, but realized that between her flashing gray eyes and her striking cheekbones with their scattering of charming freckles, the word didn't fit. He'd had to turn away from her at one point for fear she would detect his visible response to the magnificent figure she had revealed beneath that shapeless nightgown.

He couldn't help grinning again when he remembered the ridiculous nightcap she had been wearing. Where had she gotten such a thing? There had been the promise of a wealth of burnished hair constrained beneath that prim cap, as he was sure there was a wealth of passion constrained beneath Miss Devlin's prim exterior.

Kerrigan sobered. He had no business thinking such thoughts about the local schoolteacher. He had other matters to attend to, and once he did, he would be leaving this town to move on to another. He was a drifter. A hired gun. There was no time or place in his life to tangle with a sharp-tongued spinster like Miss Devlin.

It was nearly midnight by the time Kerrigan arrived in town, and the saloon was still noisy with the sounds of Saturday night revelry. The Dog's Hind Leg was like dozens of other such establishments Kerrigan had seen in his lifetime, only on a smaller scale, and he easily passed it by in favor of the Townhouse Hotel across the street.

But appealing as he found the idea of a room with a bed that wasn't as hard or lumpy as the ground, Kerrigan was too keyed up to sleep. After setting his gear at the foot of the four-poster bed, and rinsing his face in the bowl of water on the washtable, he headed back downstairs to the saloon.

A man wearing a badge stood at the door to the Dog's Hind Leg, barring Kerrigan's entry. "Leave your weapon outside," the deputy said.

"My gun stays with me," Kerrigan replied, distastefully perusing the disorganized pile of handguns on a nearby table.

The deputy surveyed the gunslinger, noting his height, the breadth of his shoulders, and the way his gun was tied down low. "Don't want no trouble," the deputy said.

Kerrigan smiled, and for the second time that evening said, "I'm a peaceful man."

The deputy waited, but the tall stranger stood there, hard as whetstone. Deputy Joe Titman wasn't used to being defied. The local cowboys knew that if they didn't obey Deputy Joe, they would have to deal with Sheriff Reeves, and that was a different matter altogether. But that wasn't going to help him now. The stranger looked touchy as a teased rattler. Deputy Joe took an involuntary step back from the menacing man and said, "Sheriff Reeves ain't gonna like it."

As Kerrigan stepped across the threshold into the saloon, he glanced over his shoulder at the fidgeting deputy. "Tell the sheriff to see me if he has a problem."

Kerrigan didn't give either the sheriff or his deputy another thought, simply stepped up to the bar and ordered a whiskey. The bartender gave him a wary look when he realized he was still wearing his gun, but hurried to serve him. Kerrigan picked up his whiskey glass and turned around to lean his elbows on the bar. He hooked his boot on the footrail as he surveyed the room. He could have drawn a line down the middle of the saloon based on the division between nesters and cowboys.

He heard numerous voices with a Texas drawl coming from the cowboy tables, reminding him of home. Then, to his surprise, he heard a distinctive voice he recognized as Texan on the nester side of the room. That was odd enough to make him seek out the owner of the voice—and find the skinny face and gut-shrunk form of Levander Early. A scant year ago Kerrigan had run Levander out of Montana for rustling cattle. What was a man so handy with a running iron doing on the nester side of the room?

While Kerrigan was staring, Levander glanced up and the hired gun saw the yellow cat's eyes that had plagued him in the recent past. Levander turned and said something to the man seated next to him, then rose and headed toward Kerrigan.

Levander Early was thin as a bed slat and short as a tailhold on a bear. The coveralls and heavy farmer's boots he wore made him look like a boy dressed in a man's clothes. Kerrigan wasn't deceived. Levander Early might have been a young man, but he had long since reserved himself a seat in hell.

Levander ordered a whiskey from the bartender, and once it arrived drank it all down before he turned to face Kerrigan.

"When I told you to head south from Montana and keep going," Kerrigan said, "I had a mite farther south in mind than northeastern Wyoming."

"I'm sure you did," Levander said with a disarming grin. "But I gotta tell you, Kerrigan. When I got this far they were practically givin' away land, just givin' it away! Homestead Act or some such. I said to myself, Levander, I said, this is heaven. And suspectin' how I gotta spend the next life in the otherwheres, I decided to spend this one here."

"Are you trying to tell me you really are a farmer?" Kerrigan asked incredulously.

"I surely am," Levander confirmed. "Got me a house built, got land plowed, even got a few cows of my very own—the kind that gives milk. So you see, I'm a reformed man."

"I see." But Kerrigan was having a hard time believing.

"I come over to ask you not to spread the bad word about me. I done started over fresh. And I figger I deserve a second chance same as the next 'poke."

Before Kerrigan had a chance to respond to Levander's plea, he was distracted by a crescendo of murmuring voices. A single glance told him what he needed to know. Sheriff Reeves had arrived. When Kerrigan turned back to Levander, he discovered the new-made farmer had slipped away. Levander never had been one with much use for the law. That, at least, hadn't changed.

"From my deputy's description I had a feeling it might be you," Sheriff Reeves said. "Damn if it ain't."

"Howdy, Felton. Been a coon's age." Kerrigan extended his hand and the sheriff reached out and shook it. "Never thought I'd see you wearing a badge. Used to be you got called when I was too busy to take the job."

The sheriff merely smiled at the friendly jibe and said, "You here in Sweetwater on business, Kerrigan?"

"Sure am."

"I was afraid of that."

The two men knew each other well, yet they were a study in contrasts: one was light, one dark; one asked, one demanded; one shared himself with others, one didn't; one had settled down, one was still drifting.

"I don't have to ask who hired you," the sheriff said. "The only one with a bankroll big enough to pay you is the Association. Oak made a mistake hiring you, Kerrigan. I want you to ride out of here tonight."

Kerrigan took a sip of whiskey. "You know I can't do that, Felton."

"That's too bad. I've got enough problems in Sweetwater without adding a gunslinger to the lot."

"You know I never slap leather without honest provocation."

"Problem is, you're liable to get it here," the sheriff said. "Things are bad, Kerrigan. I don't intend for them to get worse."

"Time was we got along peaceful as two six-guns on the same belt," Kerrigan said.

"More like two bobcats in the same sack," the sheriff retorted.

It was hard for two men who had ridden so many gullies together to find themselves on opposite sides of the fence.

"Damn you, Kerrigan," Felton said with a snort of disgust. "I wish it'd been somebody else Oak got to do his dirty work. I like you too much to be the one who ends up hanging you."

Kerrigan grinned. "I'm a long way from that, I hope. What brought you to Sweetwater, Felton?"

"Got tired of traveling, being lean in the belly and on the run from the law. Decided I wanted a place of my own, a wife and kids."

"You make enough as a lawman to have all that?"

"I do well enough," the sheriff said, averting his eyes.

"You still a gambling man?"

"I play poker now and then."

"You still a ladies' man?"

Felton thought of Darcie Morton, the madam over in Canyon Creek who had been taking care of his needs since he had become sheriff of Sweetwater. While he and Kerrigan had shared women in the past, he found himself reluctant to mention Darcie's name. He smiled and said, "I ain't seeing anyone I'd care to share with the likes of you, if that's what you're asking."

"You're just mad because Doralee Smithers liked kissing a clean-shaven face like mine better than one with a prickly old mustache like yours."

Felton smiled and stroked his bushy blond mustache. "That's all right. I'm sure the lady I got picked out to be my wife won't give you the time of day."

"So, you really are settling down. If I know you she's a real looker."

Felton returned Kerrigan's grin. "Maybe you don't know me as well as you think. Actually, she's a plain-looking woman."

"Then it must be true love."

"Love has nothing to do with it."

At Kerrigan's questioning glance the sheriff explained. "A man who's wintered hard as many years as I have needs a special kind of wife. Miss Devlin is going to lend me the respectability I need to be a big man around here someday."

Kerrigan felt a prickle of unease at Felton's naming of his chosen bride. Surely there couldn't be *two* Miss Devlins in Sweetwater. "This Miss Devlin of yours, she wouldn't happen to be the local schoolteacher, would she?"

"How'd you know?"

Kerrigan bit down the epithet that sprang to mind. It was no business of his who Felton married. No business at all. Miss Devlin would sure clip his horns, all right. Aw, hell. If Felton Reeves wanted her, Burke Kerrigan wasn't going to stand in his way.

"I wish you luck in your courtship, Felton," Kerrigan said as he shook hands with the sheriff.

Once the congratulations were over, the gunslinger considered himself well rid of the spinster. He stood at the bar with Felton and drank to old times, to fast draws and faster horses.

Nevertheless, Miss Devlin's flashing eyes, her sharp tongue, and her tall, seductive form stayed on his mind the rest of the night.

Chapter 3

When you got nothin' to lose, try anythin'.

MISS DEVLIN HAD COMFORTED BLISS AS BEST SHE could and promised she would somehow find a solution to the dilemma that beset her young pupil. Miss Devlin had also reassured Bliss that while the gunshot wound in Hadley's shoulder was serious because he had lost so much blood, it wasn't deadly. With rest and care, he would recover completely.

After walking Bliss home, Miss Devlin spent a restless night plagued by unsettling visions of herself being held in the arms of a tall, dark-eyed man who bore a suspicious resemblance to the gunslinger. Such thoughts were so totally outside the normal realm of Miss Devlin's dreams (which, while adventuresome, had never included a dashing male figure) that she wasn't sure how to escape them. So instead she fully indulged them, reasoning that once she had let her wayward thoughts run their course, she would be free of them.

It was a foolish idea, Miss Devlin later conceded, because she awoke to find herself aching in new and quite alarming places. When Eden viewed herself in the mirror as she performed her ritual toilette, she was stunned to find her gray eyes almost lambent. Somehow, although she had never left the chaste confines of her bedroom, she felt disgracefully compromised.

Quite abruptly the dreamy look left her eyes, to be replaced by outrage. How dare that *rude, violent, unprincipled gunslinger* intrude on her private life! She simply would not allow it. Miss Devlin grimaced at her image in the mirror. She hoped she would have more success controlling her thoughts than she was having in confining her burnished curls in the tight bun arranged low on the back of her neck.

A narrow-brimmed hat, banded by a rust-colored ribbon that matched her dress, hid the worst of the rebellion. She straightened the tatted ivory lace collar that was the only decoration on the practical merino dress, draped it with a navy blue shawl, squared her shoulders, and marched out the door for church muttering denials of the potent stirrings the gunslinger had aroused in her.

Even in church she encountered unpleasant reminders of the awful situation that had brought the gunslinger to town. Nesters sat on hard wooden pews along one side of the chilly town meetinghouse that also served as a church, ranchers on the other. A narrow aisle that ran down the middle of the room might as well have been the Powder River, so little was the chance that either group might cross to greet the other. Miss Devlin found it especially uncomfortable because the simple act of sitting down meant having to choose sides.

Oak Westbrook never came to church because he contended, "God knows where to find me if he wants me," so Regina sat alone. Yet the sharp-eyed look the rancher's wife gave Miss Devlin made it clear she didn't wish for company. Eden settled herself next to Bliss and her family, thinking at least she would be able to determine how the troubled child had passed the night.

The absence of Hadley Westbrook and Big Ben Davis had cast a pall over the congregation that no amount of Reverend Simonson's uplifting words could conquer. Miss Devlin secretly felt the reverend's failure might well have resulted from his sermon entitled "Love Thy Neighbor."

Through whispers spoken as the collection plate was being passed, Miss Devlin discovered that Bliss had spent a sleepless night. She promised to ask Regina Westbrook for the most recent news on Hadley's condition and report back to her concerned pupil.

The congregation left the church like stiff-legged dogs and cats forced to walk the same narrow bridge—with equal likelihood that a spat would ensue. Miss Devlin lengthened her stride to catch Regina Westbrook before she stepped into her Concord spring-top buggy for the drive home.

"If you please, Mrs. Westbrook, I would like a moment of your time."

Regina responded to the authority in Miss Devlin's schoolteacher voice by turning around. But, immediately recovering herself, she replied, "I'm not sure what we have to say to one another."

"I hoped you could tell me how Hadley is feeling this morning."

The older woman's eyes filled with tears that she quickly blinked back. "The doctor promised Hadley will be himself again in a matter of days, and up and around before long. But I've never seen my son so pale. And Hadley swears he isn't hungry, but how will he get well if he doesn't eat? I confess, I'm worried about him."

"How long before he'll be well enough to receive visitors?"

"Not for a while, I'm afraid," Regina said in a frosty voice, her gaze skipping to where Bliss stood watching them from afar. "That is, some visitors will be welcome, of course. For instance if *you* want—"

"What about Bliss Davis?"

"That girl's father shot my son. His daughter isn't welcome in my home," Regina retorted.

"I thought Sheriff Reeves said Hadley didn't see the man who shot him, so he couldn't keep Big Ben in jail."

"Well, no, Hadley didn't. But everyone knows—"

"What people want to believe is quite often a far cry from the truth. Won't you please reconsider allowing Bliss to visit Hadley?"

"Never!" Regina turned abruptly, stepped up into her buggy, and sat down on the dark green leather-upholstered cushion. Taking the reins into her hands, she said a curt, "Good day, Miss Devlin."

The instant the buggy pulled away, Bliss was at Miss Devlin's side. "Is Hadley going to be all right? Can I come and see him?"

Miss Devlin put a comforting arm around Bliss's shoulder. "Hadley's going to be fine, Bliss. But Mrs. Westbrook says he isn't well enough for company yet. You'll have to wait a little longer to see him, I'm afraid."

Under the circumstances, Miss Devlin thought Bliss took this news with commendable stoicism.

"So long as I know he's going to be all right I can wait," she said. "Thank you, Miss Devlin. I'm going home now. I didn't get much sleep last night."

Miss Devlin followed Bliss with her eyes until she reached the welcoming embrace of her mother.

"You handled that very well."

The rumbling bass voice in her ear startled Miss Devlin, but she quickly regained her composure and smiled as she looked into a pair of friendly blue eyes. "I hardly expected to find you here today, Sheriff."

"It was the one place I could be sure of finding you."

"Me?"

"I was hoping you'd agree to have dinner with me."

"Dinner?"

"You don't have other plans, do you?"

"No."

Miss Devlin was aware how ridiculous her one-word responses must sound, but she wasn't sure what to say. The sheriff's invitation had come as a complete surprise.

When Felton Reeves had come to Sweetwater, she had noticed him right away because he was an attractive man, and one of the few tall enough for her to look up to. However, not once in the past two years had he expressed an interest in courting her. Fortunately, that also meant she had never used any Big Words to discourage him.

Since he had never expressed any personal interest in her in the past, Eden naturally presumed he must have some other reason for asking her to dinner—and a ready explanation came to mind. The invitation to join him must have something to do with the shooting. That settled in her mind, Miss Devlin smiled at the sheriff and said, "I'd be glad to dine with you."

To Miss Devlin's dismay, when she walked into the Townhouse Restaurant with Sheriff Reeves, the very first person she saw was that no-name gunslinger, sitting with his back to the wall. As big as he was, and dressed all in black in a cheerful room full of red-checked tablecloths, he was hard to miss.

She planned to ignore him, but Felton made a point of raising his hat to the man as they headed past him on their way to the sunshine-brightened tables by the front window. Miss Devlin nodded but kept her eyes averted from the gunslinger's face, agitated anew by memories of the previous night's encounter. To her utter disgust, she felt her face begin to flush.

She had a vain hope that the gunslinger would keep his mouth shut, but he didn't.

"Good afternoon, Miss Devlin."

She would have walked right past him without responding, except Felton had a politely supporting hand on her elbow and was able to stop her. She lifted her chin, determined not to end up in another confrontation with the stranger. "Good afternoon."

"You two know each other?" Felton's surprise and distress were evident in his frowning face and disapproving voice.

"Miss Devlin and I have only a passing acquaintance," the gunslinger replied. "In fact, we've never been properly introduced."

"There's no need—"

Miss Devlin was cut off by Felton's brusque, "This scoundrel is Burke Kerrigan. You'll do well to avoid him."

The flush on Miss Devlin's face darkened at Felton's rudeness, but the gunslinger only smiled and said, "Your introduction is only half complete, Felton. To whom do I have the honor of being presented?"

"My name is Eden Devlin."

"This is the respectable lady you were telling me about, Sheriff?"

Miss Devlin was confused by the gunslinger's comment, which suggested he had been discussing her with Felton, and irked by the way he had said *respectable lady* as though she were no such thing. Why, everyone knew Eden Devlin was the soul of propriety! The gunslinger's eyes slowly raked her from ribbon-trimmed hat to high-button shoes, and she realized suddenly that the only other time she had met him she had been wearing a nightshift and spectacles.

Miss Devlin's jaw slackened in horror. There had been a perfectly good reason why she had answered the door in her bedclothes last night, and if the gunman had suggested otherwise to Felton Reeves, why— She turned to Felton for some clarification of Kerrigan's statement, but the sheriff avoided her eyes. Taking a firm hold on her arm, he urged her away from Kerrigan's mocking glance.

Miss Devlin refused to take another step. Her eyes darkened as she pinned the gunslinger with an icy stare. That rogue had obviously told the sheriff some slander about her. No wonder Felton had invited her to dinner today. He probably planned to warn her off the man. As if she would ever have anything to do with Burke Kerrigan again!

Eden's temper got the better of her. "As a respectable lady," she began tartly, "I trust I will be safe from the unwelcome attentions of a gentleman like yourself." She left no doubt when she said *gentleman* that she meant exactly the opposite.

Kerrigan grinned. "You're right, of course. A gentleman like myself could hardly be expected to have a conversation with a lady—especially if the lady in question is determined to act *respectable*."

Eden opened her mouth to retort and found herself with nothing to say. That man had a way of turning her own words against her that she found totally reprehensible. Chagrined literally beyond words, and anxious to escape the scrutiny in the dark eyes that followed her, Miss Devlin allowed Felton to escort her to their table.

Felton was furious with Kerrigan. Why his former friend had stuck a spoon in the stew with Eden Devlin, Felton had no idea. If he hadn't known better, he would have thought, from the sparks flying between them, that the two had a long-standing feud. But Kerrigan had just gotten into town last night, so that was clearly impossible.

Still, he didn't like it. Felton had told Kerrigan about his serious intentions toward Miss Devlin. Maybe Kerrigan didn't realize that meant the "share-and-share-alike" rules they had followed with women in the past didn't apply in this instance. He would have to make sure Kerrigan got the message before he provoked another scene with Miss Devlin.

"What possible reason could you have for talking to that man about me?" Miss Devlin demanded when they were finally seated across from each other.

Eden waited while Felton cleared his throat, refusing all the while to meet her eyes. She suddenly found the sunshine uncomfortably warm, and the glare through the windows began to give her a headache.

At last the sheriff met her gaze and said, "I'm sorry if you was—"

"Were."

"Huh?"

"The correct form of the verb is *were,*" Eden said.

"Uh. I'm sorry if you *were* embarrassed by what Kerrigan said. But I ain't—"

"I'm not."

"You ain't embarrassed?"

"No! I mean, yes! I was embarrassed. I was correcting your grammar, Felton. *I'm not* is the correct form of *I ain't.*" Miss Devlin could see they might spend the whole meal misunderstanding each other if she kept interrupting, and vowed to bite her tongue at whatever grammatical irregularities there might be in the rest of Felton's confession.

"What I'm trying to say," Felton continued doggedly, "is that I ain't—*I'm not*—always going to be just a sheriff. I got plans to buy me land and start a ranch hereabouts. One day I'll be a man of position in Sweetwater, and I'll need a woman like you by my side. What I mean is, I want to court you, Miss Devlin, with the intention of marrying you."

Miss Devlin's instinctive reaction was to tell Felton

Reeves in Big Words she had no interest now, or in the future, in his courtship. A day ago, even a week ago, the words would already have been out of her mouth. Now she forced herself to stop and consider his proposition carefully.

As far as she could tell, the two of them had nothing in common. From what she had heard of him, and in a small town that was a lot, Felton didn't like to read and he preferred games of sport, cards in particular. Significantly, she couldn't seem to stop correcting his grammar, which was embarrassing for them both.

Staring down at her gloved hands, which were gripped tightly together, she admitted she wasn't getting any younger. With the shortage of single men her size in Sweetwater, this might very well be her one chance for the kind of marriage she wanted and, more importantly, a family before she was too old to have children.

To the good—considering she had vowed not to love the man she married—she felt no affection for Felton. But to her consternation, neither could she imagine allowing him to touch her as intimately as a husband must if they were to have a family. She thought that perhaps, with time, she might grow to like him enough to conceive of such familiarities between them. And, if he was willing, she could help him improve his grammar.

She was a little surprised he had waited so long to declare himself, but brushed the thought aside. His offer would allow her to be a wife and mother, goals she had feared beyond her reach. So, instead of the sharp setdown that had been on her lips, she found herself saying instead as she carefully tugged off her gloves, a finger at a time, "I would be pleased to accept your suit, Felton."

The beaming smile on his face below his bushy mustache was reward enough for her generous response. He was so genuinely nice and thoughtful for the rest of their meal together that Miss Devlin began to think perhaps she might have an easier time learning to like him than she had presumed.

She was conscious all the while of the man dressed in black sitting across the room. It vexed her that she knew the exact moment he rose to leave. Instead of heading for the door, he turned in their direction. She quickly forked a bite of pork chop into her mouth and began chewing vigorously.

"I assume from the smile on your face, Felton, that congratulations are in order," the gunslinger said.

"I ain't going—"

"I'm not . . . going." Miss Devlin bit her lip, but the damage was done.

Felton's jaw muscles worked for a moment before he continued, "I'm *not* going to invite you to kiss the lady's hand if that's what you was—"

"Were . . ." Miss Devlin turned her head away, feeling a sudden, desperate need to investigate an interesting knothole on the windowsill.

"—*were* angling for," Felton finished determinedly. "But I'm pleased to say Miss Devlin has agreed to see me with the object of marriage."

Miss Devlin turned back to observe what effect Felton's words had had on the gunslinger. To her utter disbelief, and right before Felton's frankly challenging eyes, Kerrigan took Miss Devlin's hand anyway—the one not holding the fork—and raised it to his lips.

The instant his lips touched her skin it was as though a lightning bolt streaked up her arm. She tried to jerk her hand away, but he had a firm hold on her and wouldn't be denied.

"May I wish you happy, Miss Devlin?" the gunslinger said, his breath warm and moist against her skin.

"It appears you're going to do so despite Felton's wishes," she said.

"Felton knows me well enough to allow the familiarity," Kerrigan countered.

"Well, I don't," Miss Devlin said, recovering her hand from him at last. She opened her mouth to give him a sharp setdown for his audacity, but was interrupted by Felton, who saw which way the wind was blowing and wanted to avoid the scene he felt sure Kerrigan would be happy to create.

"You ain't—"

"Aren't!" Eden snapped.

Felton flushed and Eden could have bitten her tongue off in remorse. If it hadn't been for that awful gunslinger, she would never have lost her temper with Felton, who couldn't help his atrocious grammar.

"—*aren't,*" Felton continued doggedly, "welcome company here, Kerrigan. So I'll thank you to be moving on."

Eden stared up into the gunslinger's eyes and saw the mocking humor was finally gone, leaving them cold and hard and not at all friendly. She wondered what she had ever seen in him to allow him to invade her dreams. She swallowed the masticated lump of meat in her mouth with difficulty and said, "Anyway, I'm sure my happiness is no concern of yours."

If possible, his eyes were even colder when he replied, "Pardon my presumption, Miss Devlin. Felton." He tipped his hat in a gesture that was insolent in the extreme before sauntering out the door.

It was lucky she had already swallowed the pork chop because Eden's throat closed so tight, she might otherwise have strangled. She set her fork down and hid her trembling hands in her lap. "Ooooh! That man! I'd like to shake him."

"Don't let Kerrigan upset you, Miss Devlin. He's more

than likely going to find himself jailed, or hanging from the business end of a rope, in the not too distant future."

"Can't you arrest him now?"

"He ain't broken any laws in Sweetwater."

Catching herself in the nick of time, she let Felton's poor grammar pass, but said, "You mean you have to let him kill someone before you can do something?"

"What would you like me to do?"

Eden felt an uneasiness around Burke Kerrigan—almost agitation, not quite irritation—that made her nearly desperate to avoid seeing him again. It was nothing she could explain with words, but she would have been quite happy at the moment to know he was confined anywhere she wouldn't accidentally run into him. Jail sounded pretty good, actually. But she could see Felton's point. He could hardly put Burke Kerrigan in jail simply for being annoying.

Eden drew her kid gloves on, anxious to make her escape. "I'm sorry, Felton. I took out my anger at that gunslinger unfairly on you. I hope you'll forgive me."

Felton captured her gloved hand in his. "Certainly, Miss Devlin. Don't worry," he reassured her. "I can handle Kerrigan."

Miss Devlin noted she felt nothing remotely like the electricity with Felton that she had experienced with Kerrigan and felt relieved . . . but also somehow disappointed. She refused to think further on the matter. In fact, she couldn't sit still for another instant. "I have to go now. I have some papers to grade this afternoon."

"I'll walk you home."

"No! I mean, no thank you, Felton. I'd like to be by myself for a while, to think."

"All right. Can I—"

"May I—Oh, I'm so sorry, Felton. I just can't seem to stop myself."

"It's all right," he said with a rueful smile. "So long as nobody else is around," he hurriedly added.

Eden relaxed and smiled back at Felton, who then said, "*May* I call on you later this week?"

Miss Devlin hesitated so long, she wondered herself what her response would be. But her pragmatism got the better of her. Felton Reeves wouldn't be a bad husband. He was certainly attractive enough to face every morning across the breakfast table, with his wavy blond hair and light blue eyes. More to the point, he was not put off by her plainness, or her height— or the fact she felt compelled to correct his grammar. If she didn't enjoy his company, or if she discovered any disagreeable bad habits, there would be plenty of time later to cry off. "Of course, Felton. I'll look forward to seeing you."

Miss Devlin used the solitary walk home to think about how she could help Bliss and Hadley, since dealing with the problems of others was infinitely preferable to dealing with her own. If only there were some way to end this war before it got started. If men would just learn the lessons history had to teach, they would know that violence never solved anything. It was seldom, however, that women were able to convince them otherwise—though they certainly had tried their best throughout the ages.

If only there were some leverage she could bring to bear to make the ranchers and nesters see reason. Women had so little ammunition they could use—tears and pleading exhausted her list. Unless, of course, she considered ridiculous options like the one used by the women in the bawdy Greek comedy *Lysistrata,* which she had been reading when the gunslinger interrupted her last night.

In the play, the women of Greece had all taken a sacred oath not to perform their marital duties until their husbands ended a destructive war. Amazingly, the women's ploy had worked. Miss Devlin grinned at the thought of

Regina Westbrook or Persia Davis vowing to withhold the
pleasures of the bedroom from their husbands until they
agreed to settle their differences peaceably. Why, the very
idea was—

Miss Devlin stopped in her tracks. She had to be out of
her mind even to be considering what she was considering. The very idea was crazy!

Why not? she thought. Desperate situations required
desperate measures. After all, men today weren't so very
different from the men of ancient Greece, were they?

It would never work. How could she even broach such a
subject to the rancher and nester wives?

The Sweetwater Ladies Social Club was meeting this
very afternoon. Every woman in Sweetwater belonged, although lately, they divided into factions the instant they
walked through the meetinghouse door. All she had to do
was show up and . . .

And convince the wives to withhold S-E-X from their
husbands? The very idea was absurd.

In the first place, how was she going to introduce such a
delicate subject? It made her cheeks pink even to think
about it! Although, what one must do, one could do.

In the second place, when the rancher and nester husbands found out what their wives were doing they
would—When she thought about it, what could they do? It
was hardly likely Oak Westbrook could intimidate Regina.
And despite his size, Persia Davis was well able to stand
up to Big Ben. Surely, if she could talk Regina and Persia
into supporting her idea, the others would follow their
lead. Miss Devlin felt a spark of excitement. The whole
business was so farfetched, it might even work.

She reversed her direction and began walking back
toward town so fast, she was practically running. The
ladies of Sweetwater would—

Miss Devlin stopped again.

The ladies of Sweetwater would think she had lost her mind. They would tell her to go home and mind her own business. Or worse, she would find herself out of a job and run out of town. Besides, she wasn't even sure Regina or Persia still enjoyed conjugal relations with their husbands. And she would be too embarrassed to ask.

But unless somebody did something, there was going to be more suffering and bloodshed. Bliss Davis and Hadley Westbrook would never be able to get married and raise their child in Sweetwater. Her chin jutting in determination, Miss Devlin marched the distance to the combination town meetinghouse and church where the Sweetwater Ladies Social Club would just be gathering.

Sure enough, when Miss Devlin entered the wooden frame building the women had rearranged six of the benches that had served as church pews into two semicircles facing either side of the stove. The nester wives had taken the set of benches in one corner to work on squares for a quilt they were making for the Christmas bazaar. The rancher wives worked on squares for the same quilt in the opposite corner. The ladies were talking quietly among themselves and didn't notice her at first.

"Good afternoon, Persia, Mabel, Amity." Miss Devlin nodded at the three nester women while she pulled up an empty chair and sat precisely in the center between the two quilting semicircles.

Miss Devlin turned to the rancher women in the other circle and said, "Good afternoon, Regina, Claire, Lynette."

In a town as small as Sweetwater, everyone knew everyone, so Miss Devlin was at least acquainted with the other women, who included the wives of the butcher, the blacksmith, the wholesale and retail grocer, the boot and saddlemaker, and the owner of the Townhouse Hotel.

"What brings you here, Miss Devlin?" Persia asked. "Not that you aren't welcome," she hastened to add.

"As long as she's not here to make trouble," Regina muttered, glaring at Persia.

Miss Devlin saw the battle lines had already been drawn. It might be too late for the women to join forces, but she had nothing to lose by presenting her idea—if she could only think of a way to do it.

She picked up a half-finished quilt square from each of the two circles and dropped them in her lap. She stole a needle from a nearby pincushion and began to thread it, stalling while she thought of how to begin. In the end, she realized there was no easy way to say what she had come to say. So she just opened her mouth and started talking.

"What would you ladies say if I told you I've found a way to get the rancher and nester menfolk to settle their differences peaceably?"

"I'd say that would truly be a blessing," Persia replied fervently.

"I'd say it would truly be a miracle," Regina said dryly.

Not allowing herself to be dissuaded by Regina's sarcasm, Miss Devlin continued, "What if I said your participation—agreement by all of you to get involved—is crucial to my plan?"

"What do you have in mind?" Mabel Ives asked.

"I don't care what it is," Amity Carson interjected. "I'd do anything to get things settled down the way they used to be. Ollie spends half of every night oiling his shotgun."

"I want to see an end to the violence," Lynette Wyatt said. "If I could I'd have stopped it long ago."

In her quiet but earnest voice Claire Falkner added, "I don't see what *we* can do to stop the fighting. We're only women."

"That's precisely why my plan will work," Miss Devlin said.

Persia set her quilt square down in her lap and gave Miss Devlin her full attention. "What do you have in mind?"

You could have heard a pin drop on the varnished wooden floor, it was so quiet. Miss Devlin took a deep breath and blurted, "It worked for the Greek women. I don't see any reason why it won't work for you."

The multitude of confused stares demanded an explanation, which Miss Devlin struggled to provide.

"I got the idea from a Greek play I've been reading. The women of both Athens and Sparta—that is, the women from both sides of a conflict—got tired of their men fighting one another. So, they refused to perform their marital duties until the men agreed to settle their differences. It worked. The men capitulated to the women's demands and the war ended."

A moment of stunned silence was followed by a babble of excited female voices.

"I never heard of such a thing!"

"I couldn't say no to Ollie."

"Rusty would break down the door if I tried to keep him out."

"You've got to be joking!"

"Did she say what I thought she said?"

"My Bevis would never stand for it."

"Ladies! Ladies!" Miss Devlin's schoolteacher voice quickly pierced the din and the assembled ladies fell silent. Miss Devlin had hoped for immediate support of her proposition, but it looked like she had her work cut out for her.

"I know what I've suggested sounds outlandish," Miss Devlin conceded.

Someone giggled.

"But before you reject my idea, let me warn you that unless something is done, and done soon, Big Ben Davis won't be the last husband or father who's jailed for shooting someone. And Hadley Westbrook won't be the last son or brother who's seriously injured—or killed."

"She's right," Persia said. "Ben didn't shoot Hadley—"

Regina Westbrook harrumphed.

"—but I know it's only a matter of time before he's provoked to violence. Since he got out of jail, he never goes to the fields without his Winchester."

"But Persia, you aren't seriously considering Miss Devlin's suggestion, are you?" Amity Carson demanded.

"I am," Persia answered.

"What if our husbands threaten to leave us?" one of the women asked Miss Devlin.

"They won't."

"Suppose they go to someone else?" another wondered.

"I'll talk to the ladies at the Dog's Hind Leg. We'll get them to join us," Miss Devlin said.

"Suppose my husband drags me by the hair into our bedroom," Claire Falkner suggested dramatically.

"Hang on to the doorposts."

"What if he threatens to beat me?"

"He wouldn't dare!"

"What if he flies into a rage and . . . takes me anyway," Claire said in a breathless voice.

Every woman in the room waited with bated breath to hear Miss Devlin's reply.

"Then, of course, you yield. But you can lie there like a . . . like a dead fish, denying him—and yourself—any pleasure. I shouldn't have to tell you there can be no joy for him if you don't share it."

"I could never do that to Bevis," Mabel Ives wailed.

"Of course you can," Persia snapped. She turned to Miss Devlin. "You have to know that even if *we* manage to make our husbands capitulate to our demands, unless *everyone* joins in, our efforts will be wasted." Persia glanced significantly across the room at Regina.

Regina's eyes narrowed in speculation. "It just might work. And contrary to what *others* might think, I am as anxious as the next person to see this ridiculous feuding settled." Regina glanced significantly across the room at Persia.

"Good," Miss Devlin said. "If you're all agreed—"

Miss Devlin wasn't expecting opposition at this point, so Lynette Wyatt's shrill voice startled her. "It's easy for you to say we should bar our bedroom doors, *Miss* Devlin. Since you've never enjoyed the pleasures of the marriage bed, you don't know what you're missing. Quite frankly, I'm not sure I could stand it for very long."

There was a prolonged silence while Miss Devlin swallowed the intense mortification she was feeling. "I may not know the precise nature of the deprivation I'm asking you to endure," she said in a surprisingly steady voice, "but I assure you that were I in your bloomers, I would not hesitate to keep them up—and sacrifice the pleasures of the bedroom—for the promise of peace."

A single pair of clapping hands applauded this statement before Regina intoned, "I'm sure your sentiments are in the right place, Miss Devlin. It really is too bad you won't have a chance to put your principles to the test."

A titter and a girlish giggle punctuated Regina's observation, but sharp looks from several women in the room quickly squelched the laughter. Anyone even mildly acquainted with Miss Devlin agreed it was a shame the spinster schoolteacher hadn't found a husband yet. Not that they hadn't tried to arrange things here and there over the years she had been in Sweetwater. But somehow the man had never suited. No one had ever been so cruel as to suggest it was Miss Devlin who had been found wanting.

Under the circumstances, no one regretted more than Miss Devlin the fact that she wasn't in a position to make the ultimate sacrifice. She promised herself she would not be so quick to dismiss Felton Reeves when he came calling, as he had promised to do.

"Lynette has a good point," Regina continued. "How long do you suppose we'll have to carry on this charade?"

"I can't help but think a concerted effort on the part of every married woman here will yield results in a very few days. To be certain, I would suggest—if you're going to emulate the Grecian ladies—that you do your best to flirt with your husbands, to tease them and make them desire you, even as you refuse them."

Claire's breathy voice floated into another silence. "Why that's . . . that's . . ."

"The most devilishly sneaky trick in the book," Regina finished for her with a smile.

Persia grinned. "I can't wait. It sounds like it might even be fun."

"For a while," Mabel cautiously agreed. "Exactly how long is it likely to take them to give in?"

"In Ollie's case, not very long," Amity said as she looked down at her fifth daughter, who was nursing at her breast.

The warm, wholesome laughter that greeted Amity's tart comment came from both circles. For the first time in the nearly eight months since the first fences had been cut and the first cattle had been rustled, both rancher and nester women were in accord.

"We're willing if you're willing," Persia said to Regina.

"We'll do it if you will," Regina answered.

"The Greek women took a solemn oath, and sanctified it with a toast of wine," Miss Devlin said, tapping her chin thoughtfully with her forefinger.

Lynette Wyatt pointed to the kettle brewing on the stove. "We've got some hot apple cider."

"That'll have to do," Miss Devlin murmured. "Everyone gather round and get a cup of cider."

Excited by the adventure on which they were all about to embark, the rancher and nester wives clustered around the cider kettle until everyone was holding a steaming cup of the potent brew.

"Each woman here swears there will be no more conjugal relations until her husband agrees to seek peace. And you all take an oath to that effect. The oath the Greek women took started something like this:

"On this sacred cup of . . . of friendship
We swear this oath of sacrifice.

"I guess I'll have to make up the rest, since I don't remember it exactly. But you repeat it after me as I say it," Miss Devlin instructed.

"From this day forth until peace is declared—"

"From this day forth until peace is declared—"

"Although my heart aches for my husband's love—"

"Although my heart aches for my husband's love—"

"And though he seeks me out afire with passion—"

Several sniggers were heard before the ladies repeated, "And though he seeks me out afire with passion—"

"I will take no man into my bed."

"I will take no man—"

"I can't! I can't take such an oath."

Every eye in the room focused on the woman crying hysterically in their midst.

"Stop it, Claire," Regina said.

"I can't do it," Claire sobbed.

"You *must*!" Regina captured Claire's free hand in hers. "We must all stand firm together, or this will never work. Now, repeat after me: I will take no man into my bed."

"I will take no man into my bed," Claire wailed.

"She'll probably take him on the floor," Persia muttered under her breath.

Everyone laughed again, and Miss Devlin had to quiet them before she could say, "I think under the circumstances there should be a little more to this oath. Repeat after me: *And if he overcomes me by sheer force—*"

"And if he overcomes me by sheer force—"

"I'll lie as cold as ice and not respond."

"I'll lie as cold as ice and not respond."

"Now you've taken the oath. You have to pledge it by drinking the cider."

The women all tipped their cups and took a swallow of the pungent brew.

The Sweetwater Ladies Social Club broke up not long afterward, with each woman wondering—and in some cases deliciously anticipating—how her husband would react to the oath she had taken, with more than one thinking that abstinence just might make the heart grow fonder.

Miss Devlin watched with mixed feelings as the rancher and nester women left the meetinghouse united by their cause. She was convinced that if all the women held firmly to their oaths, her plan could bring peace to Sweetwater. She wondered how many of them would actually be able to do what they had promised, and just how long the men could last without the comfort and sexual succor of their wives.

She glanced out the window and discovered the gunslinger leaning indolently against a wooden column on the second-floor balcony of the Townhouse Hotel. He was wearing a black shirt, but it was unbuttoned and pulled out of his Levi's, exposing a chest covered with curly black hair.

Miss Devlin was confused by the feelings that assaulted her as she stared up at him. She couldn't understand why she found him so compelling, or why she found it so pleasing simply to look at him. She quickly put a firm rein on the nebulous *something* she was feeling. She simply was not going to let herself think about that *awful, horrid, rude* man. Miss Eden Devlin was above that sort of silliness. She had hope that her courtship with Felton

Reeves would prove fruitful. If so, she soon would have a husband, and someday children, without the necessity of ever losing absolute control over her emotions. That way lay disaster, as she had learned from her mother's tragic experience.

Eden turned around and forced herself to look up at the gunslinger. He had been joined on the balcony by one of the ladies from the Dog's Hind Leg. She watched in awe as the half-clad woman brushed up against him, her nearly bared breasts teasing his hairy chest.

Miss Devlin stepped back from the window, frightened by feelings she didn't dare identify. She placed a hand against her belly where a tight, achy sensation had arisen. Suddenly, she was glad she had no husband to resist. Because it appeared the feelings she had so long denied, and had kept so rigidly under control, were more powerful than she had ever suspected.

She straightened her shoulders and stuck her chin up in the air, more determined than ever that she would *not* feel those feelings again. Surely as a rational, educated woman she could avoid the pitfall of allowing her emotions to control her life. At least, that was what she told herself as she left the meetinghouse for home.

Miss Devlin kept her gaze straight ahead as she marched past the Townhouse Hotel, gritting her teeth against the shiver caused by the sensual male chuckle that drifted down from the balcony as she passed by.

Chapter 4

A man don't get thirsty till he cain't get water.

"THE SWEETWATER STOCK GROWERS ASSOCIATION won't be needing your services after all, Mr. Kerrigan."

"Just Kerrigan. No mister."

"Certainly . . . Kerrigan."

Burke Kerrigan calmly perused the uncomfortable men sitting timidly on the delicate chairs and sofas in the drawing room of the Westbrook mansion. The weather-hewn cattlemen in their leather chaps and spurs seemed out of place in a room lit by a brilliant crystal chandelier and featuring rose-point lace curtains, a fireplace fronted with English tile, polished parquet floors, and handcarved cherry woodwork. He presumed the house had been built for a woman, for while a man might take pride in its appearance, and appreciate its beauty, the cowmen he knew would not readily welcome so domesticated a stomping ground.

The members of the Association would have been surprised to know the agitation he felt at the announcement that he had wasted his time coming to Wyoming. Kerrigan had already made plans for the balance of the money he was supposed to have earned for this job. He had been thinking lately about the future. Most hired guns didn't live to see their hair turn gray. Kerrigan already sported a touch of silver at the temples. He figured to get out of the business before his luck ran dry. Every job moved him one step closer to that goal. So he was more than a little disappointed that this deal was going bust.

Kerrigan's voice revealed none of what he was feeling when he asked, "You got rid of the rustlers on your own?"

Oak Westbrook chewed on the soggy end of his unlit Havana cigar—Regina forbade him lighting it anywhere except his study—before he slid it to a corner of his mouth and said, "Not exactly. Uh, something has come up . . . uh . . . I'm not sure we're going to be able to wait the length of time it would take you to find the rustlers before we have to come to some accommodation with the nesters."

"I don't understand," Kerrigan said flatly.

"Uh . . . it's not something I can easily explain," Oak hedged.

"Just tell him," Rusty Falkner said in an irritable voice.

"Tell me what?"

"We're being blackmailed," Cyrus Wyatt blurted.

"By whom?" Kerrigan asked.

"Our wives," Oak answered through jaws clamped tight on his cigar. Although the gunslinger stared at him in patent disbelief, that was all Oak could bring himself to say. He had no intention of admitting the hoops Regina had put him through last night. First the teasing, the taunting, the kind of anticipation he hadn't experienced in thirty years, and then the ultimatum given in soft, dulcet tones before the bedroom door slammed right in his face. He shook with anger as he remembered pounding on the door in vain. Only Regina's warning that he would disturb Hadley had made him turn tail. He had spent the night in the guest room. On a too short bed. With a scratchy wool blanket. And a pillow with feathers that made him sneeze.

He hadn't felt any better when Rusty and Cyrus and a half-dozen other husbands had arrived at the Association meeting ranting about equally high-handed treatment from their wives.

"I told her she was getting a mite too big for her britches," Cyrus had related, "and you know what she said? There was no chance she was going to be 'getting big' anytime soon unless this business with the nesters is settled!"

There were veiled hints to Cyrus that he should have taken his wife anyway, if he wanted her, to which he had replied in heated tones, "I tried that. She just laid there like . . . like . . ."

"Like a bumpy log," another man volunteered. "That's what my wife did," he mumbled when he became the object of all eyes.

From what the members of the Association had been able to piece together before Burke Kerrigan had arrived to silence them, all the wives in Sweetwater—including the nesters' wives—had joined in the game. The rough-and-ready cattlemen exchanged guilty glances, wondering how they were going to admit to the gunman from Texas in what particular way they were being bullied by their wives.

"Maybe if I knew what your problem is, I could help solve it," the gunslinger volunteered.

Several of the men snickered. Another coughed nervously. One blushed.

"It's a . . . hmm . . . a delicate matter," Rusty said.

The gunslinger rose and glanced around the room of miserable, even surly, faces. "Then I guess if you don't need me, I'll be heading back to Texas."

Kerrigan hadn't gone two steps toward the door before

Oak rose and cried out, "Wait!" He turned to the others in the room and said, "I hate like hell letting those rustling nesters get the best of me. What have we got to lose if we let Kerrigan in on the plot against us?"

"Our pride," someone muttered.

"In my opinion, that's a small price to pay if we get satisfaction," Oak opined in a somber voice. "We ought to at least give Kerrigan the chance to help us find a solution that doesn't involve outright surrender."

Kerrigan stood patiently while the men in the room made up their minds.

"Well, are you with me?" Oak demanded of his friends.

"Aw, for chrissake, Oak. Go ahead and blab," Cyrus said. "I don't think I can get any lower in the lip than I already am."

The gunslinger crossed to the fireplace and rested an arm on the brass-trimmed walnut mantel as he waited for the head of the Association to spill the beans.

"It isn't a pretty story," Oak began, "but the gist of it is, our wives have joined forces with the nester wives in the cockeyed notion of keeping us out of our bedrooms until we settle our differences with the nesters."

Kerrigan was hard pressed to keep from laughing, but he could see from the belligerent faces around him that it would be a mistake. "Why not simply stay out of the bedroom until you catch the rustlers?"

"That could take weeks!" one man said.

"Months!" another exclaimed.

"There are other women besides your wives who could take care of your needs," Kerrigan suggested.

"I already tried that," someone interjected.

The gunslinger raised a surprised brow.

"The ladies at the Dog's Hind Leg are in cahoots with our wives," he explained in a disgruntled voice.

"I see," Kerrigan said, turning toward the fireplace to

hide the grin he couldn't control. "Of course, you can't be expected to last indefinitely without your wives," he said, "but surely you could last long enough for me to track down the rustlers. At least that would give you a bargaining chit with the nesters."

"He's right," Oak said. "I can last a . . . a month. How about the rest of you?"

No man was going to admit he was so tied to his wife's apron strings that he couldn't last so short a time without her—they had all been on cattle drives that long and more.

Rusty couldn't help remarking, "It ain't goin' to be easy."

"Nothing worthwhile ever is," Kerrigan advised sagely.

In short order all those present had agreed to resist the charms of their wives—which had become infinitely more attractive now that they were forbidden—while Kerrigan searched out the rustlers. The Association would meet again in a month, or when Kerrigan caught the rustlers, whichever came first.

As the gathering rose from their seats to take refreshments Kerrigan asked, "Who came up with the crazy idea for your wives to barricade their bedroom doors?"

The men looked at one another with blank stares.

"I never thought to ask," one said.

"Neither did I," another offered.

Oak chomped down hard on his cigar. "I did."

"Who was it?"

Each man avoided looking at the others, hoping to heaven that his wife wasn't the culprit.

"It was the schoolteacher, Miss Devlin," Oak announced.

Kerrigan choked on his coffee.

A collective gasp rose from the crowd, followed by angry exclamations.

"Why, she ain't even married!"

"What business is this of hers?"

"She oughtta be tarred and feathered!"

"If that old maid knew what she was missing, she'd never have incited our wives to deny us," Cyrus said.

"Little chance of that," Wyatt said, "Plain as she is—"

"—and tall as a pine—" Cyrus interrupted.

"—and sharp-tongued to boot—" another offered.

"—there ain't a man likely even to give it a try," Wyatt finished.

"I disagree," Kerrigan said quietly. He couldn't have said why he championed Miss Devlin, because he knew from his own little experience with her that she was plain and tall and sharp-tongued. But she hadn't struck him as quite so awful as the members of the Association had painted her. Unfortunately, what the others heard in his statement was something far different than he had intended.

"You'd be willing to bed her?" Cyrus asked.

"That sure would take the starch out of her collar," Rusty said with a sly grin.

"Rusty's right," Oak agreed, his eyes narrowed in contemplation. "Miss Devlin could hardly incite our wives to deny us if she was enjoying the pleasures of the flesh herself."

There was utter silence in the room as the horde of disgruntled husbands considered Oak's words.

"Are you suggesting what I think you're suggesting, Oak?" Cyrus asked incredulously.

"I'm merely saying that we've hired Kerrigan to handle the trouble in Sweetwater. Maybe we should add another little bit of trouble to the job. After all, a man of Mr. Kerrigan's considerable talents should be able to seduce a plain-faced spinster like Miss Devlin." He turned to confront Kerrigan and added, "Especially when we offer him a substantial bonus for the job."

Everyone waited with sucked-up guts to hear the

gunslinger's response to this outrageous proposal. His eyelids were lowered, hiding his reaction, his voice emotionless when he asked, "How much of a bonus did you have in mind?"

"How about a hundred dollars?" Oak said.

"How about a thousand dollars?" the gunman replied.

His voice was curt, and Oak thought perhaps Kerrigan disapproved of the idea, except if he did, why hadn't he just said so instead of bargaining for more money? "That's a lot of cash."

"As I understand the situation, what you're asking me to do will be well worth every penny," the gunslinger drawled.

Oak's eyes scanned the room, getting tacit permission from those assembled. "All right," he said at last. "One thousand dollars for the seduction of Miss Devlin."

The gunslinger abandoned his negligent slouch by the fireplace and approached Oak. "It's a deal."

Oak wanted to ask how and when they would know the deed was done, but remained silent in response to the icy coldness of Kerrigan's dark-eyed gaze when they shook hands.

"I'll be in touch," Kerrigan said. Without taking the least notice of the men who stood gawking at him, he turned and left. They heard the heavy oak front door slamming shut behind him.

"How're we gonna know if he does what we hired him to do?" one man asked in the stupefied quiet that followed Kerrigan's departure.

"I imagine he'll turn the rustlers over to the sheriff," Oak replied.

The man turned beet red. "No, I meant the other. A woman don't look no different when . . ."

"For crying out loud," Cyrus said. "What makes you think he's going to be successful? I expect you're underestimating Miss Devlin. That woman would talk a man to death before she unbuttoned the first button."

There were some relieved looks on the appalled faces of those men who couldn't quite believe to what ends their desperation had driven them. It was something quite out of the ordinary to hire a man to seduce an innocent woman. Their relief was short-lived.

"On the contrary," Oak countered as he stared at the door through which the gunman had departed. "I think you're underestimating the persuasive powers of Mr. Kerrigan. To be on the safe side, however, I think we better keep this little bargain to ourselves."

There was no objection to be heard from the men shifting uncomfortably around their consciences.

Meanwhile, on the other side of the valley, a similar meeting of nesters was under way led by Big Ben Davis. The farmers had gathered at the split-log home of one of the bachelors among them, Levander Early. Although the chinks in the walls had been stuffed with newspaper, the house was drafty. It had a dirt floor and shuttered windows. The single rectangular room served as bedroom, parlor, and kitchen. The farmers who had crowded inside the crude structure leaned against the wall, perched on the brass four-poster bed and straddled the benches at the kitchen table. Levander Early had claimed the rocker by the stone fireplace for himself.

"We cain't trust the Sweetwater Stock Growers Association to deal fair," Levander said. "I say we don't make up to 'em no matter what."

"Easy for you to say," Bevis Ives argued. "You and your friends don't have wives making your lives unbearable."

Levander glanced quickly at the men who had been a part of his gang in the Montana Territory in the days before he had supposedly become an honest farmer in Wyoming. It hadn't been easy convincing Bud, Hogg, Doanie, and Stick that they could make a dishonest living in Sweetwater. He had carefully explained that being a part of the community was the perfect cover for their life of crime. They had all filed for adjoining land under the Homestead Act, and Levander had browbeaten his cohorts into plowing the land and planting crops, which they had harvested to their profit.

But Levander had greater expectations than could be realized from the pittance the land had rendered up. All his plans of future wealth depended on the upheaval he and his gang had created in the valley. He had no intention of letting the nesters make peace overtures to the ranchers. It served his purpose very well to have one side distrustful of the other. The current state of affairs he and his gang had created offered them the chance to take from both sides with neither being the wiser.

"You cain't knuckle under to your wives," Levander cajoled, "or you risk losin' everythin'."

"My wife can make me so miserable I don't *care* if I lose everything," Ollie Carson muttered.

"Levander's right, Ollie," Big Ben said. "We can't let our wives get away with this. They don't realize what we stand to lose."

"I ain't never spent the night apart from my wife—till last night," Ollie admitted. "I honestly don't think I kin stand it for another night."

"You'll have to," Big Ben said, giving Ollie a stern look. "But I agree we gotta find a way to end this foolishness, and fast. I vote we do some investigating of our own to find out who's been doing the rustling that's got the Association so riled up. That oughtta go a long way toward bringing peace to the valley."

"That's a great idea!" Bevis agreed. "If we can catch

the rustlers the 'Sociation'll be happy and we'll get our wives back."

"Don't know 'bout that," Levander said with a frown. "How're we gonna catch the rustlers when neither the sheriff nor the 'Sociation can? And it ain't only the rustlin'," Levander reminded. "Them cattlemen have got their eyes on that water we fenced off last summer."

"I been thinking about that too," Big Ben said. "Maybe we were a bit hasty there."

"Never say it!" Levander cried in a horrified voice. "If we hadn't fenced off that water there'd've been steers crossin' our land all summer to get to it."

"I'm not so sure about that," Big Ben said.

Levander could see all his fine ambitions about to bite the dust. "Hell, 'fore we make plans to go chasin' rustlers, maybe we better give the idea some more considerin'."

"I don't need to do any more considering," Bevis said. "I say we *do* something."

"Like what?" Big Ben asked.

"Start patrolling for the rustlers."

Levander snorted in disgust. "More'n likely the 'Sociation is gonna think your patrols *is* the rustlers. And that gunslinger from Texas the 'Sociation hired is liable to shoot somebody right through the gizzard—purely by mistake, o' course."

Levander was pleased to see from the leery faces around him that his words had struck home. "I heard tell this Kerrigan fellow has killed more'n a dozen men. No sense any of us takin' one of his bullets."

"But we can't just do nothing!" Ollie protested.

"That's true enough," Big Ben said. "But Levander may be right. We need to think a little more about the right thing to do. We'll just have to do the best we can to outlast our wives for a while."

Big Ben was sure that wasn't going to be as easy as it

sounded out loud. He and Persia had always had a good time between the sheets, or under a tree, or beside a stream. It hadn't mattered where they were. He always wanted her and she was always willing . . . until last night.

He had thought maybe she had arranged a special welcome home after his release from jail, she had looked so beautiful at the supper table. Her face, surrounded by honey-brown curls, had been lit up with excitement, making her green eyes sparkle, and her lips had twitched into a stunning smile whenever he had managed to catch her eye. When she had shooed Bliss and Sally to bed early, he had known it was going to be a special evening. And it had been, but not at all in the way he had hoped.

Big Ben hadn't known his wife could be so alluring. In the entire sixteen years they had been married he could never remember a night when she had taken her clothes off one piece at a time, keeping him at arm's length and forbidding him to touch. She had unbuttoned her dress one button at a time, revealing the soft white flesh that was so different from the sun-browned skin exposed to the harsh frontier sun. That was enough by itself to make him hard, but as she unbuttoned her dress she ran her hands across her small breasts, touching herself in the way he wanted to touch her, making her nipples peak. It was exquisite torture.

He would have been inside her an instant later, except she held up a hand and said breathlessly, "Wait. It'll be better if you wait."

Big Ben hurt, he wanted Persia so bad, but as much as he wanted her, he liked the feeling of wanting her more. So he had obliged her. He watched her strip to nothing more than her pantalettes. She had shoved them down in front, exposing her navel, and her hands were lost deep inside them. His heart was pounding so hard it was all he could do to hear. His mouth was so dry he couldn't swallow.

"Come here, Ben," Persia had said in a husky voice.

He was on her in an instant, his hands surrounding her breasts, his lips latched onto hers, his tongue deep inside her mouth claiming the siren who was his wife.

A second later he was bereft of the woman who had been in his arms. Persia had backed up against the bedroom wall panting hard, holding a shotgun in her trembling hands that was aimed right at his belly. Flushed and quivering, it was hard for her to speak. But speak she did, in words so unbelievable, his ears had burned.

In sixteen years he had never forced his wife to share herself with him, and he wasn't about to start now, no matter what the provocation. He had left his bedroom and spent the night in the smelly barn. On the itchy hay. In the bitter cold. By himself.

If there was any way he could get this business with the ranchers settled, he wanted it settled. He wanted his wife back. And soon. Because Persia had promised that once there was peace in the valley . . .

Big Ben shook himself from his reverie. "There's no reason why we can't all be on the lookout for rustlers," he said.

"All right," Levander reluctantly agreed. "If anyone sees anythin' s'picious, report to me, and I'll see that Bud and Hogg and Doanie and Stick gets the word to the rest of y'all. Agreed?"

Big Ben looked around the room of nodding heads before he said, "Agreed."

Levander hadn't been completely successful keeping things under control, but at least he would be able to silence any suspicions before they got voiced. It was too bad he had to share the spoils from rustling with the gang of men in cahoots with him. But then, there was a lot to share. And having help made everything so much easier.

Nobody even suspected the real source of all their troubles in Sweetwater.

Kerrigan was angry with himself. He had done a lot of dirty jobs in his lifetime—rustled cattle and horses, intimidated weaker men, even killed some who had given him no other choice—but he had never sunk to seducing an innocent woman for pay. And while he had often acted outside the law, he had always been able to argue that he was administering his own peculiar brand of justice. But where was the justice in what he had just agreed to do?

The men who'd hired him had to be blind if all they saw in Eden Devlin was a "plain-faced spinster schoolteacher." Behind her old-maid spectacles, Kerrigan had watched her gray eyes flash with defiance. She might keep her hair bound up in a bun, but he had seen her rich titian curls escaping from that silly nightcap. And they might think her "tall as a pine," but as far as he was concerned, that just meant she would fit him better in all the right places. So maybe, he realized, the reason he felt so upset was because the money tainted his enjoyment of something he would have found pleasure in doing for nothing.

The more he thought about it, the more sure he was that if he went about it the right way, a proper seduction would be good for Miss Devlin. Once he convinced her to leave off all those educated airs, and the barbed words that stung worse than a red ant bite that she used to keep a man away, she would find herself with more suitors than she could handle.

Which reminded him that Felton had a prior claim to the lady.

Kerrigan took off his hat and forked a hand through his black hair. It wouldn't be the first time he and Felton had gone after the same woman. He remembered a time down in Laredo . . . Kerrigan chuckled when he thought how Felton had won the girl with a half pound of chocolates in a heart-shaped box. Then there was the time in Lubbock . . . A hair ribbon had done the trick for Kerrigan that time. Of course, this was the first time either of them had had a notion of marrying the woman in question. But he hardly thought Miss Devlin was going to succumb to a box of chocolates or a pink hair ribbon. With her it was going to take . . .

Kerrigan tilted his face up and scratched the itchy growth of whiskers under his chin. Just what would it take to coax Miss Devlin to let down her fences? He was going to have to find out why she had put them up in the first place. Had some man hurt her in the past? She seemed too ignorant of her reaction to him for that to be the case. But he could be wrong. He had to admit his curiosity was piqued. He was looking forward to the challenge of finding out why Miss Devlin had shunned the male of the species for long enough to become an old maid.

Kerrigan grinned, creating two deep slashes on either side of his mouth. He had to hand it to Miss Devlin. Her bold plan to have the wives withhold sex from their husbands in order to force peace was a masterpiece of deviltry. Such genius deserved a compliment. Accordingly, he turned his horse in the direction of the schoolmarm's home. There was no time like the present to begin the seduction of Miss Devlin.

Chapter 5

*If you fall in a cactus patch,
you can expect to pick stickers.*

MISS DEVLIN FELT LIKE THE LOSER IN A GREASED-PIG contest—worn out, frustrated, and darned foolish. And she had no one to blame but herself.

Her students had picked up on the tension between their parents caused by the silent sexual warfare she had instigated, and today they had been even more irascible than usual. For reasons she chose not to examine too closely, her own mood had been little better. She couldn't seem to keep her mind on teaching. The school day had started out badly and gone steadily downhill.

Sally Davis had dipped Henry Westbrook's blond braids in an inkwell. The twins, Glynne and Gerald Falkner, had put a frog in Emmaline Carson's lunch box. Wade Ives had tripped Daniel Wyatt so he fell into a pile of horse flop. Things were decidedly out of control. At thirty minutes before the school day officially ended, Miss Devlin was at the end of her rope.

She checked the top button of her dress to make sure it was secure, shoved a straggling curl out of her face (not even her hair was cooperating today), and said in a carefully controlled voice, "Please take out your *McGuffey's Readers*."

"Somebody stole my book," Felicity Falkner complained.

Miss Devlin's gaze shifted to the guilty face of the freckle-nosed girl sitting next to Felicity. "Enid, do you have any idea where Felicity's book might be?"

"No, Miss Devlin."

"Then I guess you and Felicity will have to share a book."

"But Miss Devlin—"

"Don't say another word!" The sharpness of Miss Devlin's voice surprised her as much as it did her students.

"But Miss Devlin—"

"I said—" Miss Devlin shut her mouth abruptly when she followed Enid's pointing finger to the door of the schoolhouse and found herself staring into the questioning eyes of the gunslinger from Texas. It was the final straw.

"What are you doing here?" she snapped.

"I came to see you."

"We were going to read from our *McGuffey's*," she said, struggling to rein her flaring temper. "Perhaps you would like to join us?"

The gunslinger grinned as he walked past her and slipped onto a bench at the back of the room. "Be glad to."

Nettled that the gunslinger had accepted her sarcastic offer, Miss Devlin turned her attention back to the class—in time to catch Keefe Wyatt throwing a punch at Jett Ives. Jett was quick to return the insult. The boys launched themselves at one another and a free-for-all erupted in the middle of the schoolroom floor.

"Keefe! Jett! Stop that this instant!"

Neither boy had a chance to react to her command before they were each grabbed by their collars and hauled onto their feet—their toes, to be exact. Each boy hung like a sack of potatoes from one of Burke Kerrigan's powerful hands.

"You want to kill each other?" he said in a quiet voice. "I can give you a hand with that."

The gunslinger dropped the two gangly teens, who barely managed to stand on their shaky legs.

"Here." He handed one of the startled youths his Colt .45 and the other a small pearl-handled derringer from his boot.

"Now," Kerrigan drawled, "all you have to do is cock your gun and pull the trigger. Don't worry," he said to Jett, who held the smaller gun. "That derringer'll do the job at this distance. Now you two can settle your differences once and for all."

Both boys were white-faced, but with all their friends looking on, neither wanted to be the one to cry quits.

Keefe cocked his gun.

Jett cocked his.

Miss Devlin was shocked to her core. This couldn't be happening in her schoolroom. "This has gone far enough. I want you both to—"

"Be still." The gunslinger's quiet command startled Miss Devlin into silence. He never took his eyes off the two boys and kept up an easy banter. "You see, boys, when a man makes up his mind to do a thing, he should do it. The fellow who straddles the fence just gets a sore—" He stopped, as though suddenly aware of all the eager young ears listening, and finished "—tailbone."

A film of perspiration had built on Keefe's brow. Jett swallowed so hard his Adam's apple bobbed up and down. Neither boy's hands were steady. The tension built until it seemed like the room and everything in it might explode.

Miss Devlin's heart was in her throat, her pulse pounding in her temple. One—or both—of these innocent young boys was going to die. And that gunslinger was to blame.

She balled her trembling hands into fighting fists. Burke Kerrigan would pay for this. She wouldn't let him get away with murder—for that's what this was, even though he might not be the one pulling the trigger. He was a man of violence. He didn't belong here. She should never have invited him to stay.

"I guess you don't want to kill each other as much as you thought," Kerrigan said in a calm voice. "Real easy, now, let your hands drop to your sides. Slow and easy. Let 'em go."

For a moment it seemed they wouldn't comply. But ever so slowly Keefe's hand dropped to his side. Jett's hand wobbled as he lowered it.

Kerrigan quickly retrieved his weapons, uncocking them, holstering one and slipping the other into his boot in a surprisingly graceful motion.

Then all hell broke loose.

"You idiot! You crazy lunatic! How dare you give guns to children? You asinine—"

"Hadn't you better send these kids out of here before you get wound up and say any more?"

The grim smile on Kerrigan's face brought Miss Devlin back to her surroundings, and she realized she was nose to nose with the gunslinger, her hands holding fistfuls of his dark wool shirt. She turned to find fifteen wide-eyed pupils staring at her.

"School is dismissed."

When no one moved, Miss Devlin whirled, her pleated skirt flaring, and put her fists on her hips. "I said school is dismissed!"

"I'll be glad to stay if you think—" Keefe began.

"I'll stay if you—" Jett interrupted.

Keefe and Jett glared at each other until they realized what they were doing, then turned sheepish faces toward Miss Devlin.

"We'll *both* stay if you think you need us," Keefe said, warily eyeing the gunslinger.

"I'll be perfectly fine," Miss Devlin assured them. "Right now I want some privacy to speak with Mr. Kerrigan."

Reluctantly the boys trailed out of the room at the tail end of the departing pupils.

Miss Devlin slowly turned back to face the gunslinger. "I don't know what you were trying to prove, but you chose a deadly way of making your point."

"In a few years, those boys'll be grown. Better to let them see now what it means to consider killing a man."

"What if one of them had shot the other?" Miss Devlin demanded in exasperation.

"They didn't."

"No thanks to you! Violence isn't always the answer, Mr. Kerrigan. Might isn't always right."

"It'll do till the next best thing comes along."

"How can you say such a thing?"

"Because I know what it means to turn the other cheek," he retorted. "I tried doing things the peaceable way once upon a time. I learned pretty damn quick that might may not always be right, but it goes a long way toward setting things square."

"But violence—"

"—isn't always the answer. I heard you, Miss Devlin." He paused and said, "Sometimes it's the only answer."

Miss Devlin paled. "I . . . I refuse to believe that." Violence only led to more violence. She had learned that lesson from her father, and she had never forgotten it. "Violence never solves anything, Mr. Kerrigan."

The gunslinger snorted his disdain. "Then why did you suggest that outlandish plan to the rancher and nester wives?"

"But my plan doesn't involve violence," she protested.

"Like hell it doesn't!"

"I don't understand what you mean."

The gunslinger smirked. "Of course you don't. A spinster lady like yourself wouldn't know the danger of playing with that kind of fire."

His eyes took a lazy tour of her face and form, lingering at last on her mouth. Miss Devlin was uncomfortable with the growing ardor in his gaze as his lids lowered over his dark eyes. She thought he might be mocking her again, but she hadn't enough experience with this sort of thing to know for sure.

"If you have something to say, Mr. Kerrigan, why don't you come out and say it?"

"Sex can be a powerful weapon."

"What?" Miss Devlin flushed. She should have expected a scoundrel like him to use *that* word in mixed company.

"At least, you've turned it into one, the way you've got wives making demands in exchange for their favors. Frightening when you think about it. . . ."

He let his voice trail off, leaving Eden to contemplate the enormity of his accusation. "I only wanted to offer a peaceful solution—"

"You call dallying with the bedroom affairs between husbands and wives *peaceful*?" he asked incredulously. "Where did you ever get a crazy idea like that?"

"I . . . I just thought—"

"—a thought based on ignorance. You, of all people, should know the importance of making educated decisions, Miss Devlin. I could give you a lesson—"

"I don't have to know—"

"—right now that would give you a pretty good idea of the powerful passions you've set in motion."

He stepped closer as he spoke, and Miss Devlin was suddenly aware of how tall he was, how broad his shoulders, how narrow his hips. He was close enough that she could see the fine laugh lines at the corners of his eyes, the slanting scar on his cheek, the shadow of dark beard on his face. She could actually smell him, the scents at once foreign and familiar. Saddle leather. Sweat. A musky smell both strange and alluring.

His entire posture challenged her, daring her to stand her ground. The urge was there to retreat. But she had already learned that when she ran, he pursued. Miss Devlin wasn't about to give him another chance to play fox and hare with her. She stood rigidly in place, chin up, shoulders back, defiant. She swallowed despite the dryness of her mouth and demanded, "What kind of lesson did you have in mind, Mr. Kerrigan?"

"A kiss, Miss Devlin."

"That's all?"

"That's enough," he said with a roguish grin.

She shivered and told herself it was from the chill in the schoolroom, although that hardly seemed likely with the heat from his body nearly scorching her. She vehemently denied to herself any possibility that what she had experienced was a quiver of anticipation. It was a lot more likely she was shaking with fear of . . . of the unknown.

Miss Devlin had only been kissed once, when she was thirteen. It hadn't been a particularly moving experience because fourteen-year-old Roger Freeland's lips had been chapped and cracked from the cold. He had mashed her lips against her teeth so hard she had been glad when it was over. Eden found it hard to believe a simple kiss could be as dangerous as Mr. Kerrigan suggested. Yet she definitely felt threatened right now.

She subconsciously licked her lips and rubbed her sweaty palms against her merino skirt. "You're saying that if I kiss you I'll regret the course of action I've taken with the rancher and nester wives?"

"I'm sure of it."

"We'll just see," she said. "Go ahead and kiss me."

Miss Devlin's voice was calm, but her pulse was racing. She squinted her eyes closed and tipped her chin upward, pursing her lips for his kiss. She waited a moment, but nothing happened. Then she heard a burst of rich, masculine laughter.

Startled, she opened her eyes to find the gunslinger shaking his head, his eyes alight with humor, his mouth an insolent grin spilling chuckles of sound.

Her face burned with humiliation. "If you're finished amusing yourself, I have work to do." She turned to scoop up a stack of papers off her desk.

"Wait!" The Texan's hand on her shoulder spun her back around, sending papers scattering across the floor. At the same time he captured her in the warm circle of his embrace. His voice was tender and soothing, his arms strong and comforting.

When Miss Devlin was tempted to accept the comfort he offered, she forcefully reminded herself he was a gunfighter, a man of violence—like her father. Eden knew his kind from bitter experience.

Kerrigan's hands continued roaming up and down her back, soothing her as he would a nervous filly. She refused to feel pleasure, but neither was she able to withdraw.

"Relax," he coaxed.

She wanted to, but she couldn't. This moment in time wouldn't last. She was already seeing him dead, gunned down by some kid trying to prove he was faster, or shot in the back by someone afraid to face him on the street. She wasn't going to be fooled into thinking there was anything wonderful about being held in a gunfighter's embrace.

"I didn't mean to hurt your feelings," he said. "I knew you were innocent, but I had no idea—"

Miss Devlin glared at him, her gray eyes darting angry sparks. "Since when is innocence a crime, Mr. Kerrigan?"

"It isn't," he soothed. "But ignorance can cause you to make costly mistakes."

She was a big woman, but he held her as though she were not. Resisting his strength only reminded her of her helplessness, so she stood quiet and stolid as a stone in his embrace.

"I'm going to kiss you now," he said.

She stared at him, unmoving, until his mouth was so close she could feel his moist breath on her face. At last she had to close her eyes to keep them from crossing. But she did not lift her face, or move her mouth in any way, afraid of making a fool of herself again.

He angled his head so his lips feathered over hers. That brief touch was replaced by his entire mouth, covering hers. His lips were surprisingly soft as they brushed hers once, twice. When he lifted his head, she opened her eyes and stared at him—stunned.

Kerrigan had been surprised at the jolt of desire he felt the instant his mouth touched hers. There was something infinitely dangerous about her innocence. The soft, whimpering sound she had made as his mouth covered hers had caught him somewhere in the gut. He lowered his mouth to hers again searching for . . . something.

Miss Devlin was ready this time for the firm lips that softened as they tasted her, but that didn't mean she was any less devastated. His teeth nibbled at her lower lip and she quivered in response to the stab of desire she felt. She fought the urge to arch her body toward him, forcing herself to go rigid again. She opened her mouth to tell him the lesson was over and his tongue came seeking the sweetness within.

Eden had never tasted another human being this way. The warmth, the wetness, the closeness, was overwhelming. Telling herself it was only curiosity that kept her in his thrall, she remained perfectly still as Kerrigan's tongue gently ravished her mouth, touching the underside of her lip and her teeth and the roof of her mouth. When he withdrew she felt more frightened than she had ever been in her life.

Because she wanted him to kiss her again.

Eden couldn't have moved to save her life. When Kerrigan's tongue came seeking honey again, she felt as though a drawstring had pulled her insides up tight. A spiral of need began below her waist and worked its way up inside her, until her nipples peaked in an embarrassing way. She clenched her hands at her sides to keep from reaching for him and shuddered with the unbelievably strong feelings that assaulted her.

Eden didn't know how long she stood there, eyes closed, lips damp, nipples peaked, before she realized Kerrigan had stopped kissing her. Slowly she opened her eyes, appalled at her reaction, afraid she would find him laughing at her again. But his dark eyes were hooded, lambent with need, his nostrils flared for the scent of her, his body riveted by tightly leashed desire. That musky male smell reached her senses again. She recognized it now as man, wanting woman.

Oh, this was dangerous, this kissing. It left her . . . wanting. Was this how her father had enslaved her mother? What on earth had she been thinking to allow Kerrigan such liberties?

It took her a moment to remember why she had permitted Kerrigan to kiss her in the first place. He had wanted to prove how powerful a weapon passion could be. Well, he had made his point. But she would never give him the satisfaction of knowing it.

"I'm afraid you've wasted your time, Mr. Kerrigan," she said in a hoarse voice, her eyes glazed with desire.

"I have?"

She cleared her throat and said, "Yes. You see, what

you've shown me only makes me even more certain I've chosen the right course to follow."

"How so?" he demanded.

"I'm assuming that if you could make those feelings happen for me, I could make them happen for you. Am I right?"

The gunslinger's body tautened as he thought of the schoolteacher returning his kiss with fervor. He nodded curtly.

"Then I'm sure this war between the spouses will be over soon."

"Why is that?"

"Because no man is going to choose fighting over feelings like that," she announced with a smug grin.

The man from Texas stared stunned for a moment before he threw back his head and bellowed with laughter. He tipped his hat to her and said, "I concede the battle, Miss Devlin." He grinned and added, "But not the war."

"What is that supposed to mean, Mr. Kerrigan? Do the ranchers still intend to hire you despite this new . . . complication?"

Now was the time to tell her the ranchers intended him to solve this new complication by seducing her. She was the lamb and he was the big, bad wolf sent to devour her. Damn her innocence! He hardened his heart against the soft feelings she raised in him. He couldn't afford to allow those feelings back into his life. This was a cold, cruel world, and the sooner Eden Devlin learned that, the better.

"The Association still wants to find out who's rustling their cattle," he said brusquely.

Miss Devlin stooped and began gathering up the papers that had gone flying when the gunslinger took her in his arms. "And you think you can succeed where Sheriff Reeves has failed?"

"It's happened before."

Miss Devlin stopped and stared. Her brow rose in confusion. "I didn't know you'd met Felton before you came to Sweetwater."

"We've crossed paths" was all he would say. "Do you have a plan to catch the rustlers?"

"A thief is like a calf. Give him enough rope and he'll tangle himself."

"I just can't imagine any of the husbands and fathers I know rustling cattle," Miss Devlin said.

"Then how do you explain the fact that cattle are missing?"

Miss Devlin sat at her desk and began putting the homework papers in some semblance of order. "I don't know. It doesn't make sense."

"Not any more sense than a woman like you going unkissed for so many years," he agreed.

Miss Devlin rose abruptly from her chair, alarmed at how quickly Kerrigan had turned the discussion back in a direction she wanted desperately to avoid. Before she could escape, he stepped up onto the platform that held her desk, effectively blocking her exit. She held the papers up in front of her, hoping they would provide a shield.

They didn't.

He took a step toward her.

Maybe being blunt would work. "Stay away from me."

"I find that impossible. I don't see how you've managed to stay unmarried, Miss Devlin. Your being plain might explain it, except I can't believe no man has seen the fire in your eyes when you're angry."

"You're about to get burned all right, if you don't—"

His callused thumb brushed her cheek.

"Or the way the sun shines off that pretty red hair of yours."

"My hair is no concern—"

He took a wayward curl and tucked it behind her ear.

"And it's a wonder no man has wanted to take this waist in his hands . . . and hold a woman like you in his arms . . ."

"I don't want you to—"

He placed his large, strong hands on either side of her waist, using just a little pressure to draw her toward him, and then slid his arms around her and pulled their bodies together so her breasts nestled against his chest and her belly slid into the cradle created by his hips.

"Kerrigan, don't—"

"You're just the right size—"

"Not for most men," Miss Devlin denied in a raspy voice.

"—for me."

For the briefest second, Eden surrendered, her lips softening under his. Then she remembered her mother's tears. Eden Devlin wasn't going to cry her eyes out for any man.

An instant later Kerrigan found himself with an iceberg in his arms. It was either release her or chance a case of frostbite. He dropped his hands and sat a hip on the corner of Miss Devlin's desk. He tipped his hat back off his forehead and asked, "What did I do wrong this time, Miss Devlin?"

"Why all this attention for the spinster schoolteacher?" Eden demanded. "Surely a man of your immense charms can find more compliant—not to mention more beautiful—female company, Mr. Kerrigan."

Kerrigan's eyes shifted away from her probing gaze. He had gotten so caught up in the pleasure of what he was doing that he had forgotten his less than honorable purpose in coming here. He had never imagined Miss Devlin would be astute enough to question his motives. He realized with a start that he was ashamed of what he had agreed to do. It had been a long time since he had suffered that emotion. Miss Devlin was going to have a lot to answer for when they were finally naked in each other's arms.

"I don't know what came over me," he said with a dry laugh. "I must have been blinded by your great . . . intelligence."

Miss Devlin paled. Of course he hadn't said "beauty." She knew what she looked like. But it still hurt. "Now that you've recovered your sight, I expect you can find your way out," she said acidly.

"I expect I can," he agreed. He didn't look at her again, simply headed back out the door the way he had come in.

Miss Devlin stared after him, distressed by what had just transpired. Somehow whenever he got near her she felt . . . things . . . she didn't want to feel. How had he managed to breach her defenses so quickly? Now that she had felt these . . . feelings . . . was she going to have to worry about feeling them with every man she met? She felt vulnerable as she never had before. And she didn't like it one bit.

That devil dressed in black, with his dark eyes and his dark past, had come into her life and turned everything upside down. Kerrigan had shown her what life could be like in a dangerous man's embrace. She saw now the temptation her mother, Lillian, had faced when she had met her father, a man called Sundance—the lure of danger, the blatant desire in a man's eyes, the mystery of his past.

Eden had watched her mother die a little every time her father drew his gun and killed another man. Until finally the day had come when Sundance hadn't drawn fast enough, and he had been the one to die. She had mourned her father's passing, and taken comfort in her mother's arms.

But Lillian hadn't wanted to live without the man she loved. When Eden buried her mother, she had vowed never to repeat Lillian's mistake. A man who lived by the gun, died by the gun. Along with danger and mystery came violence and death. Loving any man—especially a gun-slinger—wasn't worth the risk.

The walls Miss Devlin had built so carefully over the past twenty-nine years might momentarily have come tumbling down, but she would just get a little mortar and bricks and put them back up again. Eden wasn't foolish, and she wasn't stupid. From now on she would make sure Burke Kerrigan kept his distance from her. Or at least that she kept her distance from him.

Miss Devlin continued sternly lecturing herself as she walked the short distance to her gingerbread house, a shuffled stack of homework papers in her arms. She would not let herself like the gunslinger from Texas. She most certainly would not let herself fall in love with him. He could be as charming as he wished. She would have nothing more to do with him.

Chapter 6

You can't head off a man who won't quit.

☼
IF MISS DEVLIN HOPED SHE HAD SEEN THE LAST OF the gunslinger she was sadly mistaken. At first she attributed their frequent encounters over the following week to coincidence. Upon reflection, she was forced to revise that opinion. For wherever she went, the gunslinger showed up, just like a bad penny.

On Monday she was standing at the counter of Tomlinson's General Store reading the label on a jar of Eastman's Violette Cold Cream when she noticed him entering the store. She purposefully returned to her examination of the perfumed cold cream. The label promised *"Does not contain a base of oils or other ingredients that promote the growth of unwanted hair! No refined woman desires a growth of hair upon her face, neck, or arms, and hence every careful woman—"*

Miss Devlin hadn't realized she was reading aloud, and froze when she heard a familiar Texas drawl finish *"—will use only a high grade cold cream to protect herself from this danger."*

She clutched the jar of cold cream to her breast and

grated out, "Aren't you supposed to be out hunting down rustlers?"

Kerrigan grinned. "Not much rustling going on in the bright light of day."

Miss Devlin turned to face her nemesis. Unfortunately, the gunslinger was standing so close she was practically pinned between his muscular form and the counter. His black duster was hanging open and his body was disturbingly warm. "Don't you have anything better to do than stand here bothering me?"

"Am I bothering you?" he asked in a seductive voice. "You don't really need that stuff, you know. Your skin is lovely just as it is."

While she stood there wide-eyed, his callused thumb brushed across her soft, smooth cheek.

"But if you insist on having it," he continued, "perhaps you'd let me buy it for you as a gift."

Aware they were attracting the attention of the other patrons in the store, Miss Devlin hissed, "I've changed my mind." She slammed the cold cream down on the counter with a satisfying bang, threw her shoulders back, and marched out the door with the sound of the Texan's mocking laughter echoing behind her.

By sundown Florence Grady, the butcher's wife, who had been standing in the corner of Tomlinson's holding a ribbed-pattern lemon squeezer, had told everyone she met—and a few she contrived to meet—of Miss Devlin's confrontation with the gunslinger.

On Tuesday when Miss Devlin arrived home from school, she found a package on her front porch wrapped up in brown paper and tied with a pretty pink ribbon. At first she thought she must be seeing things. She looked left and right, but there was no sign of anyone about, nor was there a note. Eden wasn't used to finding items on her doorstep—especially not something that looked suspiciously like a present. Her heart beat a little faster as she carried it with her straight through the parlor into the kitchen.

Miss Devlin laid the mysterious package in the center of her kitchen table while she crossed to fill the coffeepot and set it on the stove to heat. The package sat there worrying her like a bowl of ice cream that would melt if it wasn't eaten. She sat down abruptly in front of it. Slowly, carefully, she untied the pink ribbon and unwrapped the brown paper to reveal—a jar of Eastman's Violette Cold Cream.

A flush rose on Miss Devlin's face, and she put her hands to her cheeks to cool them. This could only have come from one person. She fought down the feeling of pleasure she felt, forcing herself to concentrate instead on the gall of the man. Imagine buying her something despite her explicit request that he *not*!

Of course she couldn't accept such a gift, especially from *him*. It would be highly improper. She opened the jar and sniffed the soft violet scent, but resisted the urge to dip her finger in. She couldn't imagine why he had sent it—except perhaps to aggravate her. She quickly put the lid back on and set the jar down with a bang, as she had once before. Only it wasn't nearly as satisfying a sound without Kerrigan there to hear it.

Well, no disreputable gunfighter was going to put Miss Eden Devlin in a compromising position. She would just return the cold cream to Mr. Tomlinson and let him refund Mr. Kerrigan's money. And she would do it before the sun set. Eden quickly wrapped the cold cream back up in the brown paper and threw her shawl around her shoulders for the walk into town.

Miss Devlin entered the general store and marched directly up to the counter, heaving a silent sigh of relief that there were no other customers in the store. Mr. Tomlinson had his back to her putting some yard goods on the shelf, so she cleared her throat and said, "I've come to return something."

The balding man turned and smiled. "Why, hello, Miss Devlin. How can I help you?"

"I've come to return this cold cream."

At that moment Florence Grady entered the store.

"Is there something wrong with it?" Mr. Tomlinson asked in a concerned voice.

Conscious she now had an audience, Miss Devlin stuttered, "No . . . that is . . . yes . . . that is, I've decided I don't want it."

"The gentleman who purchased it for you seemed to think you did."

"Well, he was wrong!"

"I see," Mr. Tomlinson said. Although it was clear from the look on his face, he really didn't.

"I want you to refund the cost of this cold cream to Mr. Kerrigan," Miss Devlin said.

"I'm afraid I can't do that," Mr. Tomlinson said.

"Why not?" Miss Devlin demanded.

"Mr. Kerrigan expressly said that if you returned the cold cream I should give you whatever else you wanted in exchange."

Outmaneuvered. Again. Miss Devlin felt the heat on her cheeks. Aware of Florence Grady eyeing her from behind the button table, she gritted her teeth and said, "Please tell Mr. Kerrigan for me that I don't care to have anything in exchange."

She turned a stony eye on Florence Grady's knowing expression, and marched out the door with as much dignity as she could muster.

On Wednesday Miss Devlin overslept and was almost late to school. She had been in the throes of a disturbing dream in which she had been running, trying to escape . . .

something . . . and had been caught by a tall, dark-eyed stranger. He had cradled her in his arms while his hands roamed across her violet-scented skin. She awoke with a start when his hand reached for—a place it had no business being! She was totally mortified that her thoughts could have strayed so far from where she wanted them. It was enough to keep her up late reading at night, just to avoid sleep.

She had been relieved to discover, as she hurriedly dressed for school, that the *real* reason she had overslept was that her Waterbury Sure-Get-Up Alarm Clock had stopped ticking.

After school she headed directly for The Gold Shoppe, broken alarm clock in hand. However, she was stopped in front of the saddler's by Claire Falkner, who claimed, "I just happened to be in town on an errand, and when I saw you I just had to ask. Is it true what I heard?"

"What did you hear?" Miss Devlin asked cautiously.

"That he gave you a gift," Claire said in breathless wonder.

"He?" Miss Devlin said, tilting her chin up and eyeing Claire down the length of her nose.

"The gunslinger."

"I don't know where you heard a thing like that," Miss Devlin said in a daunting voice.

"From Lynette Wyatt," Claire admitted.

Miss Devlin's neck hairs prickled in alarm. She wondered how many people knew about her confrontation with Burke Kerrigan and the return of his gift.

"Why didn't you keep it?" Claire asked.

"It?" Miss Devlin said distractedly.

"The perfume."

"Perfume?" Miss Devlin's eyebrows rose in two pointed arches.

"Why, yes. He did give you a bottle of Violette Rose Water, didn't he?"

"No, he did not!"

"Well, Lynette told me that Florence told her—"

"You should know better than to credit anything a notorious gossip like Florence Grady says," Miss Devlin said sternly.

"But Florence—"

"I'm afraid I have an appointment," Miss Devlin interrupted. "I trust you won't repeat that farradiddle to anyone."

Claire blushed, "Well, I'm afraid I already . . . but I'll be sure to . . ." One look at Miss Devlin's face sent Claire hurrying down the boardwalk to do an errand of her own.

To Miss Devlin's dismay, Claire was only the first of several ladies who stopped her before she got to the jewelers. Every conversation led to the "gift" she had received from Burke Kerrigan. Eden's patience quickly deserted her and she donned an expression intended to convince the ladies of Sweetwater she "really did not want to discuss the matter." But since she couldn't be rude to her pupils' mothers, Miss Devlin had no choice but to endure.

"Whyever did he give you such a gift?" Mabel Ives had questioned speculatively.

"I have no idea," Miss Devlin replied.

"And of course you had no choice except to return it," Amity Carson had whispered.

"No choice at all," Miss Devlin said, her nose pinching.

She gratefully closed the door behind her at The Gold Shoppe, hoping for a respite from the curious eyes and probing questions that had followed her down the street.

"What can I do for you, Miss Devlin?" the jeweler asked.

"Can you fix my alarm clock, Mr. Gold?"

"Let me see, Miss Devlin. Ah . . . a Waterbury . . . very good clock . . . just take a second to . . ."

Eli Gold disappeared behind a curtain at the back of the shop, leaving Miss Devlin to wander around looking at the jewelry on and under the glass counters. A collection of silver baby spoons displayed on blue velvet caught her eye.

She picked up a tiny shell-shaped spoon and ran her fingers along its scalloped surface, imagining how the texture would feel to a baby using it for the first time. Her hand found its way to her belly as she imagined what it would be like to feel a life growing inside her.

"Friend of yours expecting?"

Miss Devlin froze. She recognized that drawl.

"No?" the voice continued. "Thinking of the future then? Toward the day when you'll need a spoon like that for your own child?"

Miss Devlin whirled in the direction from which the taunting voice had come, only to find herself staring out the plate-glass window of The Gold Shoppe into the interested face of Florence Grady. Miss Devlin whirled the other way and encountered the white-toothed grin of the Texas gunman.

"What are you doing here?" she said. "I'm the talk of Sweetwater after what you did yesterday."

"Your skin looks lovely." His thumb brushed her cheek so quickly that her slapping hand missed his. "Did you use the cold cream?"

"You know very well that if I could have done so without causing even more talk, I would have thrown that cold cream right in your face. How dare you follow me in here!"

"Follow you?"

"Yes, follow me."

"I'm here on legitimate business."

Miss Devlin had already opened her mouth to contradict the gunman when Eli came back into the room with her alarm clock. She snapped her mouth shut and planted a beatific smile on her face. "Did you find the problem?"

"A broken spring. I fixed it."

"What do I owe—"

"Oh, hello, Mr. Kerrigan," Eli said, seeing Miss Devlin was not alone. "I have your pocket watch all ready, sir. A minor adjustment. Quite a unique watch. One of a kind. Beautiful couple pictured inside. Who might they be?"

It had been a friendly question, but Eli was reminded in the awkward silence that followed, as the gunslinger's dark eyes narrowed and a muscle in his cheek flexed, that while one might ask questions in the West, one did not always get answers. "Wait just a moment, sir, and I'll get your watch," Eli said, making a hasty exit.

Miss Devlin refused to look at Kerrigan, so she missed the changes in his demeanor caused by Eli's unfortunate question. "It appears you do have business here after all," she said, her body stiff with embarrassment.

"Forget it."

"I shall be glad to forget ever having met you," Miss Devlin said with all the disdain she could muster. "In the future, I would appreciate it if you do not find yourself compelled to offer any more tokens of . . . of . . ."

"Affection?" Kerrigan supplied.

"Irritation!" she retorted.

"You didn't like the cold cream?"

"It wasn't a matter of liking," Miss Devlin said, gripping her gloved hands tightly together. "A lady does not accept gifts from a gentleman who is not . . . is not . . ."

"A gentleman?" Kerrigan said with a sardonic twist to his mouth. "You're more of a prude than I thought, Miss Devlin."

Eden opened her mouth to deny his accusation and snapped it shut when Felton Reeves opened the door—

carrying a package wrapped in brown paper and tied with pink ribbon.

Felton pulled his hat off as he walked up to her, frowning when he realized Kerrigan was with her. He acknowledged the other man with a curt "Kerrigan."

Kerrigan nodded and leaned indolently against the jewelry counter.

Felton turned his attention to Miss Devlin. "I heard you was in town, and wanted to give you this." He thrust the package into Miss Devlin's hand, giving her no chance to refuse it.

"Why, thank you, Felton."

He stood eyeing her expectantly, turning his battered hat in his hands. "Ain't you going to open it?"

"Now?" Miss Devlin caught a glimpse of Kerrigan's smirking face and said, "Yes, of course." She laid the package on the glass counter and carefully unwrapped it.

When Miss Devlin said nothing, Felton blurted, "I hope you like chocolates."

Miss Devlin opened the heart-shaped box and saw that indeed, it contained a dozen chocolate bonbons which, in fact, she liked very much. She turned and smiled to ease Felton's nervousness. "Thank you. I do like chocolates. I'm having Reverend Simonson and his wife over for dinner Friday night. Perhaps you could join us?"

"Friday night?" Felton stared at her blankly. "I . . . uh . . . can't Friday. I . . . uh . . . have to be out of town . . . on business."

Miss Devlin repressed the notion that Felton's refusal sounded suspiciously like he didn't want to come. Why on earth would he bring her chocolates if he wasn't serious about courting her? "Perhaps another time, then."

"Right. I'll be seeing you." Felton slapped his hat on his head and a moment later was gone from the shop.

"I'm free on Friday night," Kerrigan said, popping one

of Felton's chocolates into his mouth. "I'll be glad to join you for dinner."

Miss Devlin quickly slid the lid back in place on the chocolate box. "Hell will freeze over before I invite a hired gun to dinner, Mr. Kerrigan."

She glanced up and found Kerrigan's features taut, his eyes remote. She refused to say anything more, unsure what had caused his swift change of mood and unwilling to chance further antagonizing him. The instant Eli returned, she paid him what she owed him and raced from the store.

By dusk Florence Grady had passed on her opinion that there was definitely something going on between Miss Devlin and the gunslinger, and furthermore, Felton Reeves seemed to be involved.

That night Miss Devlin stayed up as late as she could, toes tucked under her, spectacles perched on the end of her nose, rereading *Romeo and Juliet* in bed. It was both as romantic and as tragic this time as every other time she had read it. Despite the fact her eyelids were drooping, she forced herself to read on to the bitter end, reasoning that if she were sufficiently tired when she fell asleep, she wouldn't be plagued by the disturbing dreams of the past few nights.

When at last Eden finished the play, she pulled off her spectacles and wiped the dampness from her eyes with a lace handkerchief. Swallowing over the lump of emotion in her throat, she carefully set her spectacles on the bedside table, turned down the lamp, and pulled the covers up over her shoulder. Very soon she fell asleep.

And dreamed of a baby.

It had black hair and soft pink skin, and it suckled at her breast as its father looked on in approval, his coal-black eyes both tender and hungry for his wife. The scene was so vivid, Miss Devlin was surprised when she awoke to discover it had all been a dream. And appalled that her thoughts could run so rampant.

On Thursday afternoon when she returned home from school, Miss Devlin found a present wrapped in brown paper and tied in a beautiful blue ribbon on her front doorstep. Her first thought was that it had to be from Kerrigan. Then she remembered Felton had wrapped his present in brown paper too. Exasperation warred with anticipation, curiosity with trepidation.

Eden carried the package inside and set it on the kitchen table. If it was from Kerrigan, she didn't even want to open it. But maybe Felton had put it there. In which case she should be glad, because that would mean he was avidly pursuing their courtship.

Miss Devlin frowned. She didn't understand her feelings at all. Because she found herself feeling anxious no matter who had put the package on her doorstep.

Once Eden removed the brown paper she simply stared for a moment at what she found. Her astonished face reflected back at her in the polished silver. She smoothed her fingers across the shell pattern on the baby spoon. It was from Kerrigan, of course. He had seen her gesture as she touched her womb; he had glimpsed her dreams. Felton wouldn't have known how she wanted the tiny spoon, what it represented. And of course there was no question now that she must return it.

But not today. There was no reason why she had to do it today. She didn't have to give the gossips in Sweetwater another tale to tattle so soon.

She carried the spoon into her bedroom and opened the wooden "Wish Box" on her dresser. In it she kept certain things she had collected over the years that meant a great deal to her, because each one represented a wish she had for her future. She carefully laid the spoon inside.

When she finished her supper, Miss Devlin headed

back to school, where she had unfinished business. She was glad, as she watched the sun begin its descent in a colorful wash of pinks and purples, that she had decided not to return Kerrigan's gift today. She welcomed even a brief respite from the gossip and innuendo that had followed her since that scoundrel had come to town.

On the other hand, she thought as she wiped the perspiration from her brow, she could use a little of that tall Texan's muscle right about now. The past half hour spent splitting kindling had been brutal, not that she had anyone but herself to blame for the situation. One entire side of the schoolhouse was lined with cords of firewood to heat the school through the winter. Each day, the boys took turns chopping kindling that she used the next morning to start the fire in the schoolhouse stove.

Today it was Hadley Westbrook's turn, but he was not back in school. By the time she realized no one had chopped any wood, it was too late to get a substitute. She could have waited until morning and had one of the boys do it then, but it was so cold lately, the children wouldn't have learned much bundled up in their scarves and overcoats waiting for the schoolroom to warm up.

She had worn her mittens to protect her from the cold, and realized too late that what she really needed was leather gloves to protect her hands. Miss Devlin hissed in a breath of air as her new-made blisters made contact once again with the hickory ax-handle.

"Got a problem?"

Miss Devlin nearly chopped her big toe off when she dropped the ax in alarm.

"Be careful there, you might hurt yourself," Kerrigan said as she lifted the heavy ax from the dirt at her feet.

"Stop sneaking up on me," Miss Devlin virtually snarled. "I don't like it!"

"You didn't return the spoon this afternoon."

Miss Devlin stood stunned for a moment. "I will tomorrow."

"You don't have to, you know. No one will know where it came from."

"I'll know."

Kerrigan hefted the ax and neatly split a block of wood into two even pieces. "You're much too hard on yourself, Miss Devlin. It's all right to dream."

"Dreams are illusions. I prefer facing reality."

"Even when reality is disappointing?"

"I can deal with disappointment."

He set the ax down and eyed her speculatively. "I can see how well you've dealt with it."

A flush of color rose in her cheeks. "I never said my life was disappointing."

"So you're happy being a spinster?"

Miss Devlin tilted her chin up. "Are you happy being a hired gun?"

"No."

Miss Devlin's mouth rounded in surprise. "Then why do you keep doing it?"

"Why aren't you married?"

"You answer my question and I'll answer yours," Miss Devlin retorted.

Kerrigan turned and leaned a hip against a stack of firewood. "I started out seeking revenge. Once I had it I realized it didn't bring back what I'd lost." He shrugged. "By then it didn't seem to matter so much what I did with my life. I had met a man who knew I was good with a gun and who needed my help. Word spread and pretty soon I had a reputation that brought me more work than I could handle." He shrugged again. "I've just never had a good enough reason to quit."

Eden couldn't get over how matter-of-fact Kerrigan's explanation was. Or how awful for him. Had that been what happened with her father? Had he so easily slipped into a life of violence? "Do you think you ever could?" she asked.

"Could what?"

"Quit. Put down your gun."

A muscle worked in his jaw. "I think it's your turn to answer my question."

Miss Devlin swallowed hard. "I don't know what to say."

"Tell me why you never married."

"I just never wanted to."

He raised a brow in disbelief.

"It's true."

"Why not?"

Eden could see he wasn't going to let her slide around the subject. But neither did she want to explain the pain of her past. "I never found a man I liked enough to marry," she hedged.

"You mean loved enough to marry."

"I meant exactly what I said," Miss Devlin corrected in her best schoolteacher voice.

"I see."

"Do you?"

Her chin was up again, and Kerrigan recognized it for the defensive gesture it was. "I see your nose is red. It's time you got in out of the cold."

"Oh." Miss Devlin quickly covered her red nose with a mittened hand, as though to make it disappear.

"Is there anything more I can do to help you finish up here?"

"I can handle it." Miss Devlin let go of her nose so she could scoop up a handful of kindling to carry it into the schoolhouse. She was gently bumped aside by the gunslinger's hip as he relieved her of her burden.

"I'll bring that. Why don't you go open the door for me? If we don't hurry it'll be dark before we finish."

That thought sent Miss Devlin scurrying for the school-house door. She held it open while the gunslinger carried in the load of kindling. The setting sun left the room in shadows. Kerrigan's eyes glittered in the dark as he stood, after depositing the load of kindling in the wooden box beside the stove.

"All finished," he said. "Is there anything else you need done?"

"Nothing, thank you."

"I'll walk you home."

The look in his eyes made Miss Devlin exceedingly uncomfortable. "That won't be necessary." She was suddenly conscious of being alone with him. And that his eyes were . . . hungry. Abruptly, she turned to flee, accidentally grabbing the bell rope as she yanked open the door.

The school bell clanged loudly.

Kerrigan grasped her hand to prevent her escape, causing her to wince and cry out in pain.

"What the devil? What's wrong with your hand?"

"Blisters."

He yanked off a mitten, exposing several huge bubbled blisters on her palm. "Foolish woman!" He had her backed up against the door he had slammed closed again and could feel her trembling. "A dab of that cold cream would be good for what ails you."

"I took it back."

"I know. Guess I'll have to find another way to soothe these."

Before she knew what he had in mind he lifted her hand to his mouth and his tongue touched the center of her palm. She could no longer feel the blisters for the startling sensation caused by his tongue on her flesh. The feelings were frightening in their intensity. More so because she wanted him to continue and knew she should not.

"Don't," she said. "Please."

"Does it still hurt?"

"Yes. No."

He kissed each fingertip, and then her wrist.

She shivered. "Why are you doing this?"

"You don't like it?"

"You must know I do," she admitted bitterly.

Her tone of voice brought his head up and he stared into her defiant eyes. "I'm surprised to hear you admit it."

"I'm human, Mr. Kerrigan."

"I was beginning to wonder," he muttered. He caught Eden's balled fist just before it reached his face.

"I hate you!"

"You hate what I make you feel," he said.

"It's the same thing."

"Is it?"

"Let me go."

He released her and stepped back. "I'll walk you to your door."

She straightened her shoulders and lifted her chin. "That isn't necessary."

"It is to me." He opened the door and gestured her ahead of him.

Miss Devlin marched in silence through the cold, gathering darkness toward her front door, knowing that a dangerous man trailed in her wake. Not a woman of faint heart, she nevertheless admitted she was afraid of what would happen when she reached her door. She was determined not to invite him inside. She simply couldn't stand such close proximity to so much . . . so much . . . man.

Suddenly she was home.

Miss Devlin turned so abruptly, Kerrigan ran right into her and had to grab her to keep her from falling. Her breasts were crushed against his chest, her belly shoved up hard against his. Her head was flung back so her face titled up toward his. His hands tightened on her shoulders. For a horrified moment she thought he was going to kiss her.

But he didn't.

"My fault," he said brusquely, releasing her.

She stepped back to regain her balance and pulled her shawl more tightly around her. "I just remembered I have laundry hanging inside," she prevaricated. "I think it would be best if I said good night here."

She saw the glint of humor in his eyes and knew she hadn't deceived him for an instant. Or maybe he was picturing her bloomers hanging from a clothesline in the middle of her parlor. Miss Devlin gritted her teeth in chagrin.

"Good night, Miss Devlin. I'll look forward to dinner tomorrow night. That is, if you think your laundry will be dry by them."

"Don't you dare come here tomorrow night. You're not invited! Don't you—"

He had disappeared into the night, but his echoing laughter remained to haunt her.

Chapter 7

You cain't never tell which way a pickle will squirt.

KERRIGAN WASN'T SURE WHY HE HADN'T TOLD MISS Devlin he was thinking seriously about quitting the work he'd done for the past fifteen years. Maybe he resented the way she made him feel like his life was a waste. He hadn't built a cattle empire like Oak Westbrook or etched out a farm on the landscape like Big Ben Davis, but it didn't mean he couldn't have if he'd wanted to. Kerrigan snorted in disgust. Who was he trying to fool? He hadn't even managed to settle down in one place for more than a year. Even Felton Reeves had managed that. His one consolation was that he was good at what he did. Which reminded him he had a job to do.

Kerrigan had found enough signs to make a guess where the rustlers might strike next. They seemed to be working in and around a canyon that ran along the northern border of the Solid Diamond, where it edged a couple of the smaller spreads, thus giving access to several different herds of cattle at once. The area consisted of grassy hills and valleys, with a lot of dips and gulleys where the rustlers could hide if they were pursued. Then there was the rocky canyon itself, with its twists and turns, leading to a dead end where he suspected rustled cattle had been secreted in the past. He planned to set a trap there to catch the rustlers the next time they showed up.

He could be wrong. The cow thieves might have moved on to another territory. But his instincts told him he was right. Kerrigan lived on hunches. The life of a hired gun was a contest of wits and skill that he took pride in winning; losing could be deadly.

Kerrigan let his mind wander as his paint gelding picked its way down through the canyon in the dark. Sure enough, like a tongue drawn to a sore tooth, his thoughts ended up on that spinster schoolteacher.

Kerrigan wasn't sure quite what to make of Eden Devlin. She wasn't a garden of delights, as her name might suggest. More like a forest of briars. She was prickly, all right. Yet he felt certain that if a man could ever get past the thorns, there was a rose of great beauty to be found. Not that he had the time, or the interest, to plumb Miss Devlin's depths. No, he had a job to do, pure and simple. He was bound to seduce her. And Kerrigan intended to succeed.

Which left him wondering why he hadn't kissed her tonight when they'd been thrust together at her doorstep.

He remembered the feel of her soft breasts crushed against his chest. And how surprised he was to realize that her extra height caused her hips to cradle him in just the right place. She had been pliant, soft, as she never had been before. It was the sudden look of fear in her eyes that had stopped him.

His brow furrowed. There had never been a time when he'd used force with a woman. There hadn't been the need. He found himself bemused by the spinster's reaction to him. Perhaps the simple fact that she was a spinster explained everything. Miss Devlin obviously had no experience with men. Maybe he needed to slow things down a little bit. Take it one step at a time. As with any campaign, strategy was everything. But he wasn't going to back off too far. He didn't have much time to do what had to be done.

Kerrigan saw the paint's ears pivot forward and tensed in the saddle. Then he heard iron-shod hooves on stone. Another rider was coming up the canyon toward him. He slid out of the saddle quietly, pulling his rifle out of the scabbard. He left the reins trailing and slipped into a crevice along the canyon wall to wait.

It wasn't long before the rider came into sight. The man was easily identifiable when moonlight caught the star pinned on his cowhide vest.

Kerrigan stepped back onto the trail, the rifle held easily his hands. "Howdy, Felton. Surprised to find you here."

The sheriff halted his horse. "Just checking things out. You?"

"Thought I'd check things out too."

Felton frowned, then spoke. "One of the nesters, man named Pete Eustes, got shot and killed today. A fire near where he was found still had a hot running iron in it. Wouldn't happen to know anything about that, would you?"

"Nope."

Felton took off his hat and forked a hand through his hair. Having both hands busy at once was a gesture intended to show he trusted Kerrigan, and Kerrigan duly noted it.

"I wouldn't have thought Pete was rustling cattle," Felton said, "but the evidence is pretty damning."

"Sounds that way," Kerrigan replied.

"Looks like somebody took the law into his own hands."

"You accusing me?"

"Just asking."

"You're barking up the wrong tree."

"What're you doing here in Sweetwater Canyon, Kerrigan?"

"My job."

Felton rested his hand on his thigh, away from his gun. "I expect this killing—even if the man was rustling, which ain't been proved—is going to bend a lot of folks out of shape."

"Probably so."

"Point is, you catch anybody breaking the law, you come see me. I'll take care of it."

"You know that's not how I work."

"Then I suggest you change your habits," Felton warned. "I'll hang you if I have to, Kerrigan. I won't like it, but I'll do it."

"You do what you have to, Sheriff."

Fair warning had been given—by both men. Felton pulled his hat down and spurred his horse. When he reached Kerrigan, he reined his mount to a stop. "One more thing."

"What's that?"

"Stay away from Miss Devlin."

Kerrigan grinned. "Sorry, Felton. Can't do that."

"Damn you, Kerrigan. That woman's going to be my wife."

"She's not your wife yet. You're not even engaged."

"Leave her alone."

The smile slipped from Kerrigan's face. "Don't push, Felton. Leave well enough alone."

Felton started to argue, but something in the rigid set of Kerrigan's jaw told him further talk would be futile. He spurred his mount and headed up out of Sweetwater Canyon, damning Burke Kerrigan the whole way.

Kerrigan stood and watched Felton until he rounded a bend out of sight. Then he turned and looked back the way Felton had come. What had the sheriff been doing down in the canyon? If Felton was perceptive enough to have figured out the rustlers were working here, why hadn't he caught them before now?

Kerrigan swung into the saddle in a lithe move that didn't involve putting his foot in the stirrup, and kicked his horse into an easy trot. Maybe there was some clue down there he hadn't found yet. He would just take a look and see.

The death of Pete Eustes created havoc in Miss Devlin's schoolroom on Friday, because now there was fear as well as anger for her pupils to contend with. She watched the rancher and nester children eye one another with distrust.

Eden didn't have to wait long for a fight to erupt. This time it was two of the girls, Henry Westbrook and Sally Davis. She managed to separate them before anything more damaging than a little hair-yanking occurred. But between hot tempers and cold quiets her schoolroom hardly provided a climate that encouraged learning.

Miss Devlin heaved a sigh of relief when the day ended, hoping that over the weekend she could figure out some way to ease the tensions seething at school.

Unfortunately, her pupils weren't the only ones living with new fears. Eden had been distracted all day with concerns of her own—all of them leading back to that incident at her front door last night when Burke Kerrigan had almost kissed her. It wasn't the kiss she had feared so much as her own feelings. Because, for a moment, she had *wanted* him to kiss her. And that had terrified her.

There was no logical reason for her to be attracted to the man. In light of his similarities to her father, she had every reason to hate him. But the truth was, she didn't hate him. Just as he had claimed, what she really hated was what he made her feel. Desire. Longing. Need.

Eden had believed herself above those sorts of feelings. After all, she had a bright, educated mind. She knew better than to let herself get carried away by the baser emotions. Yet, whenever that gunslinger came around, wants and needs rose up inside her clamoring for the nourishment they had been denied for twenty-nine parched years. It was unsettling, to say the least.

It didn't help to know that Kerrigan had threatened to come for supper tonight. She found it tremendously comforting to know that if he was brazen enough to show his face, Reverend and Mrs. Simonson would be there to act as a buffer.

Eden hurried to the butcher shop right after school, hoping to get a good steak to serve for supper. To her dismay, that nosybody Florence Grady stood behind the counter with her husband. Not that Miss Devlin had anything to hide. But after the day she'd just had, Eden didn't feel like dealing with the town gossip.

"Good afternoon, Miss Devlin," Florence said with a sly smile. "What are you doing here?"

"Buying beef."

"What will you have, Miss Devlin?" the butcher asked.

"A three-pound steak, Mr. Grady."

Florence raised a knowing brow. "Expecting company for dinner, Miss Devlin?"

Miss Devlin was unwilling on principle to satisfy the gossip's curiosity. "If I am, Florence Grady, it's no business of yours."

"A steak like that would feed a big man," Florence said.

"Yes, it would," Miss Devlin agreed with a benign smile. Reverend Simonson was a very big man—from side to side.

"Here you go, Miss Devlin," the butcher said, handing the paper-wrapped steak over the counter. "Need anything else?"

"Not right now, Mr. Grady." Miss Devlin turned and left the butcher shop without saying another word.

By day's end, the entire town of Sweetwater knew Miss Devlin had invited "someone with a man-size appetite" for dinner.

Felton Reeves never listened much to gossip, but a week's worth of innuendo about "Miss Devlin and the gunslinger," followed by his encounter with Kerrigan in Sweetwater Canyon, had made its mark. When he heard the rumors about the huge steak the schoolteacher had purchased from the butcher, he decided to pay her a call before he headed out of town on business. But first he had to go by the undertaker and see what kind of bullet had killed Pete Eustes.

Meanwhile, Miss Devlin was less than her usual calm and collected self. Her dinner guests would be walking in the door in an hour, and things weren't going quite as planned.

She had covered the oak pillar extension table (minus the extension) with her best Nottingham lace cloth, and put out her brass candlesticks with new pink tapers. Three places had been set with her mother's china and silver. All the furniture in her house, from the sideboard, to the combination oak bookcase and writing desk, to the birch parlor table that held her Bordeaux lamp, glistened with English Beauty's Best Grade Oil-base Wood Polish. The setting was perfect.

Unfortunately, her mashed potatoes were lumpy and her snap beans had long ago passed from brilliant green to the sickly yellow color of grass that's spent a week under a flower pot. The pumpkin pie planned for dessert had come out of the oven both too soon and too late, because the undone center had sunk far below the burnt crust. There was no hiding her mistake, because she had forgotten to stop by the Davis farm for whipping cream on her way home.

She still had some hope for the steak reposing bloodred and raw in the skillet. But after viewing her disastrous efforts with the pie, she had lost confidence in her ability to make the best use of her Acme four-hole coal and wood stove.

What made her failure so frustrating was the fact she knew she could be a good cook if she had a little more practice at it. Unfortunately, she had never spent much time cooking for herself. It didn't seem worth the effort.

She had learned today, to her chagrin and surprise, that it wasn't as easy as she had thought to make everything come out just right. It didn't help to know that she had let herself get distracted reading and completely forgotten about the food on the stove.

Now that she might have a husband to cook for sometime soon—assuming Felton's courtship came to fruition—Eden realized she couldn't afford to be quite so cavalier in the future about her cooking.

However, what was done was done. She would simply have to make the best of the situation. All that remained was for her to contrive a way to entertain her guests in the parlor while she cooked the steak in the kitchen. She realized now that a wiser woman would have prepared a pot roast that could have been ready to eat when her guests arrived. It was woefully apparent that Miss Devlin hadn't entertained much, just the reverend and his wife now and then, so thankfully they were prepared for a dinner charred around the edges.

Right now, all she wanted to do was get this supper over with so she could lie down and indulge the painful headache pounding behind her eyes.

Suddenly she realized the pounding sound in her head was not her headache but someone knocking at the door. It was way too early to be her guests. For a second she thought of Kerrigan's threat. Surely he wouldn't dare come here tonight. She shook her head at the thought. Probably the Simonsons had come early after all.

She reached around to untie the allover gingham apron she had worn to protect her dress while cooking, then realized she would only have to put it back on again to fry the steak. She looked down at the unsightly smudges of pumpkin and flour and eggs and butter on the checked material, and wished fervently that she owned a dainty white lawn apron with a nice ruffle or two. But being such a practical woman, and ruffles not being in the least practical, she didn't.

In a rash of indecision, she finally yanked her apron off, telling herself her action had nothing at all to do with the possibility she might find Burke Kerrigan standing on her doorstep.

Eden spent the entire trip to the door fiddling with a few recalcitrant curls that had escaped the bun at the base of her neck. A deep breath, an exhaled sigh, and she opened the door with complete calm—to find herself facing Sheriff Felton Reeves.

"Why, Felton . . . what a surprise! How are you?"

"Cold. May I come in?"

The growing scowl on Felton's face made it plain Miss Devlin was hesitating too long before answering. Recovering her wits, she said, "Why, of course. Come in. I thought you were going to be out of town tonight. I can set another place—"

"I only stopped by to say hello."

He walked over to examine the table set for *three*. So much for the gossip. He decided it couldn't hurt to ask anyway. "Seen Kerrigan lately?"

"Why, yes. He came by last night."

Felton looked ready to kick his own dog.

Resigned to an unpleasant interview, Miss Devlin asked, "Is there something I can do for you, Felton?"

"You can stay away from Kerrigan."

He was angrier than she thought he had a right to be, under the circumstances. "Who I choose to entertain is none of your business."

"I'm making it my business."

"You can—" Miss Devlin bit her tongue. In Felton's shoes, she might have been equally frustrated and angry. It would be imprudent to say things that would shut the door on any hope of a future relationship with this man. Now that she owned that silver baby spoon (which she had decided not to return after all), she had begun to have all sorts of fantastical ideas about herself as a wife and mother.

There were many ways to deal with an angry man, and Miss Devlin used the conciliation that had worked so well to turn aside her father's wrath, saying, "I certainly didn't invite Kerrigan here. He just showed up."

Felton wasn't listening.

Eden followed him as he made his way to the kitchen, where he stood staring down at the raw meat in the skillet. "Doesn't look like twelve pounds of steak to me," he muttered.

"Twelve pounds!"

"That's what I heard," he mumbled, his angry blue eyes daring her to laugh.

"Listen, Felton, it never occurred to me that you would be upset by—"

Loud knocking interrupted her carefully planned speech and left Miss Devlin staring in the direction of the front door, hoping that was the rest of her company.

"You going to answer that?" a surly male voice demanded.

Miss Devlin hurried to the front door and opened it to discover Burke Kerrigan standing on the doorstep. "You!"

"Supper ready yet?"

"I told you not to come here."

Felton arrived at the kitchen door in time to see Kerrigan step inside and close the front door.

Miss Devlin stood stunned while the gunman slipped a sheepskin coat off and dropped it on the sofa. Kerrigan was wearing a three-piece black suit with a starched white shirt and collar, which somehow did nothing at all to make him seem less dangerous. He was carrying a black Stetson, and although his Colt was nowhere in sight, she had no doubt the derringer was tucked in his boot.

It was easy to note the instant he realized Felton's presence, because suddenly the fact he was wearing a suit did nothing to keep him from looking like a wild thing trapped in too-close confines. Eden could almost see his neck hairs bristle, feel the tension in his muscles build until they threatened the seams of his suit. The civilized man was gone. In his place stood a barely leashed feral animal, ready to claim what was his.

Only she didn't belong to him, any more than she belonged to Felton Reeves.

"It looks like you already have company," Kerrigan said.

"Felton just stopped by—"

"For supper," Felton finished.

"I thought you had business out of town," Kerrigan countered.

"So did I," Eden muttered under her breath.

"It'll wait," Felton said.

The two men stood their ground, but it would only have taken one wrong move to set them at each other's throats. Eden didn't want any fighting in her home, and most especially not over her person. She stepped back, glancing from one man to the other. Felton's blue eyes had turned to ice. Kerrigan's dark eyes burned hot as fire.

"Before either one of you starts acting like an idiot, I suppose I'd better set two more places at the table."

"I forgot to tell you," Felton said.

"Tell me what?" Eden asked, her hand on the beveled glass door to the china cabinet.

Felton cleared his throat. "I ran into Reverend Simonson when I went to check on Pete Eustes at the undertaker. The reverend asked me to tell you he's going to spend the evening with Pete's brother. So he and his wife ain't coming to dinner."

Eden's jaw dropped. "Oh." She looked from Felton to Kerrigan to the table. "I guess I have the right number of settings after all."

The two men circled stiff-legged around each other toward the table, resembling nothing so much as two wolves ready to do battle for a bitch in heat.

"I thought you understood Miss Devlin is mine," Felton said through gritted teeth.

"That remains to be seen, doesn't it?" the Texan answered with a dangerous smile.

Miss Devlin cleared her throat to speak, and both men immediately glared at her. While she had been the source of their animosity toward each other, she no longer mattered in the scheme of things. This was male against male. She might as well not have been there. For a moment she considered simply walking out the door. Until she realized that really wouldn't solve anything.

"Why don't you two have a seat while I finish supper."

"I'd rather stand," Kerrigan said.

"Me, too," Felton said.

Totally exasperated, Miss Devlin said, "Suit yourselves. I have to go cook the steak."

But she didn't move, because the Texan's dark eyes were intent on her, telling her without words just how well her paisley linen princess sheath conformed to her waist and bodice. She closed her eyes in an attempt to thwart the feelings curling up inside her. Damn him! How could he do this to her so easily? And why didn't it happen when Felton looked at her?

When Eden opened her eyes, Kerrigan was grinning. And Felton's face looked like a thundercloud about to burst.

"I'll be back soon." She turned and shoved the door open between the dining room and kitchen—and immediately saw the relish tray she had prepared earlier. She hurried over and picked up the tray, which contained slices of raw carrot, sweet pickles (which were all she could abide), and pickled peppers, and hurried back out to the parlor.

"Can I offer you gentlemen something to whet your appetites while I finish dinner?"

She thrust the crystal dish into Felton's hands so he had no choice except to take it.

"I'll be back in just a minute. Make yourselves comfortable." She gestured vaguely toward the reception chair and sofa in the parlor, and hurried back into the kitchen, letting the door between the two rooms swing closed behind her.

Suddenly she realized she hadn't offered the two men anything to drink, and rushed back the direction she had come. Only Felton had obviously had the intention of joining her, because as she came out of the kitchen he was heading in. The swinging kitchen door slammed right into the crystal relish dish in his hands, sending the contents flying into his face and across the front of his shirt. He stood there stunned for a moment, with sweet pickle juice dripping from his nose and chin.

"Oh no! I'm so sorry." Miss Devlin took the crystal dish out of his hands and set it on the table. At the same time she grabbed a linen napkin and began dabbing ineffectually at his sticky face. "This is awful! Your shirt—your vest—"

"Don't worry about the shirt, I—"

She had Felton's vest halfway down his arms when he grasped her hands to stop her.

"I don't care about the shirt," he said. "It doesn't matter."

Eden's face was a picture of distress. "I'm so sorry, Felton. I never thought . . ."

"Look, Miss Devlin. I think maybe I better not stay—"

"Oh, no. You *must* stay. I mean ”

Felton watched Miss Devlin's glance fly to Kerrigan and back. His lips flattened as he pressed her hands and said, "I think maybe it would be better if I came to supper another time."

"But it's all ready," Eden protested. "Except for the steak, of course, and—"

Felton applied enough pressure to her hands to cut her off. "I'm a little too sticky to enjoy sitting down with company right now. Besides," he said with a glance over his shoulder, "two's company. Three's a crowd."

"But I—"

"Good night, Miss Devlin."

"I—" Eden's eyes widened as he released her hands and headed for the door. She turned accusing eyes toward Kerrigan, and waited only until the door had closed behind Felton to hiss in outrage, "This is all your fault!"

"Does this mean you don't want me to stay for supper?"

Miss Devlin fought the urge to throw something. "I want you out of my house."

"It's a shame to let that steak go to waste," he said with a grin.

"It can rot for all I care!" Miss Devlin felt tears of frustration filling her eyes and fought to keep them back.

Kerrigan started toward her.

"Stay away from me. Don't touch me. I—"

She tried to evade him, but his arms encircled her, his hands offering comfort as they roamed across her back.

"Hey. You aren't going to let a little spilled pickle juice get you down, are you?" he teased.

She kept herself as rigid as she could, her head turned away from him, her eyes staring blankly across the room as she spoke in a choked voice. "I didn't think anything else could go wrong tonight, you know, because my mashed potatoes turned out lumpy, and the pumpkin pie is burnt—but raw on the inside—and the snap beans are ruined. But then Felton showed up. And you showed up. And now he's gone. And you won't leave."

"No," he murmured. "I'm here to stay."

"You can't stay."

"Why not?"

"Because I don't like the way I feel when . . ."

"How do you feel, Eden," he said in a voice that was soft, coaxing.

Somehow she found herself cradled in the Texan's arms, with her head on his shoulder, and his chin resting against her temple. His hand reached up under her coiled hair and caressed her nape. Eden felt her body relaxing and forced it back to rigidity. "This is ridiculous. Let me go."

"All right. As soon as you tell me how I make you feel."

Eden's head snapped around to face him. "No!"

The callused fingers at her nape thrust up into her hair, and he used his hold to tug her head back so she was staring up into his dark, fathomless eyes.

She closed her eyes to shut out the need in his eyes . . . fearing he would see the answering need in hers. The hold on her hair tightened and she opened her eyes against the beginnings of pain.

"Don't look like that," he said in a fierce voice.

"Like what?"

"Like a green-broke bronc in a thunderstorm. Skittish. Ready to run. What are you so afraid of, Eden?"

The quiver in Miss Devlin's chin warned her she was about to lose control. She never got the chance.

Kerrigan's lips came down hard on hers. It was an angry kiss, his mouth rough and demanding. She had no time to feel frightened; she was too busy feeling other things—anger, and then passion, hot and biting, and totally overwhelming in its intensity. His touch softened, and his tenderness was even harder to resist.

She was panting hard when Kerrigan finally wrenched his mouth from hers. Her hands were tangled in his hair, while his hands—were in places they ought not to be.

"How dare you!"

"I think we've been through this before," he said sardonically, letting his hands slide (one up, one down) to her waist.

"Let me go."

"Yes, ma'am."

Suddenly, she was free.

Kerrigan walked away from her to retrieve his sheepskin coat from the sofa, hooking it over his shoulder with two fingers. "I'll be in touch." He dropped his Stetson onto his head and quietly closed the door on his way out.

Miss Devlin slumped into the reception chair, her body still tingling from the aftereffects of Kerrigan's kiss. She couldn't understand what had come over her. He could make her feel . . . so many things. It would be lying to say she wasn't attracted to him. She was. But it was more important than ever not to let her heart lead her head. She had to do a better job of keeping her distance.

But that was going to be much harder after this kiss, and all the firsts that had come along with it. The first time a man had nibbled on her lip in a touch racing the border between pleasure and pain. The first time a man had touched her breast, the brush of his thumb against her nipple causing it to harden against his hand. The first time a man's hand had soothed the flesh along her hip. The first time a man had pulled her close so she could feel the hard evidence of his desire for her.

Miss Devlin moaned. No wonder Claire Falkner had cried out against taking an oath to forgo such pleasures. She could see now how the kettle of worms she had opened could easily become rattlesnakes.

Miss Devlin moaned again. Tomorrow night was the annual Sweetwater Halloween Party and Dance. She would have to face all those husbands and wives knowing she was responsible for keeping them apart. Not even her plan had been enough to avoid another shooting—this one resulting in death. She would need to speak to the women to make sure this latest incident did not deter them from the course they had set. It was more important than ever that they remain firm.

At least she wouldn't have to worry about running into Kerrigan at the dance. After dark he disappeared out onto the plains in a deadly hunt for rustlers. She wasn't worried about the Association's hired gun. Eden Devlin wasn't going to let herself care enough for any man to worry about him. But she did want peace in the valley. And that was how she justified the thought that sprang into her head.

Please, please, let Kerrigan find the rustlers without any more violence.

Chapter 8

Buckshot leaves a mean and oozy corpse.

CLOUDS COVERED THE MOON, CAUSING THE KIND OF blackness you would expect for a truly bloodcurdling Halloween. Kerrigan smiled at his sense of the ridiculous. He had promised himself he would dance with Miss Devlin at the Halloween celebration being held at the town meetinghouse, but it didn't look like he was going to get his wish. An itch at the back of his neck warned him the rustlers would strike tonight. He trusted his instincts because they had kept him alive through more than one ambush.

So instead of whirling Miss Devlin in a lively polka, he was sitting in the dark on his paint horse in the bitter cold waiting for the rustlers to make their move. He had picked a spot in a stand of pines on Solid Diamond land that provided cover and still gave him a good view of the herd grazing on the grassy plains below him. On a hill in the distance he could see the line shack where Oak Westbrook had stationed a couple of hands to help keep an eye on things.

The light in the shack had gone out over an hour ago. The lonesome melodies from a mouth harmonica he had heard coming from the darkened shack had ceased. It was quiet, except for the lowing of cattle now and then.

Kerrigan warmed his gloved hands with his breath. The weather would soon put a stop to rustling for the duration of the winter. If he hoped to catch the cow thieves, he needed to do it soon, before the snow left drifts too deep to move a rustled herd to the nearest railroad head.

The clouds had drifted by, revealing moonlight so bright that he saw the rustlers long before he heard them. They came from the south, five of them, muffled up in heavy coats, their hats tied down with bandannas against the bitter wind. He couldn't see their faces. They worked as a team and quickly cut out about twenty head and herded them off in the direction of Sweetwater Canyon.

Kerrigan smiled grimly. If luck was with him, he might make it to the Halloween dance after all.

The church pews had been moved along the walls, and the town meetinghouse now served as a dance hall. Husbands stood clustered in groups of three and four on one side of the room, while wives stood in similar circles on the other side. The trio of musicians played to a dance floor bereft of revelers.

The men's groups remained divided along rancher and nester lines, but their vow of celibacy had united the women in a common bond that had nester and rancher wives exchanging war stories with desperate animation.

So far, the traditional Sweetwater Halloween Party and Dance was a dismal failure.

Miss Devlin approached the hen clutch that contained Regina Westbrook and Persia Davis and asked, "Isn't anybody going to dance?"

"I'm not speaking to my husband, thanks to you," Regina said.

"And my husband isn't speaking to me," Persia added with a brittle smile.

"Then why did you bother to come?" Miss Devlin wondered aloud.

"I'm not going to give Oak the satisfaction of knowing I'm upset that he's not in charity with me," Regina said. "And since Hadley insisted he was well enough to come, here I am."

"Where is Hadley now?" Miss Devlin made a glancing search of the room, without seeing her pupil. She knew Bliss had hoped to be alone with Hadley at the dance, so she could tell him about the baby. "I saw him earlier," Miss Devlin continued, "surrounded by young people. I believe he appeared something of a hero with his arm in that sling."

"Hadley's the main reason I haven't given up on this fool idea of yours," Regina said.

"Then you think it's working?" Miss Devlin asked, unable to hide her excitement.

"If you mean, are our husbands ready to kill us for keeping them at arm's length, then, yes, it's working," Persia agreed. "I don't think anyone is ready to give up yet. Especially after what happened to Pete Eustes. Big Ben is the stubbornest man I ever met."

"He's no worse than my husband," Amity Carson complained.

"Or mine," Claire Falkner added vehemently.

"How long are we expected to keep this up?" Mabel Ives asked.

Miss Devlin let her gaze move from wife to wife around the circle, knowing all of them were appalled by what had happened to Pete Eustes, and feared more such incidents. "Until it works," she said hesitantly. "Unless someone else has a better idea?"

None of the ladies could meet her steady gaze, and

apparently no one else had a better idea. "Every one of you must have the fortitude to keep your vows," Miss Devlin said. "Surely, your husbands can't resist your feminine wiles much longer."

Regina and Persia exchanged a knowing look before Regina said, "I don't suppose the rumors we've been hearing this week about you and Felton and that gunslinger have anything to do with your confidence that we'll succeed."

"I don't know what you mean." But the two spots of color on Miss Devlin's cheeks left her words in doubt.

"I mean," Regina persisted, "that maybe you understand a little more about what we're going through now."

"I don't know—" Faced by so many pairs of accusing eyes, Miss Devlin couldn't lie. "Perhaps I do," she conceded.

"Just remember," Persia warned, "you took the oath to abstain the same as we did."

"You're forgetting I am not a married woman," Miss Devlin said indignantly.

Regina chuckled. "That never stopped a determined man."

"I never—"

"Excuse me, ladies. I want to ask Miss Devlin for the pleasure of this dance."

The rumbling bass voice was familiar, but not the one Eden had fretted about hearing. She pasted a welcoming smile on her face before she turned to greet the sheriff. It was the first she had seen of him since their confrontation the previous evening.

"Good evening, Felton. Are you sure you want to dance? It doesn't seem to be the evening for it." She gestured to the barren dance floor.

"Then we can be the ones to break the ice," he said. "I insist."

He already had her by the elbow, urging her toward the center of the room. There was no way she could escape without causing a scene. Naturally, the moment they reached the center of the floor, the music ended. There was nothing for them to do but stand there waiting for the next tune to begin.

"I didn't expect to see you. Did you ever finish your business?" she asked.

"I decided to postpone my trip."

Miss Devlin found herself staring at the sheriff's bushy mustache, wondering whether it was soft or not, and what it would feel like against her face during a kiss. Mercifully, before she could follow those thoughts any further, the music, a slow waltz tune, began.

"Shall we?" Felton placed one hand firmly at her waist and held up the other, waiting for her palm to be placed in his.

To Miss Devlin's surprise, Felton was quite an accomplished dancer. His step was easy to follow, and since she had so little experience dancing, she was grateful for his firm lead. If she hadn't felt quite so self-conscious about being the only ones on the dance floor, she might actually have enjoyed herself.

She compared the feeling of being comfortable in Felton's arms with the anxiety she had felt being held by Kerrigan. Somehow Miss Devlin thought she ought to feel something more than comfortable and less than anxious when a man held her in his arms—although she wasn't sure exactly what.

As Felton had predicted, several single gentlemen asked ladies to dance, so they were not alone on the dance floor long. Nevertheless, she was glad when the dance ended.

"Thank you, Felton." Miss Devlin's intended retreat to the ladies' side of the room was quickly halted when Felton once again snagged her elbow.

"Surely I deserve another dance."

The tone of voice and the choice of words, especially after the scene with Kerrigan the past evening, raised Miss Devlin's hackles. "I'm afraid this dance is promised."

"To who?"

"To whom."

"To *whom*?" he grated.

"To me."

Miss Devlin whirled and found herself face-to-face with Hadley Westbrook.

"Bound to be a little difficult to dance with that broken wing. How about letting me step in for you?" the sheriff cajoled with a confident smile.

"I'll manage," Hadley replied with an equally determined smile.

"Excuse us, Felton. The music is starting."

Fortunately it was another slow waltz, and Hadley was able to manage by putting one hand on Miss Devlin's waist while she rested one hand on his shoulder and the other on the crook of the arm he held in the sling.

"That was quite gallant of you," Miss Devlin said. "But I could have managed without your help."

"I wanted to talk to you in private," Hadley said. "This was the only way I could think of to do it."

"What's wrong?" Miss Devlin asked, responding to the urgency in Hadley's voice.

"It's Bliss. I haven't been able to get near her. My father has me watched like a hawk. I wondered if there's a way you could help. Maybe Bliss could come see you and I could meet her—"

"If you don't get together tonight you'll surely see Bliss in school on Monday. I can't help you sneak around behind your parents' backs, Hadley. It wouldn't be right."

"To hell with what's right!" Hadley snarled in a voice that was all the more vicious for the control he exercised to keep it quiet. "I need to talk to Bliss, to be alone with her. And I will see her, with or without your help."

To Miss Devlin's dismay, Hadley left her standing in the middle of the dance floor and stalked away in high dudgeon. He never even glanced in the direction of Bliss, who stood surrounded by the protective wool skirts of her mother and the other nester wives.

Miss Devlin took one look at the longing in Bliss's eyes as her gaze followed Hadley out the door and knew she was going to help the two lovers get together. She would deal with her conscience later.

As though nothing out of the ordinary had happened, she strolled back to the distaff side of the room. Regina had seen Hadley's precipitous departure and was at Miss Devlin's side as soon as she reached the edge of the dance floor.

"What got into Hadley?" his mother demanded. "I never raised my son to be rude. What did he say to you? What did you say to him?"

"What did I . . . ? Nothing! As a matter of fact, if you must know," Miss Devlin said, thinking quickly, "I told him he would have to make up all the work he missed in school, and that I wasn't going to excuse him just because he'd managed to get himself shot, however romantic his wound might seem to his friends."

"Is that all?"

"It was quite enough to set Hadley on his ear."

Regina shook her head in confusion. "I don't understand what's gotten into him lately. I can't talk to him anymore, he's so contrary, and for no good reason that I can see. At first I thought he was bothered about that Davis girl. Of course, I warned him to stay away from her, forbade him even to mention the creature in my presence, but you know boys when they get an idea into their heads."

In light of those sentiments, Miss Devlin wondered

what would happen when Regina Westbrook found out she was about to become a grandmother, and that the mother of her grandchild was the "creature" she had forbidden her son to mention in her presence.

"I'll talk to Hadley," Miss Devlin promised. "Maybe I can find out what's troubling him."

"I hope so," Regina said, "because really, I've had about enough of this nonsense. If you'll excuse me, I think I could use a cup of hot spiced tea and a slice of pumpkin pie, although whoever made that pie needs a cooking lesson. It looks raw on the inside and burnt on the edges."

Miss Devlin didn't even have time to feel chagrined at the insult to her pie before Bliss Davis arrived at her side.

"What's the matter with Hadley, Miss Devlin? I saw him leave. He looked so angry! My mother won't let me out of her sight, so I haven't been able to speak to him all evening." Which meant she hadn't been able to tell him she was going to have his child.

"Hadley's parents have forbidden him to talk to you," Miss Devlin said with a sigh.

"How could they? What are we going to do?"

Seeing Bliss on the verge of tears, Miss Devlin cautioned, "This is no time to be lily-livered. Besides, I've decided to help you and Hadley meet—so you can talk—and I suppose it'll have to be at my house so I can act as your chaperone," she continued, thinking aloud. "I'll get word to you when to come. Just be patient."

"Thank you, Miss Devlin. You're an angel of mercy. Thank you so much."

Miss Devlin did her best to cut off Bliss's effusive praise, because it only served to convince her she was treading dangerous ground helping the two impetuous lovers get together in the face of their parents' disapproval. Tragedy had resulted from such meddling in *Romeo and Juliet*. But really, what else could she do?

They deserved all the help she could give them. She might even learn something from them in the process. For, in the face of tremendous obstacles—the objection of their parents, a threatening range war, their youth—they had the courage to reach out for happiness.

Eden, on the other hand, had spent a lifetime refusing to take risks, fearing the pain that might result. She was beginning to have an inkling of how much she had given up.

It was Kerrigan, with his kisses and his questions, who was forcing her to face the fact that she couldn't simply deny certain feelings and have them cease to exist. The feelings were there. Repressed maybe. Under control maybe. But there.

Now that she had acknowledged them, she wasn't quite sure what to do about them. Certainly she could never go back to the way things had been before. Eden needed to find the courage somehow, somewhere, to come to terms with these new feelings.

Having gotten that far, she began to examine her feelings for Felton. And for Kerrigan. She didn't like what she found. Because the emotions Kerrigan aroused in her were far stronger than her feelings for Felton.

But it was Felton who was offering marriage and a home and family. Kerrigan only wanted . . . her. Besides, Kerrigan was a hired gun. It would be crazy, not courageous, to hope for any sort of happiness with a man who was bound to get himself killed.

And it was pretty far-fetched to imagine Kerrigan changing his ways. Impossible to imagine him behind a desk. Or even behind a plow. Perhaps he could work for one of the ranchers in the area. But Eden realized it was impossible to imagine Kerrigan taking orders from someone else. He was a leader, not a follower.

Her dreams of reformation faded. Kerrigan was a gunslinger. He lived with violence. He would die that way.

Letting herself dream about him, about a future with him, was futile. She should know better. She should know—

Miss Devlin's bitter thoughts were interrupted by an outbreak of the very violence she so abhorred.

Eden hurried over to see if she could help stop the fracas in the corner. She couldn't see who was involved, but it was obvious from the shouts of the crowd, and the way they were arranged in the circle surrounding the fight, that it was rancher against nester.

To her horror, she found mild-mannered, over-the-hill, rattlesnake-lean rancher Cyrus Wyatt fighting tooth and nail with an equally unprepossessing, equally weathered, and equally lank farmer, Bevis Ives. Nearby, Lynette had a firm hold on a banged-up twelve-year-old Daniel's suspenders, and Mabel restrained an equally bloodied eleven-year-old Wade by the ear.

Apparently a fight begun between the men's younger sons, who had obviously not learned a thing from the lesson taught by the gunslinger to their older brothers, Keefe and Jett, had been taken up by the fathers. While the mothers had been able to subdue their sons, they stood powerless in the face of their husbands' wrath. The men in the outer circle egged the combatants on, despite the shrill cries of their wives to end the fight.

Cyrus already had a black eye and a bloody lip, and Bevis had a cut on his cheek that was dripping blood into the sawdust on the dance floor.

"Stop it! Do you hear me? Stop it!" Miss Devlin's cries were lost in the confusion. "Somebody get the sheriff," she shouted. "Where's the sheriff?"

But Felton Reeves had disappeared and nobody seemed to know where to find him.

•   •   •

Kerrigan realized it would be a mistake to confront the rustlers in the open where the odds were in their favor and they could make a run for it. Better that he follow them. He felt a grim satisfaction when he saw the rustlers broach the head of Sweetwater Canyon. Once they started down into that dead-end canyon, they would be trapped. They couldn't run, and there wasn't any way out past him. He followed them down the trail, keeping his distance so he wouldn't spook them.

When the rustlers reached the end of the blind canyon, where a boarded-up line shack stood, they built a fire with some dry grama grass and a few cow chips. Soon they'd have a red-hot running iron. It wouldn't take them long to alter the brands, and then they'd be heading back up out of the canyon. He would be waiting for them. One way or another, he would be taking the rustlers back to town.

But the rustlers seemed to be in no hurry to finish their work. The longer it took them, the more uneasy Kerrigan got. It was as though they were waiting for something . . . or someone. The skin prickled on the back of Kerrigan's neck and he took a quick look around. Suddenly he felt the sharp threat of danger like cockleburs on a coyote.

He ducked and threw himself off his horse just as he heard the shotgun go off. The blast that would have taken his head off passed by harmlessly. He rolled out of his fall and was on his feet in an instant, running down the canyon, zigzagging in a path impossible for the bush-whacker to calculate, looking for cover. It was pure bad luck that the second shotgun blast hit him square in the back, knocking him flat on his face.

The pain kept him semi-conscious, so he felt the pounding footsteps of the men who soon surrounded him. He was unable to recognize more than the grating edge of nervous voices and the words they spoke.

"You got 'im! Good thing you got here when you did. I was gittin' nervous."

"That buckshot sure put a hole in 'im!"

Someone kicked him and he groaned.

"He ain't dead yet."

"Another blast'd finish 'im for sure."

"No sense wastin' shot. He ain't goin' nowhere. Nobody'll find him in this canyon. If the cold don't do him in, the wolves will. Take his guns and his horse. Then let's get the hell outta here."

"Hey! His horse bolted. Want me to run 'im down?"

"Naw. Forget it. Probably halfway to the stable in town by now."

The last thing Kerrigan saw before he fainted was the glimmer of moonshine off a roweled Mexican spur. The silver center of the rowel held a distinctive design. He'd seen it somewhere before. When? Where?

It was still dark when Kerrigan regained consciousness, but he had no idea whether it was the same night or the next. For a second he thought he might be paralyzed, but with painful effort he was able to move his legs, and he realized it was the bitter cold that had robbed him of feeling in his hands and feet. He supposed he ought to be grateful for the wintry weather, because that same cold had apparently kept him from bleeding to death. He felt a breath on his face and froze for a moment, afraid it was a wolf or cougar come to make a meal of him.

But the soft lipping motion on his hair was the way his horse had woken him from sleep in the past. "Howdy, there, Paint. Nice of you to drop by."

The horse lipped his ear, and Kerrigan knew that if he didn't move, the gelding would bite him next. It was a game they had often played, but Paint wasn't known for his patience. This time Kerrigan was afraid he might lose an ear before he managed to get his body up off the ground. He wanted to laugh, but that was sure to hurt like the very devil, so he contented himself with a wry smile. If he still had a face to smile with, all was not lost.

The reins trailed close by, and Kerrigan reached out and grasped them in his hand. Even that much effort took a great deal of will, but he was evidently not as close to death's doorstep as the rustlers had hoped. Of course, if his horse hadn't come back, he'd have been a dead man. Now at least he had a chance. His back hurt like the devil, and he felt damn weak, but he wasn't going to die out here alone if he could help it.

He wrapped the reins around his gloved hand a couple of times, planning to use them to lever himself up. He put his mind on things other than the pain. His only chance of survival was to get up and get on his horse.

It was a journey of inches, and several times Kerrigan thought he wasn't going to make it. When he was on his knees, he managed to grasp a stirrup, and used that to help him get all the way to his feet. A hand on the horn kept him upright. He led his horse to a nearby outcropping of rock and used it as a stepping-stone to get into the saddle.

He sat there slumped, wondering where to go. The way he figured, it might not be such a bad thing to let the rustlers think they had succeeded in killing him. He would have the advantage of surprise on his side when he was ready to deal with them again. Meanwhile, he needed a place where he could recuperate, sight unseen. Someplace close.

"Giddyap, Paint. Let's go see if that spinster lady is as good at nursing as she is at cussing a man out."

Miss Devlin was furious. She started the walk home with her gloved hands balled into fists. Men! They were totally impossible! Ornery. Disgusting. Unreasonable. Foolish.

Bullies. Why did women fall in love with them? Why did women choose to mate and spend their lives with them? She would never be able to understand it if she tried for a million years.

Sheriff Reeves never had been found, and nobody had bothered to send for Deputy Joe. The fight had ended only when both men were too tired to stand up anymore. As the battle wore on, the ladies of Sweetwater had exchanged despairing glances that forewarned Miss Devlin their resolution was faltering. She had made a point, when the melee was finally over, of taking Regina Westbrook and Persia Davis aside to talk with them.

"You see what will happen if you don't stand firm, don't you?" she said to the two irresolute faces before her.

"Your plan isn't working fast enough," Regina said. "At this rate there won't be a man around who can see how attractive his wife is, let alone appreciate her efforts to deny him his conjugal rights."

"We might as well give up now," Persia agreed. "We're wasting our time."

"You're not wasting your time," Miss Devlin argued. "You're doing something to force your spouses to see reason. There's too little of that around here right now. If you give up, there will only be more violence, and more and more—"

"I get your point," Regina interrupted. "But I can't see any reason—"

"I'll give you a reason," Miss Devlin said. "Think of your children. Hadley and Bliss—"

Miss Devlin barely got the names out before the two mothers rushed to deny any attraction one child might have for the other.

"I hope Hadley knows better than to see that girl—"

"Bliss is too good a girl to be wasted on the likes of—"

"That's quite enough. From both of you!"

Regina and Persia stared at an enraged Miss Devlin in astonishment. She took advantage of their silence to make her point.

"Suppose—just suppose, I say—that your children should decide that they love each other and want to get married."

"Bliss would never—"

"Hadley would   "

"Just suppose—" Miss Devlin interrupted fiercely, "that they *did* love each other and decided to get married. Don't you see they could never be happy if their fathers were as ready to kill one another as not? Just remember the fight tonight started between two children. It was only carried on by their fathers.

"For your children's sakes you must stay firm, and convince the other women to do the same. You are making progress. The testiness of the menfolk tonight is proof positive that they aren't unaffected by the situation at home. You have to believe that this plan will work, and you must reinforce that belief in the others who've taken the oath. Because if it doesn't work—"

Miss Devlin halted abruptly. Her chest heaved, her eyes sparkled with tears of frustration she refused to shed, and her hands trembled with emotion. She clasped them together in front of her and lowered her eyes to stare at her whitened knuckles. It was frightening how much this mattered to her. Her whole being vibrated with outrage against the violence for which they all seemed destined. Such a useless, senseless waste of life. Was she the only one who could see where they were headed? She had to make them understand.

"Because if it doesn't work," she continued in a hoarse whisper, "there will be such bloodshed in this valley that what happened here tonight will seem like a picnic."

Miss Devlin cleared her throat. "The vow you took may

seem silly to you. I felt a little foolish myself when I suggested it. But it *will* work. It *must* work. It *can* work. If only you will stand firm. Will you convince the others? Can you?"

"I'll try," Persia said.

"Don't try. Do it! And you, Mrs. Westbrook?"

"I'll do my part, never fear."

She'd had to be satisfied with that. By the time her white frame house finally came into sight, her anger was spent and she felt exhausted.

When she came around the corner of the house, the last thing she expected to see was a distinctive paint horse tied to her hitching post. What was the gunslinger doing here this time of night? As she walked past she saw something gleaming on the saddle in the moonlight. She stopped and stared for a moment, her heart in her throat. Surely not. Please, God, no. She took her glove off, almost afraid to touch. Her fingers swiped across the shine on the saddle. It was wet, almost sticky. Blood. A lot of blood.

"Damn him! Damn him, damn him, damn him!" If that gunslinger had gotten himself killed she would—

Then she noticed the light inside the house. He was alive! Or had been when he arrived. She stared at the light, afraid to hope, afraid not to. She took one step toward the door, another, and then she was running. He had to be alive. "*He is alive. He is alive,*" she chanted as she yanked open the door and stepped inside.

He sat in the reception chair, which he had dragged off the India carpet. His eyes were closed. She saw why he had moved the chair. A pool of blood had gathered on the hardwood floor beneath him. His face was gray. There wasn't a sign of life. She walked slowly toward him, her body blocking the light and making a shadow on his face. Apparently that was enough to rouse him. His eyes opened and he looked at her from beneath lowered lids, appearing almost drugged.

"How are you?" she whispered.

"I've felt better."

"What happened?"

"Got shot."

"Who did it?"

"Don't know."

"What are you doing here?"

He grinned crookedly. "Reckon I'm bleeding to death."

Chapter 9

A year of nursin' don't equal a day of sweetheart.

"WHY DID YOU COME HERE? WHY DIDN'T YOU GO into town to see Doc Harper? You need—"

"The men who did this left me for dead. I don't want them to know they made a mistake."

"If you don't see a doctor, they won't have!" Miss Devlin snapped. "You've lost a lot of blood—"

"Look," the gunslinger reasoned, "my back is full of buckshot. You can likely pick that out as easy as the doc can. Then all I need is plenty of rest and a bite to eat now and then and I'll be right as rain . . . unless I'm already too far gone. And in that case, the doc won't be much help, will he?"

Miss Devlin feared the events of the evening must have left her a little crazy, because what he said made a lot of sense. At any rate, if she didn't want to have to drag him into her bedroom alone, she had better make use of what little strength he had left to get him there.

"Wait a moment while I turn down the sheets," she said decisively. "I'll be right back to help you into the bedroom."

A few moments later she turned and found him braced

in the doorway of her bedroom, his face ashen, his lips a single line of determination.

"Don't you know when to quit?" She hurried to support him. "Lean on me." She was surprised when he did, but obviously his will was no longer able to support his wounded body. He was easily as far gone as she had thought he was the first time she had laid eyes on him tonight. It was amazing he hadn't keeled over dead arguing with her.

His body hugged hers from hip to shoulder, and she was aware of the hard muscle under his clothes. Maybe if he hadn't been hurt, she would have found the contact troubling, but right now there wasn't time to think about anything but getting him across the room and into her bed.

Her mind was frantically calculating how she was going to keep his presence a secret for the several weeks it would take him to get well enough to fend for himself. And how on earth was she going to hide his distinctive paint horse?

When she got him angled right, the Texan pretty much fell face-first onto her bed. He turned his head to free his mouth from her pillow and mumbled, "Don't let anyone know I'm here."

"Surely you want to let the Association—"

"Better if they don't know. Then they won't have to lie when they're asked what happened to me."

He was out cold before she even had his boots off. It wasn't easy getting him undressed. The sheepskin coat was bulky, and she realized, as she struggled to get him out of it, that it had probably saved his life. That, and the fact that buckshot was used to best effect up close. From the pattern of pellets on Kerrigan's back, he had been some distance away when he had been shot.

Although he was bleeding again, at some time blood had dried his coat to his shirt, and his long johns to his battered skin. She was glad he was unconscious by the time she got everything unstuck and he was naked to the waist.

The upper half of his back and shoulders had the appearance of a sculpted statue, with every muscle and sinew defined. The lower half looked like raw beef. There was also buckshot along the upper edges of his buttocks, so she unbuckled his belt and undid the top button of his Levi's, sliding them down just enough to do what had to be done.

It wasn't easy finding the buckshot in that mess, but with a lantern set close, her spectacles perched on the end of her nose, and the aid of a pair of tweezers, she finally managed to remove all of it. Or what she hoped was all of it. She used some peroxide to cleanse and disinfect the wound, and was slightly nauseous by the time she finished bandaging him with a torn sheet. She poured herself a glass of water from the pitcher beside her bed and drank it down, hoping that would settle her stomach.

Her knees felt too weak to support her, but she knew she wasn't done yet. She had to get the gunslinger's horse rubbed down and settled into the lean-to out in back of her house. That would serve to hide the animal, at least for now. She had to scrub the blood off her floor and do something about the blood on the upholstered seat of her reception chair. Then she had to figure out where she was going to sleep. And then . . .

The bright November sun on her face woke Miss Devlin. She was curled up in the rocker beside her bed, and her neck had a crook in it from sleeping hunched over under a heap of quilts. She had started the night on the sofa, but it was too short for comfort, and she was afraid she might miss hearing the Texan if he woke in pain during the night. But he hadn't. In fact, his breathing was so shallow at one point, she had felt for a pulse at his throat, afraid he had died. But he hadn't. He hadn't moved. He hadn't moaned. He hadn't done anything but lie there.

Only a few coals remained in the bedroom fireplace, and she could see her breath. She didn't want to leave the warm haven she had created in the rocker, but the sooner she rekindled the fire, the sooner the room would warm up. The kinks made themselves felt as she straightened slowly out of the rocker and stepped into an icy pair of slippers. She quickly stirred the fire and added kindling and more wood.

Then she stood, still draped in several layers of quilt, and stared at the man stretched out on her bed, feeling an abundance of confusing emotions.

Relief. At least he wasn't dead, and with luck and care, he wouldn't die.

Reluctance. It was folly to touch him, nurse him, care for him. She felt things around him that she had no desire to feel.

Resentment. How dare he put her in such a compromising position! Imagine what the ladies of Sweetwater would say if they found the gunslinger from Texas in Miss Devlin's bed.

Eden braced herself before reaching down to brush an unruly lock of black hair from Kerrigan's forehead. That slight brush of her fingertips against his skin informed her he was feverish. That was to be expected. He must need water, some sort of nourishment, but she had no idea how to feed an unconscious man. The bullet that had hit her father had killed him instantly. Before that fateful day, Sundance had never even been wounded.

Miss Devlin laid her fingertips against the Texan's cheek, unable to resist the impulse to feel the beginning of a dark beard that shadowed his face. It was rougher than she had thought it would be. Her fingers traced the line of his jaw, but she withdrew her hand before she reached his mouth, aware of the awful imposition of such actions on his person. Whatever was the matter with her, touching this man without his permission? That left her feeling another emotion.

Rage. She wasn't going to let this gunslinger turn her into the proverbial spinster begging for a kind word or look from a stranger. Nor was she going to act the fool. She certainly wasn't about to make the same mistake as her mother, and let herself care one tiny little bit about a man of violence. Miss Devlin, spinster schoolteacher, was a damn sight smarter than that.

The knock on her door startled her, turning rage to irritation. Who could that be? Miss Devlin hurriedly pulled off her sleeping cap, shoved the heap of quilts off her shoulders into the rocker, and pulled on her robe, shivering as the cold flannel encircled her. She tightened the tie at her waist and pulled the bedroom door closed behind her as she headed to the front door.

A look through the lace curtains at her front window didn't reveal anyone. "Who's there?"

"It's me, Hadley."

"What do you want, Hadley?" Miss Devlin asked through the door.

"Can I come in and talk? I want to apologize for what I said last night."

Miss Devlin groaned. She had completely forgotten about the promise she had made to Bliss last night to help the two lovers meet. Eden wanted to tell Hadley to go away, but she couldn't keep everyone at bay for the next few weeks. She might as well start figuring out how to see people without revealing Kerrigan's presence.

An over-the-shoulder glance around the parlor before she opened the door assured her there was nothing to reveal she had a wounded man in her house. "I haven't even had a cup of coffee yet this morning. Come on in and I'll make us some."

Miss Devlin briskly ushered Hadley through the parlor to the kitchen in back, which had a small table and two elm spindleback chairs where they could sit and talk. She noticed a bloody rag she had left in the sink and quickly covered it with a dish towel.

She lit the kindling in her four-hole Acme stove, then filled the coffeepot from the pump at the sink and set it on the stove to heat while she ground some coffee beans. Eden reached for some cups from the top shelf of her kitchen cabinet, then got spoons from the long drawer below. Following her normal morning routine gave her time to concentrate on what she wanted to say to Hadley.

Miss Devlin had promised Bliss she wouldn't tell Hadley about the baby, but the teacher had urged her pupil to give Hadley the news soon, so the couple could plan together what was best to do. "I talked to Bliss last night," Miss Devlin began. "I promised her I'd help the two of you find a way to meet—to talk."

"You won't be sorry," Hadley said soberly.

"Hadley, have you thought seriously about what your future with Bliss will be like if your parents and hers never make peace with one another?"

"As a matter of fact, I have. My dad's taught me a lot, Miss Devlin. There's bound to be a ranch somewhere that needs a good hand. A few years from now I'll make a good foreman. Someday maybe I'll have enough saved to start a spread of my own."

Hadley was clearly willing to take a man-size responsibility on his young shoulders. His blue eyes stared back at her with innocence and sincerity. He believed young love could conquer all. Maybe he was right. But he didn't know yet that there would be three mouths to feed on a cowboy's pittance, rather than two. That might change things.

They both started at the sound of someone else knocking on her front door. "Wait here," Miss Devlin said, "while I see who it is." The fewer explanations she had to make, the better, but she could hardly keep Hadley's presence a secret, since his horse was tied up out front. When she reached the door she called out, "Who is it?"

"It's me, Miss Devlin. Bliss."

Miss Devlin yanked the door open. "What are you doing here? I said I would send you a message when—"

"I couldn't wait. I had to see you." Bliss charged inside, her nose and cheeks pink from the cold. "I saw Hadley's horse outside. Is he—"

Hadley stood in the doorway to the parlor.

Bliss's eyes were full of hope. "Hadley. You're here."

Miss Devlin watched as the two young people stared at each other with longing and disbelief. Hadley reached out to Bliss and she rushed into his one-armed embrace. It was as though Miss Devlin no longer existed. They hugged, and then they kissed with such abandon that at first Miss Devlin was too embarrassed to stop them, and then too filled with sympathy for their plight. She discreetly turned her back and gazed out the window.

When she heard them murmuring a short time later, she turned back and said, "Why don't you take Bliss into the kitchen, Hadley. You can both have a cup of coffee and talk there while I get dressed. I'll be back to join you in a few minutes."

Miss Devlin felt her eyes burn with unshed tears when she saw the grateful look in Hadley's eyes. Through a watery film she watched the solicitous way Hadley drew Bliss into the curve of his arm and led her through the swinging kitchen door, carefully closing it behind them. Eden smiled. She wanted to be a fly on the wall when Bliss told Hadley he would become a father in seven months.

Eden's smile broadened when she heard the clatter of a

coffee cup in the kitchen a moment later, followed by Hadley's elated shout of hosanna. She hoped their happiness lasted longer than it took Hadley to realize the complications this child would cause in their lives.

Miss Devlin stepped into her bedroom and rummaged in her chest for clean underthings. Inside her oak wardrobe she found a simple merino princess dress she often wore around the house.

The sight of the gunslinger lying facedown on her bed reminded her that she had no place to dress in private, yet Hadley would be sure to wonder if she returned to the kitchen in her nightclothes. She eyed the Texan sideways as she began to untie her robe. He looked done in. It was a safe bet he would stay that way long enough for her to dress.

Miss Devlin had pulled on clean pantalettes and was buttoning the top button of a clean chemise when the gunslinger opened his eyes. A confused frown formed on his face which slowly became a smile. Eden knew then why she had never become a gambler.

"If you'll kindly close your eyes, I'll finish dressing," she said.

"I'm enjoying the view too much to want to miss anything," he murmured, his voice husky from sleep.

Twin spots of color grew on Miss Devlin's cheeks. "You, sir, are not a gentleman."

"Never said I was."

Miss Devlin turned her back on the insolent man and quickly slipped several petticoats on. Her heart was pounding rapidly as she lifted the princess gown down over her head. Its graceful skirt, created by back draping that resulted in a low-slung pouf, was somewhat full over the hips, but the front skirt was arranged into a semi-hobble effect. The twelve-inch ruffle trim of the underskirt was accordion pleated. Unfortunately, the shapely bodice had at least a dozen buttons leading from the high round neck down an inch below the fitted waist, and her fumbling fingers didn't seem to want to cooperate.

"I'd be glad to lend you a hand," the Texan said, noticing her difficulty. He tried to lift himself up, but winced with pain and dropped to the bed again. "But you'll have to come over here."

"I'll manage." And somehow she did. When she turned back to face him, he was still staring intently at her. She looked down quickly at the clinging bodice, afraid she had missed a button or, worse yet, that she had buttoned the dress up cockeyed. But everything seemed all right. Nervously, she smoothed the fine wool at her waist and down over her hips.

"You look fine," he said. "I like your hair down. It's beautiful. Does it always curl like that?"

Her hands grabbed for her hair and she realized then why his dark eyes had never left her. She must look like a wanton, with her hair draped over her shoulders and falling down her back. Once her sleeping cap was off, she had never given her hair another thought.

Eden had a good brush—with a mahogany back and eleven rows of long black Russian bristles—that she had ordered through the Montgomery Ward mail catalog. Grabbing it from the top of her dresser, she set to brushing with a will. She faced the mirror over her dresser, and saw that Kerrigan's gaze never left her. She was disturbed by the look in his eyes, but hesitated to chastise him because then he would know that she had noticed in the first place. Eden took out her frustration on her hair, which was badly snarled. Her fierce brushing brought tears to her eyes.

"Are you upset because I said your hair is beautiful?"

The brush dropped onto the dresser. "Why should I be?"

"You tell me."

"I assure you," Eden said as she twisted her hair into a

bun at the base of her neck, "that your opinion doesn't matter to me in the least." She stuck a hairpin in to emphasize her point.

"Then why are you in such a hurry to pin it up?"

Eden jabbed another pin in. And another. "I'm not in a hurry."

"No?"

Eden frowned. As usual, curly tendrils had escaped at her temples and around her ears.

She had started to brush them smooth when the Texan's voice stopped her. "Don't. You've got the rest of it tied up tight. Let those few curls be. That fiery hair of yours is too damn pretty to hide in an old lady's bun."

She whirled on the gunslinger. She wanted to tell him what she did with her hair was none of his business, but the clear admiration in his eyes stopped her short. She wouldn't have believed him for a heartbeat if he had said her *face* was pretty. She had been looking into a mirror too many years to believe that. But she had thought sometimes, when the sun glinted off her burnished curls, that they looked quite nice. If she had always kept her hair pulled back in a bun, it was only because she thought leaving it down would be like putting a too-rich frame on a nondescript painting.

Confused by her feelings, needing to censure Kerrigan but unwilling to deny his compliment, she snapped, "Keep your voice down. We have company."

He arched a questioning brow.

"Hadley Westbrook and Bliss Davis are here."

"Westbrook, the rancher's kid . . . and Davis, the nester's kid? Sounds like trouble to me."

"There are some . . . problems. Nothing that can't be handled. They just needed a place to talk."

"Ahhh. She's pregnant."

"What makes you say that?"

He arched a knowing brow and Eden shook her head in disgust. "All right. Maybe she is. But you'd better not say—"

"Anybody else know?" he interrupted.

"No. And I think it's best kept secret until things are settled between Oak and Big Ben."

The gunslinger whistled low. "That's for sure." He glanced at the door and back to her again with a rueful grimace. "I hate to bring this up, but I need—"

"Miss Devlin? Are you dressed?"

"That's Hadley," Miss Devlin whispered. "I'll send him and Bliss on their way and be right back."

She squeezed through her bedroom door and closed it behind her. Hadley's face beamed with pride, yet his blue eyes were troubled.

"I assume congratulations are in order," Miss Devlin said with a smile.

"Yes, thank you. I'm sure you'll agree that Bliss and I have to be married soon. We're probably going to have to go to Canyon Creek to find a preacher who won't go running straight to our fathers."

"Getting married is a good idea. But you'll both be missed if you try to leave town right now," Miss Devlin said. "You'll have to wait. And plan."

It was plain from the look on Hadley's face that he didn't want to wait. It was equally plain that he could see the wisdom of planning. After all, Miss Devlin hadn't vetoed his idea, only encouraged him to act wisely in carrying it out. "All right," he agreed. "We'll make plans to get away so that neither of our parents will be the wiser."

"You still won't be able to live together, even after you're married," Miss Devlin warned. "Unless this plan of yours to get married also includes running away."

Hadley had difficulty meeting her probing gaze. He had bragged about how he was a cowman, how he would get a job and earn a living. But he was aware, as he knew she was, that he would have a hard time supporting a family on a cowman's wages. His wife and child deserved better. If things got settled in Sweetwater, they would have better.

"Bliss and I talked it over, and we're willing to keep our marriage a secret in the hope that things will get settled between our families before the baby . . ." Hadley gulped. ". . . before we have any explaining to do."

Miss Devlin put one hand on Hadley's shoulder, and lifted Bliss's chin with the other hand. "You're both being very wise. Things will turn out for the best. Right now, I think you'd both better get home, before your parents miss you."

Once she had the young people out the door Miss Devlin squared her shoulders and headed back to her bedroom.

"They're gone," she said as she shoved open the door.

Kerrigan was sitting on the edge of the bed facing her, wearing nothing but his unbuttoned Levi's and socks. She hadn't paid much attention to his chest the previous evening, and gaped at the broad expanse covered by a pelt of curly black hair. He looked magnificent—if you ignored the scowl on his face.

"I tried reaching for my boots, but I'm having a problem bending over. I could use some help," he admitted in an irritable voice.

"You aren't going anywhere. You're too weak—"

"If you won't help me, I'll do it myself." He bent over and nearly fainted.

She caught him and discovered he was trembling with pain and exhaustion. "I'm not going to help you finish the job those rustlers started," she said angrily. "Now lie back down."

He turned a baleful eye on her, but didn't move. "As I started to explain once before, I have some needs to tend to first."

Miss Devlin stared for a moment until she realized what "needs" he was talking about. Her face flamed. There was no way he could walk all the way to the outhouse. And no way she could carry him that far either. As weak as he was, he couldn't make it on his own. "There's a chamber pot under the bed," she said.

His mouth thinned. "If I could bend over, I could put on my boots."

Miss Devlin bit her lip in an agony of indecision. What was she supposed to do? Her practical nature came to the rescue. She bent down and pulled the pristine flowered chamber pot with its porcelain lid out from under the bed and set it beside him. "Call me when you're finished," she said. Then she turned and left the room.

Miss Devlin paced the parlor anxiously. The situation was embarrassing for her, but it must be even more so for him. They were stuck together until he was well, so she was going to have to get over any squeamishness she felt about what had to be done. Eden must have paced for ten minutes, but he hadn't called for her. Worried, she walked up to her bedroom door and knocked softly. No answer. She knocked a little louder. Still no answer.

"Kerrigan?" she whispered. Why was she whispering? There was no one in the house but the two of them. She twisted the doorknob and slowly opened the door.

He was lying facedown on the bed. He had managed to set the covered chamber pot on the table beside the bed. He appeared to be asleep. Or unconscious. She quickly grabbed the pot and started out the door, hoping to be gone before he awoke.

"I could use a cup of coffee when you get back."

She didn't answer, just glared at him, pink-faced, and hurried out the door with her burden. That horrible, despicable man! He had been awake all along and had waited to catch her at the most awkward . . .

Eden grinned. She had gotten a good look at his face—at the mischievous grin on his face—before she escaped the room. Well, two could play that game. If he wanted to match wits, he had certainly met his match.

Eden returned with a cup of coffee, only to find that Kerrigan really was asleep this time. Except for brief moments of consciousness, when she would pour some chicken broth down his throat, he stayed that way through most of the night. She quickly realized that the embarrassment she had felt when she removed the chamber pot wasn't the last of the indignities they would have to endure.

In the early morning hours, as she sponged his face and shoulders with cool water to try to get his fever down, she realized her efforts would have more success if she sponged all of him down. She wouldn't even have considered such a thing, except the fever kept him from being conscious most of the time. If he wasn't awake, neither of them would suffer as much embarrassment at his nudity. Once the thought took hold, she decided to act quickly before she changed her mind.

As soon as she stuck her hand into the warmth between his body and the sheets to unbutton his trousers, she had second thoughts about what she had decided to do. She wasn't sure she could bear to see him naked. She told herself it was just a body. He wasn't even conscious. Still, what she was going to do was so . . . personal. Once she had seen Kerrigan naked, she was sure it was something she wasn't going to be able to forget.

Eden pulled her hand back and sat down on the edge of the bed, trying to think of whom she could go to for help. But anyone she contacted would find out she had allowed Kerrigan to spend the night here. She would be exposing herself to gossip that might very well force her to leave Sweetwater. And that she did not want to do.

She rolled up her sleeves, gritted her teeth, and slid her

hand back into the cocoon of warmth between his belly and the sheets. The hairs on his stomach tickled her.

Suddenly a hand clamped down on her wrist and a raspy voice demanded, "What the hell are you doing?"

Eden sat there stunned. What could she say?

"I'm not in the mood," he grumbled. "Go away."

Eden's face flamed. Did he think she . . . ? "You've got a fever," she said through bared teeth. "I was trying—"

Suddenly he opened his eyes, and she watched as the confusion cleared. His lips quirked. "I've got a fever for you, lady, that's no lie. But you're going to have to wait till I'm feeling a little—"

"Will—you—shut—up!" Eden gritted out. "I was trying to get your pants off—"

"No kidding."

"—to sponge you down," Eden persisted. "To try to get your fever down." She defiantly met his dark eyes, which glittered with the fever that indeed was ravaging his body.

His lips curled down in a cynical twist. "You ever seen a naked man, Miss Devlin?"

"No, I have not."

"You're determined to do this?"

"I don't see that I have much choice," she said, shifting her gaze to the fireplace on the opposite wall. "I have to get you well to get rid of you."

"All right."

He didn't sound happy.

She wasn't either.

He released her hand and she rubbed her wrist where he had held it.

"How do you want to do this?" he asked.

"I . . . uh . . . can you manage the buttons yourself?"

He tried. He couldn't.

"If you could lift up a little, I'll do it," she said. Eden found it difficult to breathe. It was one thing to undo the buttons on an unconscious man's Levi's. It was quite another thing to do the same task when the man was awake and watching with a frankly challenging look on his face.

The jeans had worn soft and the buttons slipped free easily. Too easily. Eden's eyes narrowed as she looked at Kerrigan's face. His eyes were closed but his lips were curved in a self-satisfied smile. Kerrigan had tricked her. He could well have done this himself. But he hadn't, knowing full well that if she did the chore for him, she couldn't help but feel . . . him. The instant the last button fell free, Eden pulled her hand away. Her cheeks were beyond pink. She swallowed and tried to steady her breathing. It was a hopeless task.

Her voice had a distinct touch of acid when she said, "If you'll lift up just a little, I can pull your Levi's off."

With a knowing smile, he obliged.

Eden grasped the trousers at his hips and tugged them down over his buttocks, exposing a pair of long johns. She reached down and pulled the denim over his feet and a moment later dropped the Levi's on the floor beside her bed.

"The long johns have to go too," she said in a constricted voice. Eden stood there staring down at him, unable to reach for the form-fitting piece of clothing that was all that remained.

A minute passed.

Kerrigan turned around and looked at her. "I knew you'd be too chicken-hearted to do it."

"I'm not chicken-hearted," Miss Devlin retorted.

"Like hell!"

"Don't swear at me."

"Then do what you have to do," he challenged.

Eden stared defiantly into his dark eyes as she grasped the waist of Kerrigan's long johns. She was completely unnerved by the heat of him as her fingertips brushed his skin. Her eyes glazed and became unseeing as she peeled the long johns down as quickly as she could, exposing Kerrigan's taut buttocks and his muscular thighs and calves. In what became a dramatic gesture of victory, she finally stripped them off over his feet.

Kerrigan never made a sound, but Eden wasn't oblivious to the tension in the ridged muscles that stood out on the lower half of his body.

"I'm done," she said in a whisper.

"No kidding."

Stung by the mockery in his voice, she quickly covered him with a quilt. "I'll go get some more cool water." As she fled the room with the water bowl in her hands, she heard him mumble, "Damn fool spinster schoolteacher."

Kerrigan wasn't sure what kind of game she was playing, he only knew he wasn't winning. That woman had more guts and gumption than he'd thought. He hated being helpless. He hated depending on anyone. Most of all he hated having her see him like this. It wasn't that he hadn't been naked with a woman before. He had. Lots of times. But except for one other time, the woman had never been . . . innocent.

Miss Devlin put on a good show of disinterest and aplomb, but he'd heard her gasp when she'd pulled his long johns down. And seen the rosy cheeks she couldn't hide. And felt her hands tremble as they skimmed down his legs along with the long johns. Oh, she was not quite so calm and collected as she wanted him to think. But she had spunk. And he'd always believed, the wilder the colt, the better the horse.

He hadn't planned on pursuing Miss Devlin from the sickbed. On the other hand, he had been given a rare opportunity to jump several steps in his seduction of the spinster schoolteacher. He'd be a tomfool to overlook the chance to breach of few of her defenses while she was lulled into thinking he was a helpless invalid. He was looking forward with relish to the day when he had the pleasure of returning the favor Miss Devlin had done for him today.

Meanwhile, the instant Eden left her bedroom, she put a hand over her pounding heart to keep it from leaping out of her breast. She hadn't been prepared for the feelings of tenderness and need that had welled inside her when she had unbuttoned Kerrigan's jeans, nor the heat she felt as she stripped him bare. She was angry with herself for letting her feelings get so out of control. She was his nurse, for heaven's sake! *Nothing more.*

Eden poured out the water from the bowl into the sink and pumped some more. She found a multitude of things to do in the kitchen to keep her busy for nearly a half hour. At long last, she took a deep breath and headed back to her bedroom.

To her surprise and relief, Kerrigan was asleep when she sat down beside him again. That left her worried that his fever had gotten worse. She felt his forehead and, sure enough, it was on fire. She dipped the sponge into the cold water and squeezed it out and ran it over his face and shoulders. Too soon, she had covered all the unwounded parts of his upper body.

Slowly Eden pulled the quilt down to uncover the rest of him. All the while she sponged his body, Eden marveled at how perfectly he was formed. Because he was unconscious, she allowed the sponge to caress, as well as soothe, although she was careful not to actually touch his skin with her fingertips. The one time it accidentally happened, she felt a frisson of excitement race up her arm. The reaction stunned and dismayed her. Where did these rebellious emotions come from? How was he able to make her feel things she had no wish to feel?

Eden prayed the fever would pass quickly, and that the gunslinger would get out of her house and out of her life.

But she was not to be so fortunate. Infection set in, worsening the fever, and she was forced to touch him again and again, until it became a kind of torture.

After the first night spent in the rocker, she made herself a pallet in front of the fire in her bedroom, which was considerably more comfortable—when she was able to find time to sleep. She spent most of the next few nights sitting at Kerrigan's side, sponging him, talking to him, urging him to take broth, or comforting him when the nightmares came.

The first time he flailed out at her, she had been caught by surprise. His fist had connected with her jaw and she had gone sailing across the bedroom.

"I'll kill you!" he had raged, trying ineffectually to push himself upright.

She had been able to subdue him easily, but she had been more careful after that. There were moments when she thought he was lucid. One night he had woken and asked, "What time is it?"

"Nearly morning," she had answered.

"I have to leave," he said.

"You're not going anywhere," she'd replied, leaning over him, speaking into his ear and gently pressing him back down against the bed.

"I'm going to kill them all."

A chill had gone down her spine. "Who?"

"Every damn one of those murdering bastards who massacred my family."

Then she had realized he wasn't lucid after all. It was the fever talking. She knew she ought to find a way to make him stop. He wouldn't want her to know these things about him. But there wasn't much she could do outside of gagging him or leaving the room, and she wasn't willing to face the consequences if she tried either.

"I didn't even have a goddamn gun in the house," he

raved. "I thought I was through killing. But it never ends, does it?" he said in a despairing voice. "I'll make them pay, Colby, for what they did to you and Susanna. And Elizabeth . . . Oh, God, not Elizabeth, too! Please, no. God, no."

She watched helplessly as the tears squeezed from his closed eyes. She couldn't bear his pain. There was nothing she could do except murmur, "Wake up, Kerrigan. It's only a bad dream. Wake up."

As abruptly as the tears had begun, they stopped, and there was a look of such savage exultation on his face that it frightened her.

"Burn in hell, you bastards! I only wish you were all alive so I could kill you again." His face contorted, and he said in an agonized voice, "Nothing is going to bring my family back. Even killing you won't bring them back, God damn you!"

Suddenly her hand reached out to touch his face. "It's all right, Kerrigan. It's all right."

His hand grasped hers and pulled it to his mouth. She shuddered when his lips pressed into her palm.

He murmured, "Love you. Love you so much."

She jerked her hand away and stood up, backing away from the bed. He was out of his head. He didn't know what he was saying. *Who was it he loved?* She felt a horrible wrenching inside her. The tears came before she could stop them. She knew she was only crying because she was exhausted and her defenses were down and she felt sorry for him. It had nothing to do with discovering that she was beginning to care for a man who was much too much like her father. A man who had killed other men. A man who obviously loved someone else.

After that, when she sponged Kerrigan down, she kept her touch as impersonal as she could. When he recovered, he would be his same rude, irascible self, and she would cease to feel sympathy for him. And he would recover. She would not let him die.

On Wednesday, Sheriff Reeves came to see her after school. Instead of offering him a cup of coffee and a seat, she asked, "What brings you here?"

It was obvious he expected a better welcome, but she was feeling limp as a neck-wrung rooster, and that was the most hospitality she could muster.

"What happened to your face?" he asked.

Eden's hand rose to her jaw, where Kerrigan's fist had left a bruise that was past the purple stage and starting to yellow. She gave him the excuse she had given her pupils when they first saw the mark. "Ran into the kitchen door."

Since Felton had had experience with the swinging door himself, he was able to grin and quip ruefully, "You ought to get rid of that door."

Eden found herself smiling back. "I suppose you're right."

"Are . . . are you sure you're okay?" Felton asked. "You look a little tired."

His concern touched her, and she felt awful for having been so rude to him when he arrived. "I'm fine, really. It's just that . . . the children have been a bit unruly at school."

"Guess everybody's tense now that more cattle have turned up missing from the Solid Diamond."

"Is it ever going to end?"

Felton knew what she was asking. He forked a hand through his blond hair, leaving it disheveled. "I wish I knew. Kerrigan was supposed to help by finding the rustlers, but nobody's seen hide nor hair of him for days."

Eden stiffened.

Felton noticed. He tried to make his voice sound casual as he asked, "Has he come by to visit you?"

"What makes you think he'd come here?" Eden quickly

added in a more conciliatory voice, "I mean, I hardly know the man."

"He showed up for dinner here," Felton said flatly.

"Not because I invited him," Eden retorted, bristling.

Felton's lips pursed. "The gossip about you and that gunslinger was flying thick and fast last week—"

"You should know better than to listen to gossip, Felton. You'll end up chasing after twelve-pound steaks."

He turned his hat in his hands for a moment, refusing to meet her challenging gray eyes. "All right, Miss Devlin. If you say you haven't seen Kerrigan, I'll take your word on it. But it's beginning to look like he's in some kind of trouble." He turned to leave, but stopped and said, "If you hear anything, anything at all, be sure and let me know. I'd like to help him if I can."

At that moment, Miss Devlin was sorely tempted to confide in Felton. Despite Kerrigan's request for secrecy, she could see no reason why she couldn't tell the sheriff that the Association's hired gun was alive. Except, there was no way Felton would understand why she had agreed to keep Kerrigan's presence in her home a secret.

And although there was certainly no reason for it, she felt sure Felton was jealous of Kerrigan. No telling what her suitor would think if he learned she had kept a man he considered his rival in her bed for the past week. Better to let things be. It wouldn't be long before Kerrigan was back on his feet and could make his own explanations to the sheriff—ones that wouldn't involve her.

She opened the door for Felton and said, "If I see Kerrigan I'll let him know you're looking for him. Goodbye, Felton."

Eden watched regretfully as the sheriff rode away. She had just committed herself to caring for the gunslinger on her own until he was back on his feet.

It was a responsibility that wore on her. She tended to

Kerrigan's needs before she left for school, raced back during lunch to check on him, then came directly home at the end of the day. Haggard didn't begin to describe how she looked by the end of the week. Exhausted didn't begin to describe how she felt.

She was irritable with the children and, discomfited by her short temper, they were even more fractious. When Bliss finally asked on Friday if Miss Devlin was all right, she merely replied, "I'm worn to a frazzle worrying, that's all."

"Don't worry about me and Hadley," Bliss said, mistakenly assuming she was the source of Miss Devlin's concern. "We have everything all worked out. We're going to Canyon Creek next Saturday. We'll be married by noon and back before suppertime. Of course, we'll need you to provide an alibi for where I'll supposedly be all day—if that's all right?"

Although she had reservations, Miss Devlin said, "I suppose so. If you're sure—"

"That's wonderful! Hadley and I will come see you when we get back, so it won't exactly be a lie when I say I've been with you."

Miss Devlin couldn't make herself think that far ahead right now. She was too worried about Kerrigan. He wasn't getting any better, but he hadn't gotten any worse either. After a week of listening to his feverish ramblings, she knew more about him than she wanted to know.

To make things worse, there was one more clue to Kerrigan's past that had totally intrigued her when she discovered it—the watch Mr. Gold had adjusted for him.

Eden had found the gold pocket watch in Kerrigan's shirt pocket when she emptied it before disposing of the ruined shirt. She hadn't been able to resist looking inside the back of the watch to see the handsome couple the jeweler had mentioned.

One picture was of a much younger Kerrigan. The other was of a stunningly beautiful young woman, beautiful enough that Eden was stung by a totally new emotion— envy. If that was the kind of woman Kerrigan admired, there was no way he would ever be attracted to a woman as plain as Eden—not that she wanted him to be, of course.

Miss Devlin was convinced the picture had to be the woman Kerrigan loved. She wanted to know more about the woman. Who was she? What was her relationship to Kerrigan? Eden promised herself that when the gunslinger recovered from his fever, she would find out.

When Eden got home from school on Friday, she didn't bother to knock at her bedroom door, just shoved it open and stepped inside—to find a naked man sitting up in bed glaring fiercely at her.

"Where the hell are my pants!"

Chapter 10

*When a woman starts draggin' a loop,
there's always some man willin' to step in.*

"I'M NAKED AS A PLUCKED CHICKEN."

"Yes, you are, Mr. Kerrigan." Miss Devlin felt the blush rising despite her best efforts to prevent it.

His eyes narrowed. "How long have I been here?"

"About a week."

Kerrigan groaned in disbelief, then groaned again as he tried to get up. "I have to get moving. Those bushwhacking rustlers probably—"

She watched him grit his teeth as the pain took hold. She reached over to help cover him up again and he shoved her hand away, gasping as the sudden movement caused the pain to grab him again.

"What the hell did you do to me? I'm weak as a baby."

She could sympathize with his feelings of helplessness, but it wasn't her fault, and she wasn't about to take the blame. "You're lucky to be alive! You can hardly expect to be up and around in a matter of days with the kind of wound you had. Which is why you have no need of your pants, Mr. Kerrigan."

"We'll see about that," he muttered.

"Look, I'm not any happier to be stuck with you than

you are to be here," she said with asperity. "But you'll get well a lot quicker if you cooperate and do as I say."

He shook his head in disgust, but her reasonable appeal must have had some effect on him because he asked, "What do I have to do?"

"Stay in bed and give your body a chance to heal. Are you hungry?"

Miss Devlin watched, fascinated, as he scratched his stomach. "I guess I am."

"Supper should be ready soon." She rose, wondering how she had let herself get roped into this situation, and headed out of the room.

"Hey! Wait a minute. What—"

She didn't give him a chance to argue, closing the door quietly but firmly after her. When she reached the kitchen, she sat down at the table and took a deep breath. It was going to be infinitely more difficult to nurse Kerrigan now that he was on the road to recovery. She thought she had gotten over her embarrassment at seeing—and touching— his naked body over the past week. She had anticipated having no problem dealing with Kerrigan's nakedness when he awoke from his fever.

But bathing the limp form of an unconscious man was a far cry from watching the ripple and flex of muscles moving under his skin as he scratched and stretched. She liked what she saw. She wanted to touch. And that she absolutely, positively, could not do.

What worried her even more was the fear that he would somehow discern her need and take advantage of her, as he had with the buttons on his Levi's. He was a scoundrel, no doubt about it. She would have to be constantly on guard against him—and her own feelings—from now on.

By taking his time, Kerrigan was able to inch his legs over the edge of the bed. But there was no getting around it. He wasn't going anywhere anytime soon. He leaned his elbows on his knees and dropped his head in his hands. Even that little bit of movement stretched the skin on his back and let him know he had been shot.

He thought back to the ambush to see if he could remember and recognize any of the voices he had heard. Nothing. Then he recalled the unusual roweled spur. Where had he seen it before? Montana. Levander Early had worn Mexican spurs with that distinctive etching of longhorns in the center of the rowel.

Kerrigan's brow furrowed. He should have suspected Levander sooner, but had given him the benefit of the doubt. If he had trusted his instincts he'd have spent some time following the farmer-rustler around. Well, he owed Levander for a bullet in Montana. Now he owed him for a round of buckshot as well. This time he would make sure he didn't leave the job half done.

What Kerrigan needed now was proof. He had to catch Levander and his gang with the rustled cattle, or find some other way to tie him to the rustling. It was a big help, though, to know where to look when things started happening.

It was frustrating not to be able to go after the rustlers right now. But he did have an alternative. He rubbed his hand against the itchy week's growth of black beard on his face. Normally he worked alone, preferring that to trusting the local law, because more often than not, the local law was in somebody's pocket.

But he knew Sheriff Reeves, and Felton would do to ride the river with. It would be better to involve Felton than to take the chance of having more cattle rustled while he was flat on his back or—to be more precise, in light of his wound—his stomach. He gingerly settled himself back with a pillow between himself and the carved headboard of the bed.

A knock on the bedroom door was followed shortly by the appearance of Miss Devlin with a tray of food.

"I think I could eat a horse, saddle and all," he said with a welcoming grin.

"You'll have to settle for beef stew," she said, arranging the tray on his lap.

"This wasn't how I expected to have my first dinner with you," he said as he tried to catch her gaze.

"If you're smart, you won't remind me about that," she murmured, keeping her eyes carefully lowered.

"Not your best day, huh?"

"Not by half."

When she started to leave, he said, "Stay a minute. I need to ask a favor."

Miss Devlin debated the wisdom of hanging around when he might bring up other embarrassing questions she was certain he wanted to ask, but she was curious enough to stay, settling into the rocker beside her bed. Instead of telling her what he wanted, he ate, savoring each bite as if it were ambrosia.

Kerrigan might have been hungry, but his stomach had shrunk so much that he had swallowed no more than a few bites before he was forced to set down his fork. He looked ruefully at the nearly full bowl before him. The stew was too salty, and the carrots were still raw, but he appreciated her efforts, so he said, "You're a fine cook, Miss Devlin. I'm sorry I can't do your supper justice."

"There's no need to lie, Mr. Kerrigan. I oversalted the stew and the carrots are raw. I can only excuse myself by saying I got distracted by some papers I was grading."

His lips quirked. "You believe in calling a spade a spade, don't you?"

"I'm well aware of my shortcomings, if that's what you mean."

"You're awful hard on yourself. I've found more in you to admire than not."

Eden arched a brow. There he was, saying nice things to her again. If he kept that up, she might have to start revising her low opinion of him.

"Of course," he added, "that's not to say you couldn't stand some improvement."

Miss Devlin's lips pressed flat. She might have known he would spoil it. "What did you have in mind?"

"Well, for one thing, you could smile a little more."

"I see nothing to smile about so long as the ranchers and nesters in this valley are at one another's throats. I've done everything I can—"

"It's not your fight," he said in a harsh voice. "Stay out of it."

Eden rose to confront him, fists on hips. "Since when do you tell me what to do?"

"Since I know more about this kind of fight than you do. I've seen how ugly things can get. I'm warning you, for your own good, stay out of it."

"Of all the impertinent, audacious, hubristic—"

Kerrigan burst out laughing. He managed to control himself long enough to chortle, "Hubristic?"

Eden's chin jutted. "It means having exaggerated pride or self-confi—"

He burst out laughing again.

"I don't see what's so funny," Miss Devlin said.

"You are. I thought we agreed it was a waste of time for you to use big—obscure, abstruse, obtuse—words to put me in my place."

Kerrigan knew he had misspoken the instant the words were out of his mouth. Eden's face whitened and her fisted hands disappeared into the folds of her skirt. It had become clear to him that while Eden Devlin might be sensitive about her looks and her height, she was plainly *hubristic* about her intelligence. By discounting what she considered her one strength, he had struck a low blow. He hadn't meant to hurt her feelings, but damnit, he didn't know what else to do to get past those fences she kept throwing up at him.

"Look," he began. He opened his mouth to say he was sorry, and shut it again. He wasn't sorry.

Eden reached out and took the tray from his lap. "If you're done, I'll remove this."

When she started out the door with the tray, he said, "Wait. Don't go."

Eden looked down the length of her nose at him. "I don't see that we have anything else to say to one another."

"I want you to get a message to Sheriff Reeves."

"Why not wait until you're well and talk to him yourself?"

"I wouldn't ask you if it wasn't important," Kerrigan said.

"What do you want me to tell him?"

Kerrigan met her troubled gaze and said, "Tell him I want to talk to him . . . here."

"That's impossible."

"Why?"

"You know why!" Miss Devlin slammed the tray down on the bedside table. "I don't want anyone to know you've been here. Most especially not him."

"Oh, so that's the way it is."

"That's the way it is."

He leaned his head back against the pillow and looked her up and down. "I didn't know things were that serious between you and Felton Reeves."

"They're not . . . yet." His continuing stare made her wonder if her hair was falling down, or her buttons un-looped, and she began self-consciously to check them. "But inviting Felton to meet you here . . . letting him find out you've been here all along when I told him straight out that you weren't—"

"Felton was here?"

"He came asking about you earlier in the week when you turned up missing. I told him I had no idea where you were. To let him find out that I lied would be as good as a slap in the face to a proud man like him."

"And you care so much what Felton Reeves thinks?"

Miss Devlin turned away so Kerrigan wouldn't see the conflict on her face. She did care . . . and she didn't. The truth was, she hadn't had a chance yet to find out. But she wasn't about to end any hope of a life with Felton before she knew for sure whether she wanted one. She turned back to him and said simply, "You know he wants to marry me."

"And you're taking him up on the offer?"

Miss Devlin had no idea why Kerrigan sounded so angry, but she was confused and upset enough to answer him in kind. "I don't know what I'm going to do. I only know I don't want to make it impossible for Felton to ask when, or if, the times comes."

"All right," Kerrigan said brusquely. "I'll tell you what I want him to know."

"Very well," she said, threading her hands in front of her to keep him from seeing how agitated she was. "I'll have one of my pupils take a message to him on Monday. Is that soon enough to please you?"

He could see she was confused by the attitude he had taken toward her relationship with Felton. Try as he might, though, he couldn't get the sneer off his face. He wasn't sure of the source of his anger, but he knew it was real. "I'm surprised that with this great romance you two have going Felton doesn't drop by to see you every day."

"Oooooh! You're impossible!" Miss Devlin whirled and started out the door.

"Wait!"

"I have nothing further to say to you," Miss Devlin gritted out between clenched teeth.

"You forgot the tray," he said, extending it to bar her way.

She couldn't very well leave it. She reached out for it, and when she did he grasped her arm with his other hand and quickly set the tray on the bedside table.

"Don't leave mad," he said. "I had no right to say those things. What you do with Felton Reeves is your business."

"You're damn right it is!" She met his gaze, her body trembling with fury.

"Yeah," he said, his voice rueful. His fingers caressed her wrist to soothe the tiny bruises he had made.

Miss Devlin wasn't in a forgiving mood. "I have to clean up the kitchen. Let me go."

"Will you come back later to talk to me?"

Eden opened her mouth to tell him absolutely not, but what came out was, "All right."

He looked as surprised as she felt. She was halfway to the kitchen when she heard him call after her, "Bring another cup of coffee when you come."

Miss Devlin was soon having second thoughts about her impulsive agreement to spend more time in Kerrigan's company. She was a perfect idiot to fall for the coaxing plea in his dark eyes or the beseeching summons in his voice. But the fact was, she liked looking at him. And she liked hearing him say nice things about her.

Eden chided herself severely for believing Kerrigan's compliments. He probably found pretty words to flatter every woman who crossed his path. However, she had taken his compliments to heart precisely because he had been so honest about what he didn't like about her. As she washed dishes Miss Devlin found herself thinking seriously about changing her behavior—resorting to Big

Words less often—as a result of his comments. That was when she knew she was in serious trouble.

Miss Devlin decided she would deliver the promised cup of coffee and make a quick exit. Once she had the dinner things washed up, she came back to her bedroom with a hot cup of coffee in each hand, fully intending, if he grabbed her again, to spill it on him.

"Kerrigan? May I come in?"

"Come ahead."

She managed somehow to get the door open and hand him his coffee. Seating herself in her rocker, she allowed herself to relax for the first time in days. She rubbed the back of her neck with one hand while she balanced her cup of coffee in the other.

"You look tired," he said.

"It's been a long week."

"Come here. I can do that for you."

She stopped rubbing her neck abruptly. "Never mind, I—"

He set his coffee aside and said, "Come on. I promise not to bite." His lips twisted up on one side in a self-deprecating grin as he carefully levered himself over to make room for her.

"I really don't think it's a good idea for you to be . . . touching me."

"I'm just going to be rubbing a few sore muscles. Where's the harm in that?"

He sounded perfectly innocent. She couldn't accuse him of having designs on her person without seeming ridiculous. Quite frankly, it would be nice to have him rub out the soreness in her shoulders. "All right. If you're sure you're feeling up to it."

Eden sat on the bed with her back to him, her buttocks resting against his thigh. He took her coffee cup from her and set it beside his on the table. His large, strong hands encircled her neck, his thumbs pressing hard into her stiff shoulder muscles.

The instant he touched her she knew she had made another mistake. Because she didn't just *like* the way his hands made her feel, she *loved* it. She tried to convince herself she should get up and leave, but the sensations were so wonderful, she wanted to stay and enjoy them. After all, no one was going to know this had ever happened.

She groaned.

He paused. "Am I being too rough?"

"No, no. It feels wonderful. Don't stop." Her head lolled forward and a shiver of pleasure rolled down her spine.

Kerrigan felt her response to his touch. The little wisps of hair that had escaped from the old-lady bun onto her neck were the only thing between his lips and her enticing skin. The muscles were bunched in her shoulders, and he wondered if he was the reason she was so tense. "How's school been going?" he asked to get his mind off what he was thinking.

"If you're asking whether Jett and Keefe have been fighting lately, the answer is no," she said with a chuckle. "You seem to have made a permanent impression with that little demonstration you staged. But with one thing and another every day is a challenge."

"Why do you stay here, with all the trouble in the valley? Why don't you leave?"

She turned to look at him. His hands stilled and he noticed again how sometimes, when she was upset, her eyes turned an icy blue.

"I've spent my whole adult life looking for the perfect place to settle down," she said. "I'm here in Sweetwater to stay."

She turned and looked around the bedroom, her eyes resting on odds and ends she had collected to make the room seem less transient, and his hands claimed her shoulders again. As his gentling touch soothed her, she inventoried the things that had made this place a real home.

A huge French sewing basket woven of willow and rattan and lined with red satin sat in one corner of the room. It contained dozens of spools of thread, scissors, a pincushion, and needles. The first thing she had done the summer she arrived in Sweetwater was to make the braided rag rug now on her bedroom floor out of scraps of material she had collected over the years. It reminded her of all the places she had been, and how she was here to stay.

The most damning evidence that she had settled for good was the huge collection of breakables on her dresser. These consisted of two things: medicinals and toilet preparations.

Her collection of family remedies included tasteless castor oil, a box of carbolic arnica salve for burns and fever sores, effervescent salts for upset stomach, hydrogen peroxide, lavender smelling salts, and pure Norwegian cod-liver oil.

More astonishing, even to her, was the array of toilet preparations she had hoped might enable her to appear less plain than she was. None of them had ever worked, but nevertheless, when she was a child traveling with her parents, it would have been impossible to cart such a collection of breakable bottles and jars.

The dresser held Eastman's Toilet Waters (which she had intended to use with the Eastman's Violette Cold Cream that Kerrigan had kept her from purchasing), Fleur de Lis Talcum Powder, White Lily Face Wash, Witch Hazel Glycerine Jelly, C. H. Berry Freckle Ointment, Orange Flower Skin Food, Franklin's Liquid Depilatory for Removing Superfluous Hair, and last, but most certainly not least, Mrs. Graham's Kosmeo Toilet Cerate, which promised a perfect complexion in only ten minutes a day of cleansing with her beautifier.

Miss Devlin had taken to heart Mrs. Graham's caution on the label: *When a man marries, nine times out of ten he chooses the girl who is careful about her personal appearance, the girl with the pretty complexion.*

Eden had used the product religiously, and to be honest, she did have lovely skin. But nothing she had collected, used, dusted, or sprayed had ever made her face anything but plain. Miss Devlin knew it was going to take a very special man to look past her face to the wonderful woman inside.

The saddest part of her collection (because she had never expected to need them) were items useful only to a wife and mother. Her decorated wooden Wish Box contained such treasures as a bone teething ring with a rubber nipple and a luxurious silk cord that attached to the baby's arm so it wouldn't be lost, two spools of satin and grosgrain baby ribbon (one pink, one blue, just in case), a nickel-plated steel barber clipper, and a genuine badger-hair shaving brush with a black bone handle, which she intended as a wedding gift for her husband—if she ever had one. Most recently, she had added the silver baby spoon Kerrigan had given her.

Miss Devlin had no idea how long she had been sitting there dreaming, but she was suddenly conscious of the gunslinger's hands clear down on the small of her back. While it felt delicious, she was sure something that felt that good must be equally improper.

She slipped forward, and turned to meet his studying gaze. "As I was saying, I don't plan to leave this valley. That's why I'm doing my best to keep peace here. I'm through with leaving when things start to go bad."

Kerrigan waited for her to speak again, because he wondered what kind of calamity had once made a drifter out of this tall, plain woman. When she didn't offer the rest, he asked, "You have a lot of experience with things going bad?"

She turned away and his hands began their cradling work again, mostly because he could tell she wanted to get away from him and he didn't want her to go.

"My father wasn't the kind of man people wanted to see riding into their towns. And they were mighty glad to see the back of him."

His hands moved down her back, and though she arched away, he held her fast, circling her waist, his thumbs working low on her spine, to comfort, to ease. "What kind of work did he do?"

"Whatever he was paid to do," she said evasively. "It doesn't matter, does it?"

"I guess not." It was clear that if he pressed her, she was going to bolt. So he changed the subject. "Tell me. When you were going through my things, did you happen to find my watch?"

He felt her tense.

Sheepishly she admitted, "I have it right here in my pocket." She had been carrying the watch all week long, waiting for the moment she could confront him about the pictures inside. She reached slowly into her pocket, pulled out the heavy gold watch, and handed it over to him.

He stopped what he was doing to take the watch reverently into his hands.

"I was wondering," she said, angling herself on the bed so she could see his face better, "if you would tell me about the pictures."

He popped the back of the watch open. His face took on a pinched look as he studied the two portraits. "The one on the left is me. The one on the right is . . . was . . . my wife, Elizabeth."

"She was very beautiful," Eden said.

"The most beautiful woman I've ever seen."

Eden felt a lump in her throat. From the pain on his face it was easy to see that he hadn't stopped loving her even though she was dead. She cleared her throat and said, "How long ago did she die?"

"It's been . . . fifteen years."

"I'm sorry. What about Colby and Susanna?"

"Damned Yankee carpetbaggers killed them!" he said in a harsh voice. Then, "How did you know about my brother and his wife?"

"When you were delirious—with the fever—you talked about them."

"How much did I say?" he asked bitterly.

"Just that you found the men who killed your family . . . and killed them."

His eyes were filled with hate and horror.

"Would you tell me the whole story?" she asked.

He looked out the window, and his dark eyes saw a world far away and long gone. "I've never thought it was a good idea to talk about what's done and over."

"I'd like to know."

He snapped the watch shut and huffed out a breath of air. "I suppose I owe you something for keeping me alive."

"If you'd rather not—"

"I carried a gun from the day I was old enough to heft one," he said, rubbing the etched gold watch with his thumb. "First to put food on the table and then to fight off renegade Comanches. I left Texas with gun in hand when I was twenty, to fight for the South.

"My brother Colby stayed home to keep the ranch going because his wife, Susanna, was already expecting a baby by the time the South needed boys from Texas towns as small as ours, who were as young and naive as we were then. I married Elizabeth before I left, and she stayed with my brother and his wife.

"I was lucky. I came home after the war with nothing more than this little scar on my face." He traced the long, thin scar along his cheekbone with the cool edge of the watch. "I was glad the killing was over. I was ready to let bygones be bygones. To get on with my life."

He clutched the watch in his fist and drew a ragged breath. "Only I never got the chance. When I got home, Colby and Susanna were already dead—killed by the carpetbaggers who took over our ranch. With Colby out of the way, there was no one to keep them from taking what they wanted."

"They must have known you'd come back to claim what was yours."

Kerrigan's jaw muscles tautened. "A few months before the end of the war I got separated from my outfit after a skirmish. By the time I found my way back to them a letter had already been sent to my family saying I had been reported missing and was presumed dead. Before the message that I was alive and well got to them, the carpetbaggers had already acted on the assumption I wouldn't be around to complain."

When he didn't say anything more, she asked, "What about Elizabeth?"

"My wife escaped when the killing started and went into hiding. When I got home I found her living—if you could call it that—with a neighbor. She warned me I'd have to fight if I wanted my ranch back, that the carpetbaggers weren't about to hand it over just because I had a legal claim to it. But I was tired of killing. I told her I'd had enough of guns and fighting. All that killing hadn't solved anything. I had decided to lay down my gun for good."

Eden let Kerrigan stare off into the darkness for a while, but eventually prodded, "What happened then?"

"I killed my wife."

Eden gasped.

The mask of horror on Eden's face prompted Kerrigan to say, "I didn't pull the trigger. But it was my fault she died."

"Surely not."

His guttural bark was a travesty of laughter. "It was my fault, all right. The sheriff came out and evicted those carpetbaggers, just like the law ought. But that night, while I was having a celebration dinner with Elizabeth, they came back. There I was without a gun at hand . . . no way of stopping them. And what they did to Elizabeth . . ."

The hairs stood up on the back of Miss Devlin's neck at the choking agony in his voice, and a knot formed in the pit of her stomach. "It wasn't your fault," she whispered in an attempt to bring him back from wherever his hellish memories had taken him.

"They shot me. Left me for dead. Left her alive. I tried to tell her it didn't matter what they'd done to her. I still loved her as much as I ever had. She didn't believe me." He paused, and a look of such desolation crossed his face that Eden could not bear to look at him. A moment later he finished, "The first time I left her alone, she found a gun and put it in her mouth—"

"Stop! I don't want to hear any more."

He touched one of the white scars hidden in the curly black hair on his chest. A voice so savage it frightened her said, "I lived to hunt them down, one at a time."

"But you told Elizabeth you don't believe violence solves anything. Why—"

"There are times when nothing else works, Miss Devlin. It may be hard for you to believe, but there are men out there who don't give a fool's damn about reason. A bullet is the only kind of talk they understand."

"Things have changed," she said. "The war has been over a long time."

His upper lip curled and his eyes narrowed into a mask of cynicism. "There are other wars to be fought."

How could she deny that? "I can see you've got your mind made up. I'm not going to try and change it. I know from experience how futile that can be."

Her voice was full of bitterness and irony he didn't understand. The burst of rage he had felt had pretty much exhausted him, as it always did, and with his wounds, he found he could hardly keep his eyes open. With what little energy he had, he lowered the pillow for his head. By then Miss Devlin was up and helping him. He hadn't the strength to argue that he could manage by himself. He was already half asleep by the time he said, "Be sure to get that message to Felton."

Miss Devlin sent a message to Felton saying she would like to meet him in his office. But the sheriff was out of town and wasn't expected back for a couple of days. The gunslinger was fit to be tied. It was nearly impossible to keep him still. Several times Miss Devlin had to shoo him back to bed after he made forays into the parlor draped in a trailing sheet.

On one occasion, she was grading papers at the dining room table when he suddenly appeared across from her. He had wrapped a sheet around his waist and tucked it in. It was disconcerting, to say the least, when she looked up to discover herself staring at his bare chest, with its T of black curls leading down to an exposed naval.

"You should be in bed," she said. *Or anywhere except here where I can't keep my eyes off you.*

He pulled out a chair, turned it around, and straddled it—winding the sheet around his hips as he sat down. He then took the quilt he'd been trailing behind him and settled it around him to help him stay warm. "I heard you muttering to yourself. What's the problem? Maybe I can help."

"Not unless you can think of a way to convince an

eleven-year-old boy that it's a little early to give up on learning."

"Who are we talking about?"

"Wade Ives. You've met his older brother, Jett." She eyed him significantly over the top of her spectacles. "Their father has the farm farthest south from town. Wade isn't making any effort at all to do his homework. He says he's going to be a Wyoming farmer all his life, and since he already knows how to read and write and do sums, he figures that's all the education he needs."

"What more is it you want him to learn?" Kerrigan asked.

"Geography."

"He probably knows how to get his crop from here to the nearest market."

"But he won't be able to identify the countries that could import his grain," Eden contended. "Or understand how his prices will be affected by the amount of grain grown by other countries. And then there's history—"

"We have a bad habit of repeating that," Kerrigan said. "He'll probably have a chance to experience firsthand whatever he misses in a book."

"Don't be facetious!" Eden bit her lip, waiting for Kerrigan to attack her for using a Big Word meaning "to jest in an inappropriate manner."

Instead, he grinned and said, "What else?"

"Literature," she replied with alacrity.

"Ah. You may have a point there. My grandmother Haley was a schoolteacher. She made sure I learned to appreciate a good book."

Which was where he had gotten his understanding of all the Big Words she used, Eden guessed.

Kerrigan frowned and shook his head. "Naw. A farmer like Wade Ives isn't going to have time to read. And when he does have the time, he's going to be too tired."

"You're painting an awful dreary life for this boy."

"Not dreary. But hard, yes. After all, what do you expect for someone without an education?"

Miss Devlin stared at him. Then she burst out laughing. "You don't disagree with me at all."

"No, I don't."

Finding a kindred spirit, Miss Devlin said earnestly, "I want him to keep on learning, keep on reading. Then, when life is hardest, he can turn to literature for escape— to better worlds, or more exciting ones."

"Is that why you read so much? To escape?"

His perception frightened her. "Of course not," she retorted.

"Why don't I believe you?"

"You can believe what you choose," she said. "I read because I enjoy reading. It's as simple as that."

"Why?"

Eden simply stared at him.

"Why do you enjoy reading?" he persisted.

"Why do you enjoy reading?" she countered.

Kerrigan smiled. "It's a great escape from the everyday world," he freely admitted. "And because what I read often provokes thought."

"I guess that holds true for me too," Eden agreed.

They abandoned the conversation because Kerrigan pleaded fatigue, only to pick it up again a few days later. Eden was sitting in the reception chair in the parlor mending the hem on one of her dresses when Kerrigan appeared from the bedroom, wrapped in a sheet and dragging a blanket. In short order he had settled himself (Lord help her, bare-chested again!) on the sofa, with his outstretched legs covered by the quilt.

"What is it books make you think about?" Kerrigan asked once he was comfortable.

"Well, for one thing, I think about how often fate steps

in to cause a tragedy," Eden answered. "Like in *Romeo and Juliet*. Mercutio tries to separate Romeo and Tybalt when they're fighting, and gets stabbed by mistake."

Kerrigan snorted. "That wasn't fate. Mercutio made a choice. A stupid one, as it turned out. I don't believe in fate, myself. I'm convinced we control our own destiny."

"Children don't," Eden said bitterly. "Look at the pupils in my schoolroom. What control do they have over the havoc their parents are wreaking around them? My father never once asked me if I wanted—" Eden cut herself off. Sundance was a subject she didn't want to discuss.

Kerrigan saw the troubled look on Eden's face and pursued the cause of it like a cutting horse dogging an elusive steer. "I don't say a child can control what his parents do," Kerrigan said. "But once he's grown, all the decisions are his."

"Not if his parents have limited his choices," Eden retorted. She bit her lip to keep from saying more.

"I don't see how that's possible," Kerrigan said.

"By the way they raise him," Eden said, feeling her way carefully, so as to keep her secrets to herself. "Like if Wade Ives's father doesn't make him do his homework, the only choice he'll ever have is to be a farmer. Or say a parent teaches a child to hate certain kinds of people or . . . or to fear certain things . . ."

"Is that what your parents did?" Kerrigan asked. "Taught you to hate and fear?"

"If they did, it wasn't done purposely," Eden said in a quiet voice. "I learned lessons from them I'm sure they had no idea they were teaching."

"Like what?"

Eden found his concerned eyes difficult to avoid. And then she was telling him things she had never told another soul. "They taught me that loving someone too much can be painful. And they taught me that a man who lives with a gun is bound to die a violent death." She looked Kerrigan straight in the eye and said, "Sometimes we don't have choices. Things have already been decided for us."

This time it was Eden's turn to plead fatigue. She went out to the kitchen to allow Kerrigan time to get settled on the pallet in front of the fireplace in her bedroom, which he had begun to use, insisting he could no longer deprive her of her bed.

The next evening Eden was settled on the sofa reading a book when Kerrigan came into the parlor dragging his quilt, and carrying a book of his own. Instead of sitting in the reception chair across from her, he settled on the opposite end of the sofa.

"I need the light to read," he explained.

Since the Victorian sofa wasn't a large piece of furniture, Eden could have reached out a hand to touch the soft hairs on his bare chest. They read silently together for about an hour before Kerrigan laid his book down and took them back to gnaw the same conversational bone.

"It must have been fate that brought me here," he said.

Startled by the sound of his voice, Eden looked up from her book to find his dark eyes full of mischief. "What?"

"I said fate must have brought me here."

"I suppose I'll lose all the ground I've gained if I suggest you came here on purpose to complicate my life," she said with a smile.

"If there is such a thing as fate, why have you and I been thrust together like this?" he asked. "Do you suppose our lives will change forever because our paths have crossed?"

Eden shifted uneasily under Kerrigan's steady gaze. "I really don't see that my life has changed that much since you came," she said. "Except I've had a little more practice cooking for company."

Kerrigan laughed. "I don't think I was fated to come

into your life to make you a better cook," he said. "As far as that goes, your appearance has improved more than your cooking."

"It has? I . . . I'm not dressing any differently."

"It isn't what you're wearing. It's you."

"Me?"

"Your hair looks more touchable, less severe," he said.

"Oh." It was true she had stopped brushing those unruly curls into submission.

"There's a warmth in your eyes, a kind of glow that lights up your whole face."

"There is?" Eden dropped her eyes to hide the evidence of how much she was affected by his words.

"Your mouth is . . . softer."

"Softer?"

Kerrigan reached out his thumb and rubbed it across her full lower lip.

"Yeah, softer," he said. "You don't pucker up your mouth like a prune so much anymore."

His thumb stopped the protest forming on her lips. "You look very kissable."

Eden raised her eyes to meet Kerrigan's tender gaze. In the days they had spent together he had ceased being "the gunslinger" and become just a man, one who teased and challenged and, yes, even admired her.

As he leaned toward her she thought how this moment had been fated from the first instant she had laid eyes on him. He wanted her. And, God help her, she wanted him.

His lips brushed hers lightly at first, softly, a tease, a taste. The rasp of his week-old beard against her face felt marvelous. Then his mouth was back on hers, more insistent, more demanding.

Her lips softened under his and she began kissing him back, her lips brushing, teasing. The change happened without her quite knowing it, and suddenly she was the one who became insistent, demanding.

Kerrigan's hand curled around her nape and held her captive as his tongue came searching for the honey she had withheld for so many years.

At the first touch of his tongue caressing her lips, Eden gasped in startled pleasure. He gently tasted her, then withdrew.

She returned the favor and heard him make a guttural sound deep in his throat that sent shivers down her spine.

A moment later he had the pins out of her hair and had thrust his hands into the soft, silky mass. His mouth found hers again, his tongue thrusting deep, seeking all the textures and tastes of Miss Eden Devlin, spinster.

Eden was afraid to breathe, afraid that if she did, all the magical sensations might vanish. But they didn't. They only grew stronger, until she tentatively began returning his intimate kisses, her tongue imitating his, teasing his lips open and seeking the taste of him.

Eden's whole body was trembling. She wanted more. Needed more. She wanted to press herself against him. To touch—She gently laid her hands on his chest and heard him groan with pleasure. The muscles of his chest were hard under her fingertips, the black curls so unbelievably soft.

Eden had forgotten herself so completely that it was only when Kerrigan took her shoulders and wrenched the two of them apart that she realized someone was knocking on the door.

Eden sat stunned while Kerrigan swore several oaths she had never heard before, grabbed his quilt and book, and disappeared into her bedroom.

The pounding became more insistent and she heard, "Miss Devlin, are you in there? Are you all right?"

It was Felton Reeves! "I'll be there in a minute," she shouted back.

Eden raced frantically to gather the riotous curls back from her face. She held her hair with one hand while she searched the sofa for the pins Kerrigan had let fall where they might. Moments later she had fashioned an old-lady bun at her nape. There was nothing she could do to erase the aroused state of her body. She felt hot, and her knees were surprisingly weak. Her breasts ached and her lips were puffy and sore. She wiped the dampness from her palms onto her dress and opened the door.

"My message said I would meet you in your office when you got back into town," she said in the sternest voice she could muster.

"I decided to stop by." Felton looked suspiciously around the parlor, as though he expected to find evidence of Kerrigan's presence.

Realizing she couldn't keep him out, Eden invited him inside. His first words, after she had taken his coat and hat and joined him on the sofa in the parlor, were: "Where's that killer been hiding out?"

The "killer" had carefully rehearsed Miss Devlin on what she should tell Felton, and she replied with remarkable presence of mind, "He's been moving around. He only stopped here long enough to give me a message for you."

"Well, what is it?"

Miss Devlin was put off by the curtness of Felton's tone, and that, combined with her anxiety over the fact Kerrigan was listening to every word they said through the bedroom door, made her equally abrupt. "He said to tell you that he kicked Levander Early, along with Bud Fraley, Hogg Smith, Doanie Benson, and Stick Humbert, out of Montana last year for rustling cattle. He said he thinks maybe Levander and his gang are rustling cattle here in Sweetwater now."

"That's crazy," Felton said. "Why would they bother to file for farmland if they was—"

"Were."

"—*were* going to rustle steers?"

"Kerrigan thought you might have that reaction. He said to tell you to take another look in Sweetwater Canyon. He's pretty sure that's where the stolen cattle are being hidden until the rustlers can get them to market."

"Why don't—"

"Doesn't."

"—*doesn't* Kerrigan hog-tie the rustlers himself, if he's so sure who they are?"

The truth was, Kerrigan hadn't been well enough to do more than eat, sleep, and read for the past two weeks. Knowing Felton was liable to ask this question, he had tutored Miss Devlin to say, "He's waiting to see if there's anybody clsc involved besides Levander and his gang before he rounds them up."

Felton stared a long time without saying anything, and she wondered what he was thinking. Apparently her answer had satisfied him, because he let the subject drop and asked, "How've you been? I ain't—haven't—seen you for a while. But you look . . . beautiful." Felton meant what he said. There was something different about Miss Devlin tonight . . .

Eden felt guilty because she knew that what Felton was seeing on her face was the result of Kerrigan's lovemaking. It was Felton's courtship she should be encouraging. Kerrigan was just passing through; Felton was her future. She determined to remedy her lack of attention to her suitor at the first opportunity. But this was not the time— not with Burke Kerrigan listening to every word they said.

"Thank you for the compliment," she answered without the least bit of encouragement to Felton to continue the conversation.

"I've missed you," he said, and added pointedly, "I've been waiting for another invitation to dinner."

He waited some more. Miss Devlin couldn't get the words out.

But Felton wasn't going to be denied. He scooted closer to her on the sofa and took her hand in his. "Have you been thinking about what our life together will be like, Miss Devlin?"

"Yes," she croaked.

"I would like to kiss you. Would that be all right?"

How could she say no to him when she had been willing, even eager, to kiss Kerrigan. "Yes," she croaked.

There was a noise from the bedroom, and Felton jerked his head in that direction. "What was that?"

"Uh . . . my cat."

"I didn't know you had a cat."

"There was a litter of kittens at the Davis farm. I took one," Miss Devlin blithely lied.

"Oh. Where were we? What about that kiss?"

Miss Devlin saw the bedroom door was open a crack, and one fierce dark eye was glaring at her. She clamped her jaw shut. She had given Felton the message as Kerrigan had asked. What was happening now between her and Felton was none of his business, and he should have known better than to eavesdrop. If he saw or heard something he didn't like, that was his own fault! She was entitled to a courtship. She was entitled to get married. And Felton Reeves was the only man who had offered either.

She turned to the sheriff and said, "Yes, I think a kiss would be fine."

Miss Devlin wasn't as inexperienced kissing now as

she had been the first time with Kerrigan. She had the gun-slinger to thank for the fact she wouldn't make a fool of herself now, when it was really important to make a good impression. She simply closed her eyes and waited, lips slightly apart, for Felton's kiss.

It was a surprise.

His mustache was so soft. His lips were so gentle. He tasted so different from Kerrigan.

She hadn't expected to like Felton's kiss. She hadn't ex-pected it to move her. But it did. Not with the same thrilling tingle she felt when Kerrigan barely touched her, but there was something there. And that was a whole lot more than she had expected. Perhaps, with time, that feel-ing could grow.

But if it never did, it would be enough. That, and chil-dren, and a husband who came home to the same bed every night. She wanted those things, and needed the se-curity that Felton Reeves would provide when he became the dutiful husband and solid-citizen rancher he had said he would become.

"That was nice," she murmured.

"Yes, it was." he agreed. "Again?"

"Yes, again."

Kerrigan stood behind the bedroom door with his fists balled into knots. She was kissing Felton again. And she was enjoying it. They were both enjoying it. He wanted to tear the two of them apart. He knew it would only take his stepping out of her bedroom right now to end any chance she had of marriage to Felton Reeves. What Felton had wanted most of all was a chance to enjoy Miss Devlin's re-spectability. What would Felton think if he knew the spin-ster lady had hidden Burke Kerrigan in her bedroom for the better part of two weeks?

But he had learned to like and respect Miss Devlin. He

owed her a lot. He owed her his life. He certainly owed her a chance to have a decent life of her own. And that meant a husband and kids. If Felton could give her that, who was he to interfere? He felt awful damn sick to his stomach as he inched the door closed.

Chapter 11

Don't trust a wolf for dead till he's been skinned.

"WHERE THE HELL IS THAT DAMNED KERRIGAN? HE'S plumb disappeared!" Cyrus Wyatt exclaimed.

Oak Westbrook chewed on his cigar as he perused the members of the Association assembled for an emergency meeting in his study. "We have to assume he's out there somewhere doing what he was hired to do."

"Why hasn't anybody seen him, then?" Cyrus demanded.

"How the hell do I know?" Oak answered irritably. "He's the best there is. If he can't find the rustlers, nobody can. Speaking of missing folks, where's Rusty?"

"Rusty isn't coming," Cyrus said.

"Why not?" Oak demanded.

"He promised his wife he wouldn't come to any more meetings until the Association agreed to call off that gunslinger."

"How're we supposed to call 'im off if we don't even know where the durned man is?" one man muttered.

Oak heard the grumbling, but didn't know what to say. There had been talk that Kerrigan had caught Pete Eustes rustling and shot him, but the sheriff said Kerrigan denied being responsible. Which left them all wondering who the hell had shot Eustes, and why. They should have been able to turn to Kerrigan for answers, but the troubleshooter they'd hired hadn't been seen for nearly two weeks.

Another week remained of the month they had promised to remain celibate in order to give Kerrigan time to work. But in light of the gunslinger's disappearance, Oak could hardly blame Rusty for dropping out. It was hard for Oak himself to remain resolute in the face of his wife's temptations.

He hadn't imagined Regina could be so devious. Or so inventive. He had begun to look forward to their evening encounters, even to relish them.

Last night she had come into his study bearing a tray of hot coffee. He had been entranced by the totally out-of-character flirting that followed.

What had attracted him to Regina thirty-two years ago was her confidence in herself, which she had transferred to him. Throughout the years they had been married, she had constantly challenged him to be more, to do more, to reach beyond anything he had ever thought within his grasp. That alone had made her a wife beyond compare.

What he had been seeing the past two weeks, the subtle seduction, the sexual titillation, was an entirely new and different side of his wife. Adding seduction to the mental challenge of living with Regina was putting an entirely new face on their relationship. It was like eating dried-apple pie for years, and loving it, only to discover how much the flavor was enhanced by adding cheddar cheese on top.

The fire burning low in the study last night had provided enough light to reveal Regina's shapely form through the flimsy garment she was wearing for a robe. Her figure hadn't changed much during the thirty-two years they had been married. Or maybe it had, only he still saw her the way she had been the first time he had set eyes on her, at a cotillion in Houston, long before the war. She hadn't been the most beautiful woman there, but she had possessed a dignity, a proud way of holding herself, that had impressed him much more than simple beauty.

Another man might have been intimidated by all that pulchritude. Oak had known right away that Regina was a woman worthy of her regal name. Suddenly, after years of living with her, he was seeing something so entirely different in the woman who was his wife, it had thrown him completely off stride. This woman who brushed against him so his skin felt hot frissons of desire, who eyed his body as though she wanted to eat him alive, and who taunted him with glimpses of flesh he was forbidden to touch, was a person he didn't know at all, but someone he very much wanted to meet.

It wasn't easy for him to wait and wonder along with the rest of the men sitting glumly around his study, why that goddamned gunslinger had run off without telling anybody where he was going.

"I say we give it up," one of the cowmen said.

"Yeah," another agreed.

Before approval of such an idea could spread, Oak interrupted, "We promised we'd wait a month. You men ready to raise a white flag after just three weeks? How're you going to live with yourselves if you do? More importantly, how're you going to live with your wives? You going to let them know you can't last four measly—though I'll grant you, miserable—weeks without them?"

It was easy to see that without their fellow cowmen to keep them to the straight and narrow, those sitting in the room would have given up the fight in the time it took a bronc to unseat a greenhorn. But each of them knew the ribbing—the sometimes downright harsh cowboy teasing—he would get from the others for the rest of his life in Sweetwater if he gave up now.

"All right, one more week," one of the men said. "But not a day longer. If that gunslinger hasn't delivered the rustlers by then—"

"Let's wait and see what happens with Miss Devlin before we decide what we're going to do in a week," Oak said. "After all, things looked pretty promising there for a while with the other half of the job we gave him to do."

There was uneasy shifting in the room and a few sly looks exchanged as they recalled the gossip rife in Sweetwater about the spinster and the gunslinger. It was said both Kerrigan and the sheriff had gone to her house for supper the Friday before last. It was Felton Reeves who had come riding back into town first. It was anybody's guess what Kerrigan and Miss Devlin had spent the time alone talking about. Or whether they had done much talking at all . . .

"If Kerrigan seduces Miss Devlin, we may not need to be in such a godawful hurry to look for peace with those water-hogging, rustling sodbusters," Oak said.

There were murmured assents, and a few men actually sprouted grins.

"If that's all," Oak said, "this meeting is adjourned."

Oak was still sitting at his desk in the study brooding when Regina came in. He pretended to be working on the ledger he had stared at sightlessly for the past half hour.

She walked over to the bookcase and pulled out a volume of poetry to page through it. "How did your meeting go?"

"Fine."

"Has anyone seen the gunslinger?"

"Nope."

"So what are your plans now?"

Oak took his cigar out of his mouth and laid it carefully

in an ashtray. He swiveled his desk chair around to face his wife, and leaned back with his hands templed together, the tips of his fingers resting under his chin. "You're the one who put us on opposite sides of the fence, Regina. You can hardly expect me to tell you my plans under the circumstances."

"I only meant—"

He stood abruptly. "If you meant 'Are you ready to take me up to bed now?' the answer is yes." He stalked steadily toward her, and she backed away step by step as he advanced. "I've wanted to do that for the past three weeks. You're the one barring the door."

He backed her up against the bookcase, his body pressed against hers. He was hard, harder than he had been in years, more desperate than he had been in years. He knew from the enlarged pupils in Regina's wide hazel eyes, her indrawn breath, her trembling body, that not only was she aware of his arousal, she was aroused herself. He ground himself against her once and heard her gasp of pleasure. He was angry at the need for restraint, and struggled to control the furious desire to lay her flat and take her on the parquet floor.

"Get out."

Regina stared at him, helpless, paralyzed by her own need.

He backed up a step. It was all he could manage. *"Out."*

Regina scurried away. She was both elated and devastated by the evidence of Oak's need. The anguish on her face as she fled the room would have pleased him if he had seen it. Her teasing was a two-edged sword. For she wanted him as she never had. And it was killing her to keep him at arm's length. Regina cursed Miss Devlin and the foolish pride that had made her think she could bring Oak to heel this way. No one could win in a war like this. They would both lose if they kept at it until one of them gave in.

She made up her mind then and there to confront Miss Devlin at the Sweetwater Ladies Social Club meeting on the morrow. There had to be some other way to settle the problems between the ranchers and the nesters. Regina happened to be standing beside the coatrack at the front door when Hadley passed her on his way out.

"Where are you headed, young man? I thought we agreed you would rest today."

"I'm feeling fine, Mother. I can't stand being cooped up any longer."

Hadley had given up the sling, but it was apparent from the way he favored his shoulder that his wound still bothered him. This incident had made him all the more precious to Regina, and she had begun acting like a hen with one chick. He had chafed at her mothering all week. It was time she untied the apron strings. There was always danger here on the frontier. A woman learned to live with the thought that her man might not come home at night. Somehow it was harder with her son, perhaps because she still saw him as a toddler, needing her help simply to stand on two feet.

Regina tried to look at Hadley with a stranger's eyes. He was easily a half-foot taller than she was, and lean, a little thinner since he had been shot, but still hardy. He had his father's sandy blond hair, except Oak's had turned gray ten years ago, and clear, wide-spaced blue eyes topped by bushy brows. His nose had the same narrow shape as Oak's, and his cheekbones were equally high and wide. Like his father, he had a generous mouth, with full lips that smiled easily. It was an honest face. And a determined one. "At least promise me you'll keep an eye on the weather," Regina said with a resigned smile. "It looks like a snowstorm might be on its way."

"I will, Mother."

Regina held her cheek ready for Hadley's buss, then

caught him in a quick hug before he escaped. There was a sense of suppressed excitement about him for which she had no explanation. She discounted the premonition of danger she felt, knowing it was exacerbated by the fact that the sheriff still had no idea who had shot Hadley. Would the man who had gunned down her son dare try again? She yanked open the door and yelled out to him, "Be careful!"

Hadley shook his head ruefully at his mother's concern, and waved good-bye as he kicked his horse into a lope toward town. Sometimes she treated him like he was still a kid. He was full-grown, well able to take care of himself. In fact, he thought with a grin of pleasure, when next he saw her, he was going to be a married man, with a child of his own on the way.

The gunslinger's corpse had disappeared.

Levander Early sat on his horse staring at the dried bloodstains on the ground, his back to the wind, his face wrinkled in a tense frown. A week ago he had returned to the site of the dry gulch, to gloat, actually, and hadn't been able to find Kerrigan's remains. At first he had thought he must be in the wrong place. But he had found the ashes from their fire right enough. There had to be an explanation for the lack of bones, or at least rags from Kerrigan's clothes, that the wolves' and vultures' ravaging would have left. The only explanation Levander had come up with made him shiver in his boots: Kerrigan wasn't dead.

But if the man from Texas wasn't dead, where was he? Levander looked across the rolling prairie. It was the chilling cold, not fear, he reasoned, that had caused the shudder rolling through his body.

During the past week, the sheriff had been in and out of town, and therefore hard to catch, but Levander had checked with Doc Harper, and with all the nesters he thought might have offered aid to the gunslinger, to no avail. He had gone to the Dog's Hind Leg to see if any of the cowboys drinking there might know where the Texan was. All he had heard was that no one knew where Kerrigan was, or whether he was dead or alive.

The weather had been threatening for a week now, and Levander had to move those cattle out of Sweetwater Canyon before the snow boxed them in. And before somebody else accidentally stumbled onto them.

He was lucky Pete Eustes had come straight to him with the news of what he'd found in Sweetwater Canyon, as they'd agreed at the meeting. Levander was proud of how he'd taken care of Pete and left it looking like the ranchers were to blame. He might not be so lucky next time. He needed to move those cattle.

He scratched an itch under his arm. What if Kerrigan was out there somewhere, waiting for him to make his move? He didn't like it.

He stiffened at the sound of a man's voice carrying on the wind. He drew his Winchester from its sheath and sighted along the skyline, searching for a target. His finger was tense on the trigger, and he felt beads of sweat form on his forehead despite the cold. Kerrigan wasn't going to catch him flatfooted. That lucky son of a bitch wasn't going to catch him at all.

When a phaeton-type buggy, with a fancy black leather top like the ones they rented at the livery in town, appeared on the horizon, he relaxed slightly. Kerrigan was a loner; there were two figures in the buggy. He kept his gun steadied on the one on the left. His brow furrowed when he realized who it was he had in his sights. Hadley Westbrook. That nester girl, Bliss Davis, was in the buggy with him. Levander let his Winchester rest across his thighs, his thoughts churning.

What were the two of them doing together so far from town?
He decided to follow them and find out.

Miss Devlin was ready to spit nails. Now that Kerrigan's
back was nearly healed, there was no keeping him in bed.
She had given him back his Levi's, but he had to settle for
draping one of her shawls over his shoulders, because she
had destroyed his shirt. He sat at her kitchen table looking
like someone's great-grandma. She was sure he was delay-
ing his recovery by refusing to remain in bed, but there
was nothing she could do to keep him there other than to
sit on him.

She practically threw the plate of ham and eggs down in
front of him. "You're being bullheaded. Why won't you go
back to bed?"

"A bed is best used for three things: sleeping, dying,
and loving. I'm not tired and I have no intention of dying.
As for the other . . ." His roguish smile created the twin
creases on either side of his mouth that she found so attractive. "I'm ready for bed whenever you say the word."

"That would kill you for sure," Miss Devlin muttered
under her breath.

"Yeah, but what a way to go."

Miss Devlin threw up her hands. "A gentleman would
have pretended he hadn't heard what I said."

When Kerrigan chuckled, her mouth snapped shut like
a mousetrap. He had made it clear he was no gentleman.
She would do well to remember it.

Miss Devlin poured them each another cup of coffee
and joined him at the kitchen table. "What happens now?"

"I'm going to need some things from my hotel room—
long johns, a couple of shirts, pants, a coat, and a gun. Can
you get them without being seen?"

"I have some clothes in the attic that might fit you."

"A spinster who keeps a man's clothes in her attic? That's intriguing."

Eden's mouth took on the prunish look he hadn't seen for a while. "They belonged to my father."

"I'll still need a gun—"

"There's also a gun you might be able to use."

"I need a *real* gun, Miss Devlin."

"This is a specially made Navy Colt. Ivory handle. Tooled-leather holster. You should find it to your liking," she said acidly. "It's killed a dozen men at least."

Her gray eyes had turned icy blue again, and her complexion was flushed nearly the same shade as her freckles. Felton would be getting a lot more woman than he realized. Kerrigan was starting to regret that deal he'd made with the Association to seduce Miss Devlin. Because if he followed through . . .

On the other hand, the choice was, and always would be, hers—despite what she said about fate. He wasn't going to force her into bed. And he wouldn't leave her with any illusions that it would be forever. When he had her, it would be because she wanted it to happen. And he would make it good for her. If she had regrets later, it wouldn't be about that part of it, not if he could help it, anyway.

He glanced over at Eden. From the frown of concentration on her face, he surmised there must be some bad memories connected to her father's gun. Maybe he had used it during the war. Maybe he had even died using it. Kerrigan wanted to know more, but he wasn't in fit form to match barbs with Miss Devlin, so he simply said, "If it's all right with you, I'll have a look at your father's gun after breakfast."

"Fine."

Miss Devlin refused Kerrigan's help getting her father's things down from the attic. "You'll only be in the way. And admit it, you can hardly keep your eyes open."

His lips twisted in chagrin. "As a matter of fact, I could use a little help getting back to the bedroom."

Miss Devlin eyed him suspiciously but had to admit he looked a little pale. Once she was aligned with the gunslinger from hip to breast, she was much too aware of him as a man. She could feel his breath in her hair, and the warmth and weight of his hand curled around her shoulder for support. Only a layer of cloth separated her from his naked torso, and under her hand she felt the surprising softness of the hair on his chest. Her blood quickened, and it became difficult to breathe. She kept her eyes down so he wouldn't see how much his closeness disturbed her.

"After all these years of being unmarried," Kerrigan said as they made their way to the bedroom, "why did you agree to let Felton Reeves start coming to call? What is it he's able to offer you that's so attractive?"

"Security. Stability. And he'll make a good father for my children."

"I didn't hear the word *love* in there anywhere," Kerrigan said.

Eden stepped away and left Kerrigan standing on his own. "I like Felton very much. And he likes me."

"*Liking each other* doesn't sound to me like a very strong basis for a marriage," Kerrigan said with a snort.

"That remains to be seen. Besides, it's not your marriage, so it doesn't matter what you think."

Eden had gotten progressively more angry. Kerrigan distracted her from further argument by saying, "I could use a shoulder to lean on."

She stepped back to him, but he could feel the difference when he put his arm around her shoulder. Before, she had been hugged up snug against him. Now, she was stiff as a fence post and there was no give in her. All because he'd pointed out that she only *liked* Felton, she didn't *love* him.

Miss Devlin made sure Kerrigan was settled before she

left the room. "Get some rest. If you're bent on killing yourself, I want you well and out of here before you succeed."

She turned and left him alone, shutting the door firmly behind her.

Miss Devlin used a stepladder to reach the attic. The air was frigid up there, and her fingers were cold and stiff long before she had maneuvered down the unwieldy boxes containing what she wanted. She was perspiring by the time she set the two brown-paper-wrapped boxes on the kitchen table.

Lillian had packed away all of Sundance's things with a reverence that, at the time, had baffled Eden. She had warned her mother that someday her father would be killed. She had warned her father that someday some man would come along who was faster with a gun. Neither of them had listened to her. After all, she was only a child.

And so she had watched, and waited for the other shoe to fall. Sure enough, when she was eleven, the day had finally come when she could say, "I told you so." But it had been a hollow victory.

She had refused to grieve for Sundance. But she had wept bitter tears at her mother's graveside a mere four months later, blaming her father for one more death besides his own. She had spent the next eight years at St. John's Orphanage. When she left the orphanage at nineteen to make her way in the world, Lillian's boxes had come with her. They had been stored away in attics and cellars over the years as though they were a rich dowry for her future, when really they were only a painful reminder of a painful past.

Miss Devlin cut the string on the first box with a great deal of trepidation, feeling a little like she was opening Pandora's box. Inside she found only her father's clothes, carefully folded, with tissue placed between each article. She lifted a black wool shirt and held it against her face. It was redolent with the bay rum cologne Sundance had used. In all, she found three plain wool shirts in dark colors, two pairs of denim pants, a calfskin vest with a Texas five-point star stitched on the pocket, and a fringed buckskin coat.

With Sundance's clothes arrayed before her on the table, Eden clipped the string on the other box. It contained her father's more personal items, including a lithograph of her mother, a gold pocket watch, a brass telescope, a two-bladed jackknife, a metal shaving mug, a hand-forged Swedish steel razor and a leather strop, his ivory-handled Navy Colt and leather holster, and several boxes of bullets. She lifted the gun out of the box and sat down with it in her lap. She unwrapped the soft flannel cloth in which the Colt had been stored and stared at the instrument of death and destruction.

That was how Kerrigan found her several hours later. He had called out to her from the bedroom, but she hadn't answered. He had come hunting her, and been startled to find her sitting and staring vacantly out the kitchen window with the heavy gun in her lap. He could see the streaks where tears had traveled her cheeks.

"I'll take that."

At first she held on, but he pried her fingers loose and set the gun down on the table. Her hands were ice cold, and he pulled her up into his embrace in an attempt to warm her. He was bare above the waist, and the feel of her softness against him was both a torture and a pleasure beyond telling. He reached out with one hand to sort through several of the items on the table.

"From the looks of these clothes, your father was a big man. Is that where you got your size?"

She didn't answer, so he smoothed his hands up and down her back in an attempt to comfort her, and kept talking.

"I never took after my pa much. He was shorter than me, and thicker through the chest. But he was a looker. I could see why my ma married him, even though he was a vinegary old soul, and that's no lie. Sometimes I wondered if I was going to survive that woodshed out back of the ranch house.

"The whole time I was growing up I never understood how a man so good-looking on the outside could be so mean on the inside. Later, after he had passed away, my Grandma Haley, who was like a mother to me, told me some things that helped me understand him. Like how my ma ran off with a harness salesman four days after I was born.

"I understand how you could blame a parent for ruining a kid's life. But the truth is, parents sometimes make the wrong choices too. Take your pa, for instance. From the looks of that gun, I'd say he was a man who knew which end to point. But knowing how you deplore violence, I can't help but think he was a peaceful soul. Why—"

"You'd be wrong."

He tightened his arms around her, wanting to take away the pain he heard in her voice. "How so?"

"Did you ever hear stories down in Texas about a man called Sundance?"

"Sundance was practically a legend—supposedly so fast he could draw in the blink of an eye. Heard stories how there was a wanted poster on him in every sheriff's office in the South. Mighty dangerous man. Finally met his match in . . . think it was Kansas somewhere."

"Wichita. Sundance was my father."

She was struggling to get free now, but he knew she needed holding. "Easy now. Settle down. Let me hold you."

Suddenly she stopped fighting him, and looked at him with bleak eyes. "You're just like him."

He started to protest, but she stopped him with, "Oh,

maybe you do your killing on the right side of the law, but you'll die with a gun in your hand, just like he did."

He felt something tighten inside him, a knot of hurt he couldn't explain. "Everybody has to die sometime."

"How can you stand it?" she cried. "Knowing there's always someone out there anxious to prove himself by putting a bullet in you. Life is too short——"

"So I live every day like it's my last. Which is more than you can say," he accused.

"What's that supposed to mean?"

He gripped her by the arms and held her away from him, meeting her angry gaze with fierce black eyes. "You're afraid to live life at all."

"That's not true! I'm going to marry Felton——"

"A man you *like*. Because it's easier to pretend you don't have a choice in the matter than to face the truth."

"Which is?"

"You want me," he said in a harsh voice.

"That's ridiculous!"

"You have since the first time you laid your hungry spinster's eyes on me. I didn't understand it at first, why no man has gotten near you. It's because you've kept them away with all those words of yours. Even the one you've decided to marry, a man you *like,* you've kept at arm's length."

"I kissed Felton——"

"There's no passion between you and Felton. No love."

"Love doesn't guarantee happiness."

"Ah, yes, here comes one of those life lessons you learned from your parents."

"Don't you dare talk condescendingly to me," she raged.

"You're so afraid of getting hurt that you're cheating yourself out of one of the really good things in life—the love between a man and a woman."

She lifted her chin and said, "I don't love you."

"Maybe not. But you sure as hell want me."

"That's a lie!"

"Let's just see who's lying!"

His mouth covered hers, but she had her teeth clenched against any invasion. He grabbed her cheeks with one hand and forced her mouth open, and then his tongue was inside, tasting her and she was sweet—so sweet. His fingers curled around her nape and he drew her close while his mouth ravaged hers, compelling a response from her.

He could feel her fighting her need, feel her quivering with suppressed desire. He mimicked the thrust and parry of lovers well and truly coupled—only to get his tongue bitten. He jerked away and glared at her. They were both breathing hard, both angry, both aroused, and both determined not to give up or give in.

"Witch!"

"Bastard!"

"Siren!"

"Devil!"

His hands tangled in her hair and he brought her face up close so she couldn't look away. "You want me. Admit it."

"What I want doesn't matter. I will never give you that kind of power—" She bit her lip to cut off the confession that she was vulnerable to him.

He could see she was tempted. He slowly lowered his mouth to cover hers. She groaned as his teeth nibbled delicately on her lower lip. Between kisses he murmured, "It's good between us, Eden. Let yourself go. It's all right."

She jerked out of his grasp. "It's *not* all right. It's all *wrong*. My mother fell in love with one of your kind. It killed her. My life isn't going to be a mirror of hers. I'm not going to make the same mistakes she did. So you can take your smooth words, and your fast gun—my father's gun—and get out!"

She was magnificent. If he lived to be a hundred, he would never want another woman as much as he wanted her right now. He could also see she was stubborn enough to fight him. He didn't want to see her broken, only gentled. There would be another time.

He let her go and grabbed a handful of Sundance's clothes, his shaving gear, and the holstered Navy Colt. "As soon as I'm dressed I'm going to make a little foray to check some things out. I'll be back before dark."

She glared at him. "If you're well enough to be up and out riding around, you're well enough to check back into the Townhouse Hotel."

He chucked her playfully under the chin. "I couldn't do that without letting everyone know I'm still alive. And then I'd lose the element of surprise. I'll be staying here until I know who set me up for that ambush."

"I don't want you here."

"But you won't throw me out. Because if you do, people will start asking where I've been. And then I'll have to tell them."

It was a threat, and a good one, and she was appalled to hear him voice it. "You wouldn't dare!"

"Try me." He wasn't about to give up the opportunity to learn more about Miss Eden Devlin afforded him by living under her roof. Besides, the element of surprise really was useful in the job he had ahead of him.

As soon as Kerrigan was gone from the kitchen, Miss Devlin became aware that her face was flaming. Then she realized that what she actually felt was more of a burning sensation. As she touched the tender skin around her mouth, it dawned on her what had happened.

She quickly dampened a cloth and pressed it against her stinging chin, where Kerrigan's prickly growth of beard had abraded her skin when he kissed her. She hurried into the living room to make out her reflection in the beveled glass front of her china cabinet. Her chin and cheeks looked blotchy. What if the red marks stayed? It was obvious what had caused them. How in the world would she explain them?

Her mind was in a turmoil. She paced back and forth in the parlor, moving the cool cloth from spot to spot as the stinging eased. At last she lay down on the sofa and put the cool cloth on her forehead.

He wasn't going to leave.

It had been bad enough having the man in her house when he was in no condition to be a threat to her. But that was no longer true. He had made advances to her, undaunted by either the fact she was a spinster or that she was being courted by a beau. He had as good as promised he would seduce her before he was done. He was only going to get stronger, be more dangerous.

Eden wanted nothing so much as to throw him out of her house. But she hadn't. His threat had seen to that. She should have been furious. She should have been anguished. Instead she felt . . . confused.

Because, unfortunately, there was a part of her that didn't want him to leave, a part of her that didn't want to say no to his entreaties. That part of her yearned for the touch of his hands, yearned for the feel of his body covering hers. That part of her had sought out the danger to be found in loving a gunslinger—like a moth sought flame.

Miss Devlin ran her tongue across her puffy lips and shivered. She still tasted him there. He was nothing but trouble. She could handle his taunts without trying to prove him wrong. He wasn't going to goad her into doing something she knew was wrong for her. The sooner he was gone and out of her life, the better.

She touched her raw chin and flinched when she thought of the accusations he had hurled. She had made a perfectly rational decision not to fall in love. She was afraid—with good reason—to trust her feelings to a man who lived a life of violence. It was better not to love at all, than to know your love was doomed from the start.

Kerrigan made all her fears seem foolish. After all, she was no longer a child without choices. She did not have to let the past rule her life. Loving a man was a big step to take. And yes, she was tempted to take it. Was it the thrill of the forbidden? Was that why she found the thought of loving the gunslinger so irresistible? The feel of his lips on hers, the touch of his callused hands on her skin, the delicious taste of him . . . She moaned.

Kerrigan had shaved and dressed and then taken the time to clean and load Sundance's gun before he strapped it on. It hung just right on his hip and the Colt slipped smooth as silk from the polished leather when he practiced his draw.

When he returned to the parlor, he found Miss Devlin stretched out on the sofa with a cloth over her forehead. When she moaned he said, "Is there anything I can do to help?"

She sat up abruptly and the damp cloth fell into her lap. Kerrigan was standing before her dressed in her father's trousers, a black shirt, calfskin vest, and buckskin coat. He wore the Navy Colt in the holster, which was tied down on his right leg. "The clothes fit," she murmured.

"Surprisingly well."

Here was the source of all her consternation, looking so handsome now that he was clean-shaven again . . . and so concerned. Well, she wasn't going to let her emotions get involved, no matter how concerned he seemed. Her heart was *not* going to rule her head. She stood up, grabbed the damp cloth in one fist, and shook it angrily in his face. "What you can do for me is get out of my house and never come back."

"I like the sparkle in your eyes when you're angry."

"Stop that."

"And I find your trembling lips very tempting."

"Go away."

"I'm waiting for the moment I can enjoy your fiery red hair spread across my pillow."

She pointed toward the door. "Get out!"

He grinned and started for the front door. "I'll see you later."

"I don't want to see you ever again."

He turned to face her. "I'll be back. And we'll finish what we started."

"When pigs fly!"

He pointed out the front window at a large gray snow cloud. "I think I see one now."

Before she could think of a suitable (intelligent) reply, he was gone.

Chapter 12

*It ain't no time to smoke when
you're a' sittin' on an open keg of powder.*

HADLEY TURNED TO BLISS AND SLIPPED THE SIMPLE gold band on her finger. "It belonged to my great-aunt Martha," he said solemnly. "My father gave it to me when I turned sixteen and said it was for my wife. And now you are." He turned back to the preacher. "Isn't she?"

"She sure is," the elderly man replied. "And a right pretty one, too. Don't know as I approve of you two youngsters tying the knot without family here to witness, but under the . . . circumstances you mentioned . . . I suppose this is for the best."

"We love each other, sir," Hadley said. "You don't have to worry about us. We'll be fine."

"I truly hope you're right, young man," the preacher said. "I don't understand why you had to come all the way here to Canyon Creek to get married, if, as you say, your parents don't have any objection to the match."

"We had our reasons," Hadley said. "That's all you have to know."

The preacher recognized the steely determination in the young man's voice. He eyed the gun the youngster had holstered on his hip as he rubbed the crease along his scalp, which had created a streak of pure white in his salt-and-pepper hair. He hadn't exactly come to the Wyoming Territory with a clean slate himself, so he didn't want to stir up any trouble. There were folks down in St. Louis who would pay good money to know where Sam January was. He had given up his patent medicine show years ago, however, and now he was sticking by the good book. To tell the God's truth, he'd had a lot more success with spiritual healing than he'd ever had with Mrs. Prim's Magic Elixir.

"Good luck to you both," he said, shaking Hadley's hand and nodding to his new wife. "You heading back home right away?"

"We haven't decided," Hadley said.

Now the preacher saw the nervousness he had expected the boy to evidence earlier. The young woman's blush made it plain the couple hadn't discussed what would naturally come after they were married. He smiled inside, but was careful not to let his feelings show, lest the hot-blooded boy take offense. "There's a hotel in town has a mighty fine restaurant, if you was to want to have a meal to celebrate your nuptials."

Hadley grasped at the preacher's suggestion as though it were a rope tossed to a man skittering down a shaley slope. "That sounds good. Does that sound good to you, Bliss?"

"Yes," Bliss replied in a timid voice.

"Thanks again." Hadley slipped his arm around Bliss and urged her toward the door of the preacher's simple log cabin.

It was a short walk down the hard-packed dirt street past false-fronted establishments to the Canyon Creek Hotel. Hadley's mind was working furiously on whether or not he could ask Bliss to spend the afternoon with him in a room at the hotel. He wanted to. Lord, he wanted it more than anything he could imagine.

He tried to catch her eye, but she was looking straight ahead and her bonnet shielded her from view. She was his wife. It was all right if they went to bed together. Once they returned to Sweetwater, he would be denied that pleasure for as long as it took to get things settled between their parents. There weren't going to be any lazy afternoons under the cottonwoods with the fierce winter winds now biting into them.

But he didn't have to ask her right this minute. They could have a leisurely meal first. He knew she must be hungry. They had left early and she had admitted she had been too excited to eat breakfast. But when they reached the door to the restaurant, he discovered he hadn't the patience he thought he had. Hadley grabbed his wife's arm and turned her to face him. He let the hunger show in his eyes. "Bliss?"

His heart was in his throat, because he could see she was torn. Her blue-veined lids shuttered her eyes for a moment, her lashes creating two coal crescents on her flushed cheeks. When she looked back up, she let him see that she was hungry too. All she said was, "Yes, Hadley."

It was plenty.

"Wait here." He seated her on one of the Victorian sofas in the lobby and walked over to the registration desk. He didn't give the clerk a chance to challenge him, just demanded the best room in the hotel. The man looked askance at him, but Hadley squared his youthful shoulders and faced him down. The cold key clutched in his palm, he returned to Bliss and escorted her upstairs to the last room at the end of the hall.

Bliss balked at the doorway, and Hadley had to nudge her inside. Once inside, she quickly crossed to the window and gazed out onto the short, busy main street. For a frightening moment she thought she recognized one of her father's friends, staring right at her from across the street, but an oath from Hadley at the fireplace distracted her attention and when she looked back, the man was gone. It was probably only her guilty conscience that had made the face look so familiar.

She turned back to Hadley but, too embarrassed to really look at him, her gaze skipped away and she perused the room, her eyes finally coming to rest on the large four-poster bed covered with a beautiful yellow and blue patched quilt. She couldn't look at that either. She stared at the ceiling. It had cracked from wall to wall and there was a white line where it had been replastered. "The room is . . . uh . . . nice," she murmured.

Hadley had broken three matches lighting the fire that had been laid in the brick fireplace. He rose and turned to find her gripping her Bible for dear life. He wondered if he should admit he felt as nervous as she did. He thought maybe that wouldn't really help matters, so he said, "I'll take your coat."

Once her hat, coat, and gloves were off, Bliss was less nervous, as though she were committed now and there was no backing out. She watched Hadley as he removed his heavy coat, and instead of his lanky frame, she saw the promise of the man he would become. There was something sinful about wanting your husband in the middle of the day, but Bliss couldn't help how she felt.

"I wish I had been able to wear something prettier for you," she said, staring down at the washed-out dress she had worn so her mother wouldn't suspect her momentous plans.

"I wouldn't have seen it anyway," Hadley said as he walked toward her. "It was too cold in the preacher's cabin for you to take off your coat."

"Still, you could be seeing it now."

"I'd just want to take it off," Hadley said in a husky voice. "Like I want to take this one off."

Bliss battled between running into Hadley's arms and turning tail and fleeing the room. Marriage was such a big step. What if their parents never made peace? What if her father came after Hadley when he heard about the baby? What if—

Bliss's worries melted away like snow in a spring thaw as Hadley's arms closed around her. Snug in that comforting haven, she thought she could weather any storm. He held her for a long time, his arms gradually tightening, his breath coming less easily, as she felt his body respond to the closeness of their embrace.

"Hadley," she murmured. "I think I'd like to get out of this dress."

For a moment she didn't think he had heard her. Then he lifted his chin from where it rested on her hair, and looked deep into her innocent blue eyes. "Are you sure, Bliss?"

The bit of uncertainty revealed in his tentative question was all she needed to make her certain she was doing the right thing. "I'll need some help."

She turned around so he would be able to undo the myriad buttons that ran down the back of her faded pink cambric dress. He took his time. Or maybe he couldn't work any faster, the way his fingers were trembling.

Hadley hadn't realized he would be so nervous. After all, this wouldn't be the first time he and Bliss had made love. But this occasion was special, the beginning of their lives together. He wanted everything to be perfect. And he was afraid he might do or say something to spoil the few hours that would be all the honeymoon they would have.

Bliss felt the heightening tension as the last of the plain white agate buttons came free. Hadley reached up to her shoulders and slid the dress down in front before he turned her to face him. She looked down, too shy to watch him look at her.

"Oh, Bliss. You're so beautiful."

There had been no time in their first excited coupling down by the river for them to remove their clothes. Since then, Hadley had always known the fear of getting caught. He was seeing her nearly undressed for the first time that he could really look his fill. The thin cloth didn't hide much, and Bliss knew her nipples, peaking from the cold—or was it nervous excitement—must be showing. Hadley was so obviously pleased by what he saw that she felt herself relax a little.

She looked up and quipped with a shaky voice, "Just wait until you see what's under this ratty old chemise."

Hadley met her wobbly grin with one of his own, and from then on they responded as healthy, lusty young animals, eager to see each other, eager to touch. Before long they were standing naked facing each other. Both had chill bumps on their skin—the fire had barely had time to warm the room—but both felt the warmth of the other's desire.

"You're so—" Bliss didn't know how to describe Hadley's body. His chest was all taut muscle, marred only by the red scar where the bullet had struck his shoulder. The toll the wound had taken showed in his bony ribs and a belly that was flat, almost gaunt-looking. Below that was a bush of hair and from it grew the male part of him that had thrust inside her and provided the seed for the child growing in her womb.

"I want you," she said.

"I want you too."

They both laughed, because the effect of her words on Hadley, and the truth of his response, was pretty hard to hide. Hadley reached out and lifted Bliss up into his arms.

"Hadley, your shoulder—"

"—will last until I get you to bed. I don't have a threshold to carry you over, so this will have to do."

They both looked at each other with solemn eyes, acknowledging the huge step they had taken into adulthood. Then Hadley set her down on the bed and Bliss scrambled under the covers. He quickly joined her there. She lay waiting, letting him make the first move.

The first thing he did was turn back the covers again so he could see her. He reached out a hand, but paused. "Can I touch you?"

"Yes."

She thought he would touch her breast, but instead he placed a palm on her belly, which was slightly rounded now from their child. His hand felt warm and rough on her skin as he caressed her, and she fought the urge to move under his touch.

"Are you sure this won't hurt the baby?"

A rich, happy feeling welled up inside her at the thoughtfulness of a man needing the way he did, but still being concerned enough to ask. "The baby's fine. He won't mind at all."

To reassure him further, and because she wanted to, Bliss reached out and placed her palm on Hadley's abdomen. He sucked it in, and at the same time gasped.

She immediately withdrew. "Is my hand cold?"

"Not at all," he rasped, grasping her hand and placing it back on his belly. "It just felt so good. I was surprised."

She smiled. "Then get ready for lots of surprises, because I plan to touch you everywhere."

Hadley pulled Bliss into his embrace and rolled back and forth on the bed hugging her. "I love you so much. I want us to be together all the time."

The current hopelessness of the need he expressed calmed their exuberance and made them grasp each other tighter.

"Maybe we should run away, Hadley. Maybe we should leave here and head south right now."

"And go where?"

Hadley's hands framed Bliss's face and he forced her to meet his bitter gaze. "Our future is in Sweetwater. We have to face what happens there and hope for the best."

"What if—"

"No what ifs," Hadley said fiercely. "You're mine. That's not going to change. We'll work out the small stuff later."

His lips came down to possess hers, to lay a claim as ageless as mankind. There would be a time later to deal with his father, and with hers.

Levander Early stood under the porch of the Canyon Creek General Store and watched the hotel window where he had seen Bliss Davis—no, Bliss Westbrook now—standing. That Westbrook boy had bull-sized balls, he'd give him that. The preacher man had been glad to tell Levander all about the marriage when he'd said he was a friend of the family. Imagine making the daughter of your father's worst enemy your wife!

The problem, as Levander saw it, was that this marriage was liable to encourage Oak Westbrook and Big Ben Davis to come to terms. Levander had his work cut out for him if he hoped to do something to destroy any chance of a reconciliation between Oak and Big Ben before those kids made it back to Sweetwater with the news they were hitched.

But how the hell was he going to manage it?

He thought about killing the Westbrook boy, but he knew that was apt to bring on an all-out war. It wasn't his intention to start bullets flying, because there was always the chance that he would accidentally catch one. He was more interested in keeping both sides suspicious of each other. For a brief moment he considered shooting the girl. But women were so scarce in the West that a woman-killer was universally despised by lawman and outlaw alike. Not that he'd get caught, but it wasn't worth taking the risk. There had to be another way.

Then it struck him how easy it would be to set fire to one of those shanties the nesters lived in, and blame it on the Association. He smiled grimly. And if he was going to get the most result from his effort, he knew just the shanty he ought to burn down.

"We're married," Hadley announced with a pleased grin when Miss Devlin opened her door to his vigorous knocks.

"Congratulations to both of you! How was the ceremony?" Miss Devlin asked as she ushered the beaming couple inside.

"It was short," Bliss said.

"It took forever," Hadley said.

Miss Devlin laughed, and once they got over their embarrassment, Bliss and Hadley laughed too. "I'm so glad you're back safely. I was beginning to worry about you. What held you up?"

"Uh . . . we took our time coming back," Hadley said.

From Bliss's coy glance at her new husband and the red stain growing on Hadley's cheeks, not to mention Bliss's slightly swollen lips and the small purple bruise on Hadley's neck, Miss Devlin quickly surmised the reason for their delay in returning from Canyon Creek. She could hardly blame them for their few stolen moments of happiness, but they had nearly jeopardized everything by returning so late.

According to the story Bliss had told her mother, she was spending the day with Miss Devlin to do a special project for school. Miss Devlin knew Persia would come looking for Bliss if she wasn't home by dark. It wasn't far from that now. She didn't want to burst the young couple's bubble any sooner than necessary, so she simply asked, "How does it feel to be Mr. and Mrs. Hadley Westbrook?"

"It's wonderful!" Bliss said.

"It's terrible!" Hadley said.

When he caught sight of the hurt look in Bliss's eyes, Hadley cleared his throat and explained, "I mean, it's great to be married, but it's terrible we can't be together. I don't know how I'm going to stand it."

Bliss managed a wan smile. Hadley put a protective arm around her and added, "I wondered if you would mind making sure Bliss gets home safely, Miss Devlin. It's getting dark and—"

"Don't worry. It'll be my pleasure." Miss Devlin found Hadley's concern for his new wife touching, especially since they all knew Bliss had traveled to and from the schoolhouse alone numerous times in the past.

Miss Devlin watched Hadley embrace Bliss, as though he were trying to memorize the way she felt in his arms. He stuck his nose into the curls at her neck and took a deep breath, as though to catch the scent of her hair. Then he gave Bliss a quick, hard kiss and pushed her away from him. "That'll have to hold you, sweetheart. Don't forget what we talked about on the way home."

"I won't," Bliss promised.

Hadley touched the brim of his hat in farewell and said in a hoarse voice, "I'll be seeing you, Mrs. Westbrook, Miss Devlin." Then he was gone.

Miss Devlin thought Bliss was going to cry, but to her surprise the young woman bit her quivering lower lip and waved cheerfully out the window as Hadley headed the rented buggy back toward the livery.

Once Bliss and Miss Devlin were bundled up against the cold, they headed out along the path to the Davis home.

It was cold and windy and the snow clouds that had threatened all day still hung around, creating an ominous sunset. Miss Devlin wasn't looking forward to the dark, frigid walk back home. "Are you planning to tell your mother now about your marriage to Hadley, and about the baby?" she asked Bliss.

"Hadley and I talked a lot about that on the way back from Canyon Creek and we thought . . ." Bliss took a deep breath and plunged forward, as though she had dived into an icy creek and was in a hurry to get to the other side. "We thought maybe we'd wait awhile and see how things go. I mean, the baby hardly shows, and there's a chance, a small one, maybe, but a chance, that things will get settled before we have to say anything."

"But you—"

"We also thought, I mean, we hoped, that I would be able to keep pretending that I'm working on a school project at your house and that . . . and that . . . Hadley and I could meet there sometimes and . . . and . . ."

Miss Devlin waited to see if Bliss would be able to finish her sentence. When it became clear she would not, Miss Devlin said, "I'm sorry you and Hadley are in such an uncomfortable situation, but—"

"—you aren't going to help us," Bliss finished.

"I didn't say that. I—"

Bliss took off at a run, with Miss Devlin half a step behind her.

"Bliss, wait! I didn't say you couldn't come—"

Bliss's emotions were running high from the excitement of the day, and she found the frustration of being married, yet separated from her husband more difficult than she had ever imagined. She didn't wait to hear what

Miss Devlin had to say, because she didn't think she could handle any more disappointment.

Both Bliss and Miss Devlin stopped abruptly when they saw the bright orange glow beyond the hill where Bliss's home stood.

Bliss gasped. "It's a fire!"

They both started running and didn't stop until they stood at the top of the hill, where they could see the Davis house, engulfed in sheets of flame. Bliss saw the figures of her mother and father outlined in the dusk, racing to and from the well with buckets of water. But their efforts to douse the blaze were clearly a waste of time.

"I don't see Sally!" Bliss cried.

Miss Devlin searched the area around the house to see whether she could spot Bliss's thirteen-year-old sister, but couldn't find her either. "She's probably safe somewhere away from the fire. Let's go see what we can do to help."

Bliss was already halfway down the hill. "Momma! Papa!" she cried. "Where's Sally?"

Persia Davis turned and, dropping her bucket, opened her arms wide for her daughter. "Oh, my God, Bliss. I was so worried that you might have come home while I was in the barn milking. I thought you might be inside—"

"I'm fine! Where's Sally—"

"She's all right. She ran to the Ives place to get help. I was so afraid—"

"Thank God. If anything had happened—"

"My baby, my baby. You're safe!"

Miss Devlin felt her throat closing with emotion as tears of relief and joy streamed down Persia's face.

"Is there anything I can do to help?" Miss Devlin asked.

Persia turned enough so her gaze encompassed both the schoolteacher and her husband's heroic efforts to fight the flames destroying their home. "It's too late for anyone to help now," she said bitterly. "I guess those ranchers have decided there's to be a war after all."

"No! Don't say that," Bliss cried.

"Why not?" Persia demanded. "They're all alike. Brutal. Hard. Unfeeling."

Bliss moaned and hid her face in her mother's neck.

"It's all right, baby," Persia crooned. "We'll make them pay for what they've done."

"Nooooo," Bliss wailed. "You don't understand. I don't want revenge. I don't want them to pay."

"What?" Persia shook Bliss hard, snapping her head back and forth, loosing her daughter's hair so it fell across her shoulders in fire-lit golden chestnut waves. "How can you say that, after they burned down your home?"

"You don't know the ranchers did it," Miss Devlin argued.

Persia sneered. "Oh, no? Ben saw that gunslinger from Texas skulking around here earlier. Then he noticed the fire. You can bet the Association is responsible."

"I don't think Mr. Kerrigan would do anything like this," Miss Devlin protested.

"Isn't that what the Association is paying him for? To cause trouble for us?" Her eyes bright with angry tears, Persia demanded, "Give me one good reason why we shouldn't fight fire with fire!"

Bliss's face looked horrible in the flickering light as she turned to face her mother. "Because I married Hadley Westbrook today. Because a rancher's son is the father of my child . . . your grandchild."

Persia's eyes went wide with shock and her mouth dropped open. She gasped in an attempt to force her lungs to breathe, and the heavy smoke from the fire choked her. Bliss tried to pat her mother on the back, but Persia wrenched herself away from her daughter. "Don't touch me! How could you have done such a thing? What were you thinking?"

"I love Hadley," Bliss cried. "I—"

"Love!" Persia snarled the word so it sounded like a curse. "You don't know the first thing about love if you could let yourself care for a boy whose father is capable of *that*." Persia waved a hand at the crumbling cinders, the skeleton of burning timbers that had once been their home. "Oh, my God. I can't believe this is happening." Persia covered her face with her hands and began to sob, her chest heaving as she gulped air.

Bliss stared at her mother, then turned to the woman who lately had helped her find a way to resolve every dilemma. "Miss Devlin?"

Miss Devlin didn't have any answers at the moment. She wasn't sure what to do now. She was certain Kerrigan couldn't be responsible for the fire that had destroyed the Davis home. She had spent enough time with him to believe him incapable of such a senselessly destructive act.

What concerned her now was what could be done to keep the nesters from retaliating. Maybe Kerrigan would have some idea. Because unless something was done soon to stop these incidents of violence, there would soon be no stopping a bloody range war in Sweetwater.

Chapter 13

Every man is afraid of somethin'.

꙰ IT HAD TAKEN MISS DEVLIN SOME TIME TO CONVINCE
Persia that she should wait to convict the ranchers until
there was more evidence they were guilty than the mere
fact that Ben had sighted the gunslinger a short while before the fire broke out. Miss Devlin had also argued that
Bliss's marriage to Hadley, and the coming grandchild,
made a powerful case for trying to maintain peace in the
valley, despite this recent act of violence.

The Davis family had gone to spend the night at Bevis
and Mabel Ives's place. Before she left to head home,
Eden had gotten Persia to promise she would keep Bliss's
pregnancy and marriage a secret from Big Ben, who might
be provoked into doing something rash if he got that startling news right after the catastrophe that had just occurred. Miss Devlin suggested it might be best if Persia
confronted Regina at the Sweetwater Ladies Social Club
meeting on the morrow to decide how they should handle
this latest crisis.

Then Miss Devlin had trudged home in the dark alone.
Kerrigan would probably be there when she arrived. Eden
realized she was looking forward to having someone with

whom to share her feelings of anger and frustration. She had high hopes Kerrigan would be able to suggest some way to cool tempers and stop the violence. She heaved a sigh of disappointment when she spied her darkened house and realized he wasn't there.

Kerrigan had said—promised, warned—he would return, so Eden waited up until nearly midnight to confront him with Big Ben's suspicion that the Association's troubleshooter had set fire to the Davis home. Since Ben had spotted Kerrigan, there was no further need for him to hide at her house. To Eden's dismay and disgust she actually felt a sense of disappointment that he would be moving back into town.

The later Kerrigan was in returning, the more fearful Miss Devlin became that something dreadful had happened to him. Maybe he was lying hurt somewhere. . . .

When she found herself nodding off in her reception chair, she decided enough was enough. She stomped into her bedroom, where everything reminded her of him, from the shaving mug, strop, and razor he had left on her dresser, to the tangled sheets in which he had once slept. Furious with him for being so late, and with herself for worrying about him, she yanked on her nightgown, tucked her hair up into her sleeping cap, turned down the lamp, and curled up in bed with the covers pulled up to her chin.

It was just as well he hadn't shown up tonight. She would be better able to handle kicking him out with a good night's sleep.

Assuming I can sleep.

But sleep eluded her.

She had changed the sheets before she lay down, but the taint of the gunslinger remained in her bed. She sniffed once, twice, then realized her pillow smelled distinctly like . . . him. It wasn't a particular scent she could identify, just something musky and male and . . . him. Was it any wonder she couldn't relax? Where was he?

Miss Devlin spent the entire night restlessly tossing, imagining Burke Kerrigan dead somewhere, his vacant eyes staring into the night. She envisioned all the ways he could meet his end: shot by an angry nester, his body broken when his horse stepped into a gopher hole, branded by a vicious rustler with a hot running iron, struck by a rattlesnake. By the time the predawn light began making shadows in her bedroom, she had his scalp hanging from some renegade Sioux's war shield.

The worst of it was, she knew that in all likelihood he was holed up in bed with one of the Soiled Doves at the Dog's Hind Leg. She punched her pillow hard to make a comfortable spot for her head. She was *glad* he hadn't come back. Because now she could face the women of Sweetwater at the Ladies Social Club meeting this afternoon with an absolutely clear conscience, albeit with dark circles under her eyes, knowing she was no longer giving the Association's hired gun sanctuary in her bedroom.

"Howdy there."

Miss Devlin shot up in bed, clutching the sheets to her chest. It took her only a second to find Kerrigan standing in her bedroom doorway. "Where have you been all night?"

"Doing my job." He dropped into the rocker beside her bed and leaned back with his eyes closed. He was gray with exhaustion, and winced as his wounded back made contact with the frame of the rocker.

"I waited up for you." She hadn't meant to admit that, but the words had slipped out.

He opened his eyes and smiled at her. "Nobody's done that for a long time."

Miss Devlin clenched her fingers around the sheets,

fighting the urge to comfort him. She hardened her voice and said, "Did you have a productive evening?"

"I found out the rustlers have moved the cattle they stole from the canyon where I saw them last to somewhere I can't find them."

"Did they drive them across the Davis spread?"

His brow arched in surprise. "How did you know that?"

"Ben Davis saw you crossing his land . . . just before his place burned down. He thinks you set the fire."

"Aw, hell."

"Do you have any idea who did it?"

Kerrigan stared at her for a moment, realizing that she wasn't accusing him along with Big Ben, that she hadn't accepted the farmer's accusation as truth. He felt a tightness in his chest. He hadn't known how much he wanted her trust. He sighed wearily. "What difference does it make who did it? It's bound to heat things up—no pun intended—in Sweetwater. Do you suppose there's any chance Ben Davis will keep quiet about seeing me?"

"He's already told Persia, and Persia told Mabel Ives . . . it'll be all over Sweetwater by tomorrow morning."

"Aw, hell."

"You haven't answered my question," she said quietly.

He sighed again. "Yeah, I have a pretty good idea who did it."

"Who was it?"

"I'd just as soon not say until I have proof."

"What happens now?"

"As soon as I've gotten a little rest I need to follow the trail the rustlers left when they moved the stolen cattle and see where it leads."

"Are you hungry?" She bit her lower lip as soon as she said the words, afraid they held too great a note of concern.

"More tired than hungry," he said. "You ready to get out of that bed so I can get in?"

Her eyes turned a flinty gray. "There's no reason for you to stay here any more, Kerrigan. It's no longer a secret that you're alive."

"That may be so," he said with a wry grin. "But to tell you the honest truth, I don't think I could make it to town. How about that bed?"

Eden knew she should throw him out. Any sane woman would throw him out. What she said was "You can sleep on the sofa."

He arched a disdainful brow. "How do you plan to explain the man asleep in your parlor if company comes calling?"

"I—" The grim smile on his face told her he knew he had her over a barrel. Her jaw muscles worked furiously as she fought to control her temper. "If you'll kindly leave my bedroom, I can get dressed."

"How about if I promise to keep my eyes closed?" he said with an exhausted smile, his eyes already closing again.

"Oooooh!" Wrapped in the sheet, Miss Devlin grabbed clean clothes from her wardrobe, shoes, stockings, and her hairbrush, and with everything wadded up in her arms began a regal exit from the room. "The bed's all yours," she said sarcastically. But as he opened his eyes she tripped over the trailing bedsheet, and would have gone flying if he hadn't caught her.

She hadn't known he could move so fast, tired as he had appeared. But there she was, clasped in his arms, sure as snow in January.

"You all right now?" he asked.

"I'm fine," she said breathlessly.

"All right," he said. But he didn't release her. Instead he reached up and pulled the nightcap from her head. A wealth of burnished red hair flooded down over her shoulders and across his hands. His fingers tunneled up underneath the silky stuff and grasped her nape. "I already told you once you shouldn't be wearing that cap."

"My hair gets tangled."

"I like it all mussed up. It looks more touchable." He touched it. "It's so damn silky, I want to bury myself in it."

The tension built as his fingers thrust up through her hair and his hand captured her head to draw her closer.

"You look like a woman who needs kissing. Just a sweet good-morning kiss from me to you." His breath was warm and moist on her face, and in another instant his lips covered hers. A gentle touch of his mouth, a haunting taste, and then it was over.

She stood there with her eyes closed, wanting more.

"And here's the good-night kiss you missed last night."

This kiss was different. Arousing. Desirous. Demanding. This kiss was a prelude to a long night of loving. She felt her body sway toward his. She dropped the sheet, her clothes, and her shoes as her arms inched around his neck. This kiss promised so much. His tongue came searching for honey, and found it.

Suddenly she was kissing him back, her tongue touching his. The more she tasted, the more she needed. Her body began making insistent demands: touch more, taste more, take more.

Her eyes were closed so she could concentrate on the feelings that fired her body, but she also could feel the winter sunlight on her eyelids. The shadows of evening were long past, and in the cold light of day Miss Devlin forced herself to remember who this was, and why this could never be. Reluctantly she let her hands drop to the gunslinger's chest, where they caressed the muscles beneath his shirt one last time before she pushed against him.

He responded immediately to even that tiny resistance

on her part. His eyes were curious, questioning, but still lit with desire. She faced him honestly, meeting his gaze forthrightly as she said, "I enjoyed that. It was . . . nice . . . but it doesn't change anything."

"It was a hell of a lot more than nice!"

She smiled ruefully. "Yes, I expect you're right about that."

He stood staring at her as she stooped to gather up the items she had dropped. She turned one last time to look at him before she left the room. "I have to go to church, and then to the Sweetwater Ladies Social Club meeting. When I get back, I expect to find you gone."

"You're going to have to face your feelings someday," he said.

"Perhaps. But not today."

She shivered when he slammed the door behind her. She wanted to make a liar out of him. She wanted to reach out for what she wanted, without being afraid. But the past was too great a spectre to be ignored. If she wasn't careful, she would find herself repeating her mother's mistake.

It was a miracle she didn't rip anything, she dressed so fast, donning her square-necked, deep green striped polonaise gown for church. She arranged the oval-shaped pouf of double ruffles in back and the draping sides of the pleated skirt, hoping he wouldn't decide to leave the bedroom for some trumped-up reason before she finished. She gathered her hair up in a knitted snood, planning to add a flat-crowned, flat-brimmed green velvet hat. She sat down to take off the heavy wool socks she had slept in so she could put on her stockings and high-button shoes.

Only she was missing one of her white stockings.

It was quiet behind the closed bedroom door. Maybe she could sneak in and get another stocking. He was probably asleep already, as exhausted as he had claimed to be. She inched the door open. He was mostly covered by the quilt. Judging from his bare shoulder, and one leg hanging out at the side, he appeared to be naked under the covers. She examined the tangled pile of clothing he had dropped haphazardly on the braided rug. He was naked all right.

She grimaced. Maybe she could wear her socks with her high-button shoes. But that would stretch her shoes, and after all, he was sound asleep. She could see her stocking curled underneath the edge of the stack of clothing on the floor. She tiptoed into the room, knelt beside the bed, and started slowly pulling the stocking out from under the pile. It snagged on something.

She glanced up at the bed, but saw no movement, and stealthily began probing under the stack with her hand. The jingle of coins stopped her dead. A quick glance showed the gunslinger was still asleep. She hurried to finish. Just as she stood with the stocking in her hand, a triumphant grin on her face, the gunslinger grasped her by the wrist and hauled her down on the bed with him. An instant later the sheet that had twisted around his hips as he rolled her under him was the only thing saving her modesty.

"What the hell were you looking for in my stuff?" he demanded.

"Nothing!"

He pulled her clenched fist toward him. "Then what do you have in your hand?"

She opened her hand and revealed a crumpled white stocking.

"Aw, hell." He let go of her and sat up so she lay between his thighs, rubbing his eyes with the heels of his hands. "You ought to know better than to go sneaking around a sleeping man."

"I happened to be *sneaking around* in my *own bedroom* trying to find a *stocking* that *you* made me *drop*!" She punctuated her speech with a pointed finger jabbing at his ribs.

He captured her hand again. "All right. You've made your point," he said irritably.

Then it dawned on both of them that his body had reacted very forthrightly to the fact there was a soft female beneath him on the bed.

Miss Devlin felt the flush begin on her chest and work its way up to heat her cheeks. "You can get off me now," she said with as much dignity as she could muster.

"I don't think so, just yet."

His eyes were hooded and looked sleepy, but she wasn't fooled for a second. He was a predator. And she was his prey.

"Kerrigan, I—"

His finger on her lips stopped her from saying anything else. "Haven't you ever wondered what it would be like to feel a man inside you?"

"I . . ." She turned her face away so he couldn't see her eyes. He would know she was lying if she said no. And saying yes would be an invitation she was afraid to extend.

He hadn't waited for her answer. He had gone on speaking and she only now heard what he was saying.

". . . how it would feel if a man touched you here . . ." His fingertips lightly skimmed across her bare collarbone, causing her to gasp with shock at the frisson of delight caused by the contact.

". . . or here . . ." His hand cupped her breast and his thumb skimmed across the nipple beneath the velvet trim on her dress.

She moaned as she felt her body tighten in places unused to such exquisite sensations of pleasure.

"Think hard before you do anything rash," she warned breathlessly. "I am a woman of virtue. I—"

He captured her chin and saw the panic in her eyes.

"And why—at your age—is that still true?" he demanded, angry because he wanted her and irritated because she was using words again to keep him at arm's length.

"You are well acquainted with my shortcomings as a woman, Mr. Kerrigan. I'm sure I don't have to point them out to you," she said bitterly.

"Your plainness?"

She flinched.

"Your incredible height?"

She bit her lip to keep from crying out for him to stop.

"Your superior intelligence?"

Eden felt humiliated and furious at the same time.

"Those are all excuses," he snarled, "to keep the men away. They're not the *real* reason you're still untouched, *Miss Devlin*."

"Oh no? And what is the *real* reason, *Mister Kerrigan*?"

"You're a coward."

She recoiled as though he had slapped her.

"You use your looks and your education like a barbed-wire fence to keep a man at a safe distance. Because the truth is, Miss Devlin, every time a man gets close you throw a few Big Words at him and run as fast as you can in the opposite direction. You're afraid to love a man because he might die and leave you alone—like your father did."

Eden rose from the bed like a wrathful goddess. "Who are you to be preaching to me? You want my body all right, but you don't want the things that go along with taking it—commitment—a family—a future together. If I'm a coward, so are you! Don't talk to me about running away. What have you been doing for the past fifteen years? You're not any more willing to take the risk of getting hurt than I am, Mr. Kerrigan."

"I'm not running from a damn thing," Kerrigan retorted, following her off the bed with the sheet tucked around him.

"Prove it," she challenged. "You want my body? You can have it. I'll make love to you, Kerrigan. But you have to take the rest of me too—heart and mind and soul—dreams and hopes."

The only sound in the room was their labored breathing.

Eden was convinced Kerrigan would back down rather than give anything of himself to her.

Kerrigan was convinced Eden would back off rather than let any man touch her heart.

And so he took his time undressing her, giving her plenty of chances to run away. The snood came off first, releasing a flood of titian hair. He gloried in the sight of it. He spread it across her shoulders, making a special point of curling it around her breasts.

He began to unbutton her dress, one button at a time, certain that any second she would raise her hand and stop him.

Eden was determined to force him to be the one to stop this seduction. He knew the rules. If he wasn't willing to give, he could not take. She watched his eyes, expecting him to shutter his feelings as he so often did. But to her surprise, he shared all his need, his desire, his passion, his fear, with his dark eyes.

His hands touched her freely as he bared her to his gaze. He had her lift her arms so he could get the dress off over her head, and then he patiently eliminated one petticoat after another until finally she was standing across from him wearing only a chemise, her pantalettes, and a single white stocking.

"Let's get rid of this," he said, kneeling to roll the stocking down and off her leg.

He stood and said, "You take the rest off yourself, Eden."

She knew what he was doing. He was forcing her to

take the initiative if she wanted to go any further. If he was right, if she was still running as he had accused, she wouldn't be able to take this last step toward seduction on her own.

Eden's whole body was trembling. Her mouth was dry. She was afraid. She wanted Kerrigan to help her, and she looked at him with that plea in her eyes.

"I can't make the choice for you, Eden," he said. "You have to make it yourself."

He was saying he couldn't *make* her love him enough to let him into her life. She had to find the courage to do it of her own free will.

Eden wanted reassurance from Kerrigan that he would keep his part of the bargain before she went any further. Reassurance that if she took down the walls, he wouldn't storm the castle and then ride away into the sunset. She was willing to take a step in his direction, if he would take a step in hers.

"I'm telling you that I'm willing, Kerrigan. Would you . . . would you kiss me a little first. So I won't feel so . . . brazen."

Kerrigan felt his heart thumping heavily in his chest. He reached out a hand to Eden and saw it was trembling. He leaned down and kissed her on the shoulder as he began unbuttoning the chemise. He kissed her on the other shoulder, and the garment came open.

When Kerrigan stepped back, Eden let the chemise slip off her shoulders and fall on the floor. She put a hand on Kerrigan's nape and drew his head down so he could kiss her naked breast.

Eden gasped. It was the most exquisite thing she had ever felt. "I . . . I . . . think I can manage the rest now."

With an awkward innocence that Kerrigan found endearing, Eden shimmied out of her pantalettes. She took the trailing edge of the sheet that was still tucked around his waist and used it to cover her own nakedness.

"Guess we're not either of us going anywhere without the other now," she said with a rueful grin.

Their eyes met, revealing both awe and delight that they should find themselves in this situation.

Eden reached out and touched the hair on Kerrigan's chest.

He lifted a brow in surprise and she explained with a shy smile, "I like the feel of it. It's so soft."

He reached out and cupped her full breast.

Eden stood very still, and arched a questioning brow.

He grinned and said, "I like the feel of it. It's so soft."

They both laughed, and before Eden knew what Kerrigan intended, he had swept her up in his arms and laid her on the bed. He made sure the sheet would no longer be a barrier between them, before settling himself on top of her.

Eden sucked in a breath of air as she felt Kerrigan's flesh pressing against her from breast to thigh. To her surprise, she didn't feel crushed by his weight, just conscious of a rich sense of rightness at the solid feel of him.

He kissed her for a long time, his tongue tasting her lips, her teeth, the roof of her mouth. He encouraged her to kiss him back, and she enjoyed the textures and tastes of his mouth. His hands were not idle, and Eden found herself overwhelmed by what he could do with his fingertips as he traced her breasts and the length of her arms, then fondled each rib. His teeth and tongue sent shivers scurrying across her neck and shoulders. The instant he reached down to touch her upper thigh, she automatically clamped her legs together like the scared virgin she was.

"Eden?"

She couldn't meet his eyes. "You won't hurt me, will you, Kerrigan?"

He took her hand away from the portal it guarded and kissed each fingertip. "I'll be as gentle as I can, Eden. But sometimes, the first time for a woman, there can be pain. I can't help that. I promise you I won't do anything you don't want me to do."

She looked up and there was so much tenderness, such caring and concern in his gaze that she was moved to say, "I trust you, Kerrigan."

Kerrigan felt a swell of protectiveness inside him so strong, it made his throat ache.

Eden was still tense when his fingertips touched her again, but he was more gentle with her than he'd ever been with a woman before. He felt like shouting when he discovered she was already slick and wet with desire for him. He used a finger to open her and found the proof of her virginity. He was nervous because he wanted this to be good for her, and he knew now there would be pain.

He placed his hips between her thighs and kissed her as he slowly eased himself inside her. He felt her body tense as she stretched to accommodate him, and murmured against her lips, "If you want me to stop, say the word."

She bit her lip against the pain, welcoming it as a sign that she had stopped running from the past, that she was ready to give herself wholeheartedly to the man in her arms.

"Kerrigan?"

He tensed and withdrew immediately. "Is something wrong? Are you all right? Did I hurt you?"

"I . . . It's all right. I mean the pain is not unbearable. I had no idea it would be like this."

"I am hurting you," Kerrigan said flatly.

Eden grasped his shoulders before he could lever himself away from her. "No! I mean, yes, there's some pain. But I don't want you to stop. I only . . . I was a little nervous, I guess."

Kerrigan managed a smile. "Me, too."

"Can you pick up where you left off?"

Kerrigan chuckled. "You are so unbelievably innocent . . ." He had completely lost his erection when he'd thought he was hurting her.

"What's wrong?" Eden reached down to touch Kerrigan's belly and he groaned with pleasure.

"Nothing at all. But how about if we go back a few steps and get a running start?"

"Is it all right if I touch you?" she asked, letting her hand slide down to envelop him.

"Oh, God, Eden, you're going to kill me!"

She immediately withdrew her hand. "Did I do something wrong? Am I hurting you?"

Kerrigan laughed and shook his head, then took her hand and put it back on what had become a very hard part of his body. "You're doing everything just right. But now I'm going to have to help you catch back up with me again."

Eden wasn't sure what he was talking about until his mouth closed over her breast and his tongue laved, while his teeth nipped, causing her belly to react as though a drawstring had pulled up tight. Without her quite realizing how it happened, her hands were threaded in his hair and she was holding him there, wanting him to make her feel the feelings again.

Kerrigan was happy to oblige her. He suckled at her breast, bit her nipple just to the edge of pain and then licked to soothe what he had hurt. Meanwhile, his fingers caressed her belly and thighs, feeling the soft curves, the concave belly, the bones in her hips. His hand curved around to grasp her buttock and pull her closer to him so they were belly to belly.

There had been something different about making love

to Eden, and now he realized what it was. Because she was so tall, they fit together perfectly. He was able to love her without having to contort himself to match a shorter body. Kerrigan grinned with the thought of how much more enjoyable it was going to be to kiss Eden when he was deep inside her.

His hand slipped around to Eden's belly again and down into the nest of curls that protected her femininity. He heard a groan from her and couldn't tell whether it was a sound of protest or approval.

"Eden?"

"Don't stop," she gasped.

He took her at her word. He covered her mouth with his as he once again broached her with his fingers. He mimed with his tongue the dance of love he wanted her to join. His thumb found the source of her delight and she began tensing with excitement. He felt himself swelling as she groaned, a harsh, guttural sound deep in her throat.

Kerrigan raised himself over her then, and, poised at the entrance to her womb, he asked one last time, "Are you sure, Eden?"

"Yesssss."

Eden was overwhelmed by sensations as Kerrigan pushed a little way inside her, then withdrew slightly and pushed a little farther inside, until at last he had fully sheathed himself. There had been pain, but it had been a small price to pay for the pleasure of having him inside her. "I feel so full," she marveled.

Kerrigan smiled down at her. "You sound surprised."

Eden smiled back. "I suppose I am. Now what?"

"We make love," Kerrigan said.

No longer afraid of the unknown, Eden felt freer to touch Kerrigan. And she did, finding the places where he was sensitive and making him moan with pleasure as he had done with her. She touched his nipple with her teeth and when he hissed in a breath of air, she asked, "Not good?"

"Very good. Don't stop."

She bit his shoulder, then soothed it with her tongue. Found that it tickled him if she put her tongue in his ear. Kissed his neck and watched him writhe with pleasure. And smoothed her fingertips over his lean flanks, admiring the hardness of muscle under the soft skin.

Then he began to move inside her.

Eden curled her legs up around Kerrigan's buttocks to hold him inside, tipping her pelvis up to meet his thrusts. Her whole body arched into him as she felt her body tensing. She felt out of control, her emotions and her body taking off on a journey of their own.

Suddenly she was frightened again. "Kerrigan?"

He knew what was happening to her, should have known how it would frighten her. "Come with me, Eden. I'll take care of you. Trust me. It's all right."

She was strung tight as a bowstring, her body arched toward him, reaching for the unknown, surging toward the pinnacle of pleasure.

"Kerrigan," she cried again.

"Come on, Eden. Come with me."

Eden gave herself into Kerrigan's keeping. She let the feelings come, let them overwhelm her, shuddering again and again as her body arched and bowed in the throes of ecstasy.

Kerrigan growled low in his throat as he spilled his seed into her, the act of love taking him along with Eden into a paradise of their own making.

Eden panted hard, trying to find breath now that she was back on earth again. Her body trembled with aftershocks that reminded her of the ecstasy she had just experienced. She put her arms around Kerrigan and pulled him close.

"Thank you," she whispered.

Kerrigan felt his eyes burn with emotion, but managed a weak laugh. "I assure you it was my pleasure."

He slid to her side and wrapped his arms around her and held her close as they both drifted into sleep.

When Eden awoke, she opened her eyes to the sight of Kerrigan's tousled hair. She sat up abruptly. It had really happened. It hadn't been a dream. She brushed a lock of hair back from Kerrigan's forehead.

He grunted and rolled over.

Eden smiled. She looked out the window and realized with a start that she had missed church entirely. She looked at the clock by her bed and saw that if she didn't get up immediately, she would be late for the Sweetwater Ladies Social Club meeting.

She debated whether to wake up Kerrigan. Maybe he would want to make love to her again. But she still felt a little shy about what had happened between them. And to be honest, it would be easier to face him, at least after this first time, when they were both dressed. Besides, even if she wanted to, she couldn't stay in bed. Considering how the fire at Big Ben Davis's house had roused feelings, she couldn't take the chance of missing the meeting.

While Eden dressed she kept her mind blank, afraid to think too much about what had happened between her and Kerrigan. She wasn't sure if making love to him had really changed anything. As far as she knew, he still had no plans to settle down, no intention of taking off his gun. The more she thought about it, the more upset she got. There was no sense worrying about it now. There would be plenty of time to argue with Kerrigan about . . . everything . . . when she got back.

At last, Eden yanked on her stockings and shoes, slapped her hat on her head, jabbed a pin in to hold it tight, jerkily fluffed the squashed pouf of her skirt in back, and marched out the door ready to fight bear.

Unfortunately, the only bear she was interested in fighting was hibernating back in her den.

"This nonsense has got to cease!" Regina announced to the members of the Sweetwater Ladies Social Club. "If we had any hope of succeeding, I wouldn't be speaking. But I don't see that most of our husbands have budged even an inch on their stand against the nesters. And from what Persia tells me, aside from a very few exceptions"— Regina singled out Claire Falkner and Amity Carson, whose husbands had retired from the fray and rejoined their wives in the bedroom—"they haven't moved an inch in any direction either. Not only that, but it seems our boycott isn't doing much to delay the onset of violence."

Miss Devlin could see the ladies, once again divided along rancher and nester lines, were moved by Regina's speech. "I can understand your frustration, but you simply can't give up now," Miss Devlin said, mentally apologizing for her own defection from the ranks, and more aware now than ever before of just how much they were all giving up.

"Give me one good reason why not?" Regina demanded.

"If you and Persia will step into the preacher's study with me for a moment, I will," Miss Devlin replied.

"If what you have to say is so important, I don't know why you can't speak in front of everyone," Regina said.

"Believe me," Miss Devlin said with conviction, "you don't want everyone to hear what I have to say."

"Why not?"

Miss Devlin glared. "Don't push me, or I might be tempted to make you sorry you did."

Surprised by the threat in both Miss Devlin's voice and her words, Regina nodded her head and followed the schoolteacher.

Persia knew what Miss Devlin wanted to discuss, but even she was surprised to see not only Bliss, but Hadley as well, sitting in the preacher's study when they entered the room.

"What is the meaning of this, Hadley?" Regina said, confronting her son.

"If you'll sit down, Mother, I'll explain."

Regina's mood was testy, but nevertheless, Miss Devlin took her by the arm and ushered her over to join Persia on a nearby parson's bench. "I think this is news you'll take better sitting down."

"You're not going to tell me you want to marry that girl," Regina said scornfully to her son.

"No, Mother. I'm already married to her."

"We'll have the marriage annulled," Regina exclaimed, shooting to her feet. "We'll—"

"It's too late for that," Hadley said with remarkable calm. "Bliss is expecting a child. Your first grandchild."

For the first time in living memory, Regina was speechless.

Not one to let a golden opportunity pass by, Miss Devlin said in the silence, "So you see, it's more important than ever that we keep trying to do whatever we can to urge both sides to start talking to one another, to try and solve their differences peaceably, rather than by fighting."

"A baby," Regina said, her face softening. She gave Bliss a squinty-eyed look. "How long have you two been married?"

She was asking whether the baby had come before or after the nuptials, and a condemnation of Bliss hung ready on her lips.

Hadley was having no part of that. "It doesn't matter, Mother. What matters is that I love Bliss, and she loves me. We want to stay here in Sweetwater and raise our child—if we can. If we can't—we'll have to go somewhere else."

"Take my grandbaby away? You most certainly will not!" Regina said. "But Oak will be furious—"

"Ben won't be too pleased when he finds out, either," Persia interrupted.

"This isn't about Oak and Ben, it's about Hadley and Bliss," Miss Devlin said. "They're entitled to live their lives in this valley, and that will never happen unless their fathers make peace with each other. If a range war breaks out in Sweetwater, you can both say good-bye to any chance you have of watching your grandchild grow up. That's why, unless you have a better plan to offer, I say you have to stick with mine—at least a little longer."

The two soon-to-be grandmothers stared at one another in bemused silence. They were now related by their children's marriage, and soon would be related by their grandchild's blood. The foolish plan they had begun seemed too little to do to prevent a war. But since it was all they had, it would be worse than foolish to give it up.

Regina met Miss Devlin's implacable gaze. "I can see what you mean. We have to be more firm than ever before. I'm not going to be quite so subtle in my hints to Oak that he should begin negotiations with the nesters. And I'm going to do my best to find out who started that fire—and give him a good piece of my mind."

She turned to include Persia and added, "But I think perhaps we ought to keep this marriage, and the baby, to ourselves for a little while. I don't think it would be a good thing for Ben or Oak to be told. At least not until things get a little more settled."

Regina turned back to the couple. "As for you, young man . . ."

Both Bliss and Hadley stiffened, waiting for the ax to fall. Instead they heard Regina say in a voice as sweet as buttermilk pie, "Why don't you introduce me to your new bride?"

Bliss blushed as prettily as a newlywed when Regina hugged her and welcomed her to the family. "You realize, of course," Regina said, "that now that you're one of us married ladies, Bliss, we'll be recruiting you to join us by denying Hadley his marital rights until we achieve peace in the valley."

"Now, wait just a minute, Mother," Hadley protested. "What's this all about?"

"For your information, Hadley, all the wives of Sweet-water—rancher and nester alike—have banded together to deny their husbands conjugal rights until this awful wrangling between rancher and nester is settled once and for all," his mother explained.

"What does that have to do with me and Bliss?" Hadley demanded.

"Hadley," Bliss said, putting a restraining hand on his shoulder. "It would hardly be fair if I . . . if we . . . I mean, I think your mother's right."

"You've got to be kidding!" Hadley exclaimed.

"I'm afraid not," Bliss said with a mischievous smile. "Maybe you can say things to your father that your mother can't." She gazed up at him with her big blue eyes and said imploringly, "Don't you see? I owe it to our future to join the other women."

Hadley stared like a baited bear at the four women

surrounding him, then growled once in outrage and disgust before he bolted from the room.

Persia looked at Bliss. Bliss looked at Regina. Regina looked at Miss Devlin. They all burst out laughing.

Miss Devlin shook her head ruefully. It looked like she had ended up hunting bear after all.

Chapter 14

A guilty man runs when no one's chasin' him.

KERRIGAN AWOKE SOMETIME AFTER NOON TO FIND Eden gone. At first he thought she had gone to the kitchen to make him some dinner. That thought brought such a feeling of rightness and satisfaction that he was disappointed when a couple of sniffs revealed no smell of coffee perking. He frowned. The house was too quiet. It felt empty.

He rose up on an elbow and called out, "Eden?"

He got no answer. Maybe she had gotten up and left the house because she hadn't wanted to face him. That thought made him uncomfortable, because the last thing he wanted Eden to feel about what they had done together was embarrassed. What they had done together was . . . Incredible. Unbelievable. Wonderful.

He couldn't help the stupid grin on his face. He lay back, spread his arms, and arched his back in a huge stretch, then scratched his belly contentedly. He was more than satisfied with the way their argument had ended. His smile faded. But maybe Eden was having second thoughts about losing her virtue. After all, he had no way of knowing if she viewed their lovemaking the same way he did.

But he was sure she had enjoyed it. Pretty sure. All right, maybe he had been so involved himself that he wasn't the best one to judge what she had been feeling. But she had let him hold her afterward. That must mean something.

Unfortunately, she wasn't here now to tell him what she felt. Which might mean she was having second thoughts about the "loving and caring" part of their bargain. Granted, that was a pretty big step for her to take after twenty-nine years. He could appreciate her feelings if that was the case, because she wasn't the only one who had been forced to face the truth this morning. Eden had made a good point. Maybe he had been running from love himself all these years without realizing it. He had to admit the thought of settling down, of loving a woman so much that his breath quit in his chest just from looking at her, was pretty damn scary.

Kerrigan realized suddenly that Eden might be sitting in the kitchen right now, refusing to answer when he called out to her. He wrapped the sheet around himself and plodded barefoot on the cold floor into the kitchen. The instant he pushed through the swinging door he remembered that Eden had mentioned something about attending the Sweetwater Ladies Social Club meeting this afternoon. He hurried back into the bedroom, and when he didn't find either her high-button black shoes or her coat, he figured that must be where she was.

He started dressing, figuring that as long as she wasn't here, he might as well get some work done himself, so he could be back when she was. As he pulled on his Levi's, tucked in his shirt, and buckled on his gun belt, he reviewed his feelings about the momentous decisions of the morning.

It was past time he settled down. That would be easy to do if he had a woman like Eden Devlin by his side. He could spend a lifetime probing all the facets of that woman and never discover them all. But despite the fact she had let him make love to her, he wasn't at all sure she would choose to marry him over Felton Reeves. Not only was Felton an attractive man, he offered her the security and stability she had said she wanted from a husband. Kerrigan didn't have a good record where those qualities were concerned.

And Felton would be a damn good father. Kerrigan knew for a fact that Felton loved kids. Kerrigan felt his gut wrench at the thought of Eden growing round with any child except his. He didn't know if he could be a good father, but he didn't think he could help loving a child he and Eden had made together.

Finally, Felton had made plans for the future that Eden approved of. Not that Kerrigan couldn't make plans. He'd put the money from the sale of his ranch in Texas into the bank. And had added to his cache from his earnings over the years. He ought to have enough money by now to at least buy a small spread around here close to the school so Eden could keep on teaching if she wanted.

She didn't love Felton. But she didn't love him either. At least not yet. And she liked Felton. He wasn't at all sure she liked him. More like she tolerated him. She had said she trusted him. And she felt some strong emotion for him, though he thought maybe it was probably more sexual desire than anything else. Desire was a good start. But he wanted more than that.

No, he wasn't going to take it for granted that Eden Devlin would marry him if he asked. He was going to do everything he could to prove to her he was the kind of man she wanted before he took the chance of popping the question.

Meanwhile, he would have to do whatever he could to keep Eden and Felton apart. Because there was no telling what might happen now that Miss Devlin had decided to let herself start caring for a man. He wasn't about to take the chance that she might start caring for the *wrong* man.

Kerrigan saddled his horse and headed out toward Sweetwater Canyon to see whether he could find any more sign of where the stolen cattle had been moved. He approached the canyon from the south across the grassy plains, so he had a good view of the terrain around him. He was still quite a distance away when he spied a horseman poised on the rim of the canyon.

The sun was headed down, and the shadows kept Kerrigan from seeing the man's face under his hat. He approached the man from behind, keeping him in sight the whole way, and keeping his hand free to reach for his gun if he needed it.

"Howdy there, Felton."

Felton jerked his head around, completely surprised to find Kerrigan beside him. "Where the hell did you come from?"

"You're lucky I wasn't stalking you. Otherwise, you'd be dead."

"I was thinking," Felton replied sullenly, knowing Kerrigan was right. A man who wasn't aware of what was happening around him was asking for trouble.

"Must have been some pretty deep thoughts, my friend."

"I was just wondering," Felton said, "how long it would take a man with the right piece of land, a couple of good bulls, and a decent-size herd of cows, to get rich."

"Deep thoughts indeed," Kerrigan said with a smile. "I admit I've pondered the idea a few times myself."

"I've been doing more than thinking," Felton admitted. "I've been saving up to make it happen."

"You must have been living lean to save up that kind of poke since we parted ways in Texas."

"I've been doing what's necessary," Felton said guardedly.

Kerrigan heard the caution come into Felton's voice and wondered what the sheriff was hiding. Whatever it was, Kerrigan didn't have time to worry about it right now. He wanted to get this rustling business settled for the Association so he could concentrate on wooing Eden. Felton Reeves made a formidable rival. In all the years they had vied for a woman's attention it had never really mattered to Kerrigan who won. This time it did.

"I got the message you sent through Miss Devlin," Felton said. "And I took a look around Sweetwater Canyon like you asked. I saw signs of cattle all right," Felton replied, taking out the makings for a smoke. "But it was two, maybe three days old. They were long gone by the time I got there."

"That's too bad. Any ideas where to go from here?"

"I thought you were the expert," Felton said with a wry twist of his mouth. "Leastaways, that's what you always told me."

"So I did," Kerrigan agreed with a grin. "To be honest, this one's almost too easy, Felton. And that worries me."

"What do you mean?"

"I ran into Levander Early the day I rode into town. He was a big part of the biggest ring of rustlers in Montana when I ran him out of the Territory last year. I believed him when he told me he'd gone straight here in Wyoming." His lips twisted ruefully. "After all, even a dumb son of a bitch like Levander deserves a chance to start over. I would have kept on believing him, except he made the mistake of bushwhacking me and leaving me for wolf bait."

Felton raised a surprised brow. "You look pretty healthy for a dead man."

"He didn't finish the job," Kerrigan said.

"Then where have you been?" Felton asked.

"With a friend." To Kerrigan's relief, although Felton's eyes narrowed, he didn't ask "which friend."

"There's something that puzzles me," Felton said. "If you were ambushed, how do you know it was Levander Early did it?"

"In Montana, Levander wore a Mexican roweled spur with a longhorn design in the center. Lying flat on my face with a load of buckshot in my back, I got a real good look at that same spur."

"That's not proof that'll hold up in court," Felton said.

"Maybe not," Kerrigan conceded. "But I know who I'm trying to catch now. What worries me is that Levander never was real smart, and I'm a little surprised he's managed to fool everybody here in Sweetwater for so long."

"Maybe he's working with somebody else," Felton suggested. "Somebody smarter."

Kerrigan met the sheriff's blue-eyed gaze and said, "That's exactly what I was thinking. You got any ideas who that might be?"

"Don't look at me," Felton said. "I don't know nothing."

A sudden thought struck Kerrigan, one he didn't like but felt he had to pursue. "You've been talking big about having the money to buy a ranch and settle down. I have to ask myself where you're getting the money to do that, Felton. And I put that together with the fact a gang of idiots like Levander Early and his bunch have been rustling cattle for months in and around Sweetwater—where you're the sheriff—and haven't been caught. That leaves me looking to you for answers."

Dots of perspiration formed on Felton's brow, and his horse started shifting nervously, as though sensing its rider's distress. The truth was, he'd been out of town so much—on personal business—that he'd been a piss-poor sheriff lately. But he wasn't accountable to Burke Kerrigan, and nobody else was complaining.

Felton blew a cloud of smoke and said, "Look, Kerrigan, if it was me involved with the rustlers, do you think I'd have come out here to help you find the varmints?"

"You might if you thought you could keep an eye on me that way, and make sure I don't find out what I need to know to tie you to Levander's gang."

"That's crazy!" Felton blustered.

"Is it?"

"Goddammit, Kerrigan. I don't have to prove nothing to you. I'm the sheriff in this town. You're the one who better watch out. Because the first wrong step you make, you're going to find yourself looking out at the world from the inside of a jail cell."

Felton kicked his horse into a gallop and left Kerrigan choking in his dust.

Kerrigan frowned. Something was wrong here, but he wasn't sure what. Felton Reeves was a lot of things, but he had never thought him a thief. Kerrigan had been taking a shot in the dark when he described the scenario that made Felton a villain. But Felton's overreaction had certainly looked guilty enough for it to be somewhere near the truth.

If the sheriff was in cahoots with the rustlers, it was going to make Kerrigan's job for the Association a hell of a lot harder. And it was going to rip the daylights out of Felton Reeves's courtship of Miss Eden Devlin. As far as Kerrigan was concerned, that sounded like a damn good trade.

If there had been tracks in the canyon, Kerrigan was pretty sure Felton had gotten rid of them by now. Maybe he could find out something if he squeezed Levander and his crowd a little. He headed his paint horse across the grassy plains in the direction of the homes the rustlers-farmers had thrown together along the river.

When Kerrigan rode around the corner of Levander's

log cabin, he found the man sitting on the first of two wooden porch steps, his elbows on his knees. He was swinging a whiskey jug by the finger he had looped in the handle while he drew circles in the dirt with a booted foot. He apparently didn't hear Kerrigan's approach because he was singing a cowboy song with a pretty good set of lungs.

"Oh, I am a Texas cowboy
So far away from hooooome
If I ever get back to Texas
I never more will rooooooam.
Wyoming is too cold for me
The winters are too looooong;
Before the roundups—"

"Howdy there, Levander."
"Son of a bitch!" Startled, Levander jumped up, dropping the jug. It hit the ground, spilling fine corn whiskey into the dirt. Levander grabbed at it and stuck the cork in before it emptied completely.

From the back of his paint horse, Kerrigan tipped his hat as he greeted Levander's slack-jawed gang, who were strewn in various attitudes of slouching, squatting, and standing, from one end of the cabin's slant-roofed front porch to the other. "Bud, Hogg, Doanie, Stick, howdy-do?"

The four members of Levander's gang were an ugly bunch. Not that they were ugly, actually, but they were dirty and unkempt, and their yellowed, blackened, and toothless smiles showed the signs of years of neglect.

Bud had been a prize-fighter in his younger days, and looked it. He was huge, with a thick barrel chest and an oversized head set on a thick neck. He had small, piggy eyes, a crooked nose, and one cauliflower ear. To put it plainly, Bud looked mean. And, indeed, he could be. Kerrigan had seen him beat a man to death with his fists.

Kerrigan had also seen Bud down on one knee playing marbles with a group of seven- and eight-year-olds. The surprise was, Bud was equally happy doing either, because he wasn't really sure of the difference. Someone had hit him in the head once too often, and now Bud only did what he was told to do. Which made him dangerous if somebody whispered the wrong words in his good ear.

Hogg and Doanie were about the same medium size, had medium brown shaggy hair, mustaches with a week-old beard stubble, and were dressed alike in baggy bib overalls and patched plaid shirts. They looked like typical farmers.

They also wore dirty bandannas, a useful, and obviously well used, cowboy accessory, and had their bib overalls stuffed down into cowboy boots, which told Kerrigan they weren't doing as much farming as they claimed. The two men might have been attached with a rope, they stayed so close, and in Kerrigan's experience, one never said a word without checking first with the other. Which was a smart move when you thought about it, because they probably had a collective intelligence equal to one simpleminded cowboy. Their sheer stupidity made them dangerous.

Stick hadn't gotten his nickname by accident. He was tall and skinny and had the mental powers of a stick. But he could throw a sweeter loop from a roping horse than anybody Kerrigan had ever seen. His hands, legs, and neck stuck out of his clothes because he wasn't a regular size, and his legs going into his boots looked like a leafless tree stuck in a pot. Stick was like a puppy, willing to do anything for a pat on the head, including killing, maiming, and, of course, rustling.

Levander was the only one of the bunch with any brains at all, and he was dangerous because the other four listened to him. It was amazing to think this was the rustling gang that for months had been successfully evading Sheriff Reeves and the combined efforts of the Sweetwater Stock Growers Association to catch them. There was obviously more here than met the eye. Kerrigan had to be careful not to underestimate them.

"Uh, howdy," Stick said. "What brings you all the way out here, Kerrigan?"

"I'm looking for rustlers," Kerrigan said.

Doanie and Hogg exchanged guilty glances.

"We don't even eat steak no more since you run us out of Montana," Doanie said, running his hands up and down along the denim straps of his bib overalls. "We're farmers now. We eat chicken."

Kerrigan fought hard not to laugh. "*Cookin'* steak was never the problem, Doanie, it was *burnin' the rawhide* that had me bothered."

"Oh," Doanie said.

"Oh," Hogg said.

Levander shoved Doanie and Hogg out of the way. "What're you doin' here, Kerrigan? We're law-abidin' citizens. You got no right to be on our land."

"I need to ask some questions."

"Well, we don't wanta answer no questions."

"Whatever happened to those fancy Mexican spurs you used to wear in Montana?" Kerrigan asked.

"I 'member them," Stick said with a smile as he squatted down to play with one of the kittens in Bud's lap. "They shore used to shine up real purty like—"

"Shut up, Stick!" Levander said. "Why you wanta know 'bout them spurs?" he asked suspiciously.

"Because I saw a pair just like them recently."

It took Levander a moment to realize what Kerrigan was getting at, but when he did, he scowled. "I ain't the only person on this here earth wears Mexican spurs," Levander said.

"But how many have got that longhorn etched in the center of the rowel?" Kerrigan queried.

"Them little horn things was shore purty, all right," Stick said.

Levander closed his eyes and shook his head in disgust. "I tole you to shut up, Stick. Now shut your mouth!"

Stick rose and shuffled around behind Doanie and Hogg and stood with his head hanging down. "Didn't mean no harm."

"You got no proof of nothin'," Levander said.

"I haven't accused you of anything," Kerrigan said with a menacing smile. "All I'm saying is your rustling days in Sweetwater are numbered, because I'll be watching you from now on. And if I catch you being a little too handy with a rope—well, we all know what happens to cattle thieves."

"They hang," Stick volunteered with wide eyes.

"Shut up, Stick," Levander warned, his shoulders hunched up to his neck in frustration.

"Of course, you boys can always clear out now and cut your losses," Kerrigan said. He touched the brim of his hat and said, "Be seeing you, boys."

As he rode away Kerrigan had a picture in his mind of the five members of Levander's gang hunkered around the front of the house, some standing, some squatting, some sitting. He pictured them around that branding fire the night he was ambushed and tried to figure who had been standing, who had been squatting. He felt a sudden chill as he realized he had seen *all five of them* around the fire.

So who had snuck up behind him with the shotgun?

As Kerrigan disappeared over a rise, Stick turned to Levander and said, "The Boss ain't gonna like it that we can't rustle cattle no more."

"Shut up, Stick," Levander said. "Once the Boss hears what's goin' on, he'll take care of Kerrigan once and for all. But I ain't gonna stick around here waitin' on him. We're clearin' outta here now."

"C-c-c-can I bring my kitties?" Bud asked.

"There's no room for 'em where we're goin'."

"Where we goin'?" Stick asked.

"Somewhere Kerrigan can't find us if he comes lookin' again," Levander said.

Felton Reeves rode into Canyon Creek along the back alleys, the same as he always did, until he got to the Black Horse Saloon. He used the fire escape to get to the second floor and walked down the hall to the second door on the right. The room was empty, but it smelled just like Darcie, of too-strong perfume. Everything in the room reeked of too much: too many flounces on the bedspread, too many bows on the curtains, too many too-bright colors, and too many pieces of furniture crowded into the tiny room. Everything in the room said its owner was trying too hard to make up for a past that had contained too little.

Maybe that was why he felt both drawn and repelled by the place, as he was both drawn and repelled by its owner, Darcie Morton. Felton knew too well what Darcie was feeling, because he'd had the same feelings himself. That was why the money was so important. He was going to have everything he had never had. But he didn't want to be like Darcie and spend his money so people would know he hadn't always had it. That was why he had chosen to court Miss Devlin. She had taste and style. She would make a home for him that wouldn't shout to the heavens, "This here place belongs to a poor man what struck it rich."

He took off his hat and sat down on the edge of the too-soft bed and pulled off his boots. Then he lay back with his hands behind his head and waited. Darcie would be finished downstairs by midnight. Then she would come to him. He needed to feel her arms around him, needed the chance to talk to her. She understood what he was trying to do. In fact, she was the one who had encouraged him to try to better himself. That was why he felt so bad about leaving her behind so he could marry Miss Devlin. He had tried to tell Darcie about his decision, but he knew it would hurt her, so he had kept quiet.

His conscience had been bothering him lately, though not just about this. While he couldn't relieve himself of the other burdens, he could certainly do something about this one. He had made up his mind as he rode to Canyon Creek that he was going to tell Darcie tonight he wouldn't be coming to see her anymore. He would soon have all the money he needed to buy his ranch, and once he did that, he would be marrying the schoolteacher in Sweetwater, Miss Eden Devlin. And once he was a married man, he couldn't be coming to visit a whore in Canyon Creek.

He was nearly asleep when the door opened and a stream of light from the hall silhouetted Darcie. She was dressed in a shiny satin dress, cut both too low and too short for decency, and had a too-large red feather stuck in her hair. She must have seen him lying there, because she tiptoed in and lit the lantern beside the bed. That illuminated a too-large smile that he knew was because she loved him too much for her own damn good.

Lately, Felton had been fighting the good feelings that rose inside him when he saw her, hoping that if he concentrated on all the things that were wrong with Darcie Morton, he wouldn't feel so bad about leaving her. But there was a thick feeling in his throat, and a heavy feeling in his chest when he looked at her smiling down at him with her green eyes too full of caring.

Nope, she sure wasn't anything like Miss Devlin. In the first place, she didn't come no more than about shoulder-high on him. She had a tiny bosom (which she had cried over because a big one would have meant better tips), which in his opinion she more than made up for with nice wide hips and well-shaped legs. She had tiny feet, which he knew because he had rubbed them for her sometimes when she had been standing too long.

"H'lo sweetheart," she murmured, sitting down beside him on the bed.

"You look tired. You shouldn't work so hard," he said.

She turned around and he automatically began to help her out of the shiny dress. It was a ritual he had been through dozens of times with her, but it never failed to thrill him when he touched the sleek skin of her shoulders, and ran his hands down her back to her narrow waist. She always made a big production of removing her garters and stockings, and it always left him wanting her with his heart pounding so hard he couldn't hear himself think.

But not tonight. He wasn't going to let that happen tonight. He had bad news to give, and he didn't want it to hurt her any more than he could help. But he figured it probably wouldn't matter if he waited until she changed into her silk Chinese robe and got comfortable first.

When she was lying beside him enfolded in his arms, somehow the words wouldn't come. He kissed her once, feeling sorry that she wasn't ever going to have more than this too-small room, and too little attention from men who cared too little about whether she was happy or not.

"What's wrong?" she said, playing with the frayed collar of his shirt. "You're awful quiet tonight. Did this last trip pay off like you thought it would?"

"Yeah."

"And you got the money put in the bank right and tight?"

"Yeah."

She snuggled closer and he could feel her belly against his groin beneath his Levi's, and her small, pointy breasts poking through his shirt against his chest. It felt too damn good! He pushed her away abruptly and sat up, brushing his fingers through his hair.

"What's wrong?"

This time he heard the worry in her voice, and he felt awful knowing what he was about to say. "Nothing's wrong," he lied.

He hadn't fooled her, because she left the bed and came around to kneel on the floor in front of him. She took his hands in hers and looked up at him. "You can tell me, Felton. Whatever it is, I want to help."

She wasn't making this any easier. He took her hands and used them to get her to stand up. Then he lifted her into his lap and held her there. Her hands sneaked up around his neck and she started playing with the hair that hung over his collar, and his ears, and pretty soon he had to kiss her to get her to stop.

One thing led to another and pretty soon she had his shirt open and was sucking on one of his nipples. It was his own groan of pleasure that brought him back to his senses. He stood up and she fell off his lap and the only reason she didn't end up on the floor was because she had a good grip on his hair.

"Ouch!"

She let go, but by now she was getting mad. "What's wrong with you?" she demanded, the shape of her mouth, her eyes, even her eyebrows all announcing her confusion.

"Noth—"

"Don't tell me nothing, Felton Reeves. Because something sure as hell is the matter with you tonight! Now spit it out."

He forked his fingers through his tousled hair and said, "I gotta talk to you."

She gave him an exasperated look. "So talk."

"Maybe you better sit down," he said.

"Get on with it!"

"I've been courting a woman in Sweetwater and I'm going to marry her," Felton blurted.

Darcie turned completely white, and he really thought for a moment she was going to faint. He got her to sit down on the bed and pushed her head down between her knees. "Take a deep breath," he said.

She fought the hand he was using to hold her head down, and when he let go and she came up, he wasn't sure whether it was all that blood that had rushed down into her head or just plain fury that had her so red in the face. That wasn't so bad. What really worried him was that her eyes were kind of watery, and she had her jaw clamped tight, like maybe she was trying not to cry. He didn't know what he was going to do if she cried.

"Do you love her?"

That question surprised Felton, and before he could think of the right answer under the circumstances he said, "Of course not!"

"Then why are you marryin' her?"

That question put him in deep trouble. But he figured after everything he had been through with Darcie he owed her an honest answer. "Because I'm starting a new kind of life in Sweetwater, and I want a respectable wife to help me fit in."

"Did you ever think maybe I hoped someday to start over too?"

He shrugged. "I never thought about it much." And that was the truth. But maybe he should have. "You can still do it," he said.

"Not without you," she said flatly. Then she sighed and slumped onto the foot of the bed. "I guess I was just kiddin' myself." She looked up into his eyes and he felt his stomach sink clear to his knees. "I was hopin' . . . I kept thinkin' all this time . . . that you were puttin' that money away for us . . . that you were plannin' to take me away from all this. . . ." She gestured around the too-littered room, with fingers wearing too many rings. "That was pretty stupid, huh?"

She rose and walked over to the dressing table, sat down in front of the mirror, and began to take out the pins that held her coal-black hair in a mass of too many curls. "I want to be respectable too," she said. "I was hopin' that in Sweetwater, with us legally married and all, I could start over and be somethin' . . . I don't know . . . maybe better than what I am."

She turned and tried to catch his eyes again, but he kept them on the floor. "I know how you feel about this place, about how I dress and such like, and I made up my mind that when you proposed and I had that new chance, I'd change. I'd be more . . . better . . . than I am now. But I see that was just some fairy tale I was makin' up for myself."

She smiled faintly. "I can't hardly blame you for grabbin' at a chance for what I've always wanted myself, can I? But I think you better leave now, Felton. And I don't think you better come back here anymore."

"Darcie, I ⎯"

"Unless you're goin' to tell me you've changed your mind, I don't want to hear it," she said in a voice that wavered.

He grabbed his hat, buttoned his shirt, and stomped his feet down into his boots, not stopping until he had the door open and was halfway out. The hell of it was, after hearing what she had to say, he was damn close to saying he *had* changed his mind. But out of the corner of his eye he saw a garish stack of ostrich-feather headdresses that no decent lady would be seen dead wearing. If he took Darcie with him, it would mean bringing the past along. He wanted a clean break. A new life. She had said she didn't blame him. And he would have to be satisfied with that.

"Good-bye, Darcie."

"Good-bye, Felton," she said. "I hope you have a grand new life."

As Felton rode west toward Sweetwater he had a lot on his mind. He had done what he had set out to do. With Kerrigan so suspicious of how he made his money, it was best he put Darcie Morton behind him. He supposed it was excitement over his "grand new life" that had him feeling so sick to his stomach. He had no explanation at all for the lump that stayed in his throat the whole damn way home.

Chapter 15

*A man's eyes will tell you what
his mouth is a'feared to say.*

KERRIGAN FACED THE ROOMFUL OF RANCHERS IN OAK Westbrook's study and admitted, "I don't have proof that'll stand up in court, but I have a pretty good idea who's stealing your cattle."

"Is it nesters?" Oak demanded.

Kerrigan took off his hat and rolled the brim in his hands. His lips twisted wryly. "Well, yes and no."

"What kind of answer is that?"

"Not the one you wanted, I'm sure," Kerrigan said. "But that's all I'm willing to say right now, except you won't be losing any more steers."

"Give us some names and we'll go string up the varmints," one of the ranchers said.

"When I have the proof I need, I'll bring them in and turn them over to the law," Kerrigan said.

"Sheeeit," Cyrus muttered. "What do we do now? I can't stand any more waiting. My wife is driving me nuts!" He scratched the bald spot on top of his head. "I don't like bringing this up, but I gotta ask, Kerrigan. You had any luck seducing that Miss Devlin?"

Kerrigan was struck dumb for a moment. If he said the

word, he would have his thousand dollars and the ranchers would very likely have the lever they needed to end the sexual boycott Miss Devlin had instigated. But he found even the mention of Eden's name in such a context so distasteful that it was all he could do not to grab Cyrus by the throat and throttle him.

There was no way Kerrigan could voice his change of heart about seducing Miss Devlin without the need for explanations he would rather not make right now. And it could do Eden no good for him to lose his temper with Cyrus. When he opened his mouth, all that came out was a curt, "I'm making some progress."

"You got a *pretty good idea* who the rustlers are," Cyrus mimicked. "And you're *makin' some progress* with Miss Devlin. But that don't solve my problem. I want my wife back *now*!"

"I have a suggestion about that," Kerrigan said.

Suddenly he had the full attention of every man in the room.

"Oh, yeah?" Cyrus asked suspiciously. "This better not be some *maybe it'll work* kind of idea, Kerrigan, because this is one time when all I want to see is *results.*"

"You'll get them," Kerrigan promised. "But it means talking with the nesters."

In an instant Oak was on his feet and nose to nose with the gunslinger. "What the hell is this all about? If we'd wanted to talk to those no-good, sodbusting yokels we could've done it six months ago. We're paying you good money to—"

"You're paying me to make sure you don't lose any more cattle," Kerrigan said in a dangerously quiet voice. "And I'm doing my job. But you have some other matters that need to get settled. As I understand it, the nesters have claimed all along that they weren't the ones rustling your cattle. They were telling the truth." He paused to let that sink in and continued, "Did you ever stop to wonder who might be ruining the nesters' crops and cutting their fences if you weren't doing it? Or why?"

Kerrigan let them stew on that for a while.

"I suppose you have an idea who the culprits might be," Oak said.

"The same gang who's responsible for the rustling," Kerrigan answered promptly.

"That don't make no sense," one of the ranchers said.

"Sure it does," Kerrigan contradicted. "When did the nesters first start fencing off water?"

"Must've been about nine months ago, in the spring," Oak figured.

"What reason did they give?" Kerrigan queried.

"They claimed they were retaliating for us cutting their fences and running our cattle on their land," Oak said, a note of wonder in his voice as he realized what he was saying.

"And when did the rustling start?" Kerrigan asked, once again tracing the history of unrest in Sweetwater.

"Right after that, I guess."

"You all say you didn't cut any fences, or burn any homes. They all claim they didn't rustle any cattle, or shoot your son. And it seems nobody on either side killed Pete Eustes. So that leaves some third party doing all kinds of mischief," Kerrigan concluded. "And keeping both sides suspicious of each other so no questions get asked or answered."

"I'll be damned," Oak said, slumping back into his desk chair. "I'll be damned."

"I still don't understand your point," Cyrus said. "What has all this got to do with getting my wife back?"

"What I'm saying is that somebody has been playing you ranchers and nesters against one another like a fiddle and getting away with it. Maybe if you got together, you could talk out some of your differences. Once you aren't at each other's throats your wives will have the peace they want. And you'll have your wives back."

"That still leaves us with rustled cattle," Oak pointed out.

"You probably won't get back what you've lost," Kerrigan said. "Chances are the cattle have been sold and the money spent. But if any cash is still around, if it can be recovered, I'll get it back for you. That's what you hired me to do. As for getting the nesters to take down those fences around the water holes, seems to me that could be negotiated between you and them. After all, until nine months ago everything was working out all right."

"Does this mean you aren't going to seduce Miss Devlin?" Cyrus asked.

Kerrigan was upset that the subject had come up again, but managed to answer in an even voice, "If your negotiations with the nesters turn out successfully, it won't be necessary."

"How soon do you think you can set up a meeting?" Oak asked.

"To tell you the truth, I've already spoken to Big Ben Davis. How does a week from today sound?"

"Sheeeit!" Cyrus shouted. "That sounds just fine!"

Miss Devlin could hardly believe what her pupils had told her Monday morning. The Association's hired gunslinger had arranged a meeting between all their fathers to be held at the town meetinghouse. It was exactly what Miss Devlin had hoped for—a chance for a peaceful solution to the trouble in Sweetwater. But she wanted a little more insurance that the meeting wouldn't turn into a brawl than Kerrigan's claim that he would keep the peace.

She had sent each pupil home with a note suggesting that the wives of the ranchers and nesters accompany their husbands to the meeting, and if the negotiations were successful, that they celebrate with a party and dance. That way the meeting would provide an opportunity for reconciliations not only between ranchers and nesters, but between husbands and wives.

Eden expected Kerrigan to object to her initiative, so she wasn't surprised by the knock on her front door. But it was Sheriff Reeves who stood there with a light dusting of snowflakes on his hat and coat, waiting to be invited inside.

Miss Devlin smiled a welcome. "Hello, Felton. Please come in. Have you heard the good news?"

As she helped him off with his coat he said, "I heard there's going to be a big town meeting next week. But whether it'll be the answer to everyone's prayers—I have my doubts."

"Don't be such a pessimist," Miss Devlin admonished, then instructed, "That's a person who always looks at the dark side of—"

"I didn't come here for a school lesson, Miss Devlin."

"Of course not. Well, I have every confidence that the meeting will—"

"That ain't—isn't—why I come—came," Felton said, running a finger around the buttoned neck of his striped shirt, which had gotten tight all of a sudden.

"Oh." Miss Devlin settled herself on the sofa beside the sheriff.

Felton nervously shifted away from her, putting as much distance as possible between them. "Miss Devlin . . ."

Eden examined Felton's agonized expression. "Whatever it is, Felton, it can't be that bad, can it?" she asked with a whimsical smile.

His Adam's apple bobbed as he swallowed his reservations. He thrust a ring box in her lap and said, "Miss Devlin, would you do me the honor of becoming my wife?"

Miss Devlin stared at the ring box with eyes that soon glazed over. Here in her lap was a wish come true. She should have been overjoyed. So why did she feel sick instead?

You have to tell him about Kerrigan.

Eden had forbidden herself to think about what else she was giving up when she offered her virtue to the gunslinger, because she had never expected it to matter. She had never really expected to get this proposal. Now that she had it, Eden wasn't entirely sure she wanted it. Which was a good thing, because she couldn't accept Felton's proposal without confessing that he wasn't getting the prim and proper spinster lady he had been led to expect.

Tell him about Kerrigan.

It occurred to her that she should at least pick up the ring box and look inside. When she opened it, she saw a tiny diamond in an elaborate, ostentatious gold setting. "Why, it's . . ." She forced herself to finish, ". . . lovely, Felton. Thank you."

She glanced up at him, and there was such a miserable look on his face that she was taken aback. If he wasn't happy about marrying her, why had he asked? Before she could stop herself, the words tumbled out. "Why do you want to marry me, Felton?"

"Why?" His wide blue eyes filled with panic before his gaze shifted away. He had been thinking a lot about what Darcie had said, and it worried him how close he had come to changing his mind about marrying Miss Devlin. He had decided the best thing to do was to get himself committed, and that way he couldn't back out. Here he was, giving her a ring and having a devil of a time explaining why he wanted to marry her.

"I want to marry you because I think you'll make a good wife, Miss Devlin, and a good mother for my children," he said at last. Of course he had said *good,* but he meant *respectable*. Which Darcie wasn't. Which was why he was marrying Miss Devlin instead of the woman he loved.

Eden was afraid to ask Felton whether he loved her, because she was afraid he would admit he didn't. What if he asked her if she loved him? What right did she have to judge his motives for marriage, when hers weren't so lily white. "And I'm sure you'll make a good husband, Felton," she murmured, returning the compliment. "And a good father."

"Does that mean you're saying yes?"

His eyes were bleak but determined, and she couldn't look at them without feeling distraught. Even if Kerrigan finally offered marriage, it would be a mistake to accept him. He was like Sundance, the kind of man people called in when they needed help and then couldn't wait to see the back of when their killing had been done for them. She could never be happy living like that again.

Eden stiffened. Until this moment, when she had to make a choice, she had been able to hide from the awful truth. Now it reached out to grab her with a force that left her reeling.

I love Burke Kerrigan.

She loved a man just like her father. Deeply. With her whole heart and soul. Loved him so much that if anything ever happened to him, it would destroy her. The way Sundance's death had destroyed her mother. She simply could not afford to repeat her mother's mistake.

Eden stared at Felton's ring in its red velvet setting. She would never experience the ecstasy of loving with Felton. But she would never experience the agony of losing him, either. And if she was determined not to marry Kerrigan, this was her chance to have the things she had always wanted: a stable home and a husband and children. Eden couldn't throw that chance away just because she didn't like the looks of the ring her future husband had chosen . . . or the expression in his eyes when he had proposed . . . or because she was no longer coming to him untouched.

Tell him about Kerrigan.

Felton hadn't said he was marrying her because she was virtuous. He had merely said she would make a good wife and mother. She would be the most loyal and steadfast wife and devoted mother any man could have.

Tell him about Kerrigan.

"You know, Kerrigan and I—"

"Kerrigan won't ask you to marry him," Felton said in a harsh voice. "He ain't the marrying kind."

"But he and I—"

"I don't care what you've been to Kerrigan in the past, so long as once you put that ring on your finger you know you're mine."

Tell him about Kerrigan.

But Felton had already said he didn't care. Who could blame her if she chose to believe him?

Miss Devlin took a deep breath and forced a smile. "I guess this means we're engaged. Would you like to put the ring on my finger?"

"Sure," he said, his Adam's apple bobbing again.

She held out her hand and after fumbling a little, he slid the ring on her finger. It fit. It didn't look quite so bad once it was on. It took up most of the space on her ring finger below her knuckle, leaving barely enough room for a wedding band.

"You've made me a very happy man," Felton said. But his eyes said differently.

"And you've made me a happy woman," Miss Devlin replied, her gaze equally solemn. She had purposely left out the *very* in front of the *happy*. There were limits to how much lying she thought she ought to do under the circum-

stances. "Maybe we should have some kind of party to celebrate," she suggested, "and invite our friends."

"Yeah, sure," Felton agreed. Except Felton's best friend
was Darcie Morton, and he didn't hardly think he could, or
should, invite her to his engagement party. "On the other
hand, maybe we could wait and announce our engagement
at that party the town's having at the end of the week,"
Felton said. "That way everybody would already be there."

"Why, that's a wonderful idea!" Once her engagement
was public, Miss Devlin wouldn't be having all these
doubts and second thoughts. Once it was public, she
wouldn't be able to back out.

They both sat for a while, neither saying anything,
while a pall settled over them.

Felton wanted to scream, *Forget the whole damn thing!*
but just as he opened his mouth Miss Devlin said, "Thank
you again for the ring, Felton."

Miss Devlin knew she ought to *oooh* and *ahhh* over the
ring a little more, but as long as she was drawing these
squiggly lines of honesty, she didn't want to step over
them any more than necessary.

She leaned forward, expecting Felton's kiss to seal their
engagement. Instead she received a hard, punishing attack
on her mouth; there was nothing tender or loving about it.
When he was done, she had a lump in her throat and her
eyes burned with unshed tears. What they had shared
hadn't been a kiss of joy, or reverence, or even passion. It
had been an act of tumult, of vehemence, of violence.
"What's wrong, Felton?"

Felton jumped, certain Miss Devlin had read the confused state of his mind. He couldn't say the same things to
her that he could say to Darcie. And he certainly couldn't
confide his stark fear that this engagement was a terrible
mistake. So he said, "I'm a little worried, that's all, what
with such an important town meeting coming up next

week. I guess I'll be saying good night. It's been a long day. Be seeing you."

Felton was already at the door by the time he finished talking. He let Miss Devlin help him into his coat. His gut tightened when she flinched away from him as he leaned over to kiss her on the cheek. Everything would be all right once they were married. He wouldn't feel like kicking something anymore, and this sick feeling would go away.

When Felton was gone, Miss Devlin held her hand out and perused the engagement ring on her finger. She should feel enraptured. A handsome, eligible man had proposed to her. Soon she was going to be a married woman. Why did she feel positively ill?

Well, she had plenty of remedies for an upset stomach. She walked over to the china cabinet and took a silver spoon from the top drawer. She marched into her bedroom and filled the spoon from the bottle of Tasteless Castor Oil. Closing her eyes and opening her mouth wide, she swallowed the stuff down. Her face screwed up so tight, her eyes and lips practically disappeared.

When she could talk again, she said, "Whoever said that was *tasteless* just plain lied!" To make matters worse, she now felt absolutely nauseous.

Miss Devlin stripped off her clothes and slipped under the bedcovers. She didn't bother with a lamp. She wouldn't be needing any light because she couldn't bear to stay up and read. All she wanted to do was sleep until tomorrow morning. Maybe she would feel a little better about being an engaged woman in the bright light of day.

Kerrigan was troubled when he arrived on Miss Devlin's doorstep in the early evening and found her house dark. In the days since he had come to stay with her, he had gotten used to her habit of reading far into the night, with her legs tucked under her and her spectacles perched on the end of her nose. He knocked on the front door, but when no one answered he opened it and walked in. "Eden? Are you here?"

No answer.

He let himself into the bedroom. He found her lying curled up with her hands under her head, minus her spectacles, like Sleeping Beauty waiting for the prince to awaken her with a kiss. Thanks to his Grandma Haley, Kerrigan knew all the romantic fairy tales by heart. He leaned across Eden with a hand on either side of her head, whispered, "Wake now, my lovely princess," and kissed her softly on the lips.

She must have been dreaming of him because she began to kiss him back. Her lips were yielding and responsive and Kerrigan lifted her into his arms so he could bask in her warmth.

His fingertips brushed tendrils of hair away from her face as he gifted her with kisses at her temple, and on her eyelids and across her freckled nose. "You are so beautiful, Eden," he whispered. "Like an unspoiled garden of beautiful flowers, budding and blossoming in my arms."

Still half asleep, Eden thought she was dreaming his words, they were so much what she had always hoped someday to hear from the man she loved. She smiled lazily up at Kerrigan's shadowed profile and threaded her fingers through his hair. His day's growth of beard felt wonderfully rough against her cheek as he nuzzled her neck.

She giggled as his tongue tickled her ear and hunched her shoulder to keep him away. "What are you doing?"

His dark eyes twinkled with mischief. "Relax. If you don't like it I'll stop."

Eden leaned back into the supportive curl of his arm, and allowed Kerrigan to have his way with her.

He mouthed delightful kisses along the underside of her chin and along her neck on his way to her ear. He took her earlobe in his teeth and bit just until she could feel pain, and then his lips and tongue were there to soothe, sending frissons of excitement dancing along her skin.

"Feel good?" he whispered.

She gasped as his moist breath fanned her ear. "It feels wonderful," she said. "It's my turn now."

His lids were lowered and his dark eyes revealed a threatening passion barely held in restraint. "Not yet," he said.

His mouth claimed hers, or at least tried, because Eden fought him for the right to give the most pleasure, to bite and tease and taste the most. With a heartfelt sigh of surrender, he let her win. It was the first duel Kerrigan had lost since the war, but he was fully, and cheerfully, prepared to suffer the consequences.

"Your turn," he said, when his mouth was free to speak.

She laughed, and placed her hand on the bulging front of his Levi's.

"Whoa, there, lady!" He caught her hand and held it against his hardness. And felt the ring.

Eden froze, horrified, when she felt him outlining the ring with his fingers. "Oh! What am I doing? What have I done?" She tried to jerk herself out of Kerrigan's embrace, but he had hold of her hand and the harder she struggled to free herself, the tighter his grasp became. "You're hurting me!"

"Tell me about the ring, Eden," he demanded in a harsh voice.

She stopped fighting him and took several deep, calming breaths. "Let me go first."

He held out her hand so the betraying diamond glittered in the moonlight. "Tell me about the ring."

It was obvious he wasn't going to move an inch before

she told him what he wanted to know. "Felton gave it to me."

"What for?"

"It's an engagement ring."

"You got engaged to Felton Reeves? When?"

"Don't yell. Tonight."

"I'm not yelling," he yelled.

"Can I have my hand back now?"

He dropped her hand as if it were a hot coal. As soon as she was free, she sought out a lantern, breaking several matches before she finally got it lit. She sat down at the head of the bed and balled her knees up and held them tight with her laced hands.

Kerrigan jumped up and began pacing back and forth across her bedroom like a caged animal. "I don't understand you. You can't even have a conversation with Felton Reeves without correcting his grammar!"

Eden reddened.

"You sure as hell don't love him." He stopped and turned to face her, his fisted hands on his hips. "Tell me you love him."

"You know I don't."

He threw his hands up in exasperation. "Then why did you get engaged to him?"

"He asked me to marry him."

"And just like that"—he snapped his fingers—"you're going to do it?"

"I want a home and a husband and children, Kerrigan. I think I always have, though I haven't always admitted it to myself. Felton is offering me those things."

"But you love me," he said, his chin jutting mulishly.

"Yes, I do," she admitted in a quiet voice. "Do you care for me at all, Kerrigan? You've never said you love me, you know."

"I . . ."

His lips pressed into a flat line of denial, but she saw her answer in his eyes. Everything he felt was there for her to find: his pain, his confusion, his anger. She looked for more, and he let her see it. Behind the fragile facade of volatile emotions, he had painstakingly hidden the one feeling she most wanted him to share with her: his love. It was there a brief flicker of time, and then cached away to be hoarded again like a miser's gold.

"You're a hard man to love, Kerrigan," she said.

"You sure jumped into my arms quick enough tonight."

Eden rose onto her knees and grasped one of the bedposts to keep her balance. "That's not fair. I was half asleep—"

"Not for long," he said with a scornful laugh. "Have you ever thought that if you'd just hold your horses, someday I might decide to marry you and settle down on some nice little spread—"

It was her turn to laugh scornfully. "I know your kind, Kerrigan. *Someday* never comes."

"I don't want you to marry Felton Reeves."

"There's nothing you can say that'll change my mind."

"He's not the man for you," Kerrigan insisted.

"Why not?"

Kerrigan was in a quandary. He had no proof that Felton was the brains behind the rustlers. Nor did he have any proof that Felton had bushwhacked him. All he had was a whole lot of circumstantial evidence that pointed toward the sheriff as the likeliest suspect—and a powerful desire to discredit his rival.

"Felton is an outlaw."

Eden laughed in his face. "Felton is the *sheriff.*"

"Felton is also the leader of the rustlers. And he shot me in the back."

She was on her feet confronting him in an instant, her

hair a flaming banner of fury as she shook her head in denial of his accusation. "I don't believe you!"

"It's true."

She grabbed his shirt in both fists. "What proof do you have?"

"None, but—"

She let him go and stepped back away from the powerful destructive aura that surrounded him, and attracted her. He was even more like Sundance than she had thought. Just like her father he was making up lies to manipulate her to do what he wanted. Just like her father he was holding out the carrot on a stick so she would follow him around, knowing all along that he would always keep it a step beyond her reach.

"I never thought you would stoop this low, Kerrigan." Her voice quivered with anger and hurt.

"Eden, I'm not lying, I'm—"

"What you are is a dog in the manger, Kerrigan. You don't want to marry me yourself, but you can't stand to let another man do the honest thing. Get out! I never want to see you again." When he just stood there, her voice got quiet again, like the terrible calm before a storm. "You heard me. Get out."

Kerrigan's face paled. He opened his mouth and realized he wanted to beg her to forgive him—to demand she take off Felton's ring—and to insist she marry him instead. That series of thoughts, jumbled on top of one another, made him alternately disgusted (He had never begged in his life!); furious (She didn't even *love* Felton Reeves!); and horrified (He had to be crazy to be thinking of marrying a woman as mixed-up as Eden Devlin). But the next thing he knew, he was saying, "What if I asked you to marry me right now?"

Kerrigan was appalled at the look of pain that crossed

Eden's face before she lifted her chin and replied, "I think you'd better leave."

He felt both relief and fury. She hadn't said no. But the damn woman hadn't said yes, either. "Just remember," he warned, "when Sheriff Felton Reeves goes to jail, that *I told you so.*"

After the things Eden had said to him, Kerrigan was tempted to let her ruin her life by marrying an outlaw. But hell, no woman who wanted kids the way Eden did ought to tie herself to a man who was going to spend the better part of her good childbearing years in prison. Kerrigan would make a much better husband, and Eden would see that as soon as he showed her Felton's true colors.

Miss Devlin watched the gunslinger stalk from her bedroom for what she was sure would be the last time. It hurt to know she had given up the chance to have a husband who loved her. But not as much as she was certain it would have hurt some day in the future when Kerrigan got himself killed.

Eden walked over to the Wish Box on her dresser and carefully opened the lid. She fingered the bone teething ring and slid the satin ribbon through her fingers. She tested the barber snips, liking the raspy metal sound they made as the spring contracted.

At last she lifted the genuine badger-hair shaving brush out of the box and ran the ticklish bristles across her palm. She looked into the mirror over the dresser and tried to imagine her husband standing beside her lathering his face with Perkin's English Shaving Soap.

Her imaginary husband applied a razor to the stubble on his chin and the foamy soap disappeared, all except for a little spot by his ear that he wiped away with the warm shaving towel she provided. But when the towel came down, instead of Felton Reeves, it was Burke Kerrigan's face she saw.

Eden groaned. She turned her back on the mirror, the same way she had turned her back on the gunslinger. Kerrigan was nothing but trouble. She was well away from him. Felton Reeves would make a fine husband and father. She had been willing to settle for that. At least it had been enough until that low-down snake Burke Kerrigan had come along and spoiled everything. Well, she wasn't going to spend her life wishing and wanting. She was going to be satisfied with what she had.

Mrs. Felton Reeves. Mrs. Eden Reeves. Mrs. Eden Devlin Reeves. That sounded a whole lot better than Mrs. Eden Devlin Kerrigan. Didn't it?

Chapter 16

Suspicion ain't proof.

✿ KERRIGAN WAS RACING AGAINST TIME. HE HAD FIVE days to prove that Felton Reeves wasn't deserving of Miss Devlin's hand in marriage. He hadn't slept at all, talking instead to dozens of people since he had left the schoolteacher's house last night. Everyone from cowboys and farmers to whores and drunks had all told him the same thing: Felton Reeves had been out of town frequently in the past nine months. Nobody knew where he went. Nobody knew what he did. And nobody seemed to care.

Bleary-eyed from lack of sleep, frustrated by the trusting attitude of everyone in town toward a sheriff who had been making clandestine trips to who knew where for who knew what purpose, Kerrigan headed for the jail. He would confront Felton with what he had found out and see what explanation the sheriff could give for his behavior. But first he wanted to talk to Deputy Joe Titman.

He found Deputy Joe asleep in one of the jail cells, the other being empty because disturbances usually occurred on Saturday night when the cowboys came to spend their wages at the Dog's Hind Leg. Kerrigan rattled the jail bars to waken the deputy. "Hey! Deputy! Wake up!"

Deputy Joe came awake with a gun in his hand, which shouldn't have surprised Kerrigan, but did. In their one and only meeting he had judged the deputy to be a meeker sort. The man in this jail cell had woken up wild-eyed and mean.

The deputy caught him staring and snarled, "What the hell's your problem, Kerrigan? The damn sun's barely over the sill."

"I need to talk to you."

"I go on duty at eight o'clock. Come back and see me then." The deputy stuck his gun back in the holster on the floor and pulled the tattered blanket back up over his shoulder.

An instant later Kerrigan had a fistful of Deputy Joe's long johns and the deputy was blinking into the bright sunlight streaming in the jailhouse window. "It's eight-oh-five and I'm in no mood for any back talk."

"I'm the law here in Sweetwater, Kerrigan, so you better let go of me right now."

The gunslinger released the deputy, and Joe stood there in his long johns and stocking feet looking foolish and feeling feisty. "I could arrest you for that."

"You sure you want to do that?"

The tone of Kerrigan's voice said he wouldn't make it easy. Deputy Joe wasn't as dumb as Kerrigan had thought. The deputy reached for his wool pants at the foot of the bare mattress and started pulling them on. He stuck his arms in his web suspenders and rolled his shoulders through to settle them comfortably, making sure the adjustable nickel buckles etched with the word DEPUTY were facing forward on his chest.

As he reached down for his gun belt Kerrigan said, "You won't be needing that. Leastaways, not until you've had your morning cup of coffee."

Kerrigan followed Deputy Joe to the sheriff's office at

the front of the jail, which was little more than an anteroom with a desk and chair, a low-back bench for visitors, a potbellied stove, and a spur-scarred leather armchair that was situated to get the most warmth from the stove. At the foot of the chair, where he had left them the previous night, stood the deputy's boots.

Deputy Joe stuck more wood on the fire to heat up the day-old coffee before he turned to confront Kerrigan. "Now, what do you wanta know?"

"Which days over the past nine months was Felton Reeves out of town?"

Deputy Joe's eyes narrowed. "What you wanta know that for?"

"Never mind. Can you give me the dates?"

"Sure. I got them marked on that calendar there on the wall, 'cause I was in charge while the sheriff was gone."

The calendar, put out by a gun manufacturer and featuring prints of western scenes, was hanging on a nail next to a bulletin board full of WANTED posters and public notices. Kerrigan took down the calendar and laid it on the desk. Quickly paging back from November to March, he saw there were at least three days, usually during the last week of each month, that Felton was out of town.

Kerrigan turned and confronted the deputy, who by now had poured himself a cup of coffee and was sitting in the armchair by the stove with his stocking feet aimed at the fire. "Where does the sheriff go when he leaves town?"

"I don't know."

Kerrigan took a step toward the deputy. "I don't believe you."

Deputy Joe's stocking feet hit the icy floor, and he held up his cup of hot coffee to stave off Kerrigan's advance. "It's the truth!"

"You mean to say it never came up in conversation?" Kerrigan said, his voice skeptical.

"He never volunteered and I never asked. Felton would disappear for a couple of days, and then he'd come back. Rode east outta town. That's all I know."

"You never thought that was a little strange?"

"Woulda been more odd to hang around town on his days off," Deputy Joe said. "Sure as shootin' something woulda happened and he'd have to go to work. 'Sides, he was owed the time. He worked it out with the town when they hired him. Weren't no business of mine nor nobody else if he chose to go somewhere else on his days off."

Kerrigan grimaced. That certainly made sense. But he couldn't shake the notion that there was some connection between Felton's disappearances and the disappearances of the stolen cattle. Or maybe that was jealousy doing his thinking.

Kerrigan felt the cold from the open door a moment before he heard Felton's voice.

"I hear you've been asking questions all over town about me. Why not come straight to the horse's mouth?"

"Morning, Felton."

"Joe, why don't you go have some breakfast at the Townhouse," Felton suggested, only it was pretty much an order the way he said it.

"You sure you won't need me?"

"If I do, I'll shout, and I'll trust you to come running."

The deputy stepped into his boots, grabbed his coat and hat, and after a surly look at Kerrigan, grabbed a shotgun from a rack across from the desk and headed out the door.

Kerrigan had to admire the way Felton had assuaged the deputy's ego. Deputy Joe was not somebody you would want to have to rely on in a pinch. Not that Felton was ever going to need much help. If it came down to it, Felton was damn near as fast on the draw as Kerrigan was.

"Have a seat." Felton got a cup and checked to see if Joe had made fresh coffee. He swore when he tasted it. "Damn that deputy. Useless as a four-card flush." He sat down in the chair next to the fire. "So what do you want to know, Kerrigan?"

Kerrigan leaned against the bare wall where the calendar had been. He gestured with his head toward the damning evidence on the desk. "I want to know where you've been going and what you've been doing the last weekend of every month since March."

"That's none of your business."

"I'm making it my business."

Felton crossed his ankle onto the opposite knee. "Let's talk about what's really got you upset, Kerrigan."

Kerrigan's eyes narrowed. "What's that?"

"Miss Eden Devlin."

Felton had jabbed a spur where it hurt, and Kerrigan worked a muscle in his jaw to keep from losing control.

Felton drew blood when he added, "You know, the woman who's engaged to be my wife."

Kerrigan bucked under the provocation, like a greenbroke bronc. "Not for long. Not if I can help it."

"Still determined to be the one to win the girl, Kerrigan? It's too late this time. The ring is on her finger." With a hard voice he said, "Eden Devlin is mine."

"She won't have a thing to do with you once she finds out you're the fangs in this poisonous band of rustlers."

Felton laughed. "You've got to be kidding." Another look at Kerrigan's face and he sobered. "You're not kidding."

"I'm about as serious as I've ever been in my life."

"You're wrong, Kerrigan. I'm the sheriff here in Sweetwater. I've done my best to keep law and order ever since I got this job."

"How come you never caught those rustlers, Felton? You're about the best tracker I know—besides myself. And you're smart."

When Felton started to object, Kerrigan said, "Not educated maybe, but smart. Too smart not to have known that Levander Early and his gang are rustling cattle here in the valley. So I have to ask myself whether maybe you found out who those rustlers were, and then you cut yourself in, and demanded a share in return for looking the other direction.

"And I have to ask myself whether maybe having a sheriff around when those rustled cattle got delivered to the railhead didn't give those transactions a ring of honesty they didn't deserve."

Felton was getting damned angry. "I never had no reason to suspect Levander Early. And I sure as hell didn't know about any gang. I tried finding the rustlers, but the trail always went cold. I sure as hell ain't been helping any rustlers load any stolen cattle onto any rail cars on my days off!"

Kerrigan shook his head in disgust. "I don't buy it. It's too convenient that you happened to be gone from town every month while cattle were disappearing left and right. I'm going to be watching you like a hawk from now on, Felton. And I'm going to get the evidence I need to put you behind bars for a long, long time."

"You're grasping at straws, Kerrigan. Admit it. It's been an interesting contest, but this time you lost and I won. Miss Devlin is one woman who didn't succumb to your charms."

"That's enough, Felton."

"You know what's really sad about all this, Kerrigan? Even when you got the girl you never let any of them get too close. Not one. Not ever. So I can't figure what you want with Miss Devlin—other than a chance to seduce her and then leave her behind like all the others."

Kerrigan had Felton slammed up against the jailhouse wall a moment later, his hands gripping Felton's throat. "It's not the same with her. She's different."

"Choking me to death isn't going to solve your problem, Kerrigan," Felton rasped. "Your feelings about the lady—about losing her to me—are blinding you to the truth. I'm telling you right now, you're looking in the wrong direction. I'm not bossing Levander's gang."

"We'll see." Kerrigan stepped away. A good knock-down-drag-out fight would have made him feel better, but Felton was right. It wouldn't solve anything. Miss Eden Devlin had burrowed under his skin where no woman had been since he had lost Elizabeth. He owed it to himself, and to Eden, to find out the truth about Felton Reeves.

Kerrigan stalked out the door, mounted his paint horse, and headed east toward the first town large enough to have a railhead.

Kerrigan ended up in Canyon Creek. It was easy, once he started asking questions, to find out that Felton usually spent his days in Canyon Creek at the Black Horse Saloon, and his nights in the arms of a whore named Darcie Morton.

Kerrigan was sitting in the shadows waiting for Darcie when she returned to her room.

At first Darcie thought it was Felton sitting there, and the biggest, widest smile ever split her face. Her hands flung out to envelop him. "Felton! I knew you—"

Then the figure rose, and she realized this man was too broad-shouldered to be Felton. She had lived long enough in the West to be scared. She let her hands drop so she could feel the derringer tucked in her garter. "Who are you? What are you doin' in my room?"

"My name is Burke Kerrigan."

"Felton told me about you. You two rode together down in Texas." She was searching for reasons he might have come, and feared the most likely. "It's Felton, ain't it? Somethin's happened to him."

"Yes. He's been—"

"He's been shot. Is he dead?"

"I came because—"

"I knew somethin' like this would happen. I warned him that sheriff job was a bad idea."

"If you'll listen a minute—"

"Not that Felton ain't a good man with a gun, but there's too many will back-shoot and . . ." Darcie's eyes blurred and the shadowy room begin to fade. Before she fainted, strong arms captured her and she was laid on the bed.

Kerrigan felt like a heartless bastard for letting the woman think Felton was dead. She was white as a sheet, and the spirit had gone out of her like a punctured balloon. Quiet tears streamed from her made-up eyes, leaving black streaks as they slid down the sides of her powdered face.

He had opened his mouth to explain that Felton wasn't dead—or at least hadn't been the last time he had seen him—when Darcie began talking again. When Kerrigan realized the information she was giving him was what he had come to hear, he sat down on the bed beside her and listened.

"I knew that job would kill him," Darcie said in a choked voice. "I told him to quit. He had plenty of money in the bank. He didn't need to be sheriff of some podunk town anymore." She wiped her runny nose with the sheet. "He was gettin' married, did you know that?"

"I heard."

"It near killed me when he told me. He picked out this respectable woman, a schoolteacher, who was gonna help him start a new life." She sobbed and covered her face with her hands, rocking back and forth. "He shoulda stayed with me. I wouldn't have asked for much. He wouldn't have needed all that money he had to have for her."

"Felton never had a dollar to bite on when I knew him," Kerrigan said, feeling bad that Darcie had to suffer like this, but needing desperately to know the truth. He would tell her the truth in a minute, and she would feel better then.

"He's been savin'. He's got near six thousand dollars in the Canyon Creek National Bank."

Kerrigan hissed in a breath of air. Felton hadn't put that much away on a sheriff's fifty-five dollars a month.

Darcie wiped her eyes with the sheet, getting most of the blacking off. She had pretty green eyes that looked even larger because of her long black lashes. She wouldn't really have needed the makeup, Kerrigan thought, to be attractive.

He could see now that behind the hard whore's costume was a vulnerable young woman. Lots of people hid behind masks. Darcie's just happened to be made of satin and feathers and powder and kohl.

Right now the young woman—and Kerrigan was startled by how young and pretty she appeared without all that makeup—looked totally bereft. He wondered where she had come from, and what had caused her to take up such a hard life. It was clear that she loved Felton, and that Felton had abandoned her—long before she had heard he was supposedly dead—for another woman. Felton had left her not for a prettier woman, but for one with respectability. Kerrigan thought how painful that must have been for Darcie Morton. Even knowing she was a whore, he felt sorry for her.

It dawned on him that to be so sensitive about her height and plainness, Eden must have experienced the same sort of rejection in the past. Seeing how devastated Darcie looked, how choked up she was and how heart-torn her reaction to losing Felton, Kerrigan felt a wrenching in his gut for what Eden must have endured.

He was certain Eden's painful relationship with her father was what had kept her from committing herself to a man all these years. But Kerrigan was beginning to think it hadn't helped matters for a woman as intelligent as Eden to know that had she been desirous of pursuing a relationship, she ran the danger of being rejected merely because of her physical attributes.

Darcie sighed and hiccuped. Kerrigan figured she was about as composed as she was going to get until he admitted Felton wasn't dead. He wanted this finished so he could get out of here, so he asked, "How'd Felton get all that money?"

"Gambling."

"What?"

"He sat downstairs sometimes three days in a row and never left the table. He had the luck of the devil, that man." A clear crystal tear streamed down her face. "It looks like his luck finally ran out."

"I don't believe it," Kerrigan said. It was too easy—and too obvious—an explanation for why Felton had spent so much time in Canyon Creek, and how he had accumulated so much money. Kerrigan grimaced. As much as he hated to admit it, the story smacked of the truth.

Felton wouldn't have been able to gamble for the same high stakes, and very likely empty the pockets of every cowboy around, in the small town where he was sheriff. Here in Canyon Creek there would be ranchers and businessmen who came to the tables. Felton was a smooth hand with a card. He had always been a winner whenever Kerrigan had seen him play.

But if Felton wasn't the leader of Levander's gang of cutthroats, who was?

Darcie pushed herself up on one hand. It had suddenly

dawned on her that she had told this man an awful lot about Felton. "Why are you so interested in Felton's money? You got some claim on it? He leave it to you in his will, or somethin'?"

Kerrigan rose and crossed to the window. "Felton isn't dead."

Furrows of confusion lined Darcie's youthful brow. "I don't understand."

He turned to face her. "I never said Felton was dead, you assumed it. I needed some information so I let you keep on thinking what you wanted."

"How could you be so cruel?" She was on her feet now and advancing toward him like an avenging angel.

"I had to know whether Felton was doing something dishonest here in Canyon Creek."

"Gamblin' ain't dishonest."

"You don't have to defend Felton. But I had to know the truth. There's an innocent woman involved and—"

"That's what this is all about—that woman, isn't it?"

It was an intuitive guess on Darcie's part, but so sure a shot that Kerrigan blurted, "What?"

"Felton told me about how you and him used to pick out a woman and see which of you could win her favor. How you'd both go to almost any lengths to be the winner. I told him I didn't think much of a man who'd play a game with someone's feelin's like that. Is that what this is all about, Mister Kerrigan? 'Cause if it is, I'm not going to let you get away with it. Felton deserves a chance to start over. And if you're playing games with the woman he chose, well, that's your hard luck."

"Felton isn't going to marry Eden Devlin," Kerrigan said with a hard edge to his voice.

"He ain't?" Darcie couldn't help the sound of hope in her voice.

"Nope. Because I'm going to marry her." Kerrigan

hadn't realized what he was going to say until the words were out. Now that he'd said them, he felt good. He felt wonderful. And he felt sick. Because there was a long trail to travel between deciding that he wanted with all his mind and heart and soul to marry Miss Devlin—and turning that decision into reality. Especially in light of the way he had bungled things when he had proposed to her the first time.

Kerrigan had to convince Eden that she wasn't too plain or too tall or too intelligent for him. He had to find the words to make her take a chance on a man who had lived his life with a gun in his hand. He had to make her see that it wasn't a matter of having a choice.

They were fated for one another.

He needed her the way he needed water to drink and air to breathe, the way he needed to see the sun rise in the morning, and the sight of the mountains after a long, hard ride across the plains.

"I'm damn well going to marry her myself," he repeated.

"Felton will have a word or two to say about that," Darcie murmured.

"Felton doesn't love her," he retorted.

"But you do," Darcie said in a voice so soft, it barely carried to Kerrigan.

"I do," Kerrigan admitted aloud for the first time.

"And I love Felton," Darcie said.

"They're announcing their engagement on Saturday."

"So soon?"

"It sounds like we have a serious problem, Miss Morton."

"All problems have solutions, Mister Kerrigan."

"If you have a suggestion, I'm willing to listen."

"As it happens, Mister Kerrigan, I do."

• • •

Levander Early arrived at the appointed rendezvous a little early because he wanted to make sure it wasn't a trap. Ever since Kerrigan had come asking all those questions he had been looking over his shoulder, afraid of what he would see. It was a feeling he didn't like. And one he didn't intend to put up with for much longer.

"Were you followed?"

Levander froze, realizing that somehow the Boss had come up behind him without him hearing a thing. He must be losing his touch. "I come the long way," he said. "And I doubled back a couple times to make sure no one was trailin' me."

"We have a problem."

"I know, Boss. But outside of killing Kerrigan, I don't see no solution."

"Then we'll have to kill Kerrigan."

"He don't kill easy." Levander's gelding fidgeted, reflecting his rider's fear.

"As it happens, Mister Early, I have a plan."

Chapter 17

Calico fever can be fatal to a man's bachelorhood.

✿

THERE MUST HAVE BEEN SEVENTY PEOPLE GATHERED in the town meetinghouse. It amazed everyone how simple it was for the ranchers and nesters to work out their problems when it came right down to it. Kerrigan was there to keep the conversation going. Felton was there to keep the peace. The wives were there, waiting to open their arms to their willing husbands. Persia Davis and Regina Westbrook were there, anxious to acknowledge the marriage of their firstborn children and to smooth the waters between the fathers-in-law when they learned that their children had become man and wife. And Miss Devlin was there to keep an eye on everything, her engagement ring secreted in her pocket until she and Felton made the announcement that they also had decided to tie the knot, at which point Felton would publicly place the ring on her finger.

All in all, there was a great deal of incentive to resolve matters, which led to a great deal of compromise.

The nesters agreed to pull down the fences around certain water holes that would be used by the ranchers, and the ranchers agreed to keep their cattle out of nester fields and away from certain other water holes, which would remain fenced. There was to be no more violence of any kind. All problems in the future were to be resolved by a committee composed of three ranchers, Oak Westbrook, Rusty Falkner, and Cyrus Wyatt, and three nesters, Big Ben Davis, Bevis Ives, and Ollie Carson, and arbitrated by an impartial party.

Someone volunteered Miss Devlin to be the arbiter, and although there was some reluctance to put a woman in such a powerful position, there was no one else who both sides could agree would be as impartial as the school-teacher. Despite her better judgment, Miss Devlin accepted the post.

Then the benches were moved to the sides of the room and the musicians began to practice a few chords. There was a feeling of such excitement, such merriment, that the room seemed brightened by more than lamplight. The chattering flowed in alternating waves of raucous laughter and clandestine whispers.

Men and women lined up on opposite sides of the room, as they had at the Halloween party. Only tonight there was an air of expectation, of excitation, of tempta-tion, hovering over male and female. Because tonight it had been agreed the teasing and taunting would end. Tonight the long-postponed desire of wives for husbands, and husbands for wives, would come to fruition.

It was the sudden silence that caught Miss Devlin's at-tention and sent her eyes, along with every other pair in the room, searching for its source. She found it when she spied Hadley and Bliss standing in position for a waltz in the center of the dance floor. Oak Westbrook stood at his son's shoulder. Big Ben Davis stood at his daughter's side. Everyone in the room held their collective breath, wonder-ing if the armistice was to end so soon.

Already feeling the weightiness of her role as arbiter,

Miss Devlin stepped forward toward the quartet on the floor. "Is there some problem here?" she asked.

"This is between my son and me, Miss Devlin. No need for you to get involved."

"I want his son to get his hands off my daughter," Big Ben said.

Hadley kept his arm around a trembling Bliss, whose big blue eyes never left Hadley's face.

"I'm going to dance with Bliss, Dad," Hadley said.

"Like hell you—"

"Mr. Westbrook," Miss Devlin admonished. "Please watch your language. Now, I think Hadley and Bliss have something they want to tell you."

Miss Devlin had thrown out a challenge, hoping Hadley was man enough to accept it. He didn't disappoint her. Hadley turned so that he and Bliss were squarely between both fathers. He held out Bliss's left hand, which lay across his palm, so both men could see the simple gold ring on her finger.

Miss Devlin saw the surprise in Oak's eyes when he recognized the ring on Bliss's finger, and the stunned moment when it dawned on Big Ben what the ring on his daughter's finger had to mean.

"You're married to him?" Big Ben asked his daughter. "Why you—"

Bliss put a hand on her father's chest. "We love each other, Pa," she said in a voice so sweet and pure that it couldn't help but move both of the older men. Bliss dropped her chin to her chest and with lowered eyes said, "And I'm going to have his baby."

There was a tender side to Ben Davis that Miss Devlin had never imagined. The big man gently lifted his daughter's chin and made her look him in the eye. "You were willing?"

Bliss's face flushed as she nodded once. But there was a

sexual ardor in her once innocent eyes that, as uncomfortable as it made him feel as a father, convinced Big Ben his daughter had gladly become a woman.

"You treat her right," Big Ben warned Hadley in a gruff voice. "Or I'll come after you."

"Thank you, Pa." Bliss hugged her father once, tight, then turned into Hadley's open arms.

Hadley folded Bliss into his embrace and met Big Ben's probing gaze. "She'll never want for anything as long as I can draw breath, sir."

Oak cleared his throat and said, "I guess congratulations are in order, son." He thrust out his hand to his son. "It looks like you've got yourself a lovely wife."

Hadley took his father's hand and shook it, blinking furiously to stem the tears of happiness and relief that were burning his eyes. "Thank you, Dad. We'll be needing a place to live. Do you suppose—"

"Of course you can stay at the house until you get a place of your own built."

Then Oak turned to Big Ben and said, "Looks like we're going to be related. How about having a drink with me to toast our grandchild?"

"That sounds like a mighty fine idea," Big Ben said with a toothy grin.

"While we're at it, maybe there's some way I could help you get that house of yours rebuilt. I have some extra lumber and paint and nails sitting around going to waste."

Big Ben stiffened. "I don't take charity."

Eden held her breath, alarmed at how quickly things had gone back to being tense.

"Who the hell said anything about charity?" Oak blustered. "It's not charity for family to help family. Besides, what's wrong with me wanting my grandbaby to have a roof over his head when he goes visiting his Grampa Ben?" he said with an outthrust jaw.

A rueful smile grew on Big Ben's face. "Well, when you put it that way . . . I'd be pleased to have your help. What say we go have that drink."

The two men left the dance floor patting each other on the back. Miss Devlin heaved a sigh of relief, and then one of envy as she watched Bliss and Hadley begin waltzing gracefully to the music that began playing.

She looked for Felton, needing the reassurance of his company. Bliss and Hadley were not the only couple tonight who were announcing a change in their relationship. Although she had changed her mind a dozen times during the past week about marrying Felton, she was determined, now that she saw Bliss and Hadley's happiness, to go through with it. She would make Felton happy. She would make herself happy. And they would both live happily ever after.

Her search of the room stopped abruptly when she saw Kerrigan. He was standing beside a stunningly beautiful woman with black hair and green eyes. She was wearing a sedate deep green polonaise dress that fit her like a glove through the bodice, revealing a slim, almost boyish, figure to the waist, and womanly hips supporting the layered pouf in back. Kerrigan was leaning down to talk privately with her, their heads close together.

Miss Devlin felt as jealous as a hound bitch with her first litter of pups. She gritted her teeth and forced herself to walk toward the couple, intending to meet this woman who was a stranger to her.

Before she got there, the woman left Kerrigan's side and walked away toward the refreshment table. "Who is she?" Miss Devlin asked Kerrigan, looking in the direction the woman had taken.

Kerrigan felt his heart begin to pound as Eden confronted him. "Who?"

"The woman I just saw you with."

"Jealous?"

"Of course not!" She didn't want to ask again, but couldn't help herself. "Who is she?"

"A friend. That's all."

"She's very beautiful."

"Yes, she is."

"Where did you meet her?"

"I don't want to talk about another woman, Eden. I want to talk about us."

"There is no us."

"But I want there to be."

His voice was soft and seductive, and she knew she had no business standing here listening to him. "Don't do this, Kerrigan. I'm announcing my engagement to Felton tonight."

"I want you to tell Felton you've changed your mind."

"Why?" She searched his face, looking for a reason for him to say these things, afraid to believe what she hoped she was seeing.

"I love you, Eden. I want to marry you myself."

Miss Devlin swayed, and he caught her before she lost her balance. Kerrigan hurried her into the small chamber that served both as the preacher's study and a place for the town council's executive meetings.

"Why are you doing this to me?" Miss Devlin cried. "You know how I feel. If I married you it would only be a matter of time before I buried you."

"I'm going to quit hiring out my gun," he said earnestly. "I'm going to buy a spread—there's land to be had around here—and settle down. I want you to settle down with me, Eden. I want you for my wife."

It was all too good to be true, like some fairy tale. But in fairy tales there was always a witch, or a goblin or a troll waiting to step in and spoil things. She desperately wanted to believe Kerrigan was telling the truth, but she was afraid to trust him. "What made you suddenly willing to give up your gun and settle down?"

"You. I love you, Eden. I need you in my life." He said it as if he meant it, and his dark eyes were tender and full of the feelings he spoke of. He smiled ruefully and added, "I realized you and I are fated to spend our lives together as man and wife."

"Is love enough, Kerrigan? Is even fate enough to make you settle down in one place? How do I know you won't pick up and leave the next time someone comes looking for a hired gun? How do I know—"

"You'll have to trust me when I say I'm not going anywhere. I've found my paradise with you, Eden. Nothing can tempt me to leave it."

She wanted to believe him. She wanted to be swept up in his arms and kissed until she was silly. She was afraid, but the past week of imagining a life with Felton Reeves had done its job. She wanted this chance for happiness. She wanted it bad enough to try and overcome her fear.

"I believe you mean what you say," she said soberly.

Kerrigan took Eden's hands in his, looked down into her serious gray eyes, and asked, "Will you marry me, Miss Devlin?"

Eden grasped his hands and answered, "Yes, Mister Kerrigan. I will."

He started to kiss her, but she put her fingers to his lips to stop him. "I have to find Felton and talk to him. He deserves to hear from me that I've changed my mind."

Kerrigan kissed her fingertips, since that was the most she would allow, unable to believe the burgeoning feeling of joy that expanded his chest and made him feel light as air. "I'll let you go. But as soon as you talk to Felton, come and find me. I'll be waiting for you."

·   ·   ·

Felton was busy having his own evening of shocks. When he had first seen the woman in the green dress walking toward him, he had thought she was beautiful, but he hadn't recognized her. A moment later, when Darcie Morton said, "Good evening, Felton," he had gone slack-jawed with astonishment.

"Is that you, Darcie?"

She had smiled demurely and said, "I'm a little different on the outside, but it's me on the inside. What do you think?" She held out her arms and twirled in a circle for him.

Felton swallowed hard. "I never imagined you dressed like a lady."

"Will I do?"

Felton looked around to see if Darcie was sticking out like a sore thumb, but except for being more beautiful than the other women, she fit in just fine. "You're beautiful, Darcie. You look real—"

"Respectable?"

He smiled. "Yeah. You do. Where'd you get the dress?"

She was looking down, straightening the pouf in back, so she didn't see his face when she answered, "Kerrigan helped me pick it out."

"Kerrigan?" The word came out sounding kind of strangled.

Blithely, Darcie said, "Wasn't that nice? And he helped me with my manners, too. Told me how I should act and what I should say. He brought me here tonight."

"Kerrigan brought you?" Felton had never felt the antagonism when Kerrigan treaded on his relationship with Eden Devlin that he felt right now. He had murder on his mind. "Did you . . . did he . . . have you let him . . ."

Felton couldn't even ask, he was so furious. He was afraid of what he would do if he got the wrong answer.

"I didn't think you'd mind if I came tonight, seein' as

how I'm with Kerrigan, and Miss Devlin would never have to know."

Felton felt that heaviness in his chest again. He was about to get engaged to a woman he didn't love, when standing right in front of him was a perfectly good woman he loved very much. And she looked perfectly respectable to him. Everyone who came west left his past behind him. Who was to say that he and Darcie couldn't start over together right here in Sweetwater?

He dragged Darcie over to a corner where they wouldn't be interrupted. "What would you say if I asked you to marry me, Darcie?"

"But you're announcin' your engagement to Miss Devlin tonight."

"Answer the question!"

She looked up at him with eyes that had seen too many disappointments, and replied. "I would marry you in a heartbeat, Felton Reeves. If you asked."

He heard from the tone of her voice that she wasn't expecting him to. Which was the goad that made him say, "Well, I'm asking. Will you marry me, Darcie Morton?"

She looked at him steadily, even though her heart was racing, and said as calmly as she could, "When you aren't promised to another woman, you come back and ask me again, and I'll give you my answer."

Felton started to kiss her, but she put her fingertips against his lips. "When you're free," she whispered. "Come and find me. I'll be waiting."

Miss Devlin had been looking everywhere for Felton, but without much success. She thought maybe he had stepped outside on the boardwalk in front of the meetinghouse for a breath of fresh air. It was cold outside, and all she saw was a couple of ranchers at the corner of the building sipping on a tin flask they were passing back and forth. She was on the verge of stepping back inside when she heard her name mentioned along with Kerrigan's. She flattened herself against the wall in the darkness to hear what they said.

"I say he done it," one rancher argued.

"Hell, nobody coulda seduced Miss Devlin," another replied, "not even that high-and-mighty gunslinger."

"He had more at stake than most. A thousand dollars is a pant-load of money. Seems he woulda found the right words to say to get her into bed."

"Probably took one look at her without her clothes and changed his mind," one of them said with a guffaw.

"Didn't have to take off her clothes," another one said with a drunken giggle. "Only had to take a second look at her face."

"Still, hirin' a man like him to seduce a woman like Miss Devlin, that ain't something I'd want to have to do again."

There was a moment of sobering silence while they reflected on the desperation that had brought them to offer the gunslinger money to seduce Miss Devlin.

"I got me a wife inside," one said, "who ain't let me across the bedroom threshold for way too long. I think I'm gonna go get her and head on home."

"Me, too."

"Missed that goldang woman more than I ever thought I would," a third said.

Miss Devlin slid farther into the darkness as they passed by her on the way inside. She pressed herself flat against the meetinghouse wall. She was cold. And she felt a sense of impending disaster, as though an avalanche were sliding toward her, gathering force and speed. In her mind she was running as fast as she could to escape it, but however fast she ran, it wasn't fast enough. The revelations of the past few moments hit her hard and left her feeling overwhelmed and suffocated by the crushing weight of disillusionment.

Miss Devlin bolted back through the lighted door of the meetinghouse, frantically searching for a way to escape her devastating feelings. She saw Kerrigan with a smile on his face walking toward her from one direction. She turned away from him only to encounter Felton walking purposefully toward her from the other direction. She felt as if she was going to perish from the pain if she didn't do something quickly. She turned away from both of them and headed for the platform where the musicians were playing.

Her voice was strident when she spoke. "May I have your attention!" Confused, the musicians stopped playing. "Please, I need quiet!" Concerned, interested, the dancers on the floor turned to look at her. She felt every eye in the room on her.

Kerrigan was still coming toward her.

Felton was coming too.

"I have an announcement to make," she said.

Kerrigan stopped.

Felton kept coming, and stepped up onto the platform beside her. But as he grasped her arm she took a deep breath and said, "There's going to be another marriage in Sweetwater. Felton Reeves and I want to take this opportunity to announce our engagement."

There was a stunned silence and then a general hubbub of excited laughter and genuine pleasure that the spinster schoolteacher was going to be married at last.

All Miss Devlin saw was Kerrigan's pale cheeks, and the hurt and anger of her betrayal in his dark eyes.

Only she was the one who had been betrayed! Struggling awkwardly, she finally got the ring out of her pocket.

"Here, Felton. Would you like to put the ring on my finger now to make it official?"

Felton was trapped. He took one quick look and saw that all the blood had drained from Darcie's face. There was nothing he could do right now to fix things without humiliating both Miss Devlin and himself. "Certainly."

He had trouble getting the ring on her finger because both her hands and his were shaking.

"A kiss!" someone shouted from the crowd. "Give her a kiss."

The crowd wasn't going to leave them alone, so Felton kissed her on the cheek.

"Not like that. Give her a real kiss!" someone yelled.

The crowd started clapping, and shouting and whistling and stomping, until neither Felton nor Miss Devlin had a choice. Felton took her in his arms, and feeling wounded and sick at heart, he placed his lips on Miss Devlin's and gave her a kiss that pleased the crowd.

After that Miss Devlin was surrounded by couples offering their best wishes and help for planning the wedding.

"Why, you sly miss," Regina said. "Keeping us out of our husbands' bedrooms, and all the while you were being courted by the sheriff!"

Miss Devlin heard everything, listened to nothing. She was only aware of Kerrigan standing on the fringes, his anger a palpable thing. She kept her chin up and refused to let him see her humiliation at what she had heard outside on the boardwalk. He had been *paid* to seduce her. How could she have believed his lies? Their entire relationship had been dishonest. A man who could agree to do something as despicable as seduce an innocent woman was incapable of love.

At the first opportunity, Felton took Miss Devlin aside and said, "I need to speak with you alone."

"Can't it wait, Felton?"

He glanced at Darcie's devastated expression and said, "No. This can't wait. Let's get out of here."

"All right. Let's go."

Felton walked her home in silence. He came inside, but he wouldn't take off his coat. "This won't take long," he said, sitting on the edge of the sofa.

Miss Devlin took off her coat and settled herself on the sofa beside him, but as soon as she did he popped up and moved over to sit in the reception chair across from her. "What is it, Felton?"

"I've . . . uh . . . changed my mind."

"About what?"

"Getting married."

"Oh."

"That is, I ain't—haven't—changed my mind about getting married. I decided I'd rather marry somebody else," he rushed to say.

"Then why in the world did you let me announce our engagement tonight?" she demanded.

Felton let his anger show for the first time. "God-dammit, woman, you never gave me a chance to stop you! I couldn't get a word in edgewise. I should have been the one to speak, and if you'd have waited for me, I'd have told you I changed my mind before things got out of hand like they did."

"Oh."

Felton was feeling bad, but not bad enough to back off from his stand. "I'm real sorry, Miss Devlin. We can wait a little while if you like, and you can say you changed your mind—"

"The girl you want to marry . . . do I know her?"

"She ain't—isn't—from Sweetwater."

"Is she pretty?"

"Well, sure," he said, her apparently calm acceptance of

his pronouncement making this discussion easier than he had dared to hope and free of the stomach-wrenching tears he had been dreading.

"Is she tall?"

He gestured with a flat hand. "Comes about shoulder high on me."

"Is she smart?"

He grinned, in relief more than anything else that Miss Devlin was being such a good sport about all this, and showing such an interest in Darcie. "Not hardly. But she's real nice, and she loves me and . . . I love her."

"What's her name?"

"Darcie Morton."

Miss Devlin pictured the stunning woman with the black hair and green eyes that Kerrigan had introduced to her. She found a smile somewhere and pasted it on her face. "I'm happy for you, Felton. I hope you'll both be happy. When is the wedding?"

"I ain't exactly proposed to Darcie yet. I wanted to settle things between us first before I—"

"Well, we've settled things now, so maybe you should go find her."

Felton recalled the stunned look on Darcie's face at Miss Devlin's announcement of their engagement. "Yeah, I'd sure better at that."

"Oh. Wait. You'd better take your ring back now."

"Are you sure? I can—"

"Take it now." She tugged the ring off and handed it to him.

Felton left Miss Devlin's parlor with all the relief and excitement of a kid breaking free at the end of the school term.

When Felton was gone, Miss Devlin walked into her bedroom and opened the Wish Box on her dresser. Staring back at her were the teething ring and the baby ribbon and the barber snips and the badger shaving brush—and the silver baby spoon. She gritted her teeth to still the quiver in her chin. Then she picked up the box and threw it as hard as she could against the bedroom wall.

Eden didn't know how long she had been sitting in the dark when she heard the knock on the front door. She ignored it, thinking that whoever it was would go away. But the knocking became more insistent, a pounding that threatened to drive her mad. She opened the front door ready to give whoever was standing there a good piece of her mind.

It was Deputy Joe.

"You gotta come quick," he said in a breathless voice. "There's been a gunfight twixt Kerrigan and the sheriff. Kerrigan's shot bad, Miss Devlin. He's asking for you!"

Chapter 18

*If you'd like to know a man,
find out what makes him mad.*

FELTON HAD FLED MISS DEVLIN'S HOUSE IN SEARCH of Darcie Morton, afraid she would leave town before he had a chance to explain what had happened. When the sheriff stepped through the door of the town meeting-house, he found much the same merriment under way as when he had left. The celebration might have even been a little louder, the smiles a little broader.

Regina and Oak were dancing, as were Bevis and Mabel Ives, and Cyrus and Lynette Wyatt. Persia and Big Ben were sitting on a bench holding hands, and next to them were Ollie and Amity Carson. As usual, Amity had a baby at her breast, and if rumor was correct, she was already pregnant with the next. Rusty and Claire Falkner were standing at the refreshment table enjoying a glass of punch. Finally, he spied the woman he had been scanning that sea of faces to find.

Felton experienced a surge of pleasure when he saw the beatific smile on Darcie's face. As the crowd shuffled he realized three things at once: Darcie was dancing in another man's arms; the beatific smile on her face was directed at that other man; and the man embracing her was none other than his arch rival, Burke Kerrigan.

Never in his life had Felton known such rage. It enveloped him in a fiery cloud from head to toe. A fierce, animalistic urge to protect what was his propelled him toward Kerrigan. If he had been thinking rationally, he would have noticed that neither Darcie nor Kerrigan was smiling with more than their mouths, that their eyes were distressed, and that their steps were leaden.

But fear that he had lost Darcie to another man, and fury that Kerrigan would dare lay claim to his woman, sent the sheriff's fist ahead of him to greet the unsuspecting gunslinger.

Some instinctual response to a flicker of movement kept Kerrigan from taking Felton's blow square on the chin, but even a glancing contact with the sheriff's powerful fist knocked Kerrigan sideways. The gunslinger didn't stop to ask why the sheriff had hit him. He had his own reasons for hitting back. Felton Reeves had stolen Kerrigan's woman right out of his arms. A film of red glazed Kerrigan's eyes and a savage frenzy possessed him, sending him into battle against his foe.

They struck at each other like two berserker barbarians fist and foot, elbow and knee, tooth and claw. A noisy circle of anxious observers formed around them, but no one dared to interfere. Both combatants were wearing guns, and who was to say whether they might not draw on someone who got in the way?

Felton got in a good right to the eye, but Kerrigan countered with a left that nearly broke Felton's nose. The two men grappled, slugging at each other even though they were too close to get much strength into the blows. Both of them had been in fights without rules before, but neither had been so enraged during the battle. It heightened sensations, so that everything seemed to happen in slow motion.

Kerrigan followed his fist as it drove into Felton's gut, feeling the sheriff's washboard belly give way and finally resist only as Felton buckled in half. Felton watched his knuckles slam into Kerrigan's face, the flesh tearing, blood spurting, as his knuckles reached bone. They pummeled and punched. They tripped and rolled on the floor and lurched to their feet again. Their rage kept them from realizing how tired they were or how much damage they were doing to each other.

They were both bloodied and battered, wrestling in the sawdust on the floor, when the deafening roar of a gunshot brought the fight to an abrupt halt. They clung to each other for support as they staggered to their feet. The crowd cleared a space so the sheriff and the gunslinger could see Darcie Morton standing by the door to the meetinghouse with a smoking gun in her hand.

"You're both out of your minds," she said in a sobbing breath. "If you had a lick of sense you'd realize that killing each other isn't going to change anythin'. I'm going back to Canyon Creek where I belong, Felton. Don't you dare come after me."

She dropped the derringer and marched out of the room, eyes blazing, chin up, shoulders squared.

Felton had never felt prouder of anyone in his life. "That's some woman," he said, his arm wrapped around what he thought might be a cracked rib.

Kerrigan swiped the blood off his mouth with his sleeve. "So why did you go through with that engagement to Eden tonight?" he snarled.

"I didn't! I mean, I did, but—" Felton looked around and saw they still had an audience. "The fight's over. Go on about your business."

As the crowd began dispersing Felton said, "Let's go where we can talk in private."

It was slow going, as beat up as they were. Felton

draped his coat over his shoulders rather than trying to get into it. A few minutes later they were settled at a table at the Dog's Hind Leg, each with a whiskey glass that had been filled and emptied and then filled again.

"That stings," Kerrigan said as he licked whiskey off a cut on his lip. "All right, Felton, we're alone. What do you have to say?"

Felton dabbed at a cut over his eye with his bandanna. "You're the one has some explaining to do."

"I wasn't the one started swinging for no good reason," Kerrigan retorted.

Felton frowned, then winced as his battered face protested the movement. "I saw you dancing with Darcie and I guess I went a little crazy."

Kerrigan snorted. "If you wanted Darcie, why in hell did you announce your engagement to Eden tonight?"

"Wasn't me did the announcing, if you'll recall," Felton said heatedly. "I've been having second thoughts about marrying Miss Devlin all along, but I've kept them to myself. When I saw Darcie tonight . . . guess I knew then I wanted to spend my life with her and not the schoolteacher.

"I never got a chance to say anything to Miss Devlin before it was too late. I couldn't have stopped her with a forty-foot rope and a snubbin' post. She marched onto that platform and started jabbering . . . and suddenly we were engaged."

Kerrigan rolled his whiskey glass in his hands. "So what do we do now?"

Two spots of color rose in Felton's cheeks. "To tell you the truth, after I took Miss Devlin home I told her that I couldn't go through with it, that I plan to marry Darcie Morton. I told her she could wait awhile and then tell everybody she changed her mind about our engagement."

"What did she say to that?"

Felton pulled a ring out of his pocket. "She gave me the ring back and told me I'd better go find Darcie and explain things to her. Which I did, which is why when I saw you with Darcie, I guess I lost my head."

"What a mess," Kerrigan muttered.

Poor Eden, he thought. The whole town would know she wasn't the one who had changed her mind, because everybody knew she had been waiting her whole life for a man like Felton Reeves to come along. She would be so humiliated, she would probably leave Sweetwater and start wandering like some tumbleweed again. And if she did, it would be all his fault for waiting so long to tell her he loved her.

What Kerrigan didn't understand was what had possessed Eden to fly off the handle like that. Something, some catastrophe, had obviously occurred at the dance to change her mind about marrying him. But what?

"I don't know what got into her," he muttered. "One minute she agreed to marry me and headed off to find you and tell you she'd changed her mind. The next . . ."

"I saw her come in from outside looking white as a ghost and jumpy as a bit up old bull at fly time," Felton said. "Quicker'n that"—Felton started to snap his fingers but gave it up when he realized it was going to hurt—"she was up there announcing our engagement."

Kerrigan frowned. "Outside? What was outside?"

"Nothing much. Just a bunch of ranchers celebrating by passing around a flask of whiskey."

Eden would have gone outside looking for Felton . . . and found ranchers . . . with tongues loosened by all that whiskey . . . discussing certain things that were best left unsaid. It didn't take much imagination to figure out what Eden must have heard outside that had left her looking like she'd found a rattler in her bedroll.

"She heard I was being paid to seduce her," Kerrigan murmured, half to himself.

"What?"

"Nothing," Kerrigan said, his lips in a flat, unhappy line. "I think maybe we both better go do some talking with our women."

"I just hope the hell Darcie will give me a chance to explain."

"Yeah. I know what you mean. You better get going. Darcie's got a room at the Townhouse. She's probably there packing now."

"Are you going to talk to Miss Devlin tonight?"

"I don't know," Kerrigan said. "If she's hurting the way I think she is, it's going to take a lot more than talk to convince her to marry me."

"You're going to marry Miss Devlin?" Felton asked in a shocked voice.

"Yeah. What's so surprising about that?"

Felton grinned, and then moaned when his scabbed lip split again. "If you don't know, I ain't going to tell you. Don't spend too much time thinking. Just remember a woman appreciates the *doing* as much as the *saying.*"

"Where'd you learn that?" Kerrigan asked.

"From a woman with eyes as soft and green as new-grown grass, more guts than you could hang on a fence, and a heart so full of caring, we're going to need a wheelbarrow to get it down the aisle the day I make her my wife."

It was snowing when Felton left the saloon, but the wind was blowing so hard, the flakes came at him sideways. It looked like the blizzard that had been threatening was finally going to make its appearance. The snow had already drifted knee-high against the boardwalk, and the wind swept away his footprints almost as soon as he made them.

He was glad he didn't have to be on duty tonight. Deputy Joe could take care of things for a change while he settled his personal life.

Darcie hadn't checked out of the Townhouse yet. He found out her room number and headed up the stairs. He would have taken them two at a time, but when he tried it, his ribs protested and he was forced to slow down. He checked his appearance when he arrived at her door, but there wasn't much he could do without completely changing his clothes. His shirt was torn and bloody, and from the way his face felt he could only imagine what it looked like. Actually, he was hoping his appearance might wring a little sympathy out of her.

He started to knock on the door and realized his knuckles were bruised pretty badly. He turned his fist sideways and pounded once.

"Who's there?"

"It's me, Darcie. Can I come in?"

"Go away, Felton."

"It's important, Darcie. I have to talk to you."

"You got a woman now, Felton. Go talk to her."

"I ain't engaged to Miss Devlin no more, Darcie. You gotta—"

The door was flung open and Darcie stood there, her eyes wide. "What did you say?"

Felton grinned, and didn't even feel his split lip. "I said I ain't—I'm not—engaged no more. I'm a free man. Free to marry the woman I love."

A door opened down the hall and someone peered out. Felton glared and the door shut. "Can I come inside, Darcie?"

"All right." She stepped back to let him in.

They stood and stared at each other in the dimness of the cut-glass lamp beside the bed and the flickering light from the fireplace.

"You look like you had the mean stomped out of you," Darcie said with a shake of her head.

"Kerrigan don't look much better."

"Knowin' that oughta make your bruises hurt less," she said tartly. Darcie's heart was in her throat when she asked, "You wasn't—weren't—lyin' to me just now, were you, Felton? About you and Miss Devlin, I mean?"

"No. The engagement's off. She's going to maybe wait awhile to tell everyone, so's to avoid talk. But I got the ring back tonight." Felton dug in his jeans and found the tiny diamond set in the thick gold band. He held it out reverently in the palm of his hand. "Will you let me put this ring on your finger, Darcie?"

Darcie picked up the ring and held it out to the lamp, turning it this way and that so she could see it sparkle. "Oooooh, Felton. Ooooooh. It's so beautiful!"

Felton could see a big difference between Darcie's reaction to the ring and Miss Devlin's. Darcie was trembling, she was so excited, and the smile on her face could have lit up a dark night.

His heart pounding in his chest, he took the ring from her and slipped it on her finger.

It was too big. The ring had clearly been made for a larger woman, and Darcie had to hold her fingers together to keep the band from sliding off.

"We can get the size changed—" Felton said desperately.

Darcie looked up at him so adoringly that her chest might as well have been flayed open, her heart was so bare to him.

"Now that you put this ring on my finger, Felton Reeves, I ain't—I'm not—*never* gonna take it off. That is, till it's time to add a weddin' band. So you tell that jeweler man he's only got one day to get this ring fittin' right."

Felton knew right then that he had chosen the right

wife. A woman like Darcie was a rare find, and he was lucky he hadn't let his pride and his stubbornness cheat him out of the joy of living with her the rest of his life.

He wanted to make love with her. Right now. This minute. Only she was dressed like a "decent" woman. Felton had no experience with the species. The thought of helping Darcie remove her high-necked prim-and-proper dress made his skin get up and crawl all over him.

Darcie was having a different problem. She wanted Felton as much now as she ever had in her life, but he had been hurt bad in the fight. She saw in his reluctance to touch her a fear that he would end up hurting even more than he already did. As physical as their lovemaking always was, it was bound to be painful for him.

They stood there, more awkward than they had ever been with each other, at the one moment when they both wanted to express their love in the most complete way possible.

"Uh . . . Darcie . . ."

"Yes, Felton."

"Do you think you could get that dress off by yourself?"

"Yes."

"Would you take it off?"

"Right here? Right now?"

Felton swallowed hard. It would be like watching a Sunday-school teacher undress. There was something scandalous about it. And downright titillating. "Yeah. Take it off right here. Now."

Darcie took her time.

Felton's pupils dilated and his nostrils distended as he watched her slowly peel off one layer after another. First the green polonaise overdress with its twelve buttons down the front, followed by the slightly darker underskirt. The white petticoats came next, one after another, six in all. He heaved a sigh of relief when her corset came off.

She was left wearing a dainty white chemise and pantalettes trimmed in pretty pink ribbons. Felton grinned
when he noticed her prim white stockings were held up
with shocking red garters.

Darcie raised her hands to let down her hair.

"Let me do it," Felton said in a husky voice.

She stood stock-still as he took several hesitant steps
toward her. She could feel the tension in his body as his
hands reached for the sedate bun at her nape. He fumbled
with the pins and dropped several. He started to reach for
them, but she smiled and caught him before he could
stoop down. "It doesn't matter."

Felton was mesmerized by the soft, silky feel of her hair
in his hands. "Where are all the curls?"

"I left it straight after I washed it."

"I never knew it was so long." He took two handfuls of
her thick raven tresses and brought one over each shoulder
so they made a seductive shawl for her breasts. Then he
reached for the halter straps on her chemise and lowered
them. He scattered kisses across her collarbone and
worked his way down toward her breasts, finally brushing
her hair aside as he took the tip of one breast in his mouth.

Darcie's head fell back and she arched toward Felton
with a moan. She grabbed his shoulders and held on as he
took her soaring to heights that seemed higher because of
the strangeness of the place, and the clothing, and the spe-
cialness of the moment.

Felton lavished the other breast with equal praise and
then kissed his way back up to Darcie's mouth. "I love
you, Darcie," he said. "I want us to make a baby."

Darcie felt the tears spring to her eyes, and there was
nothing she could do about it.

"What's wrong, sweetheart? You don't want a baby?"

"Oh, Felton, I do! I want your baby. It's just I never
thought . . . I never hoped . . ." She smiled a beaming, silly

smile through all her tears. "I will make you the *best* wife, Felton. You'll never be sorry—"

He took her head between his hands and looked deep into her green eyes. "You don't have to convince me, Darcie. I'm yours. Forever. And ever."

"Oh Felton."

They didn't say much for the next couple of hours, just *oooohs* and *aaaaahs,* moans of ecstasy, and groans of pleasure, and once or twice pain when Darcie accidentally elbowed Felton in his bruised ribs. The loving was not quite as vigorous as it might have been if Felton hadn't spent the evening tangling with Kerrigan, but it was no less moving. Darcie stayed on top, so she could do most of the work, but that allowed Felton to touch her breasts and body more freely with his hands and mouth. When they had both climaxed and thought they were spent, Darcie happened to kiss Felton's navel and it started all over again.

Later, when they were lying naked on the mattress they had dragged from the bed to the floor in front of the fire, with Felton's head in Darcie's lap, he had simply turned and kissed her thigh, and the chain of kisses had taken him to dewy pastures that Darcie was more than willing to have him explore.

At last sated, they lay exhausted in front of the fire as it burned low with golden embers.

"Felton?"

"Hmmmm?"

"About that baby . . ."

"Hmmmm."

"How does the spring sound?"

"Hmmmm?"

"Late April or early May."

"That sounds fine."

Darcie felt a little disappointed at Felton's reaction to her news that the baby he had wanted was already on the way.

Suddenly Felton bolted upright. "April or May? That means . . . Darcie! Are you—? Is there—?"

Darcie grinned. "Yes."

Felton's gaze lowered to her naked belly. It didn't look that much different. It was just a little rounded. He stretched his hand out and she took it and laid it on her belly.

"Our son or daughter is already growing inside me, Felton. And now he's going to have a mother and a father and a home. . . . It's a dream come true for me. I want this baby to have everythin' I never had, Felton. A chance for a good life . . . a decent life."

Darcie leaned over and kissed away the tear on Felton's cheek. "I love you, Felton Reeves."

Felton swallowed over the lump in his throat. "We're seeing the preacher in Canyon Creek tomorrow."

"All right, Felton, if you say so."

"I love you, Darcie."

She brushed the hair back from his forehead as she cradled him in her arms. "I know, Felton."

They fell asleep in front of the fire, curled together with their child between them, ready for the wonderful new life that would begin on the morrow.

Kerrigan sat in the saloon for a long time after Felton left. He didn't drink, he just stared at the empty glass and thought, and worried, and thought some more.

What could he say to persuade Eden Devlin that his agreement with the Association wasn't the reason he had seduced her? It certainly hadn't been on his mind when he had finally held her in his arms. If she asked him what he *was* thinking about, he wasn't sure he had an answer. He could say he had wanted her from the first moment he had laid eyes on her, but somehow that story didn't sound very convincing, even to him. Except it was true.

He had been denying his feelings to himself, but they were there, had been there, from the beginning. He hadn't expected to desire her. He hadn't wanted to desire her. But he had. He had no explanation for why she had inspired such feelings in him, but the more time he had spent with her, the more he had been drawn to her. Until it was no longer a question of whether he would seduce her, but only of when.

He was in awe of the love he felt for her.

It had come as an unwelcome surprise. A shocking revelation. A horrendous calamity. But he was definitely in love with Eden Devlin. And while he ached for her touch, he was in agony for her devotion. He had taken the one. She had once freely given the other.

And now she never wanted to see him again.

"We're closin' the bar now, Mr. Kerrigan. Do you want some help gettin' to your room?"

"I can get there fine." Kerrigan tried getting to his feet, but between the first two whiskeys he had drunk, and the beating he had taken in the fight with Felton, it was rough going.

"Sure you don't want some help?" the barkeep asked.

"I'm sure." Kerrigan grunted with pain as he slipped into Sundance's buckskin coat. He gasped as he straightened, pulling a bruised muscle. He managed, one step at a time, to cross the room. The saloon door had been pulled closed sometime earlier in the evening and he was astonished at the blizzard that he realized now had been raging outside unbeknownst to him. He had to hang on to his hat to keep from losing it, and squint his eyes against the stinging snowflakes, as the wind shoved him across the street to the Townhouse Hotel.

It was agony getting up the stairs to his room, and he was so tired, he didn't even bother to light the lamp when he got there. He slipped his coat off and let it drop on the floor, then unbuckled his gun belt and felt in the dark for the bedstead and hung it there. He sat down on the edge of the bed, and it was all he could do to cross his legs to pull off his boots.

He let out another groan and a moan or two as he stripped to his long johns and pulled down the covers, and then he was tucked inside. The pillow was soft, and the bed, too, even though both were frigid with the cold. He knew he ought to get up and light a fire, but he was too damn tired, feeling hurt in body and spirit. There were plenty of blankets. He wouldn't freeze.

He couldn't think anymore tonight. Tomorrow the right words would come to him, and he would go see Eden and straighten everything out. He let his mind drift, and in a short while all was oblivion.

He never noticed the small piece of folded paper on the floor inside the door. It lay there unread all night. But it was the first thing he saw when he opened his eyes the next morning.

Chapter 19

Hard-boiled eggs tend to be yellow inside.

About the time Kerrigan and Felton were sitting down together at the Dog's Hind Leg, Miss Devlin was stepping up into the box frame of the spring wagon Deputy Joe had brought, supposedly to take her back to town. The instant she sat down on the padded, button-tufted seat, he slapped the reins and the two mules set off at a sedate trot. Miss Devlin grabbed the metal frame of the seat and braced her feet against the bottom board in front, wishing the deputy's urgency matched her own.

It was windy and cold, and it was snowing steadily enough that Eden suspected there would be a good covering of the white stuff on the ground by morning. But the road itself still showed numerous patches of brown, since most of the snow dashed across its flatness until it came up against some bush or a rise in the terrain where it caught and began to form drifts.

Deputy Joe kept the mules moving at a steady jog until they reached the point where the trail split. To Miss Devlin's surprise, instead of taking the fork toward town, he took the one heading the opposite direction.

"Where are we going?" she demanded. "I thought you said Mr. Kerrigan had been shot."

"He will be," Deputy Joe retorted with a vicious grin. "Just as soon as he gets the note I sent him and comes looking for you."

Before Miss Devlin could jump from the wagon, or grab the deputy, or do any one of a dozen other things to get free, the deputy shouted, "Hiyahh! Giddyap!" and lashed the mules into a run.

Miss Devlin clung to the careening wagon for dear life. The only way she could have escaped would have been to try and wrest the reins from the wiry deputy, or jump from the lurching wagon. Both of those options were sure to result in serious injury or death. Miss Devlin wasn't a foolish woman, and before she killed herself she wanted some explanation for what was going on.

"Where are you taking me?" she shouted over the rackety noise of the wagon.

"Somewheres you can't be found when Kerrigan comes looking for you."

"Then Kerrigan hasn't been shot?"

"Not hardly," he said with a derisive snort.

Miss Devlin felt a flood of joyful relief that was quickly dammed when she realized she must be part of another plot to ambush the gunslinger. Which made no sense to her. "Why do you want to kill Mr. Kerrigan?"

"That ain't none of your never mind. Just keep your mouth shut and your hands to yourself and you won't get hurt."

It didn't take much deduction on Miss Devlin's part to realize that the "you won't get hurt" part was going to last only so long as keeping her alive was useful to the deputy.

They drove for another twenty minutes at a breakneck pace. By then, the snow that had been falling when Miss Devlin first got into the spring wagon had turned as malevolent as the rest of the evening. The farther from town they got, the worse the weather became. It was as though the snow recognized their frenzy and conspired to add to it. The temperature got colder, so Miss Devlin's toes and fingers felt frozen. The wind began to whip, and enveloped them in stinging snowflake tornadoes. It soon became apparent they were in for a full-fledged blizzard.

It was appalling how fast the snow suddenly began to accumulate. It quickly covered the road and began layering drifts that made it difficult for the mules to find footing. The deputy was forced to slow the mules down to a walk or take the chance of driving off the road. A short while later, the deputy left the road and headed off toward no apparent destination.

"Do you know where you're going?" Eden asked.

"Sweetwater Canyon."

"There's no way to get into Sweetwater Canyon from this direction," Miss Devlin protested.

The deputy smiled. "That's what everybody thinks. Ain't so. There's a secret way in, leads right to the floor of the canyon. Found it myself, following a deer."

"How far is it? Are we close?"

"Not close enough," the deputy muttered, squinting at a landscape that was fast disappearing under the drifting snow.

They were going slow enough now that Miss Devlin could easily have escaped the deputy. But it would have been foolhardy to set herself afoot in the middle of nowhere at the height of what could only be labeled a blizzard.

What also became clear to her was that there was no way anyone was going to come hunting for her when it was nigh impossible to see your hand in front of your face. Just as Miss Devlin began to think she and Deputy Joe would likely be found frozen to death when the storm was over, she saw a glimmer in the distance.

"Look! Is that where we're going?"

Deputy Joe just grunted, but he turned the mules in the direction of the distant light.

Miss Devlin was the first one down when Deputy Joe pulled up in front of a boarded-up line shack. Leaving him to take care of the mules, she walked up to the door of the dilapidated hovel and knocked. When the door opened she said, "May I come in, please?"

In a million years Miss Devlin couldn't have imagined what she saw when she entered the shack. Calling it a pigsty would have been generous. Calling it a shambles was calling it close. A cowshed, a chicken coop, even a cattery, would have been cleaner. Incredibly, in the corner of the room, was a wood box containing a calico cat and a litter of tiny kittens.

There were five men crowded in a room that might have comfortably held four. She removed her coat and shook off the snow before handing it to the closest man.

In a voice she would have used on a new first-grader, Miss Devlin said, "I am Miss Devlin, the schoolteacher in Sweetwater. Would you all like to introduce yourselves?"

"Name's Stick," said the one holding her coat in his hand.

"Do you have a peg where you could hang that up to dry, Stick?" she asked.

Stick stared a moment longer at her before he replied, "Yes'm."

Miss Devlin stepped up to the two men who were sitting at the rickety wooden table in the center of the room. "And who might you be?"

"I'm Doanie."

"I'm Hogg."

"A gentleman always stands in the presence of a lady," Miss Devlin admonished.

Doanie and Hogg lurched to their feet.

"And hats are never worn indoors," she instructed.

Doanie and Hogg quickly yanked their battered felt hats off and held them in front of them like neck-wrung chickens.

"What's your name?" Miss Devlin said as she approached the largest, most ferocious-looking of the bunch, who was standing before the potbellied stove holding one of the kittens.

Bud blushed. "B-b-b-bud."

Miss Devlin put out her hand. "I'm pleased to meet you, Bud."

Bud set the kitten gently in the box with the others and then stuck out a meaty paw and carefully shook Miss Devlin's hand.

Miss Devlin turned to survey what had become, in a matter of moments, her domain, and discovered the scowling face of the fifth man, who was leaning against the wall.

"I don't believe we've met," she said, taking a step in his direction.

"We ain't goin' to, neither," Levander snarled.

"His name's Levander. Levander Early," Stick volunteered.

Levander spit tobacco juice on the dirt floor an inch in front of Miss Devlin's shoe. "You got them idjits all lickin' outta your hand, but I ain't as dumb as them, and you ain't gonna hog-tie me with your goody-goody manners. Now you set yourself down over there and keep outta my way!"

Miss Devlin looked in the direction Levander had pointed and saw nothing remotely resembling a chair. "I'm afraid I don't see—"

Levander grabbed Miss Devlin's arm to steer her toward one of the two double-deck bunks in the room, but he had barely laid a hand on her when he was grabbed under the armpits and lifted clear off the floor.

"What the hell?" he yelped.

"D-d-d-don't you be touchin' the lady," Bud said. "Not less'n she says so."

"Put me down!"

Obediently, Bud put Levander down.

"Doanie, Hogg, come get Bud so's I can take care of this bitch," Levander ordered.

"You oughn't to be callin' her names," Stick said. "Ain't nice to call a teacher names."

"Doanie! Hogg!" But the two of them stayed rooted where they were, their hats clutched to their chests. Levander threw his hands up in the air and stomped over to the filthy, much-rumpled lower bunk bed on one wall and plopped down. "You wait'll the Boss gets in here," he muttered. "You won't be so high 'n' mighty then."

"Deputy Joe is your *boss*?" Miss Devlin exclaimed.

Levander crossed his arms behind his head and his feet at the ankles and grinned, exposing a newly broken front tooth. "Sure is. Brains behind the whole operation."

"What operation?" Miss Devlin asked.

Levander smiled smugly. "That's for me to know and you to find out."

Miss Devlin didn't waste any time. She turned to Stick and said, "What's your business with Deputy Joe?"

"We rustle the cattle and Deputy Joe sells 'em and gives us our share of the money," Stick dutifully replied.

"You're the gang of rustlers Mr. Kerrigan has been chasing?" Miss Devlin asked incredulously, her glance skipping from one to the other of the simpleminded men.

"Guess we are," Doanie admitted. "Ma'am," he added as an afterthought.

"Yessir, we are," Hogg agreed. "Ma'am," he added as an afterthought.

"C-c-c-course we also cut them nester fences," Bud volunteered. "But not till Levander said it was okay."

Miss Devlin hadn't been a teacher all those years for

nothing. She recognized stupidity when she saw it. It seemed to her, however, that while these men were outlaws, they were not necessarily violent men. She spied Levander's cruel smile and amended, *at least not all of them*. Bud, Hogg, Doanie, and Stick were too ignorant to realize how they were being manipulated.

Miss Devlin took a deep breath and nearly gagged. "Well, gentlemen," she said after a fit of coughing. "It appears we have some straightening up to do to make this place habitable."

Miss Devlin had picked up a bowl caked with some sort of dried-up food when Deputy Joe came stalking in the door. It was amazing the change that came over Bud, Hogg, Doanie, and Stick. She could feel the electricity in the room, and their immediate fawning deference to the man whom they called Boss. How had ineffectual, innocuous Deputy Joe put the fear of God into these four men? She glanced at Levander and amended, *five men*.

"I want you boys to keep an eye on Miss Devlin," Deputy Joe said. "I don't want her to leave this place. If you see anybody come nosin' around here, shoot first and ask questions later. You understand?"

Four heads nodded.

"You understand what I'm saying, Levander?" Deputy Joe said.

"Yeah, Boss. I understand fine."

"We got a little hitch in our plan 'cause of the weather," Deputy Joe said. "Kerrigan ain't goin' nowhere till this blizzard blows on through. So y'all might as well get comfortable."

Miss Devlin saw no way the seven of them could be comfortable in the cramped space available—even if it had been clean, which it wasn't. The potbellied stove was belching smoke, which made it hard to breathe, even when the stench didn't.

"May I suggest," Miss Devlin said, "that we might all have a little more room if we moved some of the debris outside?"

"You can do whatever you like, long as you don't go nowheres," Deputy Joe said. "I can't stay myself. I gotta get back to town."

Miss Devlin reached out and put a hand on the deputy's sleeve. "You can't be going back out into this weather."

"What I do ain't none of your business," Deputy Joe said.

"You're going to freeze to death out there. You'll never find your way back," Miss Devlin warned.

"The mule I'm ridin' knows the way back to town."

"You're crazy!" Miss Devlin said.

As soon as she made the statement, she knew it was a mistake. Because it was clear as a lily pond before the splash that Deputy Joe *was* crazy to be leader of this particular fuddle-brained band of outlaws.

"Levander, get this bitch away from me, before I shoot her where she stands," Deputy Joe snarled, his hand already on the butt of his .45.

An instant later Miss Devlin's arm had been twisted painfully behind her back and she had been dragged across the room and thrown down on one of the bunks. She bit her lip to keep from crying out. Although the four half-wits were agitated by what Levander was doing, none of them made a move to defy him in the presence of the Boss. Levander took full advantage of the opportunity to hurt Miss Devlin as much as he could.

Deputy Joe gave one last severe look around the room and threatened, "Don't none of you forget what I said. That schoolteacher better be here when I get back." He turned and left.

As soon as he was out the door, Miss Devlin jumped up off the bunk. "Are you going to let him leave?" she demanded. "He's never going to make it back to town."

Hogg and Doanie shrugged.

"C-c-c-can't tell the Boss what to do. He don't like it," Bud said.

"You ain't gonna tell no one here what to do neither," Levander said, advancing toward her threateningly.

Once again, before he could reach her, Bud intercepted him, gently lifting him right off the ground. "T-t-t-told you. Don't touch her less'n she asks."

Levander scowled and yearningly eyed the shotgun standing in the corner. One look at the faces of Doanie and Hogg and Stick convinced him that killing Bud wouldn't help. When Bud finally set him down, Levander retreated to one of the bunks to sulk.

"Well, shall we take the deputy's advice about making ourselves comfortable?" Miss Devlin asked.

Five blank faces stared back at her.

Miss Devlin sighed and shoved her sleeves up over her forearms. "Gentlemen, we have work to do. Who would like to clean the dirty dishes off the table?"

Levander grunted disgustedly before he rolled over with his back to her and pulled his hat down over his face.

Four blank faces stared back at her.

Miss Devlin was a very good teacher. She understood how to deal with blank faces. "Let's see now. How shall we begin?"

Deputy Joe yanked on the mule's mouth, trying to get the animal to turn around. The dumb ass kept insisting on turning his tail to the wind, and Joe knew for a fact that that was the opposite direction from town. After all, the wind had been at their backs coming out of town, it ought to be in their faces now. The road had completely disappeared, and there weren't any landmarks the deputy recognized. If somebody asked him where he was, he would've had to admit he was lost. Except he had this mule. And this mule knew its way back to town. If the fool animal would only turn his head back into the wind.

The trip back to town seemed to be taking even longer than the ride out to the line shack with Miss Devlin, but Joe took advantage of the time to gloat.

He had outwitted them all.

They all thought Deputy Joe was nothing. They had dismissed him as a coward. He had seen it in their eyes. He had heard it in their voices. But he had shown them all. He had created havoc with their lives and they had never even suspected him.

If it hadn't been for Kerrigan, he would still be leading them all around like a herd of bulls with rings in their noses. Deputy Joe had called the shots until that gunslinger came along and spoiled things. Now Kerrigan was going to pay for that mistake.

Deputy Joe put a gloved hand against his left ear, then switched it to the right one. His ears felt brittle, like if he touched them too hard they would fall off. His hands and feet felt heavy, like blocks of ice. He looked around. Nothing familiar at all. Damn this mule! He kicked the beast with the big-roweled Mexican spurs he had won off Levander in a game of five-card stud.

The mule took exception and crowhopped a couple of times. Ordinarily, that wouldn't have been enough to unseat Joe, but he couldn't get a grip with his frozen knees, and he couldn't hold on with his frozen hands, and his frozen feet slipped right out of the stirrups. The next thing he knew, he was sitting on his ass in the snow, and that stupid mule was running off in the opposite direction from town.

There wasn't much chance he was going to catch that mule, and he sure wasn't going to start walking in the wrong direction. He shoved himself up off the ground and headed into the wind. He had to get back to town. His whole plan for revenge against Kerrigan depended on his getting back to his bed in the jail before the day ended, so no one would suspect he could possibly be responsible for abducting Miss Devlin.

Then he would lure Kerrigan out to the boarded-up line shack and ambush the gunslinger when he rode up to it— he had the spot picked out—and then he would give Miss Devlin the time of her life before he shot her dead, too. He had it all planned. And it would work. He was pretty smart, ole Deputy Joe.

But damn, he was cold! And tired. He needed to sit down for a minute and rest. Then he would finish walking into town. He had it all planned. He would show them all. Imagine Miss Devlin calling him crazy. Deputy Joe was crazy all right. Crazy like a fox.

Deputy Joe heard the jingle of bells on a harness. It was a sweet sound, but it seemed to come and go. He put his hands to his ears. Maybe if they were warmer, he could hear better. When he covered his ears, the sound went away completely. Deputy Joe closed his eyes and concentrated, listening for the bells. There they were. They were headed right for him.

The snow was cold. The wind was bitter. But he would have his revenge. Wait and see if he didn't.

Chapter 20

*If you wake up feelin' halfway 'tween
"Oh, Lord," and "My God," you've overdid it.*

THE BLIZZARD OF THE NIGHT PAST HAD BLOWN ON
through to the south, leaving behind it yet another batch of
gray snow clouds to defeat the sunrise. Yet there was nothing dreary about the beginning of Bliss's day, because she
awoke in Hadley's arms.

"G'mornin'," she murmured, stretching against his lanky
frame.

Hadley groaned deep in his throat and grabbed Bliss to
keep her from rubbing her naked breasts and belly up
against him. "Lord, Bliss. Don't do that!"

"Why not?" Her lower lip, already swollen from an entire night of kissing, stuck out in a pout.

"'Cause you're gonna kill me if you keep this up," he
said with a playful growl.

"This?" Bliss said, seizing the part of Hadley that was
making a tent out of the sheets.

Hadley let out a yelp of surprise, but being a glutton for
punishment, he let Bliss cup what she could hold of him in
her hands.

"I smell coffee," Bliss murmured, sniffing the air before

she stuck her nose up behind Hadley's ear. "That means it's time to get up."

Hadley smirked. "I've been 'up' all night, and it's your fault, you vixen."

Bliss laughed, a tingling, bell-like sound that reverberated off the high ceiling in Hadley's spartan bedroom on the second floor of the Westbrook home.

"Shhh! You're gonna wake up my mother and father," Hadley whispered.

"They're clear at the other end of the hall," Bliss protested.

"That doesn't mean you can make all the noise you want."

"Then you better do something to keep me quiet," Bliss threatened. " 'Cause if you don't—"

Hadley took her at her word, covering her mouth with his, and they descended back into the well of pleasure where they had dwelt the past night. Groaning aloud with pleasure, Hadley never gave another thought to whether he was disturbing his parents.

As it turned out, Oak and Regina were wide awake, the result of a lifetime spent rising with the dawn to begin a hard day's work. But today, Oak had no intention of getting out of bed anytime soon. There were times when the day's work must wait for more important matters.

Regina was lying on her side gazing out at the layer of new-fallen snow that had drifted around her pink gazebo, making it look like a charming decoration on top of an iced cake. Oak was behind her, his head resting on one hand, but he had eyes only for his wife.

"You always surprise me, Regina," he said as he ran a work-roughened hand down the curve of Regina's back to her waist, and from there over the slope of her buttocks to her thigh.

"Hmmm?"

"Even after thirty-two years together I find you a fascinating woman. And I don't mean just your mind. You know how I admire that. It's . . . it's your body, too."

"It's seen a few years," Regina reminded him.

"That only gives it character," Oak said. "It reminds me of the land, you know, how beautiful it is, all hills and slopes and valleys." Oak pressed Regina onto her back and traced the shape of her generous breasts. "These are the mountains," he said.

Regina smiled and indulged him by remaining still.

He outlined her ribs. "These are the ridges."

Her face sobered as she realized that he worshiped what he touched.

"And these are the gullies," he said as his teasing fingertips probed the folds of flesh at her waist and belly.

She smiled again, saved by his sense of humor from becoming maudlin.

"And down here . . ." His hand slipped down between her legs. "This is the valley, where the river flows. And the water is sweeter than honey."

His mouth followed his hands, and his tongue dipped and retreated as he sipped at the fount of life. Oak kissed and nipped and sucked and teased, until he felt Regina's spasms of ecstasy. For a while he lay with his head on her thigh, until she could breathe easily again and the tension had left her. Then he sat up and leaned over her, bracing himself on his palms, and kissed her, sharing the sweetness of her that was on his lips.

Regina felt her throat closing with emotion. To be loved so much, by such a man, was all any woman could ask of life.

Oak's voice was husky, and he forced himself to meet his wife's love-softened hazel eyes. "I've been dying of thirst these past weeks, Regina. I've missed you."

"I've missed you, too, Oak. I'm sorry I had to keep you away." She cleared her throat. "I'm not sorry the conflict got settled before it got started. I couldn't have stood by and watched my husband get killed in a senseless range war. I know all the other women—rancher and nester wives both—felt the same way."

His lips twisted ruefully. "If Ben Davis was going through a tenth of what you put me through, it's a wonder things went on as long as they did."

"Don't worry about Ben," Regina said. "I'm sure Persia is making it up to him. Right now I think it's my turn to touch and taste. I've been thirsty, too, Oak. More than you know."

She folded him in her arms, loving the weight of him, knowing that when they were through she would only want him again. For a while they were safe from the harsh frontier that lay beyond their door. It wouldn't be long before something else disturbed their hard-won peace. Until that day came, Regina intended to make full use of these precious moments.

Across the valley, as Regina had predicted, Persia Davis was doing her best to make up to Big Ben for the pleasure he had been denied over the past few weeks. In fact, Big Ben was thinking he had never in his life spent an evening like the one he had just been through with his wife.

It had been Persia's idea to spend the night at the Townhouse Hotel. She had pointed out that if they went home with Bevis and Mabel Ives, none of them would have any privacy. Last night, privacy had been at the top of Big Ben's list of Most Important Things in Life.

"When we get the house rebuilt, I want a bed just like this one," Persia whispered.

"This bed takes up near half the room," Big Ben protested.

"You're a big man. You need a big bed. It gives you room to express yourself," Persia said with a seductive grin.

Twin spots of color rose on Big Ben's cheeks. "If you say so," he mumbled.

It had been strange waking up with no chores to do, no cows to milk, no hay to fork, just his wife snuggled up close to him and holding him like there was no tomorrow.

"Uh . . . don't you think we should get up?" he said.

"Why?"

Blamed if he could think of a reason. But if they weren't going to get out of bed, there were other things he had in mind to try. Things he had thought about last night when Persia had first walked through the door to this room, and he had seen this big brass bed with the scroll trim at the head and foot topped with an old-fashioned canopy.

"Persia?" Her name got caught in his throat, so he cleared it and tried again. "Persia?"

"Yes, Ben."

"Did you mean it when you said you'd try anything I wanted in this bed?"

"Yes, Ben."

"Then I want you to grab hold of the scroll trim up there at the top of the bed."

"Okay, Ben." Persia slowly reached her hands over her head and curled her fingers around the cold brass.

"Now, all I'm asking is, no matter what, I don't want you to let go of that trim. All right?"

Persia felt her muscles tense as she took a tighter hold on the bedstead. He could have tied her there, but he didn't need to. The words were enough. "Okay, Ben. I won't let go."

"No matter what?"

"No matter what."

Persia knew what Ben was really asking. *Do you trust me? Do you believe I love you enough to treat you with respect, when you're helpless and can't stop me no matter what I choose to do?*

Persia had married Ben when she was only seventeen and he was twenty-two. Now she was thirty-three. Over the years there had been times when she had questioned him, contradicted him, fought like the very devil with him. This was a chance to show him that she loved him enough to trust him with her happiness. It was an awful burden to hand him. Because it would break her heart if she gave him her trust—and she was going to trust him in this—and he trod it underfoot.

"Relax, Persia," Ben murmured.

Persia felt anything but relaxed. Ben was arranging her on the bed, making sure her head was comfortable on the pillow, drawing the covers away so he could see the ribbed cotton chemise and pantalettes she had slept in. His hands created spots of heat wherever they touched. They finally came to rest at her waist. But they didn't stay still for long. Ben took her chemise in his strong hands and ripped it open down the front.

"It was in my way," he said, his voice husky. "I couldn't see you."

Persia clung to the bedstead, her heart beating a tattoo against her chest, as Ben shoved the ragged material aside and took the pebbled tip of her breast in his mouth. He suckled until she arched upward, and then his tongue became a soothing balm, only to rouse her again.

His hands were everywhere touching her. His mouth was everywhere tasting her. She kept waiting for the moment when he would rip off her pantalettes.

It never came.

Instead he gently tugged them down and off over her toes and threw them aside. "Don't want to be too predictable," he said with a teasing smile.

Then, except for the cotton scraps of her chemise, she

was bared to his heavy-lidded gaze. It was an intoxicating feeling, to lie there, clinging to the bed, seeing him so aroused, wanting to touch, and being unable to reach out to him.

He rubbed himself against her. He kissed her toes. He bit her armpit. He spread her legs and looked at her with awe and with desire.

She had never felt so revered. She had never felt such an object of love. Because even though he was pleasing himself, everything he did was for her.

He slipped inside her and stayed there a moment, not moving. She thrust her hips trying to create the friction they both enjoyed.

"Don't move," he ordered.

She lay still. And felt him inside her, filling her. She clenched her inner muscles and felt him grow inside her. She closed her eyes and bit her lip to keep herself from arching up to meet him.

He withdrew and she was bereft.

She opened her eyes and saw him watching as he connected them one to another again.

"You are so beautiful, Persia," he whispered. "And I love you so much. I dreamed this when I couldn't touch you. How I would put myself inside you, and we would be one person."

Persia felt the tear coming and turned her head into the pillow so he wouldn't see it. "That is the . . . the most beautiful thing you've ever said to me, Ben Davis. If having lots of room to move inspires you, I think I'm going to insist on having a very big bed in our new house."

Ben laughed. "Let go of the bedstead, Persia."

"You told me to hang on."

"I want you to hang on to me now—and I don't want you ever to let go."

Persia threw her arms around Ben. "I do love you so, Ben Davis!"

"Then you have my permission to *move*," he said with a grin as he thrust deep inside her.

Persia laughed and obeyed her husband.

They were making so much noise, they never heard the cry of agony down the hall as Kerrigan woke and found the note left the night before by Deputy Joe.

Kerrigan pounded on the door to Darcie's room, which was down the hall from his room at the Townhouse Hotel. "Wake up, Felton! I know you're in there."

Felton came to the door dressed in a sheet, angry at the interruption that had come at a very inopportune moment.

"Let me in," Kerrigan said.

"I ain't dressed. Neither is Darcie."

"Tell her to get dressed, and get dressed yourself. We've got work to do."

Felton raised a brow at the way Kerrigan had made them a team again, like they'd been back in Texas. "What's going on?"

Darcie donned her Chinese robe, tying it haphazardly so a great deal of skin was still exposed, then grabbed the blankets and sheets from in front of the fireplace and dumped them on the cherrywood four-poster. A moment later her head showed at the door. "You can let him in, Felton. I'm dressed."

Felton stepped back as Kerrigan stepped inside. Kerrigan had been around a lot of women in revealing robes like the one Darcie had on. When he spied the ring on Darcie's finger, he was suddenly aware that she was not some lady-for-the-night Felton was seeing, she was soon to be Felton's wife. A man did not ogle another man's half-dressed wife. Since Darcie was standing next to Felton, he didn't know where to look. He kept his eyes on the floor, trying to figure out how to pose his predicament delicately so Felton would get his point without taking offense. "Uh . . . maybe Darcie should . . . uh . . ."

It was Darcie who perceived Kerrigan's problem first and, suffused with pleasure at the gunslinger's sudden awkwardness, said, "I'll get dressed while you two talk."

Kerrigan flashed Darcie a grateful smile and she grinned back before disappearing behind a lacquered dressing screen in the corner of the room.

Felton dropped the sheet and pulled on his long johns as Kerrigan explained how he had gone to sleep in the dark the night before and found the note on the floor when he had woken up this morning.

"What does it say, exactly?" Felton asked, tugging on his Levi's.

Kerrigan read the erratic block printing.

iF YoU WAnT TO See MISS DEVLIN ALivE
CUM Alone TO the OLD LiNE ShAK
at THE NorTH ENd OF SWeeTWaTeR CanYUN
DoN'T SAy NOthIN to NO ONE.

"Are you sure whoever wrote that has kidnapped Miss Devlin?" Felton asked.

"I've already ridden over to check out her place. She isn't there. The house is stone cold."

"Any signs which way they went?"

"Wiped out by the wind and the snow."

"Who do you suppose has got her?"

"Levander Early," Kerrigan replied with conviction.

"I thought he left the Territory."

Kerrigan grimaced. "Obviously he didn't go far."

"You know, if you go to Sweetwater Canyon alone, you'll be riding into an ambush."

"What choice do I have?" Kerrigan said, his eyes bleak. "He's got Eden. What would you do if he had Darcie?"

Felton's lips flattened into a thin line. He would do exactly what Kerrigan was planning to do. Felton buckled on his gun belt after checking the five rounds he kept loaded in his .45. "There's something wrong with this whole setup. From what you've told me, Levander Early isn't bright enough to plan something like this all by himself."

Kerrigan forked an agitated hand through his hair. "It has to be him. Who else could it be?"

"Maybe there's another bad guy."

"Who?" Kerrigan demanded, his frustration apparent. "With you out of the picture, I don't have another suspect."

"Let me see the note," Felton said. He took the crumpled paper in one hand and slipped the other around Darcie, who was now dressed in another of the "decent" gowns Kerrigan had helped her pick out, this one a princess dress in a gray-green merino. "I recognize this writing," Felton said.

"You do?"

Felton frowned. "Yeah, but I don't understand this."

"What?"

"This mixture of capitals and lower letters looks like my deputy's work."

Kerrigan shook his head. "It can't be him."

"Why not?"

"Think about it." Kerrigan snorted derisively. "That man's about the most pitiful excuse for a deputy—" Kerrigan realized as he spoke that because Joe Titman was Felton's deputy he would know exactly when Felton was out of town. He would have been in a perfect position to schedule the rustling raids so the sheriff wouldn't be around to catch the culprits. Kerrigan thought back to the day he had questioned Deputy Joe, and how the man had come up off his bunk holding a Colt and looking mean. "Where is Deputy Joe now?" Kerrigan asked.

"He was supposed to be on duty last night. He should be at the jail. Unless . . ."

"Let's go," Kerrigan said.

Felton gave Darcie a swift, hard kiss. "I'm going with Kerrigan. Be waiting for me when I get back. We've got a date in Canyon Creek."

Darcie knew better than to argue. She loved Felton for the kind of man he was. Sometimes that meant staying behind, knowing he was risking his life when he walked out the door. "Take care of yourself, Felton."

"Don't worry. I've got nine lives."

"Yeah, but you've already used up a bunch of them," she called after him. "Be careful! I love you!"

Felton grabbed his bruised ribs and followed an equally careful Kerrigan down the stairs of the hotel. "How's the weather this morning?" he asked as he gritted his teeth and stuck his arms in his coat.

"It stopped snowing, but it's still clouded up and the wind's still blowing."

"That's going to make for a cold ride to Sweetwater Canyon," Felton said.

When they arrived at the jail, there was no sign of Deputy Joe. The bunk in the jail cell where he normally slept was undisturbed, and there was no coffee, day-old or otherwise, heating on the stove in the front office.

"What do you think?" Felton asked.

"I think maybe he's out on the trail somewhere between here and Sweetwater Canyon," Kerrigan replied.

"I think maybe you're right."

"I left my horse saddled at the livery," Kerrigan said. "I'll wait for you there."

"You're really going to give that lily-livered bush-whacker the chance to shoot you in the back—again?"

"You'll be keeping an eye on my back, too. That'll give me a fighting chance. That's all I'll need."

"I don't like the odds," Felton said.

"I want Eden back. And I want her alive. I don't have any choice but to spring this trap. I just have to make sure I don't get caught in it."

Felton shook his head resignedly. He knew Kerrigan when he got like this. He was a wolf on the hunt. He wouldn't give up until he'd cornered his quarry. "Well, then, I guess I better get my horse saddled up too."

Across the universe, in another time and place, Miss Eden Devlin awoke with a start. It took her a moment to focus on where she was and what had happened to her. She looked around the room of sleeping men. Bud was snoring. Doanie and Hogg were curled up on the same bed, like two little boys. Stick was hanging well off the end of the bunk. Levander slept with a gun in his hand. In the corner, the mother cat was already hard at work bathing her kittens.

Eden was sitting in one of the kitchen chairs that she had situated in the corner of the room closest to the stove. She was using her coat for a blanket, because at least that way she didn't have to worry about unwelcome vermin. She wished she could see outside, to find out what kind of day it was, but everything was boarded up tight. The wind was still howling, though, and she could feel the bitter cold.

It was hard to believe she had been kidnapped. Hard to believe that Kerrigan might be killed today trying to rescue her. Equally hard to believe that her whole life had turned so horribly, terribly upside down in a mere twenty-four hours. She closed her eyes. This was one day when she would just as soon turn over in bed and go back to sleep. Only she didn't have a bed. And she was wide awake.

She forced herself to think. The only thoughts that came to mind were painful ones. How could Kerrigan have done such a despicable thing? Maybe she had misheard the drunken men. Maybe it hadn't been like they said. She hadn't exactly given Kerrigan a chance to explain. She realized now it was because she had been afraid that Kerrigan didn't love her after all. She had not been able to face that possibility without running from it. As she had run from her fears in the past.

Without Kerrigan, her life in Sweetwater wouldn't have much meaning. Oh, she would enjoy teaching the children. They would be the closest thing to having her own. She could go to the church socials and let the town bachelor buy her picnic basket at the Fourth of July celebration. But it wouldn't be the same as having children of her own, and a man to love who loved her back. Miss Devlin wanted it all. And there was only one way she was going to get it.

After a long night on a hard chair Miss Devlin had come to the conclusion that if she wanted a life with Burke Kerrigan, she was going to have to stop running away every time she felt afraid. If she got a second chance, and with the situation being what it was, that was a little doubtful at the moment, she was going to sit Kerrigan down and ask some questions. With any luck, he would have a perfectly simple explanation for what the drunken revelers had said. And she would be able to run toward her future, instead of away from her past.

Chapter 21

*If you can't get the job done in five shots,
you better get the hell outta there.*

KERRIGAN FELT THE HAIR PRICKLE ON HIS NECK AS HE rode along the snowy rim of Sweetwater Canyon, then headed down the trail toward the boarded-up line shack that was his destination. Any second he expected to hear the crack of a rifle and feel a bullet tear into his flesh.

It never came.

He could see the line shack now. Smoke belched from a stovepipe chimney, which meant there was someone inside. The place looked too small to house Levander's whole gang, but that didn't mean they weren't all there. Kerrigan felt the sweat trickle down his spine despite the freezing cold. He had been playing life-and-death games like this for years, only this time it really mattered to him whether he wound up dead.

Maybe he and Felton had been wrong. Maybe Levander was the brains behind this gang after all. Maybe he was riding into a trap, all right, but it was one Levander had set for him.

Kerrigan's eyes scanned the horizon. He halted his paint horse, then stood in the stirrups and looked back over his shoulder. He didn't see anything suspicious, or any movement at all, except the snow blowing across the rocky surface of the canyon. Yet he knew there was at least one man—Felton—out there following him.

He wondered what Felton thought about the fact they had gotten this far down the canyon without running into an ambush. Or maybe Felton wasn't behind him. Maybe Deputy Joe had realized there were two men on the trail and had let Kerrigan pass him by and then quietly taken care of Felton.

It was dangerous to start worrying. He needed to keep his mind on the here and now. Felton was fine, probably just worried, like he was. Kerrigan kneed his horse back into a walk, his eyes searching the terrain for something out of place, something to give him a clue where the ambush would come.

When he was close enough that he could be seen from the shack, he stopped his horse in a spot where an outcropping of rock broke the force of the wind and dismounted, waiting for Felton to catch up to him.

The line shack was totally exposed on all sides, so there was no way they were going to sneak up in broad daylight. About twenty steps away from the shack, a spring wagon was pulled up next to a lean-to where they probably kept their horses. A single cottonwood shaded the lean-to, but it was bare of leaves and wouldn't provide cover. About twenty steps the other direction was a privy. It was equally exposed to view from the cabin. Paths had been stomped in the ankle-high snow to both the privy and the lean-to. Deputy Joe had chosen a good place for a standoff, if that was what he had in mind.

Kerrigan heard Felton before he saw him.

"I guess we were mistaken," Felton said, dismounting next to the gunslinger. "I thought sure the deputy planned to ambush you on the way down here. Since he didn't, what the hell do you think's going on?"

"Who knows," Kerrigan answered irritably.

"You seen anybody moving around outside?" Felton asked.

"Yeah. I've seen three of Levander's gang." He had been watching the shack long enough to see one man step outside to scrape a bunch of dishes, and for another to throw out a pan of dirty water on the snow. The third man had shaken out a blanket and hung it, along with a mattress, over a hitching rail out front.

"Were the men you saw carrying guns?"

Kerrigan frowned. "Nope."

"What were they doing outside?"

"It's hard to say," Kerrigan hedged. "I mean, I know what it looked like. But I might be mistaken."

"Well? Spit it out."

Kerrigan took off his hat and drove his fingers through his hair. "It looked like they were cleaning house."

"It's a little early for spring cleaning, don't you think?"

"I'm telling you what it looked like," Kerrigan maintained stubbornly.

At that moment the door opened. Both men tensed. The doorway was deeply shadowed, and they waited for a sign of any movement inside.

Kerrigan drew his gun and checked the cylinders. Maybe something would happen now. He drew a breath and held it, waiting. Finally, someone came through the door.

It was the huge man, the former boxer, Bud. He had a broom, and he was carefully sweeping a pile of trash across the threshold and out the door.

Felton's eyes grew wide and he looked incredulously at Kerrigan. Kerrigan shrugged as though to say, *See what I mean?*

"What do we do now?" Felton asked.

"We wait."

"How long?"

"Until dark. Or until Deputy Joe shows up."

Miss Devlin had spent a rather hectic day cleaning the line shack, with the grudging cooperation of Bud, Hogg, Doanie, and Stick. Levander had spent the day in bed playing a continuous game of solitaire. The past hour she had labored over the stove, in an attempt to make some stew. Cooking had never been her strong point, and she was anticipating a great deal of unhappy clamor when she finally presented her concoction at the table.

She surveyed the interior of the room. Bud had done most of the lifting and carrying as she rearranged the meager furniture and then helped with the sweeping. Hogg and Doanie had done the washing and dusting, while Stick had done the shaking out. The line shack was as clean and straightened as it could get, given what she had to work with. From the conversation the simpleminded men were having, even this poor place was a step up in the world from what they were used to having.

"My ma liked things clean like this," Stick said as he watched Miss Devlin stirring the pot on the stove. "Used to sweep the dirt off her floor every day. Only it was a dirt floor, so it never really got clean."

Doanie had cornered a spot at the table and waited with a plate in front of him and a fork in his hand. "Never had no ma," he said, "but my pa used to make me wash dishes every day when my schoolwork was done."

"Never went to school," Hogg said, "and never had no house to keep clean. But if I had, I woulda, 'cause it shore looks purtier this way."

Bud worked to straighten all the wrinkles from the blanket he had brought back inside from its airing, and laid it across the bunk he had claimed. "B-b-b-bud never had no bed to make up nice," he said. "Or no dishes to wash, neither. Mostly slept on the floor and ate from the can."

Miss Devlin heard in their stories the kind of start in life that might send a man down the wrong path. And none of these men had possessed much horse sense to keep them on the straight and narrow. It was a shame, really.

She had stopped being afraid of the simpleminded men when she realized how readily they followed whatever instructions she gave them. Whether she represented mother or father, preacher or teacher, in their small, hebetudinous minds, they each listened and obeyed her when she spoke. She continued to give Levander Early a wide berth and shuddered at the thought of her fate when the Boss returned.

"If you'll all please come to the table, supper is ready," Miss Devlin said.

There were only three chairs, but Levander had already said he wasn't going to sit down with them, and Doanie and Hogg had rigged a bench out of a broken slat and two half-empty five-gallon buckets of Seroco's Weatherproof Mineral Barn, Roof, and Fence Paint.

She dished out a serving of stew to everyone, including Levander, who had dinner in bed.

"A gentleman waits to begin eating until a lady is seated," she advised, when she saw Doanie about to fork in a mouthful of stew.

He held the fork in front of his mouth, waiting for her bottom to hit the chair. The instant it did, the stew hit his mouth. After that, the entire dinner became a lesson in table etiquette, with Miss Devlin no sooner catching one faux pas than another occurred. Meanwhile, she waited for a complaint about the quality of her stew.

Instead, she heard "Them's mighty fine vittles, Miss

Devlin" from Stick, followed by Bud's "T-t-t-tastes good, ma'am."

Between mouthfuls Doanie managed, "Never et such good stew," and Hogg added, "Pure deee-licious!"

Every single man—including Levander—licked his plate clean. Well, not literally, because she had advised them that picking up a plate to lick it with one's tongue simply was not done.

"Then how'm I supposed to get the gravy?" Stick demanded.

"You may sop it with a piece of bread," Miss Devlin instructed.

"I ain't got no bread."

That was true. Miss Devlin thought for a moment and said, "You have a spoon, don't you?"

"Shore do."

"Then you may use your spoon."

It was full dark by the time they had finished eating and washed the dishes. There was no sign of the Boss, and Miss Devlin would as soon have forgotten about him, except she wondered how long she was going to have to sleep sitting up.

"What do you suppose happened to Deputy Joe?" she asked. "Shouldn't he have been back by now?"

"No tellin'," Levander said. "It'd depend on how soon Kerrigan came lookin' for you when he got the note."

"What if he ignored the note?" she asked. "What if he isn't interested in finding me?"

"Then it's gonna be too bad for you," Levander said with a lascivious grin.

Miss Devlin took that to mean she wouldn't be leaving this place alive. When she looked to the other men for confirmation of Levander's threat, they refused to meet her eyes, which was really all the confirmation she needed.

With only the light from a single lantern, there wasn't

much they could do after dark. After the hard day they had spent cleaning, the four housekeepers were happy to go to bed early.

Apparently Levander wasn't tired, because he rose at last from the bed where he had spent the day and came to sit at a chair at the table, where he laid out the cards once more for a game of solitaire.

"Don't you ever get tired of playing that game?" Miss Devlin asked in a sharp voice.

"Nope."

With nothing else to do, Miss Devlin watched him play. "You cheated," she said.

"Who you callin' a cheater?" he snarled.

"I saw you with my own eyes. You took a card from the middle of the deck."

"You can't cheat when you're playin' by yourself," he argued.

"If the rules don't count, you might as well turn the cards over and pick out the ones you need," she said acidly.

Levander's eyes narrowed and his lip curled menacingly. "Why don't you shut up and mind your own damn beeswax. I was doin' fine till you horned in where you wasn't wanted."

"I simply don't understand how anyone could enjoy playing a game where there is no conceivable chance you can lose. Where is the challenge, Mr. Early?"

Outside the line shack, his back pressed against the rotted wood, Kerrigan felt his lips twitching. He gave in and grinned. Only a woman like Eden Devlin could find herself in a philosophical discussion with an outlaw over a game of solitaire.

The argument continued, and he was grateful for the distraction she was unknowingly providing. Felton was working his way to the other side of the front door, which they had discovered was the only way in or out. A moment later he saw Felton was ready.

Kerrigan signaled to Felton and then counted mentally, *One, two, three, GO!*

They crashed through the door with their Colts in their hands, locating Eden before deadly bullets started flying at the outlaws.

Miss Devlin had a second to feel jubilation before she was grabbed by Levander, the lantern went soaring past her to crash on the floor in front of the two intruders, and the bore of a loaded .45 was jabbed into her temple.

She was appalled at the speed with which the four dull-witted outlaws found their weapons in the dark and brought them to bear on the two figures silhouetted momentarily in the growing fire caused by the broken lantern.

The gunfight was over almost before it began.

"Throw down your guns or I swear I'll blow her head off," Levander shouted.

Kerrigan and Felton exchanged grim glances. Levander was going to kill Eden Devlin whether they threw down their guns or not. Felton left the decision up to Kerrigan.

Eden shook her head no. It was a slight gesture because the gun was pressed so tightly against her skull. "Don't do it, Kerrigan. You know he isn't going to let any of us live if you do."

Levander grabbed a hank of Miss Devlin's hair and pulled so hard, she cried out in pain. "Hurry up, Kerrigan! I'm gettin' an itchy trigger finger here."

Kerrigan couldn't take the chance that Levander wasn't bluffing. Eden might still get free if he kept the man talking, and he had his derringer in his boot. He let down the trigger of his .45 and dropped it on the floor. A moment later Felton's gun joined Kerrigan's.

"That's more like it," Levander said with a smirk. "You two ain't so high and mighty anymore, are you?"

"Doanie, Hogg, come on over here and get their guns."

"I can't move," Doanie said. "Bullet broke a bone in my leg."

"I got it in the gut," Hogg said. "It don't look good, Levander."

"Stick, you come get these guns," Levander said.

Stick didn't answer.

"Stick?"

Doanie said, "He's dead."

Miss Devlin closed her eyes against the pain of such waste. Her eyes flew open when Levander tightened his hold on her hair and pressed the gun into her cheek.

"I oughta kill you right now, right in front of their eyes," Levander snarled.

A second later Levander felt a pair of hands go around his chest, and he was lifted off the ground. "What the hell?"

Bud, who had put out the fire caused by the broken lantern, had come up behind Levander and had him in a bear hug. "Y-y-y-you let the teacher be," he said.

Levander's hand was caught in Miss Devlin's hair and he couldn't free it even if he wanted to. He kept the Colt pointed at her, since it was plain Kerrigan and the sheriff were waiting for a chance to grab their guns, which were still lying in plain sight in front of them.

"Put me down, Bud," Levander ordered.

"L-l-l-let her go first," Bud said, squeezing a little tighter.

Levander's hand suddenly came free of Miss Devlin's hair and he clawed at the burly arms that were crushing his chest. Miss Devlin started to move away and Levander warned, "Don't you move an inch, or I'll shoot. I swear I will."

"C-c-c-can't shoot a teacher," Bud said, his muscles bulging from the effort he was exerting.

The whites of Levander's eyes now showed, and it was clear he wasn't sure whether to keep the gun pointed at Miss Devlin, aim it at the two men in the doorway, or turn it on Bud, who was slowly but surely squeezing the life out of him.

"Bud, you gotta put me down," Levander rasped.

"C-c-c-can't shoot a teacher," Bud repeated. His grasp tightened.

Unable to breathe, Levander panicked. He swung his .45 around and shot over his shoulder at Bud.

Everything happened at once.

Kerrigan dove for Eden, enfolding her in his arms and rolling them both out of harm's way.

Felton dove for his gun and rolled the other direction, ready to provide covering fire.

Bud grunted as the slug from Levander's gun hit him above the heart. "C-c-c-can't shoot . . ." His voice faded as he used the last of his strength to break Levander's back and slowly squeeze the life out of him. When Bud no longer felt any resistance from the man in his arms, he let go, and Levander toppled to the floor. A moment later, Bud fell dead beside him.

"Oh Lordy, oh Lordy, oh Lordy." The littany of woe came from Doanie as he lay in his bunk.

"Poor Bud. Poor Stick. Poor Levander. Poor Hogg. All dead," Hogg said, putting himself in the same class as the other dead men, knowing it was only a matter of time before his belly wound killed him.

"You ain't gonna die, Hogg," Doanie said.

Miss Devlin struggled out of Kerrigan's arms and hurried over to kneel beside Hogg and Doanie's bunk. It only took a moment to realize Hogg was probably right. The chances were slim that he would survive. But there had been enough tragedy here tonight, Miss Devlin thought angrily, and surely the fates could spare this unhappy soul.

"Help me, Kerrigan. Maybe we can stop the bleeding. If the bullet didn't hit anything important, maybe we can save him."

Kerrigan was nonplussed by Eden's attitude toward a man who had been one of those holding her prisoner, but she gave him a fierce look that warned him not to argue. He did what he could to help her with Hogg while Felton took care of Doanie's leg as best he could.

"There's room for both of them in the back of the spring wagon Deputy Joe used to bring me here," Eden said. "We have to get them into town, to Doc Harper."

"Eden, chances are—"

"Don't argue with me!" Eden said in a shrill voice.

Kerrigan could see she was near the edge. After everything she had been through, he could hardly blame her. He nodded to Felton to keep an eye on the wounded men and went out to harness up what animals he could find to the spring wagon. Eden made sure Kerrigan put the box containing the litter of kittens in the back along with Doanie and Hogg.

It was a long, cold trip back to Sweetwater. It was also a quiet trip. Kerrigan had started once to talk to her about the misunderstanding between them, but the knowledge that the two in the back of the wagon, and Felton riding beside them, would overhear everything he said kept him mute.

It was Eden who finally broke the silence as they were nearing town.

"Whatever happened to Deputy Joe?" she asked.

"I don't know," Kerrigan admitted. "Maybe you can tell us."

"After he dropped me off with Levander and his gang, he said he was heading back to town. He said he was on duty at the jail and didn't want you suspecting anything. Didn't he get there?"

Felton shook his head. "His bed at the jail wasn't slept in."

Eden turned and looked all around her at the snowswept plains, an eerie sight in the moonlight. He could be anywhere out there. "I warned him the weather wasn't fit for traveling. Do you suppose he's still out there somewhere?"

"Maybe. Could be he'll turn up when there's a thaw. Or he might show up as a bunch of stripped bones in the spring."

"He was not a nice man," Miss Devlin admitted. "He frightened me. What'll happen to Doanie and Hogg?" she asked the sheriff.

"They'll have to stand trial for rustling. Most likely, if they survive their wounds, they'll hang."

"You don't have any proof they were the rustlers, do you?" Miss Devlin said.

Felton exchanged glances with Kerrigan. Kerrigan shrugged and shook his head. "Not without Kerrigan's testimony, we don't," Felton said tentatively.

"Maybe you could find jobs for them instead."

Felton stared at Miss Devlin. "I can what?"

"I am convinced that if Doanie and Hogg were given a chance to do honest work, they could both become good citizens."

Felton rolled his eyes. He had spent enough time with Darcie to know there was no arguing with a woman when her mind was made up. "I'll do what I can," he conceded.

"I appreciate that, Felton. I really do," Miss Devlin said.

When they reached Doc Harper's place, Kerrigan helped Felton carry the two wounded men inside and then came back out, leaving Eden to arrange matters with the doctor, including care for the litter of kittens.

"Where are you headed now?" Kerrigan asked Felton.

"I gotta hire someone at the livery to go out tomorrow and pick up those bodies we left behind and bring them to town for burial. Then I'm gonna hire a rig to drive Darcie over to Canyon Creek. By noon tomorrow—" He looked up at a sky that was already turning pink with the dawn and amended, "—noon today, I'm going to be a happily married man."

Kerrigan shook hands with Felton, and bid him good luck and Godspeed, envious of the excitement he saw in Felton's eyes as he looked forward to his wedding. "Are you and Darcie going to live in Sweetwater?" Kerrigan asked.

"It'll depend on what Darcie wants to do," Felton said. "I'd like to. Good grass for cattle and plenty of water. Man could have a good life here."

"Yeah, if he had the right woman by his side, keeping his house, raising his kids, it could be heaven on earth," Kerrigan said as Eden came out of Doc Harper's office to join them.

"Hmmph!" she said, marching past Kerrigan without stopping. "I should have expected to hear such an expedient circumscription of the wife's role from someone as glib-tongued as you!"

Felton turned to Kerrigan and muttered, "Circumscription?"

Miss Devlin kept on walking but raised her voice to recite, "To constrict the range or activity of; to draw a line around; to surround by a boundary."

Kerrigan grinned.

Felton rolled his eyes, tipped his hat at Kerrigan, and headed for the livery.

Kerrigan hop-skipped to catch up with Eden. "Where are you headed?" he asked, striding along beside her.

Eden stopped dead. She closed her eyes then opened

them again, and turned to look up at Kerrigan. "I guess I was running away."

"How about running toward me instead," he said, his heart in his throat.

"I . . . I think maybe it's time we talked. Take me home, Kerrigan."

Chapter 22

*If she says "no," you haven't asked
the right question—or the question right.*

A NEW DAY WAS DAWNING AS KERRIGAN HELPED
Eden back into the spring wagon, made sure the lead rope
by which Paint was tied to the rear of the wagon was secure, and climbed up beside her for the ride back home.
The wind had stopped blowing—a unique phenomenon in
Wyoming—and the sun rose toward a sky that was a clear
blue as far as the eye could see.

There wasn't much room on the wagon seat, and Eden
had to make a real effort to keep her thigh from brushing
against Kerrigan's. She held herself rigid, refusing to give
an inch. She had intended to wait until she was home before confronting the gunslinger, but after a very few minutes of poignant silence, she asked, "Is it true, what I
heard?"

Kerrigan knew that what he said now would make the
difference between whether Eden forgave him, or gave
him up. "What did you hear?" he replied in a deceptively
calm voice.

"That you were paid to seduce me."

The poignant silence returned.

"I don't know what to say to you, Eden . . . how to explain . . ."

Miss Devlin felt her stomach knot. It was true. Otherwise he would have denied it. "Why?" she whispered.

Kerrigan tried to meet her eyes, but she wouldn't look at him. Her hands were clenched together in her lap so tightly, the knuckles were white.

"It didn't seem so awful at the time," he said.

Eden moaned.

He hurried to explain, "I had just met you once, and you were so full of spunk and vinegar . . . I wanted you from the moment I laid eyes on you, and I knew I had no business messing with the spinster schoolteacher. I guess I grabbed at the first excuse somebody gave me to see you again. I don't have any better excuse than that. I'm not proud of what I did. I'd give anything to go back and do things differently."

She felt Kerrigan's eyes on her, demanding, compelling. At last she met his gaze. She searched his dark eyes, looking for something. She wasn't sure what. She saw pain. And confusion. And fear. And hope. "What kind of man are you?"

"I'm human. Sometimes I make the wrong choices. I swear to you, by everything that means anything to me, that when I made love to you, I wasn't thinking about anything except us. You and me. Nothing else. And I never let on to anyone that anything happened between us. As far as anyone in Sweetwater knows, I never laid a hand on you."

Miss Devlin heaved a sigh of relief. She hadn't realized it mattered so much to her that he hadn't bragged about his conquest.

"I'm asking you to forgive me, Eden," he said. "I meant the things I said about wanting you for my wife. About wanting to start a new life here in Sweetwater. About wanting to settle down and have kids with you."

Miss Devlin blinked her eyes to keep the tears at bay. "I . . ." She gritted her teeth to keep her chin from quivering. "I want to believe you're sincere about giving up your gun and settling down. But I wonder if you can really do it."

"I can. You have to believe I can."

When Kerrigan still saw doubt in her eyes, he knew he needed some way other than words to convince her he meant what he said. He took Sundance's gun out of the holster and set it in Eden's lap. "Here. This belongs to you. I won't be needing it anymore."

Eden stared down at the gun her father had used to kill so many men, then looked back up into Kerrigan's dark eyes, searching for the truth. Because she loved Kerrigan, she wanted to believe he no longer needed it. She wanted to stop running away from happiness and embrace it wholeheartedly. But the fear of losing him to a bullet was still very real. Very frightening. "Kerrigan, I don't—"

He could see he was going to lose her. "I promise you—I swear to you—that if you marry me I will—"

The instant Kerrigan saw the flash of sunlight off steel from within the copse of pine, instincts honed from years of living on the edge of danger came to the fore. He shoved Eden down below the floorboard of the wagon, out of the line of fire, and did a diving roll off the wagon seat into the underbrush beside the road. Seconds later several bullets thudded into the tufted seat, tearing jagged holes where their bodies had been.

Eden was stunned by how quickly Kerrigan had reacted. Still in shock, she stared at the gun in her hand, then looked over to where he was heading into the copse of trees from which the shot had been fired.

"Kerrigan, you forgot—" She bit her lip on the rest of her sentence. She didn't need to tell him he didn't have a gun. She was sure he'd already realized that fact. Yelling it out to him was only going to apprise whoever had attacked them that Kerrigan was armed with only his wits.

Kerrigan realized his mistake the same moment he took the flying leap from the wagon. Since his gun was always in his holster it hadn't occurred to him until he was in the air that he had put it in Eden's lap. When he finished his tumbling roll, he came up running on a diagonal toward the copse of pines where the bushwhacker was hiding. A bullet whined past his ear just as he reached the cover of the trees.

Kerrigan swore. It was obvious he couldn't get back to the wagon without coming under fire. And he was now too far away for Eden to safely throw him his weapon. He had the derringer in his boot, but that was only good up close. Eden was going to get her wish. He had no choice except to resolve the situation without a Colt. As long as his options were limited, he might as well give talking a try.

"Hey, Deputy Joe," he shouted. "Is that you?"

"Yeah."

"We thought you froze to death."

"Nearly did. Got rescued by a drifting peddler. Damn fellow had bells on his wagon. Thought I was going crazy. Funny how things work out, ain't it?"

"How'd you know to wait here for me?"

"I went to the line shack and saw what you done to them boys. Figured you'd have to bring the schoolteacher home sooner or later."

"It's all over, Joe. Too many people know about you. You'll have a better chance of living if you give yourself up."

"This is all your fault, Kerrigan. You gotta pay."

Kerrigan kept Deputy Joe talking, all the time working his way closer, using the deputy's voice to try to locate him. He didn't have a plan, exactly, but if he could work his way in behind the man . . .

Every time Kerrigan thought he had Joe cornered, the deputy escaped his trap. It was a dangerous game of cat and mouse, and Kerrigan kept his eye out for a mousehole he could use if things fell apart and the cat took a swipe at him with its claws.

Eden was terrified. She had wanted Kerrigan to lay down his gun, but not like this. She didn't see how he was going to capture Deputy Joe without getting himself killed. She heard them talking to each other, their voices moving farther into the pines. She kept imagining Deputy Joe cornering Kerrigan, sighting down his gun barrel and firing his gun. She saw the red blossom growing on Kerrigan's chest, a mortal wound.

Eden's whole body trembled with fear. What she had really wanted, when she asked Kerrigan to lay down his gun, was a guarantee that his life would never be in danger again. If they lived in a perfect world, a civilized world, maybe she could have had her wish. In such a world, guns would be unnecessary. But this was not a perfect world.

Certainly Kerrigan would live longer if he made his living as a rancher rather than as a gunslinger. That much she could, and would, ask of him. Even then, there were bandits and rustlers and outlaws of even worse ilk roaming the Wyoming frontier. On the frontier, a gun was sometimes necessary for survival. She couldn't ask Kerrigan never to carry a gun again. That would likely get him killed someday when he needed a gun and didn't have one—like right now.

Eden knew now why her mother had stayed with Sundance despite the pain she must have known would come some day. Lillian had known that living without the man you love is no life at all. Now that she understood that, the choice became simple for Eden.

She climbed down from the wagon, anxious to get Sundance's Colt to Kerrigan. Voices reached her, Kerrigan's and then the deputy's, taunting each other. Moving as quietly as she could, she made her way through the pines.

Kerrigan had found his quarry. Deputy Joe was walking right toward the spot where Kerrigan was hidden behind twin pines, his gun held outstretched before him. All Kerrigan had to do was let the deputy walk past and relieve him of his weapon.

The crackling of underbrush off to the left startled them both. Kerrigan watched Joe swing his gun toward the sound. An instant later Eden stepped through the undergrowth holding Sundance's gun in her hand.

Kerrigan saw Joe taking aim and knew he had to do something fast. He stepped out from behind the pines and said, "You looking for me, Joe?"

Joe swung his gun around to aim it at Kerrigan. At the same time Eden realized the danger and quickly raised Sundance's gun, aiming it at Joe.

"Hold your fire," she said. "Or I'll shoot."

Joe was in a quandary. He could see Kerrigan was unarmed. But if he shot Kerrigan, Miss Devlin had threatened to shoot him. If he turned and fired at Miss Devlin, Kerrigan was liable to jump him before he could get off another shot. His best bet was to kill Kerrigan first and take the chance Miss Devlin would either not shoot at all, or miss on the first shot.

"Give it up, Joe. You haven't got a chance," Kerrigan said in the same calming voice he had used on the boys in Eden's schoolroom.

"Everyone knows how Miss Devlin feels about guns. She ain't going to shoot me. You're a dead man, Kerrigan." Joe cocked his .45.

"You're wrong about me, Deputy Joe," Eden said, trying to keep her voice as calm as Kerrigan's and only half succeeding. "I'll kill you if I have to."

Joe turned and sneered at her. "Don't make me laugh."

"You've heard of a gunslinger named Sundance, haven't you, Joe?" Kerrigan asked.

Joe's head whirled back around to hear about this new threat. "Sundance? What does he have to do with anything?"

"Sundance was Miss Devlin's father."

"Sheeeit. You're just saying that," Deputy Joe said. But a sweat broke out on his forehead, and his eyes shifted back to Miss Devlin even though he kept the gun on Kerrigan. "He's makin' that up. He's gotta be makin' that up."

"He's telling you the truth," Eden said. "Sundance was my father. He taught me everything I know about guns."

"Sheeeit. I don't figure to get myself shot by some gunslinger's kid, even if she is a woman." Deputy Joe looked nervously from Miss Devlin to Kerrigan and back. " 'Specially when you got no proof I did anything wrong. I'm gonna drop my gun, you hear? Don't you go gettin' trigger-happy."

The instant Deputy Joe dropped the gun, Kerrigan was there. He stuck the deputy's gun in his belt and used his bandanna to tie Deputy Joe's hands behind him. He wasn't gentle.

Once he was done, Kerrigan grabbed the deputy by the elbow and hauled him over to where Eden was still standing with Sundance's gun in her hand, which was now hanging at her side.

"Eden?" he said. "Are you all right?" He took the gun out of her hand and discovered she was shivering. He pulled her into his arms and hugged her, all the while holding a gun on Joe to keep him from making a run for it. "It's all right, love," he crooned. "It's all over now. You're all right."

"Sheeeit," Deputy Joe said. "You were never gonna fire that gun at me, were you?"

Eden surprised both men when she levered herself

away from Kerrigan and answered, "I would have if I'd had to. You see, a wise man taught me that although violence isn't always the answer, sometimes it's the only answer when dealing with a sanguinary primate."

"A what?"

"A bloodthirsty man."

Eden turned and met Kerrigan's dark eyes as he said, "You're one smart lady, Miss Devlin."

"I was wondering when you would notice, Mr. Kerrigan," she said with a grin.

When their eyes locked, Deputy Joe saw his chance and took off at a run. He hadn't gone two steps before Kerrigan stuck out a foot and tripped him. The deputy lost his balance and fell. His head hit a rotted tree trunk as he went down, knocking him out cold.

"Some people never learn," Eden said, shaking her head at the sight of the unconscious man.

Kerrigan walked purposefully back to her. "We have some business to settle."

Eden's chin went up. "The answer is yes."

"I haven't asked the question yet," he said with a rueful grin.

"Then ask!"

"I'm asking for the third and last time. Will you marry me, Miss Devlin?"

"Yes! Yes! Yes!"

They both laughed as he lifted her in his arms and hugged her tight. Her arms wrapped eagerly around him and she showered him with kisses on his face and neck and eyes, murmuring, "I love you, Burke Kerrigan. Love you more than life itself."

"And I love you, Eden Devlin. Love you for now and forever."

Everything after that was done with haste. Kerrigan hefted Deputy Joe over his shoulder and walked back to the wagon. Joe was still unconscious when they got there, so Kerrigan laid him in the bed of the wagon. Since they weren't far from Eden's place, Kerrigan dropped her off, promising to return as soon as he could.

When he got back to Sweetwater, he put Deputy Joe, who by now was suffering from a bad headache but otherwise seemed all right, in his regular cell. Only this time, Kerrigan locked him in. He left the key with the clerk at the Townhouse Hotel with instructions to feed the deputy until the sheriff got back to town.

Then he sent a telegram to Felton in Canyon Creek to tell him he would have to cut short his honeymoon until he arranged to hire another deputy to take Joe's place.

Kerrigan dropped off the spring wagon at the livery and made a stop at the hotel to shave, bathe, and change his clothes. He belted on Sundance's gun, which Eden had insisted he take, before he headed down the hotel stairs, ready for the last leg of his journey back to her.

Meanwhile, Eden was a nervous wreck. She had stripped off her clothes the minute she got inside the house and taken a sponge bath. Instead of putting on a dress, she had donned a warm flannel robe that tied at the waist. Then she had gone through every toilet preparation on her dresser, trying to make herself beautiful for Kerrigan.

When she was done, she looked in the mirror and saw a face as plain as it had ever been. What if, now that Kerrigan had proposed, he took another look at her and changed his mind?

She stared at her barren ring finger. He hadn't said anything about a ring. She wanted an engagement ring, of course, but she wasn't going to ask for one. What if he didn't think of it?

She thrust her fingers through her striking red hair, which lay in a mass of curls around her shoulders. He had said he liked it down. What if he had lied to spare her feelings? She quickly drew her hair into a bun at the back of her neck, grabbing pins and stuffing them in as fast as she could. A second later she pulled them all back out again, and threw them on the dresser, helter-skelter.

Suddenly, she noticed the freckles cascading across her nose and cheeks. She had just treated them with C. H. Berry Freckle Ointment but, if anything, they were even more noticeable than before. She grabbed a puff and powdered her face. That only made her look pale as death. She grabbed a handkerchief and wiped off the powder. The freckles reappeared with a vengeance. It looked like someone had spattered her face with red paint. She tried a lighter dusting of powder and stayed away from the mirror when she was done.

Every flaw she had ever seen in herself was magnified a hundred—no, a thousand—times. She was terrified that now that she had her heart's desire, it would escape her somehow.

What if Deputy Joe slipped his bonds and attacked Kerrigan and killed him before they got back to town?

Miss Devlin snorted. Now she was making up stories so farfetched they wouldn't bear printing in a penny dreadful. She had to get hold of herself. She had to stay calm, and wait patiently for Kerrigan to come.

Where is he?

Eden forced herself to lie down in bed. She was exhausted from her travails and really ought to rest but felt too keyed up to sleep. She closed her eyes and consciously relaxed her muscles, starting with her toes and working her way up. She got no farther than her knees before she was sound asleep.

Kerrigan had knocked twice, but he hadn't heard a sound on the other side of the door. What if Eden had changed her mind? What if, after all, she had decided a tiger couldn't change its stripes, and she would rather stay a spinster than marry a gunslinger.

He ran a finger under the red bandanna he had tied around his throat, which was suddenly choking him, then opened the door and walked in.

"Eden?"

No answer.

Her bedroom door was open and he headed toward it as unerringly as a bee seeking honey from a bright spring flower. She was asleep on the bed, her hand tucked under her head, her body curled around a pillow that was clutched in her arms.

He sat down on the bed beside her, knowing that he had finally found his destiny. There was a lump in his throat as he whispered, "Wake up, Sleeping Beauty. Your prince has come."

Eden awoke to Kerrigan's gentle kiss, which became more urgent as they both sought to express the measure of their love.

"It's been too long since I've held you in my arms, Eden," he murmured.

Miss Devlin realized she didn't feel the least bit plain. The only problem with having freckles was that Kerrigan insisted on kissing each and every one of them. She laughed as he counted, ". . . thirty-two . . . thirty-three . . . thirty-four . . ."

"Enough," she said with a giggle. "I have something I want to share with you."

"This sounds serious."

She shook her head. "It's not serious exactly. It's . . . Wait here."

When she got up off the bed, Kerrigan sat up and settled himself more comfortably with his back against the headboard. He watched Eden cross to her dresser and pick up a decorated wooden box. When she got closer, he noticed the lid was broken in two.

She sat on the bed beside him with her feet curled under her. "This is my Wish Box."

He didn't say anything, just waited, curious, for her to explain.

"I collected things in it that I hoped someday I would need, if I—when I—became a wife and mother."

She set the box in front of Kerrigan.

He couldn't imagine what she had in there. He was fascinated. And terrified. What did a woman cherish? What symbols of love and marriage had Eden Devlin collected in a wooden box on her dresser?

She took them out, one by one, and shared them with him.

A pair of nickel-plated barber snips.

He insisted right then and there that she give him a trim. Laughing, she took off an inch of hair that had hung down over his collar for as long as he could remember. He felt helpless to resist her when she was done. He could see how Samson had felt with Delilah.

A genuine badger-hair shaving brush.

It was a gift, she said as she handed it to him, for the man she married. He didn't ask her how many years it had been in the box. He just accepted it and promised, "I'll use it every day."

Although he had given himself a shave before leaving town, he insisted he could use another. After all, as much kissing as they were bound to do, he didn't want to leave her face aflame. Eden found a cake of shaving soap, while he ran out to his saddlebags to get her father's razor. When he was done shaving, he set the brush on her dresser, and realized with a start that henceforth his things would always sit there alongside hers.

A baby's teething ring.

Eden admitted to him that she had always wanted a

child of her own to love, and that she had spent hours wondering what it would feel like to have another human being moving inside her. He put his hand on her womb and wondered the same thing himself.

One blue spool and one pink spool of satin grosgrain baby ribbon.

He asked her whether she would rather have a boy or a girl, and she immediately replied "Both!" So he asked which she would rather have first, and she answered, "A boy, so he could watch over his sister."

A silver baby spoon.

It was the shell-shaped spoon he had given her. He felt touched to know it had found its way into her heart and her hopes.

He felt awed that she trusted him with the feminine secrets she had harbored in her Wish Box all these years. Now that he knew how much she wanted a child, he became determined to help her make that wish come true. So he tied a snip of blue satin baby ribbon in her hair, "For luck," he said with a roguish grin, and made sweet, sweet love to her for the rest of the day.

It was while she was sleeping, as day turned to dusk, that he slipped the ring on her finger. When she woke, he kissed her, and said, "I love you, Eden Devlin. I—"

She cut him off by kissing him back.

Before he could tell her about the ring, they were both swept up in a vortex of desire that took them back to Eden's own version of paradise.

It was a long while later before either of them had any inclination to speak. Kerrigan was lying beside Eden, and she had nestled her buttocks into the curve of his sinewy body, when he finally broke the peaceful silence between them.

"Do you like the ring?"

"What ring?"

He held up her hand, and she stared at the breathtaking

emerald set in a narrow gold band that she had been too busy making love to notice. She gasped, unable to speak. Finally she managed, "It's beautiful."

"No more beautiful than you."

Eden saw that, in his eyes, she was beautiful. "Will you make love to me again, Mr. Kerrigan?"

Kerrigan grinned. "I will be happy to seduce you, Miss Devlin, for the rest of your life."

Epilogue

*A stone stops rollin' when it finds the kind
of moss it wants to gather.*

EVERYONE IN SWEETWATER WAS IN CHURCH THIS particular Sunday in June, because Bliss and Hadley Westbrook's newborn daughter was scheduled to be christened. Kerrigan and Eden had to be there because they were godparents for the newest resident of Sweetwater.

As Eden walked down the aisle with Kerrigan she noticed that ranchers and nesters still pretty much sat on opposite sides of the church. But here and there you would see close neighbors clustered together, even though they lived their lives on opposite sides of the fence, so to speak.

Eden snickered when Reverend Simonson announced his sermon for the day was "Be fruitful and multiply," because it was pretty obvious that most of his fecund congregation had long since taken the preacher's words to heart.

Sheriff Reeves was holding his new son, Frank, in one arm and had the other around his wife, Darcie. Amity Carson was nursing her sixth daughter, Eula, at her breast. As for the rest of the congregation, there were at least a dozen families expecting new additions in September, including Rusty and Claire Falkner, Cyrus and Lynette Wyatt, and Ben and Persia Davis.

Unfortunately, the former Miss Eden Devlin was among the very few who were not in the family way.

Eden knew the ladies spoke of it behind her back, because whenever she came into a room there would be a sudden hush. Her barrenness was considered a tragedy of monumental proportions. She had been at first disappointed, and later chagrined, and finally distraught, that she and Kerrigan apparently were not going to be blessed with a child of their own.

Kerrigan had never spoken to her about the fact she had not conceived. But she saw the worried frown on his brow when he thought she wasn't looking. He had held her in his arms and comforted her once when he had caught her crying because she would need the rags again.

It was Eden's privilege to hold Bliss and Hadley's daughter, Caroline Elizabeth (Persia's and Regina's middle names), while the preacher conducted the christening ceremony. Eden felt the baby's toes through the blanket, and brushed her fingertips through the fine hair on Caroline's head, under the pretense of arranging what little there was of it. There were tears in her eyes as she and Kerrigan repeated the appropriate responses along with Bliss and Hadley.

At last, she handed the baby back to Bliss and all of them turned to face the congregation.

"This is a joyful day," Reverend Simonson said. "Is there a word of gladness any of you would like to share with the congregation?"

Hadley cleared his throat and said, "I want to say how proud I am to be married to such a good woman, and that we're going to raise Caroline Elizabeth the best we know how."

There were several sentimental sniffles from the pews.

"This is a joyful day," Reverend Simonson repeated. "Does anyone else have any good news they would like to share?"

Usually, this was where a husband and wife would stand and announce they were expecting a child. It had become a painful part of the service for Eden. She felt Kerrigan's arm slip around her waist, and he pulled her close, as though to lend her courage.

Kerrigan had never felt so helpless as he had the past few months knowing that Eden wanted a child and he was unable to give her one—though it hadn't been for want of trying. This was always the hardest part of the service for him. Because it was a time when Eden, who was never at a loss for words, had nothing to say.

To his surprise, Eden turned to the reverend and announced, "I have something I'd like to say."

Kerrigan caught his wife's eye, his confusion apparent. Eden met his concerned gaze and smiled, a look so joyful that it caused a sudden lump in Kerrigan's throat, a sudden surge of hope in his chest.

Eden turned back to face the congregation and said, "My husband and I wish to share the news with all of you that we're expecting our first child at Christmastime."

There was a moment of astonished silence before the entire congregation erupted in shouts and laughter and clapping.

Kerrigan looked stunned. "Are you sure?"

Eden let her happiness shine in her eyes. "I'm sure."

He picked her up with a shout and swung her exuberantly in a circle. Just as quickly, he set her down again and asked, "Are you all right? I didn't hurt you, did I? Or the baby?"

"I'm fine," she reassured him.

He folded her in his arms and rocked her from side to side. "I am so happy, Eden. For you. For me. For us."

They weren't left alone for long. Their friends and neighbors surrounded them, congratulating Kerrigan and including Eden in all the talk she had missed, about what to do and not to do while pregnant, how to recognize the signs of labor, what to do while nursing, and all the other myriad bits of advice that mothers the world over share with other mothers.

Eden stood in the supporting circle of her husband's arms and listened and smiled and nodded. She laid a hand on her womb and thought of the child growing there. The past no longer had the power to frighten her. Life was good. Life was sweet. She had stopped running at last.

Author's Note

✿ THE GREEK COMEDY *LYSISTRATA* WAS WRITTEN BY Aristophanes in 411 B.C. as a satire on the foolishness of war. The ancient play is one of the earliest heralds for the rights and influence of women. It has been my inspiration, as it was Miss Devlin's.

Dear Readers,

Sweetwater Seduction is one of my favorites. I hope you enjoyed reading it as much as I enjoyed writing it!

Be sure to check out my modern-day western Bitter Creek series, including *The Cowboy, The Texan,* and *The Loner.* And in stores now, *The Rivals.*

I love hearing from you! You can reach me through my web site www.joanjohnston.com or send a self-addressed, stamped envelope with your remarks to me at P.O. Box 7834, St. Petersburg, Florida 33734–7834 so I can reply.

Happy reading,
Joan Johnston

Joan Johnston

"Joan Johnston continually gives us everything we want . . . fabulous details and atmosphere, memorable characters, and lots of tension and sensuality." —*Romantic Times*

☐	22201-X	*After The Kiss*	$7.50
☐	21129-8	*The Barefoot Bride*	$7.50
☐	22377-6	*The Bodyguard*	$7.50
☐	23470-0	*The Bridegroom*	$7.50
☐	22200-1	*Captive*	$7.50
☐	23680-0	*Comanche Woman*	$7.50
☐	22380-6	*The Cowboy*	$7.50
☐	23677-0	*Frontier Woman*	$7.50
☐	21759-8	*The Inheritance*	$7.50
☐	21280-4	*Kid Calhoun*	$7.50
☐	23472-7	*The Loner*	$7.50
☐	21762-8	*Maverick Heart*	$7.50
☐	21278-2	*Outlaw's Bride*	$7.50
☐	20561-1	*Sweetwater Seduction*	$7.50
☐	23471-9	*The Texan*	$7.50
☐	23684-3	*Texas Woman*	$7.50

Please enclose check or money order only, no cash or CODs. Shipping & handling costs: $5.50 U.S. mail, $7.50 UPS. New York and Tennessee residents must remit applicable sales tax. Canadian residents must remit applicable GST and provincial taxes. Please allow 4 - 6 weeks for delivery. All orders are subject to availability. This offer subject to change without notice. Please call 1-800-726-0600 for further information.

Bantam Dell Publishing Group, Inc.
Attn: Customer Service
400 Hahn Road
Westminster, MD 21157

TOTAL AMT $_____
SHIPPING & HANDLING $_____
SALES TAX (NY, TN) $_____

TOTAL ENCLOSED $_____

Name _____

Address _____

City/State/Zip _____

Daytime Phone (_____) _____